The Raunch Factor
A Novel of Provincial Life

by

D.J. Muns Blancato

Authors Choice Press
New York Lincoln Shanghai

The Raunch Factor
A Novel of Provincial Life

Authors Choice Press
an imprint of iUniverse, Inc.

iUniverse books may be ordered through booksellers or by contacting:

iUniverse
2021 Pine Lake Road, Suite 100
Lincoln, NE 68512
www.iuniverse.com
1-800-Authors (1-800-288-4677)

Originally published by Chiaro/Scuro Press

This is a book of fiction. Names, characters, places and incidents are the product of the author's imagination. Any resemblance to actual events, locations or persons, living or dead, is entirely coincidental.

Cover by D.J. Muns Blancato

Acknowledgements

For their encouragement and patience, special thanks and appreciation to my intrepid editors, Cottage Wordsmiths Nancy Gavrilis and John Metcalfe, and to my husband, Sam Blancato.

Many thanks and my gratitude to George Peter Vogt, Margaret J. "Mossie" Vogt, Carol Young Schmidt, Rosemary Hogan, Joanne McCloskey, Craig Thomson and Mildred Faye Psihoulis for their support and inspiration.

ISBN-13: 978-0-595-38230-9
ISBN-10: 0-595-38230-4

Printed in the United States of America

The Raunch Factor
A Novel of Provincial Life

For my husband, Sam, and our children, Nancy, Ann, Sam and Tom, with love; and in loving memory of their sister, our daughter, Maria Carmella Blancato.

The Raunch Factor
A Novel of Provincial Life

PROLOGUE

Lucille was lying face down when they found her.

She had been missing for three days. There were no signs of violence, or foul play, although her body was somewhat emaciated. The Coroner's report stated that she had been dead for approximately nine hours.

The abandoned shed where she apparently had spent the last moments — or minutes, or hours — of her life was completely concealed by clumps of evergreens and straggly old cherry trees intertwined with wild grape vines forming a sort of bower. It was not hard to imagine police or search parties overlooking such a spot.

A middle-aged couple had come upon the shed by merest chance. They were well away from the road, breaking their own path for a walk in the woods, when a glint of late afternoon sun reflected from a fragment of windowpane caught their attention. When they broke into the open, they found a sagging, partially-open door; a pair of feet clad in galoshes protruded at an unnatural angle over the remnants of a doorsill.

The hikers did not explore further, but left to notify the police.

An official examination of the scene revealed the presence of a fully clothed Caucasian female, age thirty-five to fifty, dead. There were no signs of injury and no evidence of a struggle. Under the left ankle of the deceased was a black leather handbag with a short strap, held closed with a gilt clasp. The handbag contained an amber plastic comb, a bottle of Valium prescribed for Lucille Blake, a small packet of paper tissues, a makeup case containing lipstick, an eyebrow pencil, mascara, and a small mirror, and a wallet. Inside the wallet were two one-dollar bills, $1.18 in change, a ticket stub from a recent concert at Gessler Music Hall featuring pianist Martha Argerich, credit cards and a photo driver's license in the name of Lucille Blake, and a small brown address book.

The body was removed and a Coroner's Inquest was begun.

An autopsy revealed a high concentration of Valium in the victim's blood, though not sufficient to cause death in itself. There was no note or other indication —such as scarred wrists —

that the victim had been suicidal. The coroner's inventory of items found with the body tallied with the police report, except for the address book, which was never found.

A profile developed from interviews with friends and acquaintances of the deceased was inconclusive. Lucille Blake had always been soft-spoken and withdrawn, and was generally considered to be the perfect wife and mother. She had invariably deferred to her husband. All her energies went into the maintenance of their large Colonial-style house, where the paneled front door bore an eagle-shaped knocker and a deeply-engraved plaque announcing "The Leonard Blake's" in Old English letters.

THE RAUNCH FACTOR

Book I

CHAPTER ONE

Daphne believed she must have been the last person who had seen Lucille Blake alive.

When Daphne drove up the gravelled driveway to the Blake's home, Lucille had come out to meet her, and had taken her on a tour through the house, pointing out, in a soft voice, the changes that she and her husband wanted to make. Daphne took notes and measurements throughout the house, and when they returned to the living room Lucille ran her hand over the gleaming ebonized piano, a studio-size grand. A Pleyel edition of the Chopin *Preludes* lay on the music rack.

"This is my favorite thing in the whole house," Lucille whispered, "this piano."

"Do you play?" Daphne asked her as she put on her coat.

Lucille was staring dreamily at the piano; slowly she turned back to Daphne.

"Oh, yes. Music is my whole, secret life. But I get very little time to practice; there's never a chance to play the piano. There are the children's activities and Leonard works so hard, I feel that they need me more than I need to make music."

They walked to the big paneled front door.

"I'll have some drawings to show you in about a week, Mrs. Blake." Daphne turned to leave.

"Oh, call me Lucille —please."

"All right. And I'm Daphne, OK? Does anyone ever call you 'Lucy'?"

"Oh, no. Never. You know, when I hear the name 'Daphne,' I always think of that English writer. The one that wrote *Rebecca,* my favorite novel."

"Daphne du Maurier?" asked Daphne, thinking, *Well, she likes Chopin and she reads books. I would have pegged her as more of a light-weight; more of a Peewee Football Mother or that sort of thing.*

"Yes. That's the one. That's the writer." Lucille's voice was slurred —the words ran together somewhat. "Just remember, Daphne, *I* like violet and lilac and cerise, but I can have those

1

colors only in my little upstairs sitting room. Everything else has to be in Leonard's colors: black and red.''

Those words were probably the last that anyone heard Lucille Blake say.

Back in her drafting room Daphne spread a brushful of lilac watercolor across the illustration board, then around the sketched-in small chairs; chairs placed around the sitting room for intimate chats. She had planned a lush, English chintz in cerise and purple for the chairs and draperies. Now there would be no point in finishing the rendering. Yet she continued the lilac wash, picking up pools of color with the sponge action of the squeezed brush, mixing in a deeper gray-purple to flow on for the shadows around the two chairs and for a feeling of texture on the mauve carpet. *Lucille Blake will never feel this carpet underfoot —or sit in these chairs —*Daphne thought as she rinsed her brush and laid it down. She watched the purple swirls in the water jar.

Beside the jar the newspaper lay where James had left it a few minutes before. He had known she would be upset, and had murmured, "I'm afraid this is bad news." He was a sweet, considerate guy. Why did it always seem to be the gay men who were sweet and considerate?

The newspaper was open to Lucille Blake's picture, the second time it had appeared; this time it was above the story about her body having been found. The memory of that last hour spent together would not leave Daphne. She studied the picture. It showed Lucille shyly smiling in an unflattering, front-faced pose, like a passport picture. It probably was; there had been European souvenirs all over the house.

Daphne put away her paints and brushes and stacked the four meticulously-drawn pencil sketches and the one partially-painted rendering on the shelf. It would have been a nice job, and she and Mrs. Blake had hit it off right away.

What made her do it? Daphne wondered. *What could have happened that made death her only choice?* She read the obituary

2

again.

> *Lucille T. (Rarick) Blake, Sunnymeade Drive,*
> *Bingham, died unexpectedly Friday, February*
> *25, 1982. Born in Doncaster, Pa., daughter*
> *of the late Leroy A. and Thelma F. Rarick,*
> *she was a member of the Garden Square*
> *Presbyterian Church, Bingham, where she*
> *sang in the choir. Surviving is her husband,*
> *Leonard D. Blake, owner of Blake Casting*
> *and Blake Valve, a subsidiary of Blake*
> *Casting. Mr. Blake is president of the*
> *Bingham school board and was recently*
> *named to the Bingham Sports Honor Arena*
> *and received the All Time Best All Around*
> *Sports Speaker award, the ABASS Bronze.*
> *The statuette of a trout fisherman has been*
> *awarded to only ten other sportsmen in the*
> *United States. Also surviving are two*
> *daughters, Christine and Ella Jean, at home,*
> *and two sons, Leonard D. Blake III, of Los*
> *Angeles and....*

Daphne stopped reading. A tractor trailer was pulling into the parking lot beside her shop, heading for the loading dock. The phone rang, and two people entered the shop. Debbie and James were on the job. Daphne could see Debbie smiling, approaching the two customers, while James went to the dock to help the trucker unload.

The phone rang again.

The delivery was probably the mahogany sideboard for which they had waited six months, an order that Mrs. Hartley had threatened to cancel. Feeling relieved, Daphne picked up the ringing phone. She could see another woman approaching the front entrance. Business at Designs for Living was picking up.

Approximately five blocks away, Allison DeVries chirped into the telephone as she flicked her cigarette into a lopsided hand-made ceramic ashtray that bore the admonition "Smile."

"Hi, Daph? Allison. Wait till you hear what I found out. Felicia's definitely pregnant."

Daphne's answering voice sounded faint. "Oh, Allison, I don't know whether to be happy or sad. She's thirty-eight and she's in very poor health. It couldn't be worse news. Herb will bounce her off a wall again when he finds out."

"She's ecstatic. So is Herb. You know how they've wanted a family. They've decided they're not going through with the divorce, and they're going to start all over again, and the baby will be a new beginning and, well, it's just super news, I think. But it's my turn to go grocery shopping and then I go to craft class. See you at the shelter tonight. Bye!" The phone slammed in Daphne's ear.

How do I meet these people? Daphne asked herself. *Allison is an air-brain, a real dingbat but she's so good-hearted and open and kind I get taken in by her prattle.*

A smirking Debbie was approaching the drafting room.

"Mrs. Malaprop is out front. She wants to talk to you."

"Deb, some day she'll hear you, and we'll be in mucho expensive trouble."

"Aw, what does *she* know from Malaprop?" Debbie sniffed. "I told her you'd be right out."

Daphne could see Mrs. Doctor Hartley in the middle of the Country Boutique, picking up and laying down toss pillows. Her massacre of the English language was always a delight to the Designs for Living staff and Daphne had named her for Sheridan's garrulous character after hearing a "Hartley Special": "It's an ill worm that blows no evil."

Mrs. Hartley's husband, The Doctor, an OB-Gyn specialist, had amassed a fortune in Hilton Head condos, a ketchup-and-plastic-zipper conglomerate, and a Ferrari accessory factory, and was reported to have said during a Semper Fidelis Club lunch (in regard to his medical specialty) "It's all just pussy to me."

"Oh hello, Daphne —" Mrs. Hartley flashed the grimace she used as a smile. "I guess I'll have to eat humble crow. I see

4

the cadenza finally came in. James took me back to see it. But it's smaller than I thought, and it has a scratch on it."

Daphne murmured but Mrs. Hartley went on, "I really don't know if we can use it or not. The Doctor is looking at a house in Chatterley Estates."

Daphne, seeing seven thousand dollars take wing, tried to smile. "Sounds wonderful, Mrs. Hartley. What kind of house is it?"

"It's southern. You know, with pillars, like in *Gone With the Wind.*"

"Oh, yes. Greek Revival."

"Hmmmm. I don't know about *that.* It's not foreign! I always thought that style was southern!" She looked annoyed. "It has a Jacuzzi and beautiful woodwork. All the doors are a couple inches thick and have them linen carvings —uh —those decorator folds."

Oh God, thought Daphne, *she thinks those fiberglass castings are genuine, carved, linenfold panels. The house is probably a Contractor Special with Bingham-Lumber-and-Supply Tudor details.*

"We may decide to let you look at it." Mrs. Hartley was arranging her enormous bosom beneath twenty-two thousand dollars worth of Andrea Cassotti-designed lynx coat; a large, round white badge with "Born to Shop" in red letters was pinned to the lapel. "It's on Connie Drive, next to Mellors Lane, where the Krock house is. That's the house with the English garden, with the jezebo."

Five miles across town, in a miniature Villa d'Este on Mellors Lane, diagonally across from Clifford Way and next to Connie Drive, wearing a maroon karate bathrobe and two blood-soaked toilet paper wads on his chin, Ed Krock put away his razor and faced the full-length mirror on the back of the bathroom door.

Not bad. Fifty-four and still a flat gut. You always used to see Jerry Ford on an exercycle, in Personality Magazine, wearing a robe like this, Ed mused. He struck a roguish pose and looked at himself out of the corner of his eye, opening his robe to inspect his plentiful though graying chest hair. He was getting gray fast. The Alchemy of Youth touch-ups he did on his temples didn't work. But he had heard somewhere that gray hair photographs well. He would look more impressive as a Congressman. Maybe a partly sideways pose would look good, with an American flag in the background. Or maybe seated at his desk with a pipe, and shelves behind him, with books; they'd have to get some books. Or standing in front of the gazebo with Bobbye. No, that would be too tony, with all the iron work and the marble dome. (Elitist was not a word in Ed Krock's vocabulary.)

Ed pulled the venetian blinds apart and looked out at the garden and the gazebo. Bobbye, in a pink jogging suit, was sitting out there in the twilight on one of the stone benches, smoking a cigarette. It was a beautiful back yard. A light snowfall made the scene even more romantic. Ed had an uneasy feeling that it didn't look too good for him, politically, to own this fancy place. Ed made a mental note. Bobbye would have to stop calling it "The Garden." *From now on it's going to be The Back Yard.*

He selected a quiet tie to go with his dark blue suit and white shirt. It was 1981, and running for Congress, he had to beef up his image. No more steel-worker down vests over plaid shirts, no more county commissioner plaid sports coats, no more state legislator blazers. It wouldn't hurt to put on a hard hat occasionally, though, get his picture taken wearing one; pose with union people. Then there would be the National Rifle Association picnic; he'd get Bobbye to wear jogging shorts with one of those tops with no straps. At least *he* was married. Everybody knew Drew Burgess's marriage was just a front. And that third party guy, Renshaw —as if he'd be any worry —was divorced. Still, he could take votes away from the Democrats

6

and the Republicans.

He heard Bobbye come in the back door. She was rattling pans. Ed barely had time for supper before he had to meet with those libbers. Crazy broads. Ed knotted his tie and gave himself that sideways look again, and winked.

Bobbye was hollering. She would probably start on him again about furniture. He already had nearly three hundred grand sunk in this spread! Maybe he shouldn't have accepted the money from the nuclear people, or the free utilities. Bobbye kept asking him where the bills were; she thought it was fishy when he said they were sent to his office. She was too smart. She smelled a rat. She had asked about January's bill, and February's.

Shouldn't have let her talk me into this place, he told himself. *It's too big and too fancy.* But Bobbye had whined and whined.

Ed tried to walk down the curved beige-carpeted stairs in a classy way, snapping his knees and bouncing on each step and rotating his rear end the way Robert Mitchum did on that HBO show. Bobbye was at the foot of the stairs scowling.

"You wearing that tight underwear again? I got you three new pair." Bobbye had no class. She followed him into the breakfast room off the kitchen. A pair of huge ceramic praying hands, more than twice life-size, with a peculiar lumpy blue glaze, sat by his plate like the hands of some pious, leprous giant. Ed felt a little sick. Bobbye was glaring at him.

"Well?"

"They're terrific, hon."

"You. Are. Lying."

"No kiddin', hon, I like that religious shit. You do that in class today?" He took a bite of corned beef quiche, another one of those weird dishes she had begun to serve after they moved in the new place. "Boy, what I'd give for a good steak. I'm glad nobody can see me eating this stuff," he said as he gulped the quiche. He pushed back his chair, a beer keg with half of one side cut out to form a seat.

Bobbye eyed the beer keg table and chairs.

"This dinette set has got to go. You promised me you'd talk about new furniture, Ed. If you want to have them fundraisers, we have to get started. I can't get it all done in a coupla weeks! Allison has a friend, a decorator I could get." Ed winced. She was starting to whine again.

"Aw, they just rob you. Isn't that decorator, what's-her-name Singleton, one of those libbers? That group I'm supposed to talk to," he looked at his watch " — in about twenty minutes?"

"Yeah, she's a little spacey in some ways, I guess, like Allison. But she's supposed to be really good. She's a designer, not just a decorator. She's done the McKelvey's and Helen and Jack Hillary's —the Hillarys have them new type window blinds that look like strips of mirror —"

"Bobbye, I gotta go clear to Doncaster." Ed put on his black vicuña and cashmere overcoat and his new Balaclava hat. He thought the fur hat gave him a diplomatic look. Bobbye began to carry the dishes to the sink.

"What are you meeting with that women's lib group for, anyway, Ed?"

"Oh, they want a zoning change so they can move that flea-bag lezzie operation of theirs from Doncaster to Bingham. They're trying to buy the old Doud place and the council don't want 'em in there. Don't want 'em in the town. Period. Can't say I blame 'em."

"What can *you* do about it?" Bobbye was getting interested.

"They want me to lean on Renshaw to get the variance through and agree to let 'em move in the Doud house. I sure wonder where they're gonna get that kind of money."

"Are you going to do it?"

"Aw, Renshaw owes me a favor, all right, but it won't do me any good to get mixed up with those libbers with my campaign coming up, but they keep calling the office. First that Singleton dame, then your pal Allison, then Singleton again. They just don't give up." Ed pecked Bobbye on the cheek and gave her rear end a pinch. "So long, Babe. I'll be home early if those libbers don't beat me up," he chortled.

He gunned the Caddie, then eased it down the graceful Hogarth-curved white gravel driveway. *Gotta get this driveway black topped,* Ed made a mental note, and glancing at the cast-iron jockey hitching post lamp at the end of the driveway, noted again, *I guess now we'll have to paint the little nigger guy's face white.*

CHAPTER TWO

Two sagging, donated sofas, two office chairs, a rickety desk and flaking industrial-green paint on the lumpy walls did little to alleviate the gloom of the office-cum-living-room of the Sojourner Shelter. Seated in a circle, the shelter staff looked to two of the shelter's founders, Daphne Singleton and Allison DeVries, for comfort. Daphne cleared her throat, "Thank you all for coming in a half-hour early. I felt that, with the news of Lucille Blake, we'd need to talk."

Ora Shaeffer, who called herself the community's full-time professional token, held out rosy-palmed dark brown hands.

"I didn't even see the paper till I come home from school. I didn't find out till I picked up Harriet." She nodded toward Harriet Freeman, "And she told me. I been in shock ever since. When I think how soon it come after that poor Sherry got shot — why, it's only two months —" They all spoke simultaneously.

"Oh God, it's so awful —"

"Another one we were too late for —"

"Yes —only two months after Sherry's murder."

"It's so discouraging —"

"Oh, Daph, it could have been prevented —"

Daphne looked at each woman, really saw them perhaps better than she had ever seen them before. They were so caring. From the beginning, when all they had was one hotel room and a hotline, they had been excited and hopeful about the Shelter, and so giving, and always showing up for their shifts, and now scrubbing and cleaning and begging, to furnish this broken-down house and run it on almost no money. Two years of struggling and now she had to tell them about the funding cut-off as well as try to console them about another lost woman — Lucille Blake.

"I know. I know." Tears filled Daphne's eyes. "I keep thinking I could have helped her. She was a client of mine, you know, and I talked to her the same day she disappeared. She seemed depressed. But then, I see many women like her. I've been seeing them for years. How was I to know —"

11

Allison touched Daphne's hand. "Don't be hard on yourself, Daphne."

A door flew open at the end of the dingy hall. A black woman holding a naked infant ran down the hall toward the office, shouting, "Commode's runnin' over, commode's runnin' over."

Three white teenagers and five children — two white and three light brown — clustered in the doorway of one of the two bedrooms.

"She's been puttin' Tiffany's Pampers in the toilet again, Allison. Don't look at us, we didn't do it." The complaining teenager appeared to be about twelve years old, complete with pimples, but she was nineteen, and the mother of a five-year-old and a three-year-old, and an infant of six months.

Water ran down the hall toward the office. Allison took over. She stopped the overflow, and emerged from the cellar, carrying two mops and a bucket.

"Jeeze, Lorene, I've asked you to put the Pampers in the cans — I've *begged*." She panted and mopped.

Ora took Lorene's baby into the decrepit bedroom which was crowded with four single beds and a crib. Lorene, muttering, began swishing the other mop. Harriet brought Pine-Sol and a third mop from the supply cupboard, and Ellen Kirchner began running water in another bucket in the kitchen. With an authority born of long experience, she gave orders.

"Lorene, Daphne, bring all the kids in here so we can wash their feet." The children, all sucking their thumbs, hopped happily around the hallway in the puddles. Ellen and Lorene and one of the other teenagers sat the children on the kitchen table. Daphne passed out sponges. The phone rang. Daphne called out to another teen mother who was known to be slightly 'slow,' "Get that phone, Kimberly, will you, honey? Just pick up the receiver and —"

There was a knock at the front door. "Do not, *do not* open the door, Kimberly," Daphne shouted.

The last time someone had opened the door without first

12

checking to see who was on the front porch, Leona's husband had pushed his way in, run into the kitchen and found Leona, and punched and kicked her savagely before Allison and the other shelterees could pull him off her and call the police. Although the man was jailed, a car circled the shelter for an hour every night for two weeks after that —Leona's brother-in-law. The children had been so frightened they could not go to sleep until midnight, even with Ora and Daphne and Ellen rocking them. Harriet had brought a cake one night and another night ordered pizza for everyone to try to cheer up Leona who, for days, just sat and cried.

Daphne put the two-year-old in one of the cribs and looked out of the front window. With that expensive coat and hat, it had to be Ed Krock. He was a little early.

She checked the chain lock, shoved aside two bags of donated used clothing, then opened wide the gouged and scarred door just as Kimberly yelled, "Daphne, lady want to know if we fuckin' have a fuckin' bed for her an' her two kids. Her husban' bust her fuckin' jaw."

Lorene, stripped down to her bra and bikini underpants, came around the bend from the hall, and three children in their underpants ran through the room to the kitchen. Lorene's baby screamed from her crib in the bedroom.

"Come in, Mr. Krock." Daphne swung the door wider. Out in the street, two cars drove slowly by, drivers and passengers ogling. What the hell. They needed to see this mess. Krock needed to see it. Everybody needed to know about it. They had to make people know.

After things had calmed down and Lorene had fled to her room with the children, a shelter volunteer was called to see about escorting the woman with the broken jaw to the hospital. Arrangements were made for bringing her two children to the shelter. "I guess we can find room for two more."

Finally, a wary staff faced a bewildered Ed Krock. His Balaclava hat on his knee and sweat gathering in the armholes of his nine-hundred-dollar overcoat, Ed tried to appear casual, not too friendly but not cold either. By God, they weren't a bad looking bunch, for women's libbers. He thought they all were supposed to have stringy hair and baggy clothes, with their boobs flapping loose, without any bras. All he had seen in the news throughout the late sixties and clear through the seventies were pictures of angry, yelling, ugly fat women. And those screwball, man-hating lezzies — you couldn't call *them* women, waving banners and shaking their fists.

Daphne spoke first, "Sorry for the delay, Mr. Krock —"

"Call me Ed."

"I hope we didn't inconvenience you. What happened here tonight is not unusual for Sojourner Shelter. We are overflowing at all times. There is never enough space. This place should be condemned, actually. There is continual trouble with the plumbing. The wiring is very bad, very dangerous. We need your help to get a bigger, more suitable location."

"You girls are troupers, I'll say that for you." Ed looked around, embarrassed. They were not smiling.

"We are not girls. We are adult women, Mr. Krock, asking for help so a desperately needed agency can continue to operate in Bingham County, so tragedies like the one reported in today's *Observer*, and the magistrate's office shooting two months ago will not happen again.

"You remember the Sherry Bailey case? Her husband followed her to the magistrate's office and shot and killed her. We didn't have room for her here, or she would probably be alive today."

Ed nodded and arranged his features in what he thought was an expression of concern. They didn't seem to like it that he had called them "girls." He had gotten off on the wrong foot. Daphne went on:

"Obviously we can't continue to shelter women and children under these conditions. When the Doud property came on the market, we were overjoyed because it is perfect for an agency like ours, and in excellent condition. Its perfect for a women's shelter. But the council is putting us off. That's the

14

main obstacle. We need a zoning variance, but because it's us —
because we're controversial, I know there are all kinds of stories
circulated —I think that's why council won't budge."

These dames are no dummies, Ed decided. *They're really
determined.*

He cleared his throat and said, "Ah, well, that Doud place
is pretty high. I mean, I hear they're asking seventy-five thou."

Daphne nodded. "Yes, we know the price. It *is* a lot of
money, but we're in touch with the Women's Shelter Coalition,
and there's funding available at all levels now —federal, state,
and local. And we'll conduct a fund drive. We've been operating
on a small amount — a grant from Community Way and
donations and volunteers. We have plans for a meeting room
where support groups can have rap sessions —just talk together
and calm down and not feel threatened. We want to be able to
shelter eighteen or twenty shelterees comfortably and have a play
place for the children and start working on day-care, and we
need a kitchen and a place for laundry, some decent plumbing,
efficient office space. A director or manager should live on the
premises if possible."

"How will you feed that many people?" The idea of women
and children not staying in their own homes —not having their
needs provided for by men —was making Ed nervous. His legs
felt funny. The broken-down chair creaked whenever he shifted
his weight. He unbuttoned his coat.

"Some of the women are eligible for food stamps when they
come to the Shelter," Daphne explained. "Others, if they are
not too badly injured or distraught, can sometimes grab some
canned goods or a bag of baby food, or they may have a few
dollars and be able to get along for a few days. But sometimes
they have to get out of the house —out of the violent situation —
so fast they don't have time to take anything with them."

Ed's legs were really bothering him. They itched. And his
neck itched. It was the overcoat. Vicuña and cashmere were not
supposed to be scratchy. The salesman at the Haber-Dash told
him it would not be scratchy. All this talk about women running

out of their houses, grabbing food and taking children and leaving home. It wasn't right. They must have done awful things —sassed their husbands. Why, if Bobbye ever went to a place like that —left him and moved into place like that with nigger women, with cheap, low, *poor* women! Women using that kind of language. Call girls. *Hookers!*

The one doing the talking now was supposed to be classy. Bobbye wanted her to decorate their own home! A woman like that —who associated with rough-talking hookers, black women.

And now Bobbye was getting mixed up in some kind of art class with that other one; she wasn't even going over the three bathrooms every other day —keeping them ship-shape —like she used to.

And, twice now, he had to take his own shirts to the laundry. That's what was scratching the hell out of his neck right now. They starched his wash-and-wear shirts.

He had to get up early tomorrow. He had a three-hour drive to the nuclear plant in the morning and he had already lost an hour tonight while they herded those hookers into the back room. It was like a cat house.

Like when he and Art Flayle and Joe Hibbert went to Ebbensville that time, when they were in high school — the hookers, and all those shanties down by the Ebbensville dump — why can't Bobbye meet some decent women —women with nice clothes —she used to look so cute in those shorty nighties he bought her at "Men's Night" at the Victor of Vegas shop at the mall, where all the models walked around in their underwear and served cocktails and you could pick out what you wanted, and in the back room they had bras with holes cut out of them and those crotchless pants that tied at the sides with string —he persuaded Bobbye to wear those a couple of times, but she seemed different — cold — when she wore them, and after a while she had absolutely refused to walk in front of the living room window with the lights out —with just the moonlight shining in, making her look mysterious and dangerous —something was happening to Bobbye, and it was somehow connected with this bunch of women —this cat house.

They must be lezzies. He had to get out of there, and *fast.*

Within twenty minutes he had not only pledged his support for getting council to approve Sojourner Shelter but also had promised to contribute toward the purchase of the Doud place. When he got into his car, he realized what he had done. He had actually talked to a bunch of women's libbers, and had actually made promises to help them.

That didn't mean he had to *do* it.

After Ed's departure, Daphne told the staff that Jean Blair could get no more money from Community Way, no more grants could be obtained anywhere without hiring a director —a director with a master's degree in social work. They were stunned.

"A degree!" Ora Shaeffer shrugged. "I need another year after my internship here. I can't do us no good *now*. But who knows more about women's problems than *us?* Most of us been battered our own selfs. Except maybe for you, Daphne, we all been in them scrapes."

Daphne nodded. "I experienced a sort of psychological battering when I was growing up — from seeing my aunts, neighbor women, hearing the whispers, seeing things covered up, when I was just a little *kid* —seeing the brutality being hushed up, swept under the rug. It affected me so that I never forgot it."

Harriet banged her fist on the desk. "Shit —shit —shit! I can't believe this. Daphne are you sure? What happened?"

"Yes, I'm sure. It's definite. I just found out that Barb Walton won't be here after the end of the month. She got that job she wanted in Florida, so she won't be writing any more grant letters for us. To qualify for funding we have to have a full-time CEO, a Board of Directors and a Rape Crisis Counselor.

"This is going on all over the United States because so

many shelters are being formed, and there's a tri-state coalition now — it's being organized to help women run the shelters, to keep them informed on what's going on all over the state — throughout the whole country."

The women were silent. They slumped in their chairs, thinking. Daphne put on her coat. She was unaccustomed to silence such as this at the shelter. The news had hit hard.

Ora stirred and began to tie her scarf under he chin. "Women's lives is such a mess." The others stared at her blankly.

"Yeah, I guess it's our fault. Right?" Allison buttoned her coat resolutely. One by one the others got to their feet.

Daphne opened the door and started to go out but changed her mind and turned and faced them. "That kind of thinking is the thinking of *victims* —permanently vulnerable victims. And no, it *isn't* our fault!"

In her stridency she surprised herself. "It is the fault of a rotten system controlled by old white men —it's a gerontocracy —that makes scapegoats of the most dependent and powerless — women and children and poor and sick people. They get made into punching bags, literally and figuratively. They get blamed for their own situation because they're beaten up, and they're beaten up because they're poor and female!" Daphne's heart was pounding.

"Well, gee, Daphne —I didn't mean —" Allison's face reddened.

"Oh, I know. I'm sorry I yelled. But women have to learn to take control of their lives — to fight back, and *not* with violence, not with brutality." Daphne waggled her head comically and put her arm around Allison and cajoled, "Let's all go get pizza before we go home. My treat."

CHAPTER THREE

Hal Renshaw — "Doctor Harold Renshaw" it said in the college catalogue —kicked the snow from his shoes, unlocked the pseudo-Tudor front door of Chalmers Hall, and walked through the sour-smelling anteroom to the offices of the Department of History. He liked to come to his office in the early morning stillness to think. It settled his brains to have coffee and Danish there, with just the quiet mustiness, without Mrs. Helbrun's typewriter going, or students milling around, or the phone ringing every ten minutes.

He hung his coat in the outer office closet. Mrs. Helbrun had another bouquet of plastic flowers on her desk. For some reason her bouquets depressed Hal. Someone had stolen the previous one — a clutch of virulent pink roses. The new arrangement was spiky and neon blue. Maybe he'd be lucky. Maybe someone would steal this one too.

Hal sipped his coffee. Through the window he could see Barry Spiegel's corner office across the quadrangle. The light was on. Barry must be practicing his French horn. Hal knew Barry was working on the horn part for Mozart's Quartet in B sharp major. The viola, violin and cello parts were in the hands of Barry's friends, to be learned for their chamber music group.

For an environmental economist, with a two-pack-a-day habit, Barry Spiegel was a damn good wind instrument player. And he was a friend to Hal —good-humored, witty, optimistic, dependable. A rare person, really. He had seemed fairly enthusiastic about Hal's decision to run for Congress on a third party ticket. "If you have the guts and the drive, Hal," he had wheezed through clouds of smoke, "...if you're crazy enough. The fact that a Citizen Action Party even exists at *all* is crazy. You have the energy, God knows. Believe me, you'll need it. But it would look better, I think, if you were married."

He had peered at Hal through another gray gust, grinning. "Forty-three, divorced, and honest, intellectual, peace-loving, anti-nuke, a third-party penniless liberal espousing *liberté, fraternité, egalité*. But it's very difficult to unseat an incumbent,

19

Hal. Drew Burgess may be a Republican —certainly not the majority party in the 10th District —but he's very slick. And I hope you don't take it too hard when Ed Krock and that Democratic machine trot out endless bucks for TV campaign ads, and when Consolidated Electric lines Honest Ed's pockets so they can go full-speed ahead on that nuclear and medical waste dump. And Krock is 'way ahead of you in his campaign." Barry singsonged in a nasal whine, "'Yew can believe in Krock, and that's no crock!' Have you *seen* those bumper stickers, Hal? Ye Gods!" Barry was a demanding mentor, and he would prove to be an efficient petitioner, cheering section and father-confessor.

Hal took another sip of coffee. He wrote on a note pad: Campaign issues:

Stop corporate flight.
Cut back on insane arms build-up.
Steel workers' obsolescence?
Three-day work week?
Stop sheriff sales.

He underlined:
Law firms buying up homes; quietly becoming rich from people's despair.
Extend unemployment benefits!

He underlined:
   Nuclear threat.
   Hazardous waste.
   Blake Casting Co's Vale Creek Mine property possible waste dump site?
   Will Senator Krock's log-rolling kill — in committee — nuclear waste ban bill?
   Has Drew Burgess done one constructive thing while in Congress?

The sun was coming out. A few wan rays lit ice-covered

branches of the locust trees outside Hal's window. He leaned on the window sill and looked out.

Several campus dogs emerged from behind the Fine Arts Building and sniffed each other, then frolicked in the center of the empty quadrangle. Jaded habitués of fraternity and sorority house gourmet garbage areas, they soon would station themselves at the cafeteria door for breakfast handouts.

The cafeteria concession featured a plexiglas blackboard over the entrance with the words, "Food for Thought" written by a chalk-held fist, in old style P.O. Peterson third-grader script. Chalky ovals and T's marched above and below in lined spaces.

In the twelve years that Hal had spent at the university level, his ten years of teaching were the best. He had loved getting the students fired up about American History. His classes were almost always crowded, and the exhilarating rap sessions after class were as gratifying to him as anything he had ever experienced. He could reach even the most turned-off, tuned-out student it seemed. He told them about the unquenchable idea of freedom, how the American Revolution had inspired the French to revolt against terrible, incredible oppression and how every major war against oppression since then —the American Civil War, the Russian Revolution —had taken a cue from that glorious, idealistic, American rebellion.

And there was the drafting of the incomparable Bill of Rights.

"Designing America," he had called his course.

Earnestly, he had instructed the fresh-faced young people in their rights: the right to dissent, to be free from censorship —he explained the founding fathers' idea in insisting that there be no religious influence, no sectarian restrictions in the shaping of their splendid document of government. The students had listened intently when Hal described a theocracy, comparing teenagers' lives in the seventeenth century to the students' own teen generation. He could make history live for them, could reach them with a picture of the way life was then. They had loved it and pressed and clustered about his desk after every class. He was doing what he loved: teaching. Teaching something that he believed in passionately.

Now, as department head, he was removed from all that. He had needed the money, after the divorce, and when Dr. Armstrong had died suddenly, Hal was the one singled out for the honor of stepping into the older man's administrative shoes. He could not refuse. Doreen had threatened to take both of the children. She made more money than he did, and the idea of life without seeing his son and daughter filled him with such dread that he agreed to take the job. It meant a little more money, a little more prestige, a lot more work and none of the joys of teaching. But he could afford to keep the children nine months of the year, and although there were few extras now, without Doreen's salary, they were getting along.

Doreen kicked in enticements —summer junkets to Cape Cod, and Aspen for Christmas, and even a five-day trip to Springfield, Illinois, to see Lincoln's home —a treat which Hal had never even dreamed of affording for himself. But he was happy for the children. They were turning out to be damned nice kids, in spite of all the fighting he and Doreen had done throughout the poor kids' babyhood and into their anxious junior high days.

"Kids are resilient," Hal told himself, over and over, but the guilt he felt, the remorse for filling his children's baby ears with the sounds of Doreen's and his screaming fights, would not abate. Hal Renshaw's conscience and intellect and trust in human decency directed his every move and would be, ultimately, his undoing.

Mrs. Helbrun stirred in the outer office. Hal cleaned the crumbs off his desk and coughed loudly, to indicate that he was in his office, although he knew she had seen his car in the parking lot and his coat in the closet. Why did he fear Mrs. Helbrun? She intimidated him, yet no matter how he planned dialogues with her she always got the upper hand. The truth was she reminded Hal of his mother, a stern but loving woman.

Passing herself off as fifty-eight, Mrs. Helbrun was a vigorous seventy-five and had at least another twenty years of voluble stamina to go. She was organized and tidy, and diplomatic and stylish in a rather flashy, dyed-haired way, and could type a mile a minute. She had been an exhibition typist back in Minnesota in the days when women typists were a novelty.

"We've come a long way since Bob Cratchit," she liked to point out to Hal. She was a Charles Dickens fan and kept Hal on his toes about the Victorian period. And she had total recall. One of her favorite stories was about her first job and how her egotistical boss had dictated a letter to the feisty, then very flame-haired nineteen-year-old stenographer, referring, in the letter, to his own pulchritude. When asked if she knew how to spell "pulchritude" and what it meant, she had not endeared herself to management by replying that, yes, she knew how to spell it, and she thought it meant "big stomach."

"Hi there. ACLU meeting tonight, Dr. R., and you have a Council meeting tonight also. Quo Vadis?" Mrs. Helbrun stuck her head in the doorway and took in everything; the paper cup and paper bag from Food for Thought, Hal's furtive fingertip dabbing at the coffee ring.

"You have a meeting today with Auditing in a half hour. Dr. Allen and the Board meeting tomorrow morning at nine. You're supposed to report on the Minute Men Conference of Collegiate Historians. That 'Minute Men' is a sexist title, incidentally. You got your notes together?"

"Yep."

"The department is expected to make a showing, Dr. Renshaw. None of the correlation committees have reported. I have not received one outline, or one audiovisual presentation account from *any* committee member —not one report from —"

"Mrs. H., let's try to get to the department heads today. Let's tell 'em to put up or shut up. They yammer about correlation but won't get their buns over here to make a presentation." Mrs. Helbrun poked at her rusty-hued outmoded Afro with a cerise plastic pick. "I hate to bring this up, Doctor, but you have to tell Bentley and Merrit the bad news before next week. They have to have their desks cleared out so the movers can get everything out. Construction begins during spring break."

Hal felt queasy. Having to give two excellent teachers the ax, ostensibly due to state funding cut-backs but at the same time, having to watch preparations for an expensive addition to the gymnasium —more locker rooms, more bleachers and three new racquet ball courts —enraged him. The Phys Ed department was a goddamned spa! They had all kinds of weightlifting equipment and saunas and hot tubs, and the women even had spot-reducing machines and hair dryers. In the meantime, his department had waited a year for two updated classroom maps. One map they had been using pre-dated World War II and showed the Austro-Hungarian Empire spread across central Europe. In fact, the map was a pre-World-War-I relic. A relic from before the time of the Great War!

The Great War.

The poet Wilfred Owen saw enough beauty in that unspeakable bloodiness to express the ineffable lines that Hal's children now were reading in English class in the private school for which Hal had to pay seven hundred dollars a month, not counting transportation and books and lunches. Celeste and Pete would not pack their own lunches no matter how much ham, bologna, cheese, lettuce, celery, wheat bread and peanut butter Hal laid in. They were simply too lazy or too sleepy, and he couldn't get organized enough to do it. He was afraid they would contract pellagra or scrofula or some other bizarre disease that Doreen could jeer at him about, so he gave them extra money to eat at a Food for Thought near their chi-chi private school. It galled him to do it. He was a goddamned elitist, for Christ's sake.

"I won't be able to make the Council meeting, I guess. I *cannot* miss this ACLU meeting. I missed the last two meetings."

Mrs. Helbrun was whistling though her teeth. Hal strained

to hear the tune. It was "Little Gypsy Sweetheart." Another relic from the Victor Herbert era. His freakish musical ear caused Hal no end of distraction. He could remember tunes and words of hundreds of songs, and even the original keys in which they were written. Mrs. Helbrun annoyed him by whistling flat, and she seemed stuck in the 1920's.

Hal dialed Daphne Singleton's number, as she had requested via Mrs. Helbrun, to tell her that he could not attend the Council meeting. Daphne's line was busy.

Beige satin with ecru lace is about as sensational a sight on a dark-haired, dark-eyed woman as anyone could hope to see, Daphne decided, as she took in her reflection in the mirrored fireplace wall of her eclectic, sun-filled sitting room. Lavish, handmade peignoirs and nightgowns were a sybaritic indulgence in which she delighted. And her morning coffee, in a gleaming, white Rosenthal porcelain cup and saucer, filled her with hope and the belief in an inevitable, ultimate good, day after day, morning after morning. Her beautiful sitting room, one of those wax logs in the fireplace, and that lovely, steaming coffee, the little porcelain pitcher of milk, the tiny delicate envelope of artificial sweetener and the linen napkin laid on her favorite brass filligreed-edged tray with scrolled handles —such simple things to afford so much pleasure!

Eight o'clock. Still a few minutes to linger over her coffee to leaf through some Katherine Mansfield short stories, or Amy Lowell's poems.

Today Daphne read Walt Whitman's great poem, *When Lilacs Last in the Dooryard Bloom'd*. Whitman's narrative of the journey of Lincoln's funeral train across America reached out to her with exquisite rhythms and imagery. There was something about lilacs that stirred Daphne — the moist perfume, the romantic color. Daphne thought of the dead Lucille Blake, Lucille, who was never called Lucy and who, a newspaper article had said after her death "never had taken the Lord's name in vain."

In the mirror Daphne saw sunlight, still slightly misty, softly outlining her beige satin shoulders. A treasured Philadelphia orchestra recording, a collector's item, of Mozart's 40th Symphony, caressed her with its elegant Ormandy strings.

The telephone's ring slashed into her reverie. Her "Hello" elicited no answer.

There was breathing.

Oh no! Not again.

Not him. Not another obscene call!

Then, the breathy, insinuating drawl, "Hello, Daphne."

It was not an unpleasant voice. It was pitched rather high, and vaguely familiar. He called every month or so. He drawled again, "Do you like to have your pussy ate?" The stertorous breathing. The outrage. The exasperation. The *awful grammar.*

Without thinking, Daphne cried, "Eaten. *Eaten*, you stupid jerk! Watch your participles." The caller slammed down the receiver.

Would they *never* give up, those creeps? Was that *all* they thought of? All they had in their misbegotten lives? Some salacious, leering phone call? A feeble mental picture of some sex act? Of some mindless, genital coupling? Her whole mood was broken. She stomped into the kitchen and rinsed out her cup and put away the brass tray.

She was giving herself a loofa sponge rub in the shower when the phone rang again. She pulled a towel around her hips and glanced at her antique glass-domed clock. She had twenty-eight minutes to get to her shop to open up for the day. James and Debby would not be in until noon. Running across the bedroom to the telephone, she turned her ankle.

"Yes?" she croaked into the phone.

"Um, Daphne Singleton?"

"Yes. Yes?" She was panting. Her ankle throbbed.

"Well, uh —"Hal cleared his throat.

Daphne was aghast. He *dared* to call again. what sick, warped nerve! Daphne shouted, "What, oh, *what* is going on in that obscene pea-brain of yours, you goddamn creep?"

Unconsciously, Hal stepped backward one step. He must have gotten the wrong number.

"I beg your pardon? This is Harold Renshaw. My secretary said —"

Dear heaven. It was Dr. Renshaw. Daphne sat down. "I thought you were an obscene caller." She rubbed her ankle. "Please disregard my previous statement."

"Well, I'm endeavoring to, Ms. Singleton."

"I really apologize. They usually stop calling if I yell. They hang up fast. But anyway, thank you for calling back. Can you be at the Council meeting tonight? Your secretary said you have a conflict —"

"I'm indeed sorry, but I cannot. Was there something specific you wanted to talk to me about" Students were shuffling past his outer office door. Hal could see the florid faced auditors gingerly taking seats opposite Mrs. Helbrun's desk. Another morning of arithmetic loomed —endless, convoluted maddening bureaucracy.

"I was told that Council would vote, tonight, on whether to permit the Sojourner Women's Shelter to locate in Bingham. A variance will be needed. Twenty-seventh Street is zoned residential and —"

Hal's ear buzzed from the unexpected shouting. Doreen never shrieked like that. Doreen had always managed to whine and howl simultaneously.

" —and Senator Krock has promised that something will be done —" Daphne was trying not to wheedle, " —and we're really counting on all of you. And now I'm going to have to run. I have to open my business in a few minutes. My decorating shop, you know, Designs For Living. It's downtown." She realized, *I'm gurgling. I sound like a gushy Yuppie.* She gushed on, "I've heard about your history classes and your Citizen Action Party. They're famous. Well, the classes, anyway. I like what you call your history course, 'Designing America.' That's very nice."

Nice? Hal thought, *It's just my whole fucking life.*

He felt acrid coffee and the ersatz Danish backing up into his throat. He'd have to put her off for a few days. Promise to talk to Krock. Get to him and the others later. He would have to begin a new phase of his life —that of trying even *harder* to please people. Trying to do some of the many things they would ask of him, yet still not cheat or lie or deceive. His thoughts flowed together. He would build the Citizen Action Party in Bingham County. He would prove that it could be done, that a strong potential membership was there waiting for leadership, wanting a voice at last, drained of hope for any future with the present military exercises that were being passed off as the U.S. government.

He wiped his mouth and adjusted his glasses. He'd never heard anything quite like it. A woman on whom obscene callers hung up. It certainly was a switch.

Driving through the Christmas-card-quaint streets of Bingham, Daphne found herself being seduced, as always, by the turn-of-the-century architecture. She slowed down as she passed her favorite Italian and French Renaissance Revival houses. Many of the most beautiful of these buildings now housed law firms. Even the tasteless renovations: new siding, squatty additions, the cheapest materials, could not obliterate the structures' superb proportions. Elegant pairs of roof cornice brackets, arched window heads and over-door pediments survived, shaming neighboring cleaning establishments, realty offices and already-run-down seventies apartment complexes.

Several streets back from, and parallel to, Bingham's wide, main street, began residential areas. Graceful Carpenter's Gothic styles were interspersed with homely, substantial 1920's four- and five-bedroom middle class single-family frame or brick homes with neat front yards. Many porches now were draped with crudely lettered bed sheets exhorting, "Yea Bingham Beat Doncaster."

A 1910 almanac had described Bingham's "many agricultural and industrial attractions, and with its easy access from every direction, it lies in the center of the largest coal and mineral basin in the United States. Its location, too, is one of great natural beauty. From its first history, Bingham society has been marked by a decided religious and intellectual tendency. Each church has several social organizations by means of which the people become united in purpose and members are joined together in a bond of sympathetic friendship."

Several stolid, massive, buttressed Presbyterian churches occupied prominent Bingham corners. A Methodist church competed with this dressed-stone Calvinist display, but on a much smaller scale, on a smaller lot, with fake buttresses. The Anglican church, an eyebrow-raising late-comer to Bingham, having picked up new members when disgruntled Presbyterians left the fold due to guild disputes, recently were able to build Phase II of their new brick sanctuary and no longer had to hold services in the basement.

A few, fast-growing, affluent Evangelical Protestant congregations kept architecturally low profiles with unobtrusive, deceptively humble frame churches.

There was an impressive yellow brick Lutheran church, and trim red-brick Roman Catholic church and parish house. An attached elementary school (with an ever-increasing number of lay teachers) occupied a third of one block.

But it was the unemotional, disciplined Scots-Irish Presbyterians who were Bingham's arteries of religious and social mores. Lifetimes were spent defining criteria for membership in the two medieval fortresses. Non-WASPS were not encouraged. A black person appearing within these Christian bastions would have caused a panic, was unthinkable, unspeakable. In fact, when a black family *was* seen on a Bingham street, they were more than likely visiting a prisoner in the county jail —this xenophobic hamlet was the County Seat.

Over the decades Bingham citizenry had actively cultivated its 19th century White Anglo-Saxon Protestant character. Only one or two Jewish families — usually dry goods merchants or beer and soft drink distributors — stayed on, discreetly, for several generations.

"You'd never even know they were Jewish!" some of the more charitable WASPS said of them.

The two or three Italian-American families were regarded with amused contempt and suspicion.

In the center of town, opposite the courthouse, there was an old-fashioned grassy square park with shade trees and benches. Caissons and cannon balls rested at the four corners of a stone-based sculpture group in the park's center; two doughboys and two Civil War Union soldiers directed their boyish bronze profiles and muskets and rifles at the courthouse. A 1925 fire had destroyed the original, ponderous, domed courthouse. The art-deco-modern design of the new courthouse, with streamlined corners and vaguely Mayanesque cast concrete plaques, clashed with adjacent antebellum buildings.

The middle-aged and elderly of Bingham walked their dogs nightly in the safe deserted town-square park. Their dogs defecated and peed at the feet of the bronze soldiers, in the tulip beds, along the gaslit concrete walks and at the bases of two old cast-iron drinking fountains that were beloved by the historical society. Guitar-laden Bingham teenagers, who, on soft summer evenings, attempted to gather in the pleasant park, were accosted by the community's three policemen and told to move on. The young of Bingham, when they finished high school, tended to move on from and out of Bingham, permanently.

Bordering the business and residential districts and overlooking a large lake and an eighteen-hole golf course and country club were the many landscaped acres of Chatterley Estates. Here physicians, lawyers and industrialists, mostly WASPs but an occasional Italian, Slavic, Filipino or Hindu medical doctor (cleansed of ethnicity by the financial power of the medical hierarchy) an Italian shopping mall developer, a Greek contractor or two and a few assimilated Jews formed their properties in a time-honored — and over-worked — metaphorical circle against the marauding working class: second- and third-generation Slavs, Hungarians, Poles, Scots and Irish, Italians, Germans, Greeks, Lebanese, Syrians, Blacks and a few still-poor but upwardly-mobile WASPs.

Shabby homes of Blacks crouched in the fringes of white districts or were clumped a few hundred yards from industrial plants. Rows of spiritless company housing (actually barracks) from the '20s and '30s, and collapsing remnants of Victorian frame cottages were dubious shelter for the large, angry black population. Although this depressed, disadvantaged group delivered up a fair share of oppressed women and children to the Sojourner Shelter, the proportion was not as high as might be expected. The shelter staff had observed that black extended family networks often cared for their brutalized members with quiet strength and warmth and a grim sort of "in" humor.

Fanning out in all directions from Bingham Borough were beautiful green townships; hills and valleys that comforted the astonishingly hardy immigrants who arrived in the great 19th century wave to work in the iron mills and coal mines and factories of Bingham County. These homesick laborers found a familiarity in the verdant European-looking Appalachian foothills. Fueled with genetic-pool vigor, they and succeeding generations worked and schemed and saved with the same enormous vitality and yearning as did their agrarian forebears to get some land out in one of the townships, with some trees and a place for a vegetable garden, a place to grow things.

They prospered and built graceless "memory" houses of dressed stone, brick or stucco, houses like those described to them by Babba or Oma or Nana —like the factory owners' sturdy homes in the Old Country.

The immigrants raised gorgeous children, vegetables and flowers, and kept large Roman and Orthodox Catholic parishes going. A few Lutheran and Baptist and Presbyterian churches were built in the townships, and Evangelical, Charismatic and Pentecostal sects sprang up along the way as the population had roused itself from the torpor and defeat of the Great Depression, and felt the beginnings of World War II anxiety.

Second and third generations eventually won, through strong and sometimes brutal unions, comfortable wages from equally brutal and predominantly WASP industrial management. The present ethnic generations began to improve their homes. They (and, curiously, many township WASPs as well) felt compelled to live underground like some atavistic tribe of super-consuming Mole People, furnishing the basements of their homes with dark brown imitation wood paneling, red carpeting, imitation leather sofas and chairs and bars and bar stools. They fitted out these subterranean abodes with spotless gadget-filled kitchens and bathrooms and TV sets, and lived the major portion of their lives here, returning at night to the rooms above grade to sleep. In these homes the unused rooms above ground — living room, dining, room, kitchen, "den" — were stiff and new looking, immaculate and still; musicless, bookless, conversationless. Each year township wives gravely inspected each other's unused show kitchens in church fund-raising tours. They seldom ventured into their show living rooms except to fasten more securely the clear plastic protective slipcovers, and wipe and polish and vacuum away, religiously each week, any dust speck, any fragment of printed matter, any sign of human life or thought.

Recliner chairs, red and gold flocked velvet wall paper, swagged draperies like those in TV movie brothel sets, prints and figurines of colonial ladies playing harpsichords —these were what most Bingham County people asked about and expected to see in Daphne's shop. They were dismayed to find that the shop had few gew-gaws, or doo-dads as they were called colloquially. Stripped pine hutches and tables, baskets, quilts, understated linen and chintz-covered furniture, hand-thrown pottery from North Carolina arranged on hand-loomed mats that were Daphne's pride, were baffling to the Mole People and were the cause of the relatively slow growth of her clientele.

Yet Daphne, too, loved Bingham County's serene hills, and stayed on and persevered despite being over-educated for most of her clientele. When consulted, she would go and stand in the middle of her prospective clients' antiseptically clean rooms that gleamed with pale blue, or pink, or lime, paint, and listen as they requested the same thing over and over again, in home after home. They wanted to have duplicated in their homes the red and black furnishings of an English pub-style restaurant chain, the CorBlimey Steakhouse and Lounge. Gently, she would try to suggest something better. Sometimes she succeeded.

In an attempt to educate their taste —for they certainly had money to spend —Daphne, from time to time taught evening classes at the Community College. Young housewives and matrons (men seldom enrolled), were attentive as she showed Metropolitan Museum slides: wonderful pictures of ancient Egypt, the Ishtar Gates, the Ghiberti Doors, France's Vaux Le Vicomte. She described the evolution of various styles, explained principles of balance and proportion, the difference between a lithograph and a mezzotint. During question periods hands would rise and Daphne would be asked how to clean a cut-velvet sofa or how to remove spots from plastic kitchen counters.

To these simple, vigorous, uneducated township people, the town of Bingham, their county seat, represented (next to a Las Vegas vacation) the highest social and cultural attainment. To them Bingham was the ultimate achievement; all that they should aspire to be. But they made few attempts to emulate actual WASP life. WASP rituals mystified them: stiff WASP weddings, the whole idea of Protestantism, the repressed, formal, affected way Bingham women talked, the AAUW, the funny, cold way WASPs treated their children —as if they didn't like them —how uncomfortable the men always seemed, even in sports clothes; the strange, unseasoned WASP food.

To the people of the town of Bingham, however, the adjacent residential community of Briarwood, also predominantly WASP, with more millionaires per square mile than any other community in the state, represented absolute social impeccability, to be emulated at all times, and to some, at almost any cost. Bourgeois Bingham matrons patterned their lives after what they thought Briarwood's pampered chatelaines' lives might be, from what they heard or read in the paper, or imagined.

Back during fabled Briarwood's early days, in the 1880s, the wives liked to keep busy with charitable activities, and they formed an exclusive club called "Children's Life," membership in which was one of the most coveted of all social coups. Bingham matrons —lawyers' and physicians' and industrialists' wives —quickly formed a similar, exclusive group, "Bulwark to Children and Youth" or BTCY, or Bitsy as it came to be known. Membership was by invitation only.

For a woman to receive a Bitsy Bid was to be assured, for all time, of her own social acceptability and that of her daughters and granddaughters. The Bitsy group gradually absorbed Children's Lifers to become the town's principal social focus.

Bitsys met at each other's homes over the years to hem diapers and belly bands and infant nightgowns for the poor (the flannel left annoying lint on their dark tailored suits and *crêpe* dresses), and they served refreshments —tea at one end of the table, coffee at the other. Almost exclusively WASP (the "Bulwark" was right out of a Presbyterian hymn), the group had an auxiliary group, Bitsy Junior, which sponsored young girls in white puffed-sleeved formal gowns and long white kid gloves at an annual Bitsy Junior Sweet Sixteen Ball in the closest thing to a debutantes' ball that Bingham County dared.

Now, with Aid to Families With Dependent Children, food stamps and that sort of thing, there was no need for diaper-hemming any more. In fact, the embarrassment of dealing with people with whom they had so little in common was alleviated for the Bitsys. But now that there was so much unemployment in the region and mills were shutting down (or stealthily moving south to non-union areas) and so many mortgage foreclosures, it was embarrassing to hold Bitsy Junior Balls. They switched to charitable, tax write-off types of events: Romantic Frolics or Coaches at Eight with guests transported to the country club in restored 19th century broughams, victorias and carriages, as well as events called Sleigh rides at Seven or Buckboards for Bingham Special Ed. Briarwood, forever anglophiliac Briarwood, was *heaven* to Bingham!

The Briarwood Mystique also colored other Binghamite areas, thoughts and acts: there were the Briarwood Country Day School, The all-Republican League of Women Voters, the Briarwood Art League with its annual "Hot Diggety" fundraiser featuring over fifty types of hot-dog and bun combinations, and there was the Briarwood "Look" —wrap-around skirts with appliqued whales or watermelon slices, pants and jackets made of what appeared to be pieced quilts, preppy blazer outfits and black watch plaid skirts, plaid scarves, plaid purses, plaid luggage; and the Briarwood men's "Look" —English gaiters and country gentleman woolen knickers and vests (favorites of Briarwood adolescent boys) and brilliantly polished handmade loafer shoes worn with everything from chino trousers and big-game hunters' coats to falling-apart jeans that the men wore when knocking about picturesque Briarwood Village; the self-consciously bucolic, quaint Village with its needlepoint and bargello schools and the colored yarns they marketed, the gourmet meat shops, equestrienne shops, fish markets, travel agencies, Porsche and Mercedes and BMW agencies, and ubiquitous pet boutiques. All this enthralled the Binghamites just as Binghamites and their indefinably charming, tree-lined streets enthralled the township Mole People.

Pulling into the parking lot beside her shop —a remodelled, former laundry now board-and-battened with alternating brick sections, evoking a Palladian feeling —Daphne noticed with pleasure that James had arranged in the three front windows a collection of country accessories: large shells and rough boxes and trunks and woven-twig-framed mirrors, with contemporary linen fabric samples in grays and corals. Daphne thought, *I swear he could take two can openers and a storage battery and make something exciting to look at.*

Mrs. Dr. Hartley was entering the parking lot in her Jaguar as Daphne switched on the shop lights and the FM classical music station that "fills the joint with class —" as Debbie put it. But, alas, Rachmaninov's "Isle of the Dead" was depositing sepulchral gloom on the baskets of coral and yellow silk tulips which Debbie and James had placed about the shop entrance. Daphne made a mental note to make some tapes, a little Eric Satie or some Debussy piano pieces. Something consistently light, not so moody.

Mrs. Hartley was heading down the aisle. Daphne forced a smile. If the Hartleys cancelled their sideboard order, Designs for Living would be in trouble. Daphne had kited a check on the assumption that she'd be getting the balance payment on the sideboard.

"Hello, Daphne. I hope I'm not persona au gratin around here." A red angora tam o'shanter set off Mrs. Hartley's rather flat features. In a forest green, burgundy and bright red plaid stole over a red wool gathered skirt, and burgundy boots, she was a Lammermoor Castle escapee. A faint bluish shadow sloped across one eye, partially hidden by the tam o'shanter. Daphne realized, with an icy brain-flick, that it was a bruise.

"I've been to Grosse Pointe for a few days. The doctor's niece got married Saturday. It was a gorgeous wedding." Mrs. Hartley stripped off burgundy kid gloves and slapped them into a seven-hundred-dollar calf handbag. Up front a youngish-looking woman entered the shop hesitantly, and was glancing around.

"The Isle of the Dead" wailed on. Debbie really couldn't be expected to turn it off, Daphne reasoned.

"They had everything from soup to nuts at that wedding! They did it up right —I can tell you. The church was decorated gorgeous. And the wedding party, well, phew! They were *something*." Mrs. Hartley settled her two hundred pounds into a delicate, emerald green damask Georgian occasional chair. "Twelve bridesmaids in apricot silk, the ushers and the groom in dinner jackets with ruffled shirts, and concubines around their waists —well —it was beautiful. And music! They had a full choir in cossacks that sang acupulco!"

"That must have been *some* wedding —" Daphne said. *But what about the sideboard?* she thought. *Jesus,* she thought, *will I ever get in the clear with this fucking business?*

"The Isle of the Dead" had given way to the 10 a.m. misogynist musicologist, Darrell Foss, who giggled salaciously about opera plots and femme fatale sopranos. The favorite, this morning, combined a (hee hee) Raquel Welch type and a (hee hee) more virginal soprano who had, still,"been around plenty." After that smarmy introduction, he played the trio from *Der Rosenkavalier.*

That man must be stopped, Daphne vowed to herself. Mrs. Hartley rattled on as the soaring voices of Octavian, the Marschallin and Sophie filled the air with Strauss's sublime music. Higher and higher the superb voices climbed. Mrs. Hartley's lips were moving. Daphne pulled herself back to earth.

" —and so, whenever it's convenient, I'd like you to come out to the house and I'll give you some of my views. Our moving date is Wednesday, so you better come out the Monday after. Let's see," Mrs. Hartley rummaged in her purse for her check book, " —I owe a balance on the cadenza, don't I?"

"I'm Senator Krock's wife." Bobbye introduced herself in the leftover gingerbread haze of Mrs. Hartley's perfume. Daphne extended her hand. "Hi. I'm Daphne Singleton. I met your husband at the Sojourner Shelter a few days ago. We had a nice visit." Daphne had a way of guiding potentially good clients, good leads, around the shop. *How small she is,* Daphne thought, *but she carries herself like a much bigger person.*

"What's *your* name, Mrs. Krock?"

"What?" Bobbye looked confused.

"What's *your* name? You told me your husband's name."

"Oh. Yeah. Okay. It's Bobbye. B-O-B-B-Y-E. I know a friend of yours, Allison DeVries. We're in the same craft class at Briarwood Art League."

"Yes. Allison's a good friend. Lots of wonderful work gets

done when she tackles anything. She's really speedy. She's manager of the Sojourner Shelter. Do you like the Briarwood Art League? They asked me if I'd teach there for the summer session. I decided to do it. Interior Design is what they want, but I'd rather do a History of Art course. With that background it's possible to develop taste far beyond a list of "do's and don't's." They walked together down an aisle of vignettes featuring intimate seating combined with unusual window treatments. A pair of lacquered Oriental side chairs didn't interest Bobbye. Before she could think it out, Daphne broke one of her own professional rules about discussing clients and confided, "That room is —was —for Lucille Blake's home." She pointed to the two colored renderings, which, for display purposes, she had finally finished painting.

"The Blake Casting Blakes? The woman who —"

"Yes."

"Did you know her well?"

"Yes. Well, no, not *well*, but I knew her. I shouldn't be discussing it — a client, a former client, but it was such a tragedy, her suicide."

"Do you really think it *was* suicide?" Bobbye said. "I heard that her husband poisoned her," she blurted.

The FM station gave a loud squawk. Through interference, Darrell Foss' last selection could be heard. It was Vanessa's solo "Do Not Utter A Word," from the Samuel Barber opera. The static continued, but the singer was identifiable as Leontyne Price. Daphne had heard clearly what Bobbye said about Lucille Blake.

Bobbye made an appointment with Daphne to look at the Krock house.

What a break, Daphne thought. She liked Bobbye, and Bobbye seemed to like her, but the sudden wave of nausea she felt had risen from her mental picture of Leonard Blake's thin-lipped grin that she had observed when he had passed her once on the street.

Outside the shop, peering through the front window and

38

seeing Daphne with a client, Ellen Kirschner went ahead
anyway, and rapped on the glass. The Sojourner Shelter situation
demanded immediate attention. Daphne motioned her in. Ellen
was more agitated than usual. She had her youngest child, Mark,
by the hand.

"Daph, you've got to do something. Ora called me. The
sewer backed up in the cellar at the Shelter! There's water up to
their knees. It's bad. I have Kathy home from school with a
cold. She's in the car now. My mother wouldn't watch her and
Mark even for a few minutes so I could run down there —
Allison and Ora are about out of their minds. They have eight
new shelterees. Leona's still there with her three, and the fire
department flatly refused to flush out the sewer again and —"

"Ellen, slow down."

"But what can we do? The last time it backed up they got
out the fire hoses and the firemen were so mad they yelled at
Allison and Harriet. It was awful. The pipes were clogged with
tampons! It's embarrassing. My *mother* found out about the
tampons. It was all over town. She was horrified. She and her
Bitsy group are always talking about 'those awful people at the
women's shelter.' That's all I hear! She wants Kelly to make
Bitsy Junior —she gave *up* on me, long ago, you know, but she
nags me about the shelter all the time —"

"Listen, Ellen, if that sewer were clogged up with jock
straps or condoms instead of tampons, believe me, it would be
another matter. They'd be joking and winking and it would be
the talk of the town —all good-natured banter and joking, and
they'd flush out the drains and the town would love it. But
because they think it's some filthy, disgusting female thing —oh,
go on home. I'll call the fire department. And I don't care *what*
those tight-ass Bitsy Biddies say. They're worse woman-haters
than the men."

Ellen started toward the door. Daphne called after her,
"Did you finish that set of Hitchcock chairs? Not the set of four
—the set of six. They're the ones I need. James can pick them
up." Ellen was forever behind schedule in restoring furniture for

Daphne.

"I'm nearly done. I need a couple more days. I'll call you." Ellen's turpentine-dried, laundry-chafed hands itched in their woolen mittens. She was tired. Kathy had awakened three times during the night, and Mark was catching her cold. And being twenty-five pounds overweight was depressing Ellen. She noticed Daphne's and the other woman's —the customer's —high fashion outfits, their cared-for skin and hair. The woman was wandering to another part of the shop. Her suede pants were gathered at the ankle in that new style. *God,* thought Ellen, *—it must be wonderful to have clothes, plenty of space to work, some free time. To feel in control, and not always feel pressure, pressure, pressure.*

Three-year-old Mark was pulling at her coat, whimpering and sniffling. Ellen picked him up and walked to the car. She felt chastened and reassured at the same time. Daphne's assertiveness was inspiring. Time after time she cut through superficiality and ignorance. She pointed out the stupid misogyny that seemed to be everywhere, in this town, in the whole world; it was everywhere! But Daphne was fearless. And she had a business to run!

But she can take more risks, be more assertive, Ellen reasoned. *She doesn't have sick children, or the expenses of a large family. She doesn't have a mother who's an insufferable snob, a mother who pulls her down all the time with her self-hating brand of ridicule and condemnation of all females. Her mother doesn't lay guilt trips on her constantly. Daphne doesn't have a mentally unstable husband who's living in a fog of war movies and sports matches and anger.*

Mark and Kathy had fallen asleep. *I'll just drive around for a while,* Ellen thought. *Anything but hassling these kids into the house.* Her head ached.

After Ellen left, Bobbye buttoned her double breasted squirrel jacket and pulled her crocheted orange cap down over curly, bleached-almost-white hair.

"Hey, you were terrific." She smiled at Daphne in open

admiration. "I couldn't help hearing. Allison's been telling me about the trouble —the crowding and everything, at the shelter."

"Oh, if you could see that place, Bobbye. It's so frustrating. There are hundreds of things we want and need to do for the women — and for the children. The situation in this county is critical, with all the layoffs, plant closings, funding cutbacks. The angry men, the brutality —it's unbelievable! We turn away beaten women —yes —and children too, for lack of space. There are incest cases, rapes. Much more than ever gets in the paper. We're required to have a Rape Crisis Counselor in order to continue receiving funding —I'm running on and on — I'm sorry —"

"Ed —my husband —says there's a building you might get."

"If most of the Council members have anything to do with it, we won't. They're voting tonight."

"I know. Ed says there's a special late meeting tonight, to vote on that issue. He can make those guys do anything he wants. He'd kill me for telling you, but he told me he never forgets when he's done someone a favor —"

Daphne was excited. "I can't express adequately how much good could be done if we had a better building! Maybe we could offer those poor dependent women some life options — hold seminars and consciousness-raising, maybe someday open a women's bank. Bobbye, if you could *see* how grateful they are —for any little thing. I've got to call the fire chief now. I have to cajole and wheedle and pry things out of these macho males." She waved goodbye.

Tell me about it, thought Bobbye, maneuvering her Corvette into her driveway, past the now-white-faced negro jockey lantern holder. Two men were measuring the driveway for a black-top estimate. They stared at Bobbye as she walked into the house. "Oh, put your eyes back in," she muttered. She went upstairs. Ed would be back from the nuclear power company about four.

41

He had said that Council would meet at nine. He'd want to relax, have a drink. It got dark out around five-thirty or six.

She stood on a stool and shuffled boxes around the top shelf of her closet. It was still there —the Victor of Vegas box. The box itself: erotic, padded pink satin with a black lace overlay. The contents: a black lace bra with cut-out nipple holes, a black garter belt and black lace open-crotch bikini pants. She laid them on her bed, then dug in her dresser for a pair of black stockings with seams —the ones she had shoved in back of her sweaters. She found a black net shorty peignoir too, and laid it and the stockings with the things on the bed.

It would be dark enough by seven to turn off the lights in the living room, Bobbye thought. She'd put the oldie "Behind Closed Doors" on the stereo, have a pitcher of Ed's favorite cocktails, Vodka Pineapple Yardarms, like they made at the CorBlimey —Ed called them "hard-ons" —all ready, and two glasses from Al's nudie glass collection.

She went downstairs and sauntered slowly past the living room bay window. Then she went out and got in the car and drove downtown to get two of the thickest steaks she could find.

CHAPTER FOUR

"Y'know, you're getting gray down here..." the voice rose from between Felicia Del Monte Haselas's thighs. She struggled to lift her head, but sharp metal stirrups pressed into her bare feet. At the end of the examining table Dr. Ernest Hartley inserted an ice-cold speculum into Felicia's vagina.

Visits to Dr. Hartley were a series of shocks. Now that her pregnancy was definite, Felicia was trying to adjust to her constant body changes; now she had to face this humiliation. She was a sheltered, sexually unsophisticated, rather prudish Italian-American housewife. Now, at the age of thirty-eight, she could feel the only man other than her husband to see her naked in her life poking and prying at her body orifices.

Dr. Hartley always called her "Hon" or "Sweetie," in a condescending tone. He leered at her and made jokes about her body. He even told her she had " —a nice pair," when he did her breast exam. In general Dr. Hartley was insulting and, to Felicia, didn't seem professional.

But what did *she* know? Her Sodality friends — and her sisters and sisters-in-law —had gone to Dr. Hartley. He called them all "Hon" too. His jokes didn't seem to upset them. Or at least they hadn't mentioned anything.

All they ever talked about was cooking or shopping or housecleaning or children. In fact they said very little about their pregnancies, the deliveries — how they felt about anything directly connected with sex or motherhood. Yet it was the only thing they really seemed interested in —acted alive about. Felicia couldn't talk to her mother either, who seemed embarrassed and changed the subject any time Felicia tried to ask her anything. Her mother had had six children, two stillborn. She must have had *some* feelings and recollections about birth.

All Felicia felt was constant exhaustion. She just wanted to sleep twelve or fourteen hours at a time. Keeping the apartment spotless and Herb's clothes in perfect order, trying to cook what he liked —all the things she had to do filled her with weary desperation.

She tried to force herself to relax now, to clear her mind of the jabbing pain of the speculum. Dr. Hartley shouted, peering over the sheet, "Whoooooeeeeee, yowza, yowza, yowza."

Felicia felt faint. How was she ever going to bake the five dozen cookies she had promised Daphne for the Sojourner's Shelter fund drive? They had raised a down-payment on the Doud house, now that the variance had gone through, and they were moving in, and an open-house was planned, to attract community interest and to raise more money. She wanted to help Daphne even though Herb ridiculed the Shelter and said he wouldn't give them one cent, and he had certainly not wanted Felicia to take the volunteer hotline one night a week.

"Okay, upsy daisy. Get into your duds. Here's your titty garage." Dr. Hartley dropped Felicia's bra and pantyhose on her chest, winked and was gone from the linoleum-floored cubicle. Eight other such cubicles contained eight other vaginas awaiting the icy speculum. *With his money, he should have a nicer office,* Felicia thought as she struggled into her clothes. She felt nauseated whenever she bent forward.

The main office, where five minutes later the doctor winked and leered at her again, was furnished with an immense oak desk and floor-to-ceiling shelves laden with sports trophies. Hockey sticks were crossed on the wall behind the high-backed leather desk chair. From where Felicia sat, the doctor's bony head appeared to fit into the apex of the angled sticks like an inverted skull and crossbones. Felicia, facing the desk, gripped the arms of the extremely low chair —one of two tacky cast-offs from the game room of the Hartley residence —and tried to ease her thighs away from her aching crotch while still keeping her ankles modestly crossed. The doctor was shuffling papers on his desk.

"Yabba dabba doo! Bippity boppity boo!" He always mumbled or sang off-handedly throughout Felicia's visits —as if it were all a joke or a game —as if she didn't matter and he was doing her a favor even to look at her. Yet he was *the* obstetrician in town. The women didn't question anything he did. Dozens of them sat in the waiting room, for two and three hours sometimes, leafing through three-year-old *Parents* and *McCalls* and *Good Housekeeping* magazines, smiling like cretins, never speaking to each other, just exchanging those vacuous smiles.

Dr. Hartley handed Felicia a prescription. "Boop boopa doop. Here's your calcium, Babe. Better get started with it. See you next time."

He disappeared before she could ask about the tiredness, about the awful fatigue. About her fear. She shuffled through the shabby crowded waiting room. Most of the women appeared to be middle-aged or near to it. There was some sort of baby boom going on. *I wonder how they feel,* she thought. *Whether they're afraid, whether they feel the same pain and confusion I feel.*

Outside by the curb in the stinging, wind waiting for Herb to pick her up, Felicia felt a welling up inside —a rush of tears and sobs that wouldn't leave her eyes and chest and throat, an inchoate plea to someone —anyone that she could talk to. An understanding woman. A friend. Friends.

If she had a car, she could bake the cookies and take them to Daphne's. She could talk to *her.* Daphne was warm and sympathetic and fun to talk to. They had gotten acquainted when Daphne came by the drapery workroom at Felicia's mother's, to bring work orders or to pick up finished jobs. Living upstairs over the workroom in one of her mother's apartments was not ideal; Herb hated it, but they hadn't saved enough for a house.

She and Herb didn't get along. Fifteen years of perfect housekeeping, making beautiful meals, never crossing Herb, trying to get along with his sisters; telling herself Greek customs weren't that different from her Sicilian ancestors' —the cooking wasn't all *that* different.

Family unity was everything: not complaining — ever — always doing what your husband and father and brothers and uncles told you. Living for your husband and children. But there had been no children. And there was no excitement in her marriage. No love, no affection. Her husband and his family frowned on friendships outside the family. They were angry, demanding, controlling, cold people.

Felicia's and Herb's families didn't know about the times he had hit her. Once he slapped her so hard that one of her gold earrings, the ones her mother placed in her small pierced ear when she was a child, ripped through her ear lobe. She had made up a story about getting it hooked on a dress button.

In the car Herb was glum, as usual. His job as manager of two CorBlimey Steak Houses, one in Bingham and one in Briarwood, made him nervous. The long hours and responsibility kept him preoccupied and irritable. He had a driven, worried expression which relaxed only when he was with his father or his uncles or when he talked to the cooks at the restaurants, all males. He didn't get along well with the waitresses, with women.

Felicia glanced at him as they drove toward their apartment. He had said little about the baby when Felicia first found out what her bouts of gallbladder trouble really were. Now he didn't even ask about how she felt — what the doctor said. Nothing. There was nothing.

"I have to drop you off and go right back." He was glowering, angry. In the waning light his glossy black hair and eyebrows contrasted with his incredibly fine pale skin. His elegant, classic profile could have been lifted directly from a Greek vase. He was so handsome that, fifteen years before, Felicia had been dazed for weeks after they announced their engagement. Their families were neighbors. There had always been an understanding about the engagement, but she wasn't even considered pretty, although she did have a plump and shapely body. He could have had any girl, though. Any at all.

"What happened at the restaurant?"

She dreaded his temper.

"One of the prep cooks quit at Bingham. Now we're short handed, and we have two banquets." He pulled up in front of their apartment building. "I'll be home late. Don't wait up."

"Herb, Herb, is that all? Can't we talk a minute?" Felicia felt tears welling again. "I'll be up pretty late myself. I have the hotline tonight. I'll take the phone out of the bedroom. I'll fix your dinner any time you come home. I made spanokopitta."

"I can eat at the restaurant. You know what I said about that women's lib shit! You just call that goddamn answering service and tell them you're not taking calls." Felicia was silent.

Later, as cookies cooled on every available kitchen counter space, Felicia sat in her immaculate living room with her swollen feet propped up. She was surrounded by snowy lace curtains, crocheted pillows and framed photographs of nieces and nephews, weddings and christenings.

She listened on the Sojourner Shelter hotline as a weeping twenty-four-year-old woman described her hopeless life. The woman's second husband, a brutal forty-eight-year-old alcoholic, refused to give her any money, provided only shelter and food for her and her two little daughters in exchange for maid service and sex.

"To feel alive," as the young woman put it, and to be able to get some clothing for herself and her daughters so she could visit friends occasionally, she had worked nights for the past year cleaning stores and offices. Five nights a week she had left her daughters with their stepfather, who she finally discovered was molesting them. When she confronted him, he threatened violence.

The woman's sobbing made it nearly impossible for Felicia to counsel her. Gradually, she regained control and could answer questions concerning her situation and options. Was she in danger at that moment? Could she get herself and her daughters to the shelter? If not (her husband was due home from work soon), could she get to the shelter the next day? Felicia had learned, through feminist-directed volunteer seminars, how to do telephone counseling. (For a while she had managed to do it secretly but had finally had to tell Herb.)

Local police also had reluctantly attended the shelter seminars, at the staff's urging, and had begun to cooperate more willingly when they discovered the shelter services actually benefitted their departments. Generally the police had a non-intervention policy regarding domestic violence, and such violence was increasing in direct ratio to unemployment. Adverse community criticism of the police handling of violence had also increased, making the whole police department look bad. The Sojourner Shelter's programs and seminars, therefore, had begun to look good to them.

By midnight, and fortunately before Herb Haselas came home and *put a stop to this shit* by ripping the phone from the wall and stomping off to bed, Felicia, shaking with fatigue, had counselled three more anguished women: a suicidal thirty-year-old whose husband was so jealous that he beat her almost weekly for no apparent reason; the mother of one child —a hydrocephalic baby —whose emotionally disturbed Vietnam veteran husband had thrown the child across the room; the frantic mother of a raped thirteen-year-old, calling from a phone booth while the hysterical child sat on the sidewalk, clutching her mother's ankles.

On that last case, Felicia had called Bobbye Krock, now rape crisis counselor for the shelter and studying for a law degree. Bobbye arranged to meet the mother and daughter at the hospital, where the medical staff, also trained at the shelter rape seminars, could discreetly care for the raped girl and perform tests. It was Bobbye's practice to stay with rape victims for hours —days, if necessary —helping them to compose themselves in order to endure police questioning. She also ran interference for the victims during interrogations, preventing any exploitive prurience in the wording of questions, any insinuations, any innuendo.

The Sojourner Shelter staff had learned that Bobbye herself had been raped as a child, had suffered unspeakable pain and trauma and then had undergone it all again when police questioned her for hours afterward in the dreary living room of her family's Doncaster home, with her mother glaring at her, red faced and accusatory —her palm stung from the blow she had delivered to Bobbye's cheek ("you whore!"). The police had persisted in asking her for humiliating details over and over, even suggesting that she must have enticed the rapist. She had experienced ghastly nightmares and debilitating fear for years afterward.

As the cold morning light began to show beneath the scalloped-edged plissé window shades of the bedroom —the room she had so wistfully and hopefully furnished for their bridal night fifteen years before —a bower for their happiness —Felicia lay trembling beside her snoring husband. She clung to the far side of the bed and tried to blot from her mind the distraught cries of the women she had counselled. There were so many who were troubled, desperate. Many other women suffered alone, feared their husbands, as she did. It was unjust. She had not thought of it clearly before. Why should only men have freedom to choose their life options? To go freely in the world? A ripple of excitement passed through Felicia. She was experiencing, for the first time, the exhilaration and energy generated by a rising feminist consciousness.

CHAPTER FIVE

Sauerbraten and potato pancakes slithered into Leonard Blake's convex, tweed-vested stomach along with applesauce, three tankards of vodka-pineapple Yardarms and a large serving of Gadzooks Olde English pudding. It was the weekly lunch meeting of the Semper Fidelis club in the banquet room of the Bingham CorBlimey Steak House and Lounge.

Ed Krock, seated on Blake's left, directed his full attention to the restaurant chain's famous two-inch-thick CorBlimey Zounds Beefeater Special, broiled rare so the blood pooled on the faux pewter trencher. Faux pewter porringers of mashed potatoes, corn pudding, lima beans, Spanish rice and sweet potatoes circled the trencher. An iced one-pint tankard of vodka Yardarms sweated on Ed's right. His individual heated gravy boat shaped like a pewter galleon steamed on his left. A wedge of coconut Stilton cheesecake awaited on the dessert tumbrel.

"Now this is what I call eating." Ed helped himself to another rum-buttered scone which nestled in a helmet-like metal basket with push-up visor lid.

The banquet room had ship's wheels, rope rigging and wall lamps made from windlasses. There were suits of armor in each corner; murals of stone parapets and unicorns, and imitation millefleurs tapestries decorated the red-, gold-, and black-flocked wallpapered walls. The CorBlimey couldn't decide which kitsch was kosher.

When he wasn't at the state capital, Ed ate at the CorBlimey more and more. Bobbye was gone most of the time, either at her classes at the university or counseling women at the Sojourner Shelter. She didn't even have time for the Briarwood Art League anymore. For a while things had been going along well between Ed and Bobbye. It was almost too good to be true. Then she drifted away again, even after he'd given council the go-ahead on the shelter and okayed the decorating of the whole first floor of their house. Twenty-seven thousand, just for openers, should have got him more than a peck on the cheek and bean sprouts and tofu in the Frigidaire.

"Gimme another hard —er —Yardarm, dear," Ed motioned to the waitress. He swivelled around to stare into her decolletage. The others at the long refectory-type table laughed.

"You almost slipped, Ed," Dr. Hartley yelled as he reached out and, in a flash, tweaked the barmaid's left buttock as she passed.

Leonard Blake laughed too as he finished his Gadzooks pudding, but he had not missed the famous Hartley sleight-of-hand. Harletta Hoskins, the pinched waitress, caught the industrialist's eye briefly as she fled the banquet room. Harletta and Blake had an "arrangement" of many years that was, among other things, helping her to put her son, Russell, through dentistry school.

After lunch, chewing licorice-flavored mints, Ed Krock and Leonard Blake sauntered together across the fake drawbridge which led over the moat encompassing the CorBlimey, linking the perma-stoned, crenellated and stained-glass hybrid structure with an asphalt parking lot and the surrounding shopping mall.

They walked to Blake's car and stopped briefly; then Honest Ed went on to his Caddie carrying a brown leather attaché case that he had not been carrying before.

"Surely you can think of *one* thing you like about yourself, Lillian." It was Harriet Freeman speaking. The consciousness-raising group was meeting in what had been the sunroom of the Doud house. Although there was no furniture yet, the well-proportioned, bright space cheered the nine women who sat on cushions on the scuffed but still-handsome parquet floor.

Thumps overhead reassured several in the group that their toddlers were supervised in the playroom —a large sunny front bedroom being equipped, gradually, as part of a twenty-four-hour child care center and nursery school. Through oak sliding doors came Daphne and Ellen's muffled voices as they organized the main office. It had taken two weeks of steady work with the help of volunteers from the surrounding communities, the whole staff, and all the shelterees to move everything from the old house they had been renting in Doncaster. Enthusiasm was high. Bingham families had brought in furniture and other donations without comment, glancing about with frank interest as they set down armchairs, lamps, tables, old rugs.

Allison now carried donated paper goods and canned fruit from her car into the kitchen of the turn-of-the-century building. Bobbye Krock was in court with the thirteen-year-old rape victim and the girl's mother. On the second and third floors, five white women, three black women and the seven children among them were distributed into eight clean rooms equipped with beds, cots and cribs. Two unfurnished rooms in the warm pleasant attic awaited promised donations. The attic bathroom and two baths on the second floor with their sturdy old-fashioned white porcelain fixtures and white tiles were in good working order. Lorene Wilton, now a member of the shelter staff, carried supplies to a second floor closet. "We in a real house now, Baby," she had told her daughter, Tiffany, that morning, as she placed the infant in one of the nursery playpens.

In the sunroom, Harriet again addressed a morose Lillian Morrison, who held up proceedings at the beginning of every CR session because she could not think of any strokes to give herself —the group began each session by having each member in turn tell two things she liked about herself.

"Try to think of just one. You don't have to do two." Everyone stirred impatiently.

"I can't think of nothing." Lillian stared at the floor drearily. "I want to pass."

"You pass every week, Lillian."

"There's nothin' *good* about me *every week*." There was general laughter.

"All right. You can pass again. But next week you have to have at least one stroke, or you can have a chance after we go around the circle."

"I have about five strokes today." It was Melba Cochran's turn next.

"Just two, please, Melba. Okay?"

"Okay. First, I told my old man I'm lookin' for a job, and if he don't like it, he can screw himself. He's always accusin' me of lookin' for guys. Second stroke. I took one whole afternoon and went to the liberry. My sister watched the baby. I'm babysittin' her kids next week while she takes her G.E.D. I didn't feel guilty about goin' to the liberry, and when my mother yelled at me —tryin' to shame me for neglectin' my housework —I told her it is my life and I like to read, and if she don't like it, that's too bad."

Audrey Hopper heaved her bulk over to the wall and leaned against the faded, ivy-patterned wallpaper, feet sticking straight out. Her eight-months-pregnant belly burgeoned beneath a blue and white checked gingham top. She was one of three black women who signed up for CR. One of the three had not returned after the first session.

"With all her reading, Melba hasn't learned any new words," Audrey laughed. "My stroke for today is I like myself because I feel like hittin' her with this knittin' bag because she has a dirty mouth. I'm enjoying sayin' it, and three weeks ago I never would have opened my mouth." The group laughed.

"Second stroke, please." Harriet lit a cigarette. Her beautiful red-blond hair, braided into one thick braid, gleamed in the afternoon sun.

Audrey inclined her head to one side. "I like the way I feel now that I'm comin' to CR. I like the way I don't get mad and holler when my boyfriend tries to get me mad, like not callin' when he gonna stay out late and that. I mean, like, I like bein' by myself okay now."

They went around the room giving the required two strokes. A few spoke readily. Most spoke slowly and painfully. It was clear that many of the group had extremely low self-esteem. But in just three weeks Harriet could see that the CR training she had learned as a twenty-year-old activist in the mid '70s had begun to help this group almost immediately. The levels of consciousness varied from group to group, but sooner or later,

The Raunch Factor

CR always worked.

It was a beautiful thing to see the women's political consciousness awakening. Neither therapy nor counseling, consciousness-raising was a process which helped women to relate themselves more realistically to a society which manipulates and exploits women and then makes them feel guilty when they become angry or feel hurt and defeated by the exploitation. In CR no confrontations were allowed, no personal disparagement or putdowns, just the steady, inexorable chipping away at what the system does to women —and to men too (for they couldn't talk about an isolated one-half of the population).

The women were fascinated by the CR process and were sorry when each two-hour session ended. They were now in meeting number five of ten sessions. The upstairs nursery enabled mothers to participate. Several of the mothers had cried at the third session —the topic was "Do Women Like Each Other?" —and they had said that before the shelter, before CR and the nursery and day care and the Life Option Seminars, they had felt isolated and lost and "out of it," and hopeless because of their children. They had felt cut off from friends —other women, someone to communicate with. They said that their husbands seemed to prefer it that way, seemed to want them to be divided —against other women. CR had helped the women to see that their friendships with other women were threatening to men. Insecure men in the community —and many women too — used the scare-label "Lezzies" or "House of Lesbians" to intimidate their wives, sisters, and daughters who were attracted to Sojourner Shelter activities and seminars.

"Today's CR discussion topic is Women and Anger." Harriet Freeman folded her long legs into a more comfortable position. Her perfect oval, unmade-up face was so bright and rosy and merry, her extraordinary large deep brown eyes so arresting that women and men alike found her appealing. She had a wonderful sense of humor and laughed often, throwing her head back and shouting a delighted, staccato bray that was infectious. All eyes were on her now.

55

"Anger *can* be healthy, no matter what you may have been conditioned to believe. It is normal to feel anger and express it. Women are taught to repress anger and to substitute another emotion —usually depression. Anger is considered a male power tool. Therefore women are warned constantly, either subliminally or directly, that they'd better not let out their anger because it belongs to men. Women give up their freedom when they cannot direct healthy anger constructively at its cause. The first question for discussion is this: How do you experience and express your anger?"

They went around the circle, one by one, Lillian passing again, and the sameness of each other's responses made them smile. "I feel such rage, sometimes, that I just cry. I feel nauseated too, sometimes." Or "I go somewhere and cry to myself." Or "I feel that I can't get my breath. I get an asthma attack. Or I cry." Or "My voice squeaks. I can hardly hold back the tears." Almost all admitted that they wept.

The next question, "How do men generally express anger?" elicited low groans. "They yell and swear. Slam things —and people —around." "That's easy. They punch somebody. Hurt someone." "Or start a war." (This from Harriet.) "Yeah. They shoot people." Or "Couldn't be simpler. If shouting doesn't work, or threats, they tear the place apart."

"Question three," Harriet continued, "concerns women's difficulty in expressing anger towards men. If they show anger towards men, women risk much: loss of a job, rape, abandonment, physical violence to their children or to themselves. It is decreed by society that women are the keepers of the peace, the emotional support of men. Women are not supposed to deviate from this role. In what ways have your expressions of anger jeopardized you? Do men run the same risks?"

"When I was little, I got whipped for showing anger, but my brothers didn't." From Harriet: "I lost my job, once, for arguing with my supervisor about a genuine injustice. I was fairly loud. They said I mouthed off all the time, but I only yelled that one time. I doubt if a man would have been fired for one offense." Or "I never show anger. I smile or laugh. It gets me a lot farther. I think men are careful who they show anger to — outwardly. It depends on who they feel equal to in power, or if they feel they are more powerful than the other person." Melba said, "You talk about anger belonging to men. I think the whole society belongs to men."

"Better make that *white* men." Lillian spoke up for the first time since CR had begun. Everyone looked at her, astonished.

Helen Yankovich —one of the few Slavic women who had sought out the shelter's services —spoke up. "This just sounds to me like man-hating. Don't men have it tough too? They have to go out and earn money —have to 'make it' financially."

"Yes. Women bug men about money all the time. It's uphill all the way for lots of men just to get from week to week, especially now." Alma Ferrance held out supplicating hands.

"Very noble." Harriet shifted her position, sitting up straight and looking from one to the other as she spoke, "You sound just like you're *supposed* to sound. You've bought into the system when you get those empathetic feelings. Remember, the system was made *by* men, *for* men, and it works for a handful of men." She nodded toward Lillian, "And you're right, Lillian, *white* men, and it's not a good system for *anyone*. It's oppressive to almost everyone. But even the oppressed men have laws and traditions that protect them; laws and traditions that have never applied to females. Yes, men *are* oppressed —the majority have to work at jobs they hate —in mines and factories or service jobs without dignity or incentive. Or they're unemployed —and in this society if you don't have money, you're not a man. But men have *us* —their mothers, sisters, wives and those poor secretaries to whom they give *one* rose *once* a year. All of us have the job of protecting men against their oppressive system, that *they* created. But as long as a few powerful men profit by it, it will go on. Women must have a say in creating a better society, but we can't begin to unless we have a base of operations —equal footing, equality. Only then can we have a chance at deciding what will make a better world. Next question. Over whom do men almost always have power?''

Alma raised her hand. ''I can speak for all of us and save us going around. The answer is somebody weaker than they are: most women, kids.'' The others nodded.

Harriet lit another cigarette. They're catching on fast, she thought. She looked around the room with satisfaction.

After the CR group left, Harriet, Daphne, Allison, Ora and Lorene met in the kitchen to celebrate their first month in the new building. Two bottles of Asti Spumante cooling in the refrigerator were donated by Ellen who took little Mark to the doctor and could not stay for the party. Ellen, who believed in rituals, especially for joyous occasions, had even found clear plastic champagne glasses for the celebration.

April sunlight slanted through the window over the sink as the group filed into the cozy, old-fashioned turquoise-walled kitchen. A second-hand refrigerator and range flanked a tall yellow pine cupboard with glass-paned door. Bacon-wrapped mushroom and cheese kabobs —also donated by Ellen —crackled in the oven broiler.

Harriet and Daphne set out the glasses. ''We ought to ask the shelterees to come down and celebrate with us. This is a milestone. An important occasion. What d'you all think? Would it cheer them up?'' Harriet set the Asti Spumante on the old-fashioned wooden sink drainboard.

Lorene ran upstairs to invite the shelterees. All but two came shyly into the kitchen a few minutes later. The children took advantage of their mothers' distraction by sliding down the two flights of stairs on donated pieces of plastic crib sheeting. Their shouts and giggles echoed through the big hallway. In the kitchen, champagne glasses were lifted, and Daphne, her dark eyes luminous, toasted, ''To a feminist future.''

They all lifted their glasses. It was a pretty gathering, everyone's face flushed and hopeful. Harriet's braided hair glinted copper-gold, bathed in the last swath of dull orange sun which, seen through the window, was sinking behind the adjacent

Gothic-roofed Catholic church, making the kitchen window of this —their dream shelter —a James Wyeth, an Edward Hopper composition, an almost prophetic artist's fantasy framed in varnished yellow pine.

"Right on," Harriet said softly, sipping her wine and remembering.

Remembering the gatherings of the angry early '70s. Remembering —the ascending consciousness, the glimmerings of understanding here and there, of friends and acquaintances — halting and tentative at first, then building into a forceful movement. Remembering —the marches and demonstrations, in all weather, but which always seemed to be blistering heat or icy rain; being jarred, jolted for hundreds of miles in ancient, unheated, uncooled busses fighting for the Equal Rights Amendment. Remembering —being reviled and ridiculed for her beliefs, by her family, by neighbors and relatives, being spat upon and jeered at by disgusted, laughing spectators who watched as she and Daphne, and five, or eight or ten other dark-robed women pulled a tolling bell on a cart through the streets of city after city, followed by eleven thousand, fifteen thousand (the newspapers, if they reported the event at all, always said "a small group") silent women —and sometimes a few dedicated men —marching to commemorate and to protest the deaths of women and children who were lost down the years, physically, psychologically beaten, brutalized by the system men made, by the men the system made.

Remembering —five, six hours of testimony after each march —from daughters, sisters, mothers, aunts, wives who lamented, over the ghostly, hollow-sounding P.A. system, accounts of the destruction of their female family members, friends, lovers. Remembering —the pain of her own failed marriage to a man she could not help loving but who hated women; a frightened, threatened man. Remembering —the many failed marriages of feminist friends as they read and learned and grew, as their anger coalesced into energetic knowledge and purpose, as across the entire United States they created and supported their new voice,

NOW, and Wilma and Karen and Ellie, and Title Seven and Title Nine and fuller life participation for their daughters. Remembering —insisting that society remove from females once and for all the burden of responsibility for male violence, male sexuality. Remembering —the shock waves as feminists exposed taboos, the hidden incest, child molestation, the truth about the actual statistics of rape. Remembering — the genesis of the Sojourner Shelter, their first twenty-four-hour hotline and the calls that poured in from that first day. Remembering — monitoring the Domestic Courts, trying to fathom the morass of child support, vanished dollars of vanished fathers, vanished from invisible (but hungry) toddlers, vanished from hurt eight- and ten-year-olds, from bewildered fourteen-year-old sons with beginning biceps and shadowy upper lips, support money vanished from confused teen daughters who had only vacuous TV sex objects for role models. Teenagers who wondered, "Who am I" and envisioned a soap opera star or a Dallas Cowgirl cheerleader role for their cute legs and boobs; who asked their moms (crocked, discouraged, easy-to-blame Mom), "Where's Dad?"

Remembering —her own alcoholic, frantic, defeated mother. Remembering — her own questions, "Where's Dad?" Remembering —the wonder of the knowledge, the beginnings of understanding, the resolve that she and her feminist friends felt together, the power of it, the exhilaration; remembering — remembering.

Asti Spumante bubbled in plastic glasses and all the way down throats unaccustomed to the sparkling wine. Soon everyone felt relaxed, giddy and hungry. Four dozen bacon kabobs disappeared quickly. Daphne brought the celebration to a jubilant peak with the news of the first lap of their fund-raising campaign which had netted them eleven thousand dollars — in time to complete the shelter down-payment. If they could win the support of the community, they had succeeded. A cheer went up.

Everyone cheered again when Daphne told them of her conversation with the applicant for the job of Chief Executive Director, Traci Bilsen-Bloom, the only one of the eight women who had answered the ad who met all of the job requirements.

"She sounded businesslike to me," Daphne said, as she divided the remaining wine. "Of course, I've only talked with her by phone. We have a meeting scheduled here for Thursday morning at ten. I hope you all can be here. And I hope I can introduce a together person —an MSW, loving, feminist —to this community in four weeks. If we can hold out for four more weeks. But enough of money matters. I feel like partying." Another cheer went up. Someone turned on the ghetto blaster and music flooded the kitchen and followed them as they boogied out into the hall, Harriet in the lead.

CHAPTER SIX

"Are you wondering what's in my obscene pea-brain?" Hal Renshaw grinned across the table at Daphne as they sat in a booth at the Copper Bottom. At her suggestion, they had gone there for drinks and a late supper.

Daphne had introduced herself after a meeting of the Society for Historic Preservation for which Hal was the evening's guest speaker. His topic was "The Influence of Jeffersonian Classicism upon American Architecture and Government." Daphne found the speech rather dry, but witty in spots. Hal was given to elaborate puns and metaphors which, tonight, were met with polite laughter and much foot shuffling from the audience, who sat on wooden folding chairs in the Presbyterian church's meeting room.

Hal had suggested that instead of concern for the pediments of the buildings of the early Republic, we should be concerned about the impediments of the structure of the present Republican government. In the audience, some of the Friends of the Gessler Museum laughed nervously, "Aha. Aha, ha. Aha." But Daphne observed Leonard Blake, widower of the late Lucille, as he stared straight ahead, inscrutable, the corner of his lipless mouth twitching. (The Society members reported around town the following day that they had expected slides of Monticello, not a political speech.)

Daphne liked Hal's voice, and he had a kind, rugged WASP face and seemed to have a trim, well-proportioned body. Now, in the dimly lit booth, they sat smiling at each other. Hal's limp, brown hair drooped over one eye. He twirled his bourbon and ice around and around. To her amazement, Daphne found herself wondering whether his hair was all that was limp about Hal.

"I guess I'll never live down that telephone diatribe," she laughed. "Dear heaven, what must you have thought?" she giggled and hiccuped.

"I was too taken aback to think much of anything at the time. But I must say, you were impressive —very forceful, for someone so feminine." He was smiling sweetly. He had very straight even white teeth.

I can't believe this, Daphne thought. "Don't you think someone feminine can be forceful?" she asked, as she slipped her arms out of her gray flannel coat and arranged it over her shoulders. Almost dutifully, Hal stared briefly at her chest. Across the room, from a plant-filled corner, an electric organ began to whine a dismal version of "Lady Be Good." The Copper Bottom's cutsie decor featured brass and copper ladles, tubs, sauce pans and fry pans leaning on and hanging from rough-hewn shelves and ceiling beams. Unmatched chairs and tables were grouped in the room's center; rustic booths along the walls were lighted with pierced-tin lanterns, or bulbs in old four-sided coleslaw cutters. Waitresses were dressed in very low-necked pilgrim outfits —pin-up puritans.

"Well, yes, of course. Femininity and forcefulness are compatible, but I always equated femininity with less overt, less direct behavior. My ex-wife would have hung up in a snit and then complained and fretted to me for hours, for *days,* if she got an obscene phone call.

"Is she feminine?"

"Well, come to think of it, not really. She has her own advertising agency."

What's that got to do with femininity? Daphne wondered. *This is a looney conversation.*

"I think femininity is a male invention," she said. "I believe in *humaninity.*" Daphne was beginning to be sorry she invited Hal for drinks *and* a meal. Maybe she could plead a forgotten appointment. No chance. It was ten o'clock.

"Well, anyway, I wanted to say 'thank you' for putting over the variance. For whatever you said to the council. The Sojourner Shelter thanks you. We are one happy bunch of weary feminists, home at last. We salute you." She raised her glass.

"I wish I could say I did something, but to be perfectly truthful, I didn't have a thing to do with it. It was all a *fait accompli* the next day. There was no stalemate, no need to call another meeting. Ed Krock has quite a bit of clout with that group. I think it was his doing, if you can figure that out. He's not exactly known for his contributions to liberal causes. He makes Archie Bunker sound like Lord Chesterfield. But I can't take any credit. Still want to buy my supper?"

"Yes, of course. The invitation still stands."

"That's good, because I have exactly four dollars in my pocket." Hal grinned again. During his adolescence his widowed mother, Hazel, had spent three thousand dollars of her savings on Hal's orthodonture, for which he was everlastingly grateful, and now he told himself that he could smile the whole fucking time if he fucking wanted to.

"I saw the announcement in the *Observer* about your running for Congress," Daphne crunched the last piece of ice in her glass. "Congratulations. What does the university think about it. Can you do both jobs?"

"Not really. If I win, naturally I'll resign. If I don't win, it's not too good either, because the university is on alert that I'm not enamored of the audits and fiscal budgets of the Department of History."

"Do you think you could win? On a third party ticket?"

"I don't even know if I'll actually run. I can't if I don't come up with the eight thousand signatures I need. The law requires signed petitions, with the number of signatures being based on a formula: you have to calculate percentage of the number of votes received by the winning candidate for that office in that district in the most recent election."

"A prudent requirement, I should think."

"Yes, one *would* think so, in a democratic process. But it is excessively prohibitive. Ballot access should not be so limited. The Republicans and Democrats in the district —they are two sides of the same coin — can collect the necessary signatures simply by going up and down the courthouse halls, as it were. I have to haunt flea markets. When we go into shopping malls we get chased out. I've gotten arrested twice. So much for the democratic process."

"I see. It's not exactly fair, is it? But perhaps that's the penalty for trying to rock the boat. For shaking up the two-party system. But do you think you actually have a chance to win?''

"I don't know. Something must be done, and soon. There must be some way to alert people. This is the only way I know. My ideas are not complex. But they *are* egalitarian. They are basic principles which I thought were the founding fathers' intent. I am a constitutionalist. The thrust, or should I say, the assaults of the present government are relentlessly anti-populist, elitist. It's certainly no *cultural* elite. It's *financial* elitism —that is, a controlling monied aristocracy. Our Constitution is in grave danger. Also in the making is a completely unconstitutional, fascistic, shadow government. What's frightening is the ignorance, the apathy of the voters. Petitioning in Philadelphia showed us that many of the electorate are embittered and lost — defeated and discouraged people. There is downright hostility to new ideas. About forty percent of the people we've talked to aren't even registered to vote. I don't think there's been anything like it before in the history of this country."

Hal downed the last of his bourbon and held up his glass.

"Wouldst quaff?" he asked, "and quaff again? I'm enjoying talking to you. I'll reimburse you later. Honest."

He ordered two more bourbons. " —And a cheese platter, too, dear," he told the waitress. Daphne groaned to herself, *I swear to God men are all alike.*

"Where, as the students say, are you coming from, politically, Daphne?"

"You should be able to conclude, from my independence, my iconoclastic feminism, that I am a dangerous liberal." She smiled.

"I would assume in your kind of work —you do decorating? —that you'd have to deal much of the time with hedonistic *Town and Country* magazine let-em-eat-cake mentalities. How do you reconcile your liberalism with such —such unbridled elitism?"

"It isn't easy. Like Thomas Jefferson, I'm an elitist by inclination but an egalitarian by conviction. I grew up with a social conscience. My father hired the first black steel mill foreman in this state, perhaps the first in the U.S., in 1937. A Ku Klux Klan cross was burnt on a hill behind our house after that, my parents told me. And after that, integrating the locker rooms in the mill was a long stressful period. My family received threatening phone calls for a long time. So you see, I come from a long line of activists, but I'm happiest working in the arts. Sometimes my work is even lucrative."

"That's quite a background. I'm impressed, really — but still, I don't see how you can reconcile your conviction —"

"Everyone needs to have a pleasant — even beautiful — place to live," Daphne interrupted. "My art history degree opened a world to me that is seldom considered by the decision makers — the men who make the rules. A world of creativity, of contemplation of natural beauty, of nature — even of *agapē* — Christian, Confucian, Taoist, Hindu, Buddhist — is of little importance in the value system of most males except in the sense that they might use some superficial aspects of the arts or of religion, of philosophy, for power moves — for manipulation." She had to gasp for breath.

"Oh, come now." Hall protested. "Aren't you selling men short? Many Oriental religions, male-inspired religions, are based almost entirely on a reverence for nature, a contemplation of nature. And then there is the tremendous Sierra Club movement —"

"Yes, but consider this: Oriental contemplators of nature, for example, encouraged — insisted upon — the mutilation of the feet of upper class women. The women's hideous bound feet were sexual turn-ons for those nature lovers because the crippled broken arches and distorted toes resembled lotus bulbs. That's not reverence for nature. That's pornography."

"And do you have a Sierra Club theory?"

"Touché." Daphne smiled a wry smile. "When I talk about reverence for nature, I don't mean just 'Save the Sequoias' demonstrations — a bunch of men with a few worshipful women in tow, women who will dutifully cook snacks for them on Coleman stoves, and be led by — right — 'Dwate Big Mans' in a plaid shirt. That kind of thing. I'm talking about a whole new kind of thinking, a whole new creativity for men *and* women that can only be possible if women break out of their half-alive dream state of having their goals defined and dictated by men."

"Do you think men are in a half-alive dream state also?" Hal asked. He leaned forward and rested his chin on his hands.

"Men are about one-half to one-quarter as alive as women, I think, because men don't have the contact with their own bodies — their senses, that women have — contact that women have fought to keep so that they wouldn't go completely mad."

"How are they being driven mad? Do you really think it's that bad?"

"Listen, I think it's astonishing that women have survived the dehumanization by males — by the male system, as long as they *have* done. With all the mixed messages, the contradictions, the script that says that they're goddesses of love and life and civilization, and this is their sole value and purpose. Then, when the women pour their hearts and their lives into this purpose, they're told that none of these things has any value — told by degrading advertising, by dehumanizing sadistic pornography, by people everywhere laughing at home-making and child-raising. Raising children and housekeeping are *demeaning*, they're told, and they find out that their sole purpose for being alive is really a sort of joke.

"In the midst of this country's stupefying affluence, millions of women and their sacred product — children — don't get enough to eat or decent medical care — they bear on their backs the poverty of the whole nation. And then, when women, many of them heads of households, are forced to work a double shift — for that's what happens when, in order to survive they go into the work force because that paycheck is essential — they're told they're not worth pay that's equal to men's pay for work equal to men's work. And if pregnancy threatens their very existence — threatens whether they'll have enough to eat or a place to live — and they need an abortion, they're told they're criminals by the same people, mostly men, who told them their sacred maternity had little value. It's a no-win situation for most women. They can't all be doctors' wives, you know."

"And you think these injustices are all the fault of men?"

"It's the fault of the system, and the men made the system."

"What system is it? How do you see the structure of the system?"

"Well." Daphne cleared her throat. "I see it as nothing more than men's 'Can You Top This' obsession. It is —on a monstrous, global, war-making, death-dealing scale —one power move after another — all disguised as free enterprise. It's supposed to be healthy competition. It's a bunch of Little Leaguers grown big, and all that 'how to play the game' hogwash. That Little League or sports analogy is the way I see it. But it only works for a few, a handful of the strongest, the best coordinated or shrewdest white males, and simply eliminates all women and, actually, most of the men too. They just don't count. Men and women who could be skilled, talented at many things —maybe dreaming up and creating a whole new society, a whole new way of organizing a better society, a better value system where good things *matter* —visual arts, music, wonderful buildings, new ways to grow more nutritious food in less space and closer to markets, new ways to experience the senses' responses to learning in order to open minds to new creative ways of thinking. But if they can't break into the power elite they don't get a chance. Men shouldn't be ashamed of being sensual. Women should be using more than one-fiftieth of a percent of their intellects. I don't think I'm making this very clear."

"When women do become empowered —when they have been empowered — they aren't always the compassionate creatures feminists assure us they will be," Hal countered. "May I cite the example of Ilse Koch, the Bitch of Buchenwald, and her handsome human skin lamp shades with the concentration camp victims' numbers for decoration. Talk about creativity!"

"One in a million. She was probably one in a million. One psychotic woman," Daphne replied wearily. "That example is always trotted out, believe me. I've heard it before, many times.

The Raunch Factor

People take that one example and use it to condemn all women *in advance*, before they've had the remotest chance. Yet, for centuries, since the beginning of time, we all have stood by, or worse —we go *along* as *men* everywhere destroy and destroy and destroy. Do people remember '*Alice* the Hun'? Caligu*lena*? Ghengis *Connie*?'' she demanded.

"Do you think I'm describing an androgynous society, Hal? Uni-sex people —a genderless lock-step mentality? That's what we have now. On the surface it's yin and yang. Oh yes, macho man and the snuggly, soft play-boy bunny, but in reality, such polarization just makes all behavior between the sexes predictable — and deadly boring; and predictability is the same as regimentation. That's the antithesis of what I mean. In my dream, the necessity to have power over something or someone would be replaced by a power —I prefer 'creative impulse' —to do something wonderful, good, beneficial for a great number — the greatest mental health and physical health and knowledge, fulfillment, pleasure and beauty for the greatest number.''

"Do you know something?'' Hal's eyes were shining. "Your last sentence summed it up. You have just described the political platform of the Citizen Action Party.''

Daphne became aware, through a growing haze —it was not the bourbon —that her heart was pounding.

Hal went on, "If you think men use art to dehumanize, which of the arts do you think lends itself best to this pandering, this prostitution?''

"I think the visual arts more than music or literature, because visual art needs only to duplicate reality to have some meaning —recognized objects, settings, photographs, everything seems to have been seen before, whereas in music and literature we deal with abstractions. Musical sounds don't duplicate anything in nature.''

"What about bird calls.''

"I'm not even going to dignify that remark by replying,'' Daphne laughed.

"Sorry.'' Hal had finished off the Monterey Jack and was

starting on a cracker-studded mound of port-wine cheddar mixture in the middle of the platter. He lifted his empty glass. "Wouldst quaff?" He motioned to the waitress.

Daphne stabbed at the vanishing cheese with a rye wafer. "Wouldst, for Christ's sake, quaff! I guess so. Do you always talk like this, Hal?"

Maybe my soliloquy on art was too strident, she told herself. *After all, he's probably on my side. He needs campaign workers. It wouldn't hurt to be nice.*

"Speaking of bird calls, I'm an expert whistler. She licked a blob of the excellent creamy, winey cheese off a cracker. "One of my hobbies is whistling Sousa marches."

"*On the Mall,* whistle *On the Mall!*" Hall leaned forward, transfixed. "You're a John Phillip Sousa aficionado?" he laughed. Cracker crumbs clung to the corner of his mouth.

Daphne felt the table move. It seemed to be going 'round and 'round. "You mean, whistle it here? With Ethel Smith at the organ. I'd be drowned out."

Pricilla Alden brought two more bourbons. Hal said jubilantly, "You're really up on minutiae, Daphne. You've got to meet my secretary, Mrs. Helbrun. She has a whole collection of Ethel Smith records. You know, *Tico Tico* and all that, and Jo Stafford and the Modernnaires and Jonathon Edwards —but please, whistle *On the Mall!*" Hal was very drunk, and ecstatic. He'd met another music freak.

Daphne leaned forward and began the first few bars.

"That's not it! You're a fraud." Hal was gleeful. "That's *Colonel Bogey's March.* You're a fake." He smacked his palms up and down on the table.

"Well, they start out the same," Daphne groused. "You whistle it if you're so smart." She slumped in the corner of the booth. Hal pursed his lips, lips which, for four years of his youth had enveloped the intricate filaments of orthodonture, and whistled twenty bars of *On the Mall.*

"There!" He was triumphant.

"I have to admit that was sensational," Daphne conceded,

"but if I don't get something to eat, I may not be able to walk out of this place."

Pricilla Alden approached again. She tapped impatiently on her tablet with her pencil. "Do you want to order? We don't have no more flaming pizza. The-kitchen-is-closed-we-can-only-serve-sandwiches, the sandwich-bar-closes-in-ten-minutes" she threatened.

"*Miserere*," Hal moaned.

"*Misericordia.*" Daphne rolled her eyes upward. She was sloshed. Pricilla Alden sniffed and swept away, grey skirts swishing, Pilgrim hat askew.

"How can we drive our cars home? We'll be arrested. You'll never win the election." Daphne slumped deeper into her corner. Hal buttoned his plaid-lined Alligator raincoat.

"Let's walk home," Daphne said. She sat up straight, cheered by her idea.

"Where do you live?"

"About eight blocks from here," she said.

He bent over her and took both of her hands in his. "Let's drive our cars the two blocks to the faculty parking lot. Then I'll walk you home."

"Agreed." She rose unsteadily from her seat, her beige wool beret falling to one side. Straightening it and hitching her purse over her shoulder, she lurched to the cash register, then to the door, a distressed-oak replica of the entrance door of historic New England's Parson Capen house. She turned in time to see Hal bowing obsequiously to a startled couple who were seated at a table by the organ.

The Copper Bottom hostess, another pneumatic Pilgrim, murmured, "Goodnight, Dr. Renshaw," and Hal walked with exaggerated dignity out to the vestibule and straight into the cigarette machine.

"Oops," Daphne said, leading him through the Parson Capen doorway.

They walked the mile to Daphne's house arm-in-arm, whistling *El Capitan*. A soft, wet snowfall began as they neared the row of square, rather oafish Grover Cleveland-period frame houses in the midst of which Daphne's pale-yellow-painted 1870s brick, French-revival cottage, sat primly, like a schoolmarm surrounded by bib-overalled bumpkins. Daphne had restored the entrance double doors to their original warm brown walnut. Eastlake-style carvings incised the glass-paned top sections. She had saved since adolescence for just the right place — for the womanly house she had fantasized for herself —the statement of and for herself that was a dream she had proudly bought for herself, by herself. They went in. "I'll make some coffee," she said.

In the living room she switched on the ceiling track lights.

Hal stood in the doorway and looked about at the beautiful room, at the soft, deep blue suede covered walls, mellow cherry shutters, glints of brass. The bleached pine floor was bare except for one worn, elegant Kilim rug by the fireplace.

A faint hint of alive, fresh early spring fragrance filled the room. It rose from four flat terra cotta saucers of tulips, hyacinths and amaryllis bulbs which Daphne was forcing. Their bright pushing flower tips seemed to burst from the tops of the old basket-woven trunks, Victorian chests and simple tables scattered about the room.

"Very nice," Hal said, emotions ever guarded. He knew it was beautiful, but he could not jeopardize himself by admitting it out loud. He never could palaver. Besides, Daphne had told him that his course in American history — his creation — was "very nice." He was still smarting from her patronizing tone.

Suddenly, Mrs. Helbrun's plastic bouquet intruded. *The Office*, he remembered. *The Department. Tomorrow.* It was past midnight.

They sipped their coffee in the yellow-walled sitting room off the kitchen.

Self-consciously, soberly, they sat, side-by-side on an Empire sofa and ate leftover tuna salad and warmed-over corn bread squares. They stared at the fireplace opposite, in which Daphne had lighted the remnant of a wax log left from one of her early morning reveries. She never seemed to have time to build a real crackling log fire.

"If I don't put a load of laundry in the washer soon, my progeny cannot attend school tomorrow." Hal looked tired and sheepish. His black turtle neck sweater was harsh against his drained face.

"How old are your children?"

"Celeste is fourteen. Pete is twelve."

"They can't run the washer and dryer?"

"No. They just never have, and it's not one of the sitter's duties. It's my fault. The kids always have had everything done for them." He stood up wearily. "I have a long walk. I live seven blocks from the parking lot. Call me a cab." (There were no taxis to be had after midnight in Bingham.)

"You're a cab." Daphne laughed at the old joke.

In the dim front hall, Hal turned around abruptly and peered into Daphne's face. He leaned forward and quickly, lightly, kissed her lips.

"Thank you for more fun than I have had in many moons." He smiled at her and, again to her dismay, Daphne found that she was thinking about different degrees of limpness. Hal was holding her hand.

"Would you care to attend a Citizen Action Party campaign committee meeting Sunday evening? Ah'd shore admire ta have ya, little lady." His voice slipped into a John Wayne twang.

"I think I can make it," she said. Everything seemed to be happening too fast. None of this was part of her plan. He was lingering in the doorway. A fragrant hint of spring nudged the snowflake-spiked air.

"*Stars and Stripes!* We didn't do *Stars and Stripes Forever,*" he said, holding both of her hands.

"Listen." Daphne pushed Hal outside gently. "I hope the marching tune you'll be whistling a year from now will be the *Washington Post.*"

CHAPTER SEVEN

Eleven of the Sojourner Shelter staff and volunteers waited in the Shelter parlor for Traci Bilsen-Bloom. They sat on folding chairs, not talking —each of them thinking her morning thoughts. They looked at one another from time to time and sipped coffee from paper cups.

This was the wonderful thing about their alliance: there was no need for strained, silly chatter; they made no quick appraisals of each other's clothing and bodies in order to pass judgement, the way male-defined traditional women had been acculturated to do to one another.

Lorene was the last to arrive. She clumped up to the daycare room with her baby, Tiffany, then clumped back down again and slipped into a seat beside Allison. Bobbye handed her a cup of coffee.

"We finally settled," Lorene said, grinning and looking around at the pleasant room. Only a few boxes remained to be unpacked. Two file cabinets and a small typing stand were the only office furniture. Shelterees, with their laundry bags and rope-tied boxes, were usually brought to this room when first admitted.

The doorbell rang.

"There she is," Allison said.

"You go, Daph."

Daphne went into the vestibule but came back in a few moments.

"It was the dryer repair man. I hope he can fix that clunker. Now that the washer's working fairly well, it really helps. Those two women we took in yesterday were able to wash a load while they went out for food stamps. They'd been doing their laundry by hand, at home. Their husbands wouldn't let them use the car to go to the laundromat."

Ora got up and walked back and forth. "Did you tell Traci ten-thirty?"

She sounded anxious. Her small salary would be cut off in a month if the Shelter did not find new funding sources or if they could not qualify for continuing grants. Ora needed every cent she made; she was just scraping by. She would soon have to drop out of school and her dream of a social work degree seemed doomed.

"I'm sure we agreed on ten o'clock." Daphne said. She looked at her watch. Harriet stood staring out the large front bay window. "I'll be glad when we finally get this settled; once we're operating again, we can get on with our work and get our personal lives organized again. I haven't played my violin in two months. Barry Spiegel gave me a part to learn. It's the *Cochran Grand Quintetto*, and I read it through exactly one time in those two months. Ellen has the piano part, and even with those six kids, she's played it for Barry several times —over the phone, yet!" Everyone laughed.

"How's Norm doing, Harriet?" asked Leona, ever-caring Leona, inquiring about Harriet's twelve-year-old son, who was mildly retarded and epileptic.

"Well, the pressure on his brain is staying down. The neurologist is talking about an operation —some new kind of shunt —but he's been getting along really well in Special Ed, and the thought of another operation —"

The doorbell rang again. Daphne, holding up crossed fingers, almost ran to the vestibule. There were murmurs, then Daphne came into the parlor with a woman. She introduced Traci Bilsen-Bloom to the Sojourner Staff and volunteers.

They all drew in the their breath in one audible gasp. Traci Bilsen-Bloom, in red and white polka dots, spike-heeled red pumps and platinum fifties hairdo, was a Marilyn Monroe clone. The resemblance was eerie, unmistakable.

Daphne cleared her throat and introduced each member of the group. Traci, standing with one knock-knee bent in a fifties pin-up pose, smiled a little open-mouthed smile at each introduction. Everyone stared, stupefied. Daphne smoothly directed Traci to a chair beside the typing stand where she could be seen by everyone. Traci sat down and crossed her legs; her red purse in her lap was an exact match for the glistening lipstick on her full-lipped slightly open mouth.

"What do you think of our new building?" Daphne asked. (Evidently, she was expected to speak first.) The group sat as if mesmerized. Then Bilsen-Bloom spoke. It was a breathy, soft, halting voice straight out of *The Misfits*.

"When I parked my car it impacted on me" — it was a drawn-out *"immmm-pact"* — "immediately, that, for policy-making on a macro-level, your communal factionalizing input will be facilitated."

"Yes," Daphne said. The others remained transfixed, immobilized. *Why don't the idiots speak up?* Daphne thought. Again, she addressed Traci.

"In your résumé you mention counselling you did at the women's shelter in California. We haven't heard from that agency yet. But then, there hasn't been enough time for any of your references to respond. We'd very much like to offer professional counseling here at Sojourner Shelter. We're all pretty much coming from a feminist viewpoint, a feminist philosophy. What is your viewpoint concerning consciousness-raising?"

Traci smiled a wrinkled-nosed smile, pulled her chin down, arched her back and looked up at Daphne. *God,* thought Daphne, *this is straight out of the scene with George Sanders in* All About Eve.

Traci gave a little gasping laugh and said, "The implementation of a feminist planning process as a model for dichotomous social reality involves problem identification, data collecting and analysis, which are the criteria of service delivery methods. Don't you agree?" She looked around the room, wet red mouth open. They were nodding their heads like zombies, Daphne observed. *This is insane,* she thought. *What is this garbage she's telling us?* She leafed through the papers in the file.

"Your résumé says that you worked for Aid to People, in Los Angeles, from 1978 to 1980, and that, due to your grant letter-writing expertise, ATP was able to buy a building and equip it for a retarded adults' manufacturing program. Then, it says, you left. Did you go on to the Stockton agency for personal reasons?''

Traci uncrossed and then crossed her legs again. She licked her lips, wrinkled her nose and said, "The fundamental reform which must occur to facilitate incorporation of feminist planning necessarily immm-packs on divergent thinking and value articulation. Therefore, my value-direction reconceptualized a continuum planning model focused on the significant other viewed as private ideology."

"You —uh —you just wanted to re-locate?"

"Yes."

"Your résumé says also that you completed your MSW at UCLA in 1977." Daphne went on, "Do you have plans for further study?"

"Emergent, evolving job-life satisfaction within established norms and structures requires that I empower myself with a theoretical framework."

"You intend to go on with your schooling?"

"Yes."

Daphne addressed the others, "Does anyone have a question?" Ora raised her hand. "Did you have women of color in the other agencies you worked for? *Negro* women?"

Ora, Ora, Daphne thought, *I love you.*

"Most of my ladies," breathed Traci, "were white victims. But in aftercare counseling I had some black ladies, colored ladies. But my victims were, of course, addicted to abuse. They weren't like your ladies."

"Most of us here been battered more than *onct.*" Ora was scowling. "We're not different from most battered women. We all do crisis care now because *onct* upon a time we needed care in our own crisis our own selfs. We understand it better than other folks." Ora sounded angry. Melba Cochran laid her hand on Ora's arm.

What's aftercare? Daphne wondered. *We don't seem to be getting anywhere,* she thought. *They're all just gawking. I've got to wind this up.*

"Any more questions?"

Allison raised her hand. "How soon could you start?"

Daphne stifled a gasp. Could Allison think there was any possibility, any chance that a person like this could even be considered —

"Within a week, if I can locate a house." Traci licked her lips. "My husband may have an engineering position at Blake Casting. But if not, he can commute, weekends."

She *could* speak English.

Daphne looked at her watch. "Traci told me she has to be in the city by twelve." Traci nodded and smiled, uncrossing her legs and undulating to her feet. Her concave, knock-kneed stance was uncanny; she could have stepped out of a fifties theater lobby poster. She was lisping, breathily, to the group, " —and we must confront the struggle for implementation of the dichotomous facilitation that immm-pacts on commitment."

"Yeah," Leona nodded. Lillian Morrison mumbled, "Right." They all watched as Daphne led Traci Bilsen-Bloom through the front doorway and across the parking lot to her car.

CHAPTER EIGHT

Traci Bilsen-Bloom was hired as Sojourner Shelter Chief Executive Director against the better judgement of Daphne, Harriet and Bobbye. Traci's fifties mantrap appearance was disconcerting only to them. The others, in their varying degrees of feminist consciousness excused it. "After all, Marilyn Monroe was the quintessential female victim," Allison commented, "so what could be more appropriate?"

Hoo hoo hoo, quintessential, yet, Daphne thought. *Allison must have stepped up her reading.*

"What could be more appropriate," Allison went on, "than for the shelter to immm-pact" — already she had picked up Traci's word —"with a shelter director who reminds us daily of the exploitation of women? Sort of a living martyr to feminism."

Daphne, astonished at the staff's enthusiastic agreement, pointed out that a Marilyn look-alike could be more distracting than instructional.

"That's a pretty convoluted rationale, Allison," she said. "Our ultimate goal, after emergency rescue work, is to convey to women the importance of being self-defined, self-sufficient — of not buying into the male value system," Daphne said. They listened grudgingly.

"The way she's tricked out —packaged, like one of those erotic TV hair spray commercials. And that whispery voice. I wonder about her seriousness, her dedication to the women's movement. This job pays twenty-two thousand to start, and there are many perks. She *could* be after the money, you know."

Daphne turned to Ora. "I know you'll have to drop out of school if we don't hire her, if we don't qualify for more funding, but —"

"Right," Ora said, glumly staring at the floor.

At home, Daphne sat at the scrubbed-pine table in her beadboard-wainscotted kitchen, sipping a restorative cup of tea, watching the late afternoon snow. She had just returned from an appointment with Mrs. Hartley at the Mellors Lane house. The Hartleys had been in Italy the week before, where the doctor had a part-interest in a Ferrari leather motorcar upholstery factory. Upon arriving back in the US they had made a side trip to Williamsburg, Virginia. Now everything in the new house was to be 18th Century English, starting with a mahogany dining table, "Shippingdale" chairs, damask "hunchback" sofas. Mrs. Hartley was *crazy* about Williamsburg! As for her Italian trip (the leather seat-cover factory was near Naples) Mrs. Hartley said no, she didn't like Pompeii because " —it was so run-down."

Archaeologically "out of it" Mrs. Hartley definitely was. She might not have grasped art history nomenclature, or ancient ruins, or what were, to Daphne, the pulse-quickening interior embellishments of the famous Lascaux or Altamira caves (indeed, the very fact that such stirring drawings existed had been a major deciding factor in Daphne's career choice), but what Mrs. Hartley understood perfectly was who her enemies and rivals were. What she wanted from Daphne was a home that was testimony to the Hartley *joie de lucre*, not the Hartley *joie de vivre*.

However fraudulently this effect was to be achieved mattered little to Mrs. H. and even less to the buttock-tweaking doctor. So what *if* the first editions on their floor-to-ceiling library shelves didn't have the pages cut?

And now, Mrs. H. wanted "scones" on the walls instead of indirect, recessed lighting, and the existing windows with snap-in plastic "muttons" were to be replaced with real twelve-over-twelve double-hung windows; this meant terrific contracts for Bingham Lumber and Supply and for the electrical contractor.

Another long, dragged-out battle with contractors, lamented Daphne.

Daphne thought back over the previous week. It had been a frenetic one. There was the bizarre Traci Bilsen-Bloom interview, shelter organizing, the donated furnishings to distribute throughout the big old homey house, and continuing with CR. The current CR group was growing steadily in confidence, self-esteem, pride. Harriet said three of the group's most backward members were now enrolled in a Community College remedial reading program, and there was a waiting list for the next CR group. The child care center and nursery were shaping up. Daphne hoped Traci would implement the changes needed to conform to state daycare requirements, and there was the Shelter open-house to prepare for.

Bingham County's citizenry cautiously accepted the Sojourner Shelter. The Radical Chic aspects of the Shelter's mission were irresistible: child molestation and wife-abuse programs were booked for women's club entertainment, and high school counselors called about possible assembly programs on rape —"if it's not too explicit," one counselor had warned.

Curiosity drew young matrons to shelter volunteer training sessions. The political activism of the '70s — women's most significant progress of the past five hundred to eight hundred years —had simply passed by these former cheerleaders. Their batons and tasseled boots had barely cooled, yet from these traditional home-makers a small dependable group began to grow.

At first their comfortable, insular, middle-class lives were jarred. The idea of wives, girls, and children in their own community being beaten up and exploited by husbands, boyfriends, and fathers stunned and even titillated them. They sat primly but with almost prurient avidity in a circle at training sessions, wearing their expensive skirts and sweaters and blazers, and listened to Allison's and Bobbye's and Harriet's instructions on telephone counseling, how to calm a beaten woman, the procedure for getting her or an injured child to a hospital. A few signed up for Bobbye's special rape crisis training.

Traci's arrival would be the culmination of the Sojourner Shelter struggle. All of the wonderful, exemplary growth of women's minds and spirits would continue. The Shelter could even serve as a model for other shelters!

The prospect of serving women's needs statewide filled Daphne with pride. A familiar restlessness signalled to her the excitement she always felt when creative ideas surfaced. She reached for the phone. She had a business to run!

Debbie, though not lazy, tended to sit around leafing through back issues of *Architectural Digest*, unless a detailed schedule was posted. Time was becoming more and more critical. Tonight was Hal's first meeting —a petition-signing event and pep talk for campaign workers. The idea of a third party —here in phlegmatic Bingham County —was so refreshing and audacious that Daphne laughed out loud.

CHAPTER NINE

"The Citizen Action Party is an answer," Hal said to the group assembled in the Odd Fellows' Hall, "and we all know the questions."

"Its name says what it is: an action party of citizens who are profoundly skeptical of one party masquerading as two in what amounts to an elected dictatorship. This dictatorship is dedicated to making the rich richer — a few white males, that is — and making the American Constitution a travesty, a mockery."

Daphne tiptoed to a seat. She had not missed much of Hal's opening remarks. He was speaking with confidence and ease.

"We are a *civil* rights, a *human* rights party, and we are growing in number daily," he continued. "We organized a Philadelphia Citizen Action group while I was teaching there six years ago, and there are CitAct groups growing fast in the Middle West and on the West Coast. The Philadelphia group now numbers in the hundreds. They ran four candidates in the last election. One of them, Karen Bowen, a black lawyer who ran for State Supreme Court, got over eighteen thousand votes. As we had gotten four percent of the vote in the election before that, Karen Bowen's high percentage gave ballot status to the Citizen Action Party.

"But you would not learn anything of this by reading the newspapers. They print every move Drew Burgess makes: tree-planting, Junior Miss Pageants, discounts on passport photos — his glorious record of service — but they black out just about everything about us. A little squib might show up on a back page occasionally, but any third party is media poison. Before we discuss the CitAct platform, I wanted to give you an idea of our credibility, our validity as a serious political party. We *can* make a difference. We are, as the buzz-phrase says, on a roll."

Why does he have to be so professorial? Daphne wondered, somewhat irritated. But he looked very good in fairly respectable jeans, blue denim shirt and corduroy jacket. The familiar threadbare raincoat lay on a pile of other threadbare coats and jackets. He didn't look like a Thomas Paine — who history told

85

us was unkempt — even if he thought like one, Daphne concluded. She glanced around the hall.

These people have no money, she realized, *There'll be never-ending money problems. How can this party possibly get off the ground here, with the steel industry about finished, the apathy, the bitterness? How? Republicans and Democrats can raise as much money as they need —always. This is madness: idealistic madness.*

Hal was asking everyone to stand and introduce themselves.

No one looked familiar to Daphne except Ted Mather. He had been active in the anti-nuke demonstrations in the '70s when the nuclear plant was being built near Doncaster. That group, though very large and seemingly active, had not lasted long. At about that time, he had joined the Bingham County NOW chapter, shortly after Ellie Smeal had come to help Daphne and six others to charter it. It had been a moving experience to meet and talk with Ellie, a real feminist. Reading and talking and watching Phil Donahue were all they had had in the way of direction until that time.

They read Betty Friedan's *Feminine Mystique* — it had thrilled Daphne —and, before that, Simone de Beauvoir's *The Second Sex* —it had both exhilarated and depressed Daphne. She had lent the books to Allison, whose then-husband had thrown them in the garbage.

But Ellie was the personification of feminism: a self-defined woman. She was the perfect leader, they had all decided.

The NOW chapter had grown slowly after that evening with Ellie. At that time, to identify with assertive women was the kiss of death to Bingham women. They believed all the lies of the uneasy males who dominated the media. Only the gutsiest women ventured into Feminist-Land.

Ted Mather, a football-player type, had surprised the members when he asked to join NOW, but in the fervor of their newly-raised consciousness they were somewhat suspicious as well as flattered. This was a guy who simply was different, they were convinced, but they never really became accustomed to seeing his six-foot-plus frame jack-knifed into a folding chair at NOW meetings. However, he worked so zealously at their fund-raising hot dog and funnel cake booths at community events that gradually he became a familiar figure, and no one thought any more about it. His being there tonight was not that unexpected. Maybe it was a good omen. Daphne waved at Ted and smiled.

The rest of the group, with few exceptions, were physically nondescript, but from their comments and questions, they seemed politically directed if not politically knowledgeable. Daphne estimated their ages to be from about twenty-two to forty-five or fifty.

A very pretty blond woman was asking a question.

"Hal, most of us are anti-nuke and pro-choice people, as you know." Hal nodded. "Will these issues be dealt with or will they just be glossed over in your platform? We're not anti-gay either, most of us. Will you be addressing the AIDS issue?"

The others stirred uncomfortably. Hal cleared his throat and said, "I want to answer as many questions as possible tonight, and yours is a composite question, Merrilee; it requires a composite answer.

"Of course we must address the issues you named. They are emotionally-charged concerns that deserve more than glib generalizations. Our party stands for participatory democracy. We want to put to an end the myth that our present elitist government calls 'democracy,' and *that* means we must meet the needs of all our country's people, of all races and beliefs, not just a few rich white males.

"It means upholding women's right to decide about abortion —the right to control their own bodies; it means the right of gays and lesbians and all minorities to live in peace without constant fear and apprehension, without being scapegoated —without the persecution of gay males about AIDS. It means making concerted efforts to find an AIDS cure, and the truth must be made known that AIDS has been discovered to have evolved long ago, among many groups of people, not just gay American men.

"It means the right of all American people to live in a life-promoting environment, not death-dealing nuclear waste dumps. It means the American people's right not to have to bear the shame of a few militarists' huge profiteering activities in Central America, or anywhere else there's a quick buck to be made —"

Hal began passing out position papers. He bent toward Daphne. "Hello, good to see you; can you help set out the refreshments?" he said. "There are doughnuts, and the coffee maker's ready to go. Just turn on the switch. In ten minutes, we'll have some coffee-flavored sludge. Get Merrilee to help you."

All this talk about women's rights, Daphne thought.

She mumbled to Hal, "Why can't Ted Musclebound help serve the fucking doughnuts?" and she stomped toward the kitchen where Barry Spiegel, who had introduced himself as Hal's temporary campaign manager, was opening a package of plastic cups. Ted Mather unfolded from one of the folding chairs and ambled to the kitchen. He nodded to Daphne on the way, "H'arya?" He had a ruddy face and a big-toothed grin.

God, he's enormous, thought Daphne. *And what is there about his voice? It sounds strained, rigid. It's as though he's just a mass of violence, waiting to happen.*

Mather was curiously asexual, in Daphne's view, but she noticed several of the women smiling at him and giggling as they opened doughnut packages.

Seated in a semi-circle around Hal, the group seemed to come to life.

Caffeine and sugar will do it every time, he thought. *If only it were that easy to inject some enthusiasm into the dispirited voters of the 10th district.*

As Barry passed out pens and petition sheets, Hal explained the difficulties of running for political office in Pennsylvania, or in any state. A third party, without the blessing of either of the accepted, major parties, found ballot access complex and expensive, and there were new obstructions all along the way.

"Tenth District Congressional candidates need nearly eight thousand signatures to run. The filing fee is three hundred dollars, which I'll pay. Your signatures tonight are the kick-off of our campaign. We must collect a lot more than the exact number required, because if *one* thing is wrong —a wrong address, or initials written instead of full names, Harrisburg will reject the whole sheet —all fifty signatures.

"And we have to register some people as we go along. They can't sign a petition unless they're registered. Many Americans just don't register or vote anymore. If you don't vote for two years, you have to register again —and sometimes it's impossible to get to a registration center. But besides *those* obstacles the people feel disenfranchised and 'out of it.' Casting a ballot is a meaningless act to them, for the two major parties have a monopoly; and poor people know that their lives won't change, and won't get any better, even if they *do* cast a vote." Hal stood up and smiled at the straggly group.

"Who'll volunteer for the petition drive? We'll teach you how." All but Ted Mather raised their hands.

"I'll help with fund raising," Ted snickered. He had a silly, snuffling giggle.

Hal nodded enthusiastically. "That's terrific, Ted. We'll need all kinds of help raising money. Why not be our fund raiser chairma —er, chairperson?"

Ted nodded, still grinning.

The petition paper was passed and signed as Hal continued to explain the complex campaign procedure. A full-time campaign manager was important, he said, someone to arrange speaking engagements, debates, press conferences, TV appearances, someone to get out a newsletter. It was a demanding job, but interesting, and there would be exciting events to attend as the campaign heated up.

"We'll want to be involved in as many public events as possible, and identified as CitAct, right up until the first Tuesday in November. We can't be on the ballot in the primary for our party's first election in this district, according to election law, but we *can* make ourselves known.

Before we form the Party Committee that the law requires,

we need a manager. Who'll volunteer for Campaign Manager?"

Merrilee Dobbs, the pretty blond woman, raised her hand.

"Wonderful." Hal beamed at her. "We haven't located an office yet, so I can't tell you where to report to work."

Daphne raised her hand. "What about *your* office, at the college? Don't you have a corner there for a desk and a couple of chairs?"

Hal's office was out of the question, he explained. "No political activities are ever allowed in schools and colleges except debates and events that assure equal representation for both political parties —notice that I said 'both' parties. This does not include third parties."

Merrilee raised her hand. "Hal, is that the same *both* parties that get equal time for broadcasts and debates?"

"Ms. Manager," he replied, "You are about to learn who put the 'buy' in bipartisan."

Daphne volunteered to fix a corner of her workshop as an office.

Now I'm really committed, she thought. *We'll have to install another telephone, and Merrilee will be in there at all hours.*

A committee was formed to ensure that in the event anything happened to the candidate —if he got sick or died before the election —there would be another candidate to take his place. Barry agreed to take on this responsibility.

Looking over the position paper with its nice photograph of a somewhat younger Hal, Daphne thought of their evening at the Copper Bottom, and her strident speech to him. The position paper's wording was not hers, of course, but it set forth the same plea for a better world. As in Daphne's dream scenario, instead of a macho get-over-on-them-before-they-get-over-on-us stance, instead of the tacit acceptance of a sneering power-and-money-are-everything stance, there was instead a proposal for Daphne's own dream-world, a world where there weren't such frightful and destructive gaps between the "haves" and "have-nots."

It was a proposal for a world where there would be no more secret shadow government, where the country no longer would be bled white with military over-equipment —so-called 'defense spending.' Hal's candidacy would raise important issues. But could he possibly win?

Why not, Daphne thought. *Why not?*

They had to be out of the Odd Fellows' Hall by ten. They joked and talked as they prepared to leave. Besides the professionals and the theorists, half the group seemed to be unemployed, while the rest worked part-time for minimum wage and no benefits, filing papers and fixing fast food.

Most of the group appeared heartened and energetic now, their faces no longer pasty.

"See you at the next meeting," they called out.

I'll get Harriet and Ora and Ellen to come, Daphne resolved. *But Bobbye can't work for her own husband's opponent. Too bad.*

Merrilee walked out with Hal and Daphne. "What a great platform," she said. "Ed Krock introduced *one* bill in his entire ten years in the State Legislature and now he won't know what hit him. Neither will Drew Burgess. It'll knock him right out of the fox hunt."

They all laughed. Ted sauntered alongside the group. "Yeah," he said, snickering, "we're gonna kick ass."

CHAPTER TEN

"With Robb in the restroom every hour and taking yoga breaks, and putting on gloves before we can pick up even a stick of furniture, we can't keep any kind of a schedule, Daph." Debbie said.

She was breaking in a new man so James could have long-scheduled foot surgery. It couldn't have happened at a worse time. The Hartley drawings were dragging, Bobbye was irritable about getting her decorating started, deliveries were piling up, and the new man turned out to be a vegetarian yoga freak in canvas gloves.

"And he smells, Daph. He says deodorants obstruct the body's cosmic forces so he puts baking soda in his fucking armpits every two hours. *Plus*, for . . . *Corn's* sake, he says his acupuncture meridians require a yoga meditation period — in addition to his hour for lunch."

Daphne sighed. "Well, he came to us well recommended. He *is* a drapery-hanging whiz. And he's a a college graduate, for whatever sake."

"Yeah, barber college," Debbie sniffed. "And he's a religious fanatic. I made him take off that five-inch wooden cross he wears before we delivered the Weinberg's chairs. *Oy vey.*"

Daphne pushed a small desk into a corner in the new Citizen Action Party Office. It was a tight squeeze, but she had promised it to Merrilee Dobbs who was in and out of the shop office daily now, typing and phoning, adding to an already tense atmosphere.

"When he comes back from lunch we're gonna have a talk, Deb, but I can't afford to start hunting for another man *now*." Debbie retreated to the drafting room where she continued to trace with ink Daphne's floor plan drawings for the Hartley living room. Daphne took two aspirins.

Well, she thought, plugging in a lamp for the desk, *at least things have worked out for the Shelter.*

Traci had arrived on schedule, and had gotten busy assembling a board of directors in addition to writing grant letters. What a relief to have everything under control *there*.

93

The phone rang. It was Bobbye. "Did you cancel CR tonight? Political crap interfering with Shelter duties? The group's complaining."

"I didn't cancel it. I'm planning to be there."

"Well, the note on the bulletin board says no more CR until further notice. I assumed you did it. Also the order for the daycare sinks was cancelled. I'm not the Shelter Manager, I know, but I thought I better try to find out what's goin' on. Without them sinks we can't keep the daycare open. And after we got a certified teacher and a nurse and everything!"

"It must be Traci." Daphne felt cold to the bone.

"Oh my God. What'll we do? We better go see her."

"Bobbye, we can't do that —just barge in like that. She's only been there a short time. But we have a right to finish this CR group. We *could* send her a memo, but this is too serious. Can you meet me at the Shelter in twenty minutes?"

"What about our appointment for the house, my dear Miss Decorator, which is supposed to be in twenty minutes? I only have an hour before I have to be in court. You can't change it *again*." Bobbye sounded really angry.

"Meet me there, Bobbye. We'll work out your house, I promise." Daphne's after-lunch talk with Robb would have to wait.

On the way to the Shelter it began to snow again, heavily. Daphne shivered in a too-light wool blazer. It was depressing to wear winter clothes in April, but it was typical Pennsylvania weather. A week later, the petition drive was likely to find her out in a blizzard for days, and bundled up in lined flannel pants, layered sweaters, muffler and hat.

At the Shelter Daphne and Bobbye found two new shelterees being checked in by Allison. Still there from the previous week were five women and three children, still waiting for their Aid to Families with Dependent Children grants. AFDC delays were straining the Shelter's resources.

The delayed group sat patiently in the lounge, staring at a TV game show.

A Bingham housewife volunteer was taking phone calls on the hotline. In the back yard a Bingham architect was measuring for the off-street parking lot required by state Department of Labor and Industry regulations. There was no sign of Traci.

"She said she was going to lunch with a lady," the telephone volunteer offered. "I think she said she was getting the lady for the Shelter board. She's taken a lady to lunch every day she's been here."

Whatever became of the word "woman," Daphne wondered. She noticed a large stack of file cards on the telephone desk. "What's all this?"

"Traci gave them to me. She said we should write down every call we get, no matter what it's about —repairmen or whatever, and if they won't give a Social Security number we're supposed to make one up, and if they won't give any information, then we're supposed to make that up, too."

"Do you know anything about the CR cancellation?" Bobbye asked while she leafed through the day book.

"Just that there's to be no more CR, and Traci said the daycare room is to be used for her courthouse counseling work —her domestic court work, in addition to her main office. She said she hates children."

Bobbye pointed to a large "X"ed page in the day book. "What's *this?* This is Ora's day, crossed out. Every one of Ora's days is crossed out."

"Yes. Traci said she hates kids and blacks. She said that when a woman calls for shelter, we're to find out if the woman is black."

"Whaaatt?" Bobbye and Daphne demanded, simultaneously.

"And she told me that every time a Daphne Singleton comes in this building, all records are to be locked in this bookcase, and we have to hide the key."

Wordlessly, Bobbye and Daphne walked out of the Shelter to their cars. "What hath Traci wrought?" Daphne murmured.

"What? Whatdja say?"

"Bobbye, we did a terrible thing hiring that control freak. There's no turning back now. I should have protested, demanded, kicked and screamed —anything to keep her out. And, Oh God, poor Ora — she went along with hiring Traci just so her job wouldn't do a fade-out. Ora has come so far. She was in sight of her degree —and what'll become of Lorene?"

"Well, let's just not accept any of this shit. We have some rights. We'll have a meeting, bring a complaint against her —"

"Bobbye, we have to take complaints to a board of directors. Officially, she's executive director and in control, but the board members have to deal with complaints. There *isn't* any board yet. She's lobbying a bunch of creeps that she can control. We've painted ourselves into a corner." Daphne paused to think.

"I'm just going to show up tonight for CR as if nothing has happened. Harriet's group was so terrific that word got around, and we have a waiting list for CR, Bobbye, a waiting list! Just think, this is the first time in the lives of the women in our group that they ever realized they had any voice at all, any power of any kind —ever. They were almost all Shelterees at one time, you know —all battered in one way or another. With CR they're being transformed —empowered to help themselves out of their dependency, and with one miserable note on the bulletin board it's all going to be stopped — wiped out — *verboten*. Damn! Damn! Damn!"

"That volunteer said she called all the CR group."

"Well, *I'm* going to call them back and cancel the cancellation."

"You promised you'd come over and get my final measurements for the draperies and stuff," Bobbye whined, " I don't know if I can even believe you ordered my furniture. I need them windows fixed up or the place won't look finished for Ed's fund-raiser and —"

"I'll call the group from your house, before I measure. Bobbye, trust me."

In call after call, Daphne was faced with intransigence; all but two of the CR group were adamant. They did not want to continue CR until they talked further with Traci.

"It's almost as if they were hypnotized," Daphne said to Bobbye.

"Maybe they were."

"What do you mean?"

"It's her droning. That drawn-out 'immm-pacting' this and 'immm-pacting' that. That voice. She nearly put me to sleep at the interview. You should be on that board of directors, Daph — or Harriet. A couple of the founders would speak up and keep her from wrecking what you worked so hard to build."

Daphne rolled up her metal tape-measure with a clang. "Are you *kidding?* She spotted me right away. She's choosing, one by one, a board of directors that she can manipulate —or —one that she *thinks* is manipulable. Wow! there's to be no more CR, and she hypnotizes the staff and the Shelter residents, and she's hand-picking a board that she'll control completely. I wonder what else she has in store for us?"

CHAPTER ELEVEN

Bronwen Burgess leaned against her kitchen planning desk, smoking a cigarette and watching as the football helmet bobbed methodically over a bowl of cereal. She rubbed the grain of the desk, once a Pennsylvania Dutch dough box, waiting for Stephanie, waiting for her seven-year-old to reach the bottom of her blue cereal bowl and find the daisy pattern painted there.

The big fiberglass helmet emphasized the slender neck supporting it. On the stereo, Ravel's *Mother Goose Suite* played softly. Bronwen had long ago discovered that Classical music had a wonderfully calming effect in her household.

Getting Stephanie dressed and fed and out to school each morning was Bronwen's biggest hurdle in each day's obstacle course. The helmet was necessary every moment Stephanie stood or sat upright, for she had epilepsy as well as Down Syndrome and her seizures, though less frequent these days, were still often violent.

"More, Mom." Stephanie held out her bowl. Her appetite had improved since she started attending Thaddeus Schaeffer's physical therapy classes at Glenview State Hospital. "Tad" was wonderful with all the Special Ed children.

"There isn't time for seconds, Steph. The bus is coming in five minutes. Now brush your teeth."

Bronwen quickly wiped the top of the antique cherry breakfast table and shook toast crumbs from the hand-woven place mat.

"Awwwwrrr." Stephanie growled a raucous growl and lurched toward the powder room.

She had been a beautiful baby. There had not seemed any way that this infant could be a Down Syndrome child.

A pediatrician had come to Bronwen's hospital room with her obstetrician; together they had given Bronwen and Drew the diagnosis the day after the relatively easy birth. Drew had been expressionless, staring with unblinking eyes, uncomprehending, denying, emotionless as the doctor spoke. When a low, animal scream of grief had burst from Bronwen, Drew had not reached for her hand, had not even touched her. This searing moment was experienced individually, and separately, by each of them.

Now Bronwen could see the bus turning around in the cul-de-sac at the end of their row of widely-spaced, well-tended, expensive houses. Soon rosy-faced Lois, the infinitely patient Lois, would be pulling up to their herringbone brick walk, blip-blip-blipping the three horn blips which sent Stephanie into a squawk of hilarity.

"Bip bip bip," she shrieked back at the bus. Bronwen tucked Stephanie's medicine into her jacket pocket.

Drew had never talked to Bronwen about that day in the hospital. But she knew that their tenuous relationship —if it could be called a relationship —had turned a corner then, just like the school bus, and pulled to a stop.

It was less than a year after Stephanie's birth that Drew decided to run for Congress on the Republican ticket. When, thanks to low voter turnout, he won — in the Democratic-dominated 10th District —the responsibility for Stephanie, the anguish, the additional trauma of her epilepsy, became Bronwen's property —her sole ownership.

Stephanie's awkward, happy, leg-flinging walk as she stumped down the brick walk to the bus was so much like Drew's long-legged, loping stride, the set of her shoulders and back so like his, that Bronwen smiled. She gasped at the suffusion of love that swept over her every time she saw her child from a distance. Up close, Stephanie's endless needs seemed to make a jumble of Bronwen's feelings and her child's persona.

I love her enough for both of us, she thought, as she waved at the departing bus. *I'll make up for him.*

Bronwen turned back to her other love. She had a flawed child, and the child's father was a mistake, but there could be something perfect in Bronwen's life: her house.

She began the list of the day's chores for Fern Slagle who kept the handsome fifteen-room English Georgian home vacuumed, scoured, dusted, mopped, brushed, waxed and polished.

And then there was a list for Gus Quip, the Chatterley Estates factotum, who planted, pruned, clipped, mowed, fertilized and watered the three-acre grounds.

Bronwen began a third list to give the caterers for the fundraising party which Dr. and Mrs. Hartley wanted to hold for Drew, and prepared a fourth —special —follow-up list of guests who got telephone invitations from Mrs. Hartley in addition to their regular printed invitations. As many as a hundred and fifty stalwarts and a hundred "hopefuls," as Drew called them, attended these fund-raiser parties with their Bitsy wives, and everything was always perfect —because she, Bronwen, made sure that it was so.

In this way, with Drew's money and her own talent and shrewdness, she paid into her personal plan for future power.

She looked in her card file for the phone numbers of the car-parking boys who had helped her at her last two parties —a benefit for the Friends of the Gessler Museum, and the Bitsy Christmas Tea, at which Stephanie had shakily handed out foil-and-ribbon-wrapped popcorn balls to one hundred sullen (but very clean) poor black children brought in buses to tour the "Historical" Burgess residence. The Burgess *noblesse oblige* was renowned.

For the fund-raiser, cars would be parked at the Burgess estate; the guests would be transported the half-mile to the Hartleys' in horse-drawn barouches or Victorias.

Bronwen turned back to her telephone invitation list. Leonard Blake's name was at the top. She frowned. She hoped he would not bring that doxy waitress, Harletta Hoskins — Bronwen savored the word "doxy."

It had been reported around Briarwood that Blake was appearing with her openly, and even had taken her to the Bitsy Ball —and so soon after his wife's death!

Rumors had always surounded the Blakes. His high profile in the community was an odd contrast to her reclusiveness. Then the peculiar circumstances of her death set off a new round of talk. Still, that was all it was —just talk. There was no public record of any investigation, but it was said that there had been no autopsy. Drew Burgess had even told Bronwen that the Coroner had been paid off —or *influenced* —to file a suicide report listing drugs and exposure as the mode of death.

Others on the list were nuclear plant supervisory people, Chamber of Commerce members, JayCees, and three Protestant ministers — all of the Catholics in Bingham County were Democrats —even though Drew had said the ministers' anti-nuke stance might cause trouble; there were members of the National Association of Manufacturers, Drew's Masonic Lodge friends, and several American Legion members who, in adolescence, had worked on the Burgess family estate.

Their shared boyhood had bonded them with Drew in some way Bronwen could not fathom, knowing that he had attended private schools and was in college during the Korean War.

With their eyes ever on patronage, two lawyers on the list had already sent their contribution checks.

One Environmental Protection Agency person on the list was circled and asterisked, meaning he was "sensitive" —important but dangerous. But the Agency people seldom showed up. Any partisan activity was cause for them to fear for their jobs.

U.S. Senator and Mrs. Trumble were underlined and exclamation-pointed, and the Reverend Krock's name got special attention —it was circled twice, and underlined, asterisked and question-marked.

Brimmie was the brother of Ed Krock, but he was a garrulous Pentecostal Republican; the Reverend Krock's radical-right rantings were an embarrassment to the low-profile Burgesses, but the Reverend's sizeable congregation was predominantly Republican, and influential in the District.

Some very affluent professional types and business men typified the membership of Brimmie's Church of Christ Rising.

At the end of the list was the one Republican County Commissioner, followed by several dozen M.D.s, a flock of stock brokers and six bank executives —all underlined.

Fern Slagle's fumbling at the back door alerted Bronwen.

The Raunch Factor

Fern always brought Melba Cochran with her on Mondays and Fridays, the days when extra help was needed. Bronwen heard them talking and clumping around in the pantry and mud room, hanging up their coats, rattling buckets. Every inch of ceramic tile in all four bathrooms would be scrubbed and gleaming by noon.

How can they stand it, Bronwen wondered, *doing the same thing over and over?*

Live-in help was disdained by Bronwen. She preferred to have no one but family living under her expensive slate roof.

The window-cleaning men drove in through the front gates, as Gus Quip rolled out of the garage on the tractor.

Fern and Melba climbed up the curving front stairs; things were being done; for the moment, at least, this much was right with Bronwen's Burgess's world.

CHAPTER TWELVE

"I have nothing in common with these women," Traci was speaking to Daphne and Harriet, while Allison hovered at her elbow. "And as for those rap sessions, they're invalidating the other women and invalidating and nonconsensual to the staff. I operate from different value bases." Traci sat at her new teakwood desk, lip-glossed lips pouting.

Traci Bilsen-Bloom hath spoken, thought Daphne. *To employ a 19th Century expression, we "took leave of our senses" when we hired this bimbo.*

"We should have been notified that CR was in question," Harriet said. Her hand shook as she lit a cigarette. " —we should have had a meeting, talked over policy. We needed a chance to talk over the residents' needs." She glared at Traci. "CR is not just chit-chat. On the contrary, residents have progressed in our CR to the extent that we have many success stories on record. These women have overcome the misogyny of the community, and found new confidence and self-esteem —some of them, when they first came here, were the losers of the century —"

Daphne turned angrily to Allison, "As Shelter Manager, it was your duty to at least call me, the CR leader."

Harriet walked to the window, "Another donation's coming in —a child's table and chair set. That's the fifth one. We're really getting a response from our childcare furnishings ad, and now you're dismantling the whole thing. Why, Traci? Why?"

Traci leaned back in her new tufted leather French provincial executive chair. A cerise silk skirt and blouse echoed her glistening lips.

"It is immmm-pacting on this facility that funds be dispersed according to my agenda. Your empowerment of me validates my and my Board Members' consensual voice," she droned breathily.

"And what about this new office furniture?" Daphne demanded, "That desk, the credenza, that chair —I know that chair cost eight hundred or more, and the Mallinger Associates people told me you were in their showroom pricing oriental rugs.

Is that why the childcare plumbing work was cancelled? Allison said bills came in from Spencer Office Equipment. No one else here has new office furnishings. We need every cent we can get to pay for this building and the fire escape and parking lot —the L and I requirements."

"Take it up with the Board. The Board meeting is scheduled for two weeks from today." Traci walked to a polished brass *étagère* where, on glass shelves, many flat *sang de boeuf*-lacquered baskets served as chic file cabinets. Gray suedecloth balloon valances had been installed over brushed silver aluminum blinds in the bay window. Lorene and Leona had spent four days painting the office walls with a hundred and thirty dollars worth of aubergine paint. Five serigraphs in smart, polished brass frames sparkled on the trendy matte-finished background.

Harriet stared at two white linen love seats.

"This looks like some corporate executive office," she said. "I know you don't want to live in the building, but there's enough bucks in this one room to do over the entire third floor apartment, and *then* some, for a live-in director or manager, but now you —"

"Take it up with the Board," Traci interrupted. She sorted through some papers, then stuffed her briefcase and swayed out of the room, silken knock-knees brushing sibilantly.

"Pull this door shut when you leave. It will lock. I *keep* it locked," she added over her shoulder.

Harriet stabbed out her cigarette in a terra cotta ashtray. "I'd like to immmm-pact her agenda and grind a tube of lip gloss in her pudding face. We are being co-opted. This is *treason*. Everything we've done —all the progress we've made —is going down the toilet. Daph — " She turned to Daphne, her blunt-fingered hands palms out.

Daphne was speechless in disbelief.

A nervous obsequious Allison excused herself to direct the delivery men in the hall. Several panel-truck loads of donated juvenile furniture had been delivered to the childcare rooms. Now it had to be relocated elsewhere throughout the shelter.

The immediate community response to the Sojourner Shelter had been astonishing to its founders. Women's club members and housewives, sensing some common bond with the battered wretches housed by the shelter, had engaged in perfunctory Robert's Rules of Order procedures at club meetings —which invariably ended in a general accord that money —or goods or furnishings —should be bestowed upon the shelter, no questions asked.

Daphne collected her wits and conjectured, "That woman knows she has hands-down community support. God only knows how many contribution checks she's intercepted by now. Allison said the staff isn't allowed to open the mail. It was Traci who mandated that all mail was to be opened by nobody but her. Bobbye has been holding envelopes up to the light to see if they're checks. She says they receive anywhere from three to five hundred bucks every ten days or two weeks. After every one of Bobbye's Women's Club rape programs, the contributions just *pour* in."

"I think we have a very big problem here," Daphne said. "We should hire a CPA firm to take over the books. Felicia's been doing a good job, but we should have a CPA, not a staff member. Our only real hope is the Board of Directors. We'll lay all this before them, and they'll see what has to be done. She just has to go. That's all."

Harriet walked around the room. In marked contrast to the high fashion atmosphere was her uniform: threadbare jeans and Frye boots and a big shirt.

"Shit, shit, shit." She kicked the waste basket, an antique leather hat box. "It looks like some Briarwood 'Gift Shoppee' in here. The Board doesn't meet for two weeks. That's enough time for her to wipe us out completely."

"Couldn't help but hear you, Harriet —" Allison said as she rushed in. "Traci said she's going after those two big grants we want. We don't have any worries. She told me last night all the dynamite plans she has for the Shelter."

"Don't tell me she works evenings here," Harriet sneered.

"No, she told me that at dinner last night at the CorBlimey."

"Dinner?"

"Yes. Her treat. Since Roscoe and I have broken up, I've been, well, in therapy with her. She's, uh, counseling me."

"Counseling you?" Daphne asked, astonished. "She's counseling you? You were doing O.K. I was impressed with your CR progress. You and Roscoe were working things out. Are you not going to continue in CR? You made a commitment to the group."

"Well, with CR discontinued and everything, I —"

"CR is not discontinued. We're going to reinstate CR."

"I think Traci is helping me, though. I feel much better. She says I can go shopping with her tomorrow. I don't know how I ever would have got over Roscoe without her support. I have to continue with her counseling. I just *have* to."

"I'm sorry, Daphne." Allison said, as she opened Traci's closet and took out an armful of exotically colored clothing. "I promised her I'd take these things to the cleaner's for her. See you."

"She acts like a zombie. Like she's hypnotized." Harriet said. She pulled apart the metal window slats and watched the departing Allison.

Daphne pulled at the drawers of the teak desk. "You're not the first to make that observation. These drawers are all locked. Everything used to be so open and above board here, Harriet. We all got along so wonderfully, we were so *close*, and there wasn't anyone I didn't trust and have faith in. We all went through so much together. What's happening?"

"Damned if I know. All we can hope for is a good Board of Directors — interested, caring, compassionate. Bobbye said there's a minister and five home-makers, a nurse —she teaches at State —and Hal Renshaw. Don't you know him? She also said Traci's working on getting a woman doctor from the Fitch twenty-four-hour center, and a woman lawyer."

"Well, they sound hopeful. The board is our only hope,

Harriet, our only hope," Daphne said, so morosely that Harriet said, "Eat at my place tonight, whatyasay? Did I ever play my Birgit Nielsen and Franco Corelli recording of *Turandot* for you? It'll cheer you up. And Norm would love to see you. He feels so rotten that he needs cheering up, too. C'mon."

They switched off the brass lamps and closed Traci's office door. It locked behind them with a sharp click.

CHAPTER THIRTEEN

The first Citizen Action Party petitioning day dawned gray, fifteen degrees above zero and snowing. The coldest April since 1880, it was a dismal beginning for the petition drive; many of the volunteers were on unpaid time off, or were soon to face the end of unemployment compensation. Working for Hal Renshaw's campaign meant hope to them. He buoyed them up and made them feel the need for action; *their* action. His idealism, his fervent belief, spurred them on —his thesis that a human rights party *could* take hold, really *could* matter, could lead people away from nuclear war, away from corporate greed, from elitism, from exploitation of minorities; away from a never-ending litany of corruption spewed out daily in media accounts of the scandal and disasters resulting from the worship of power and money.

But why did it have to be so damned cold?

Groups of three or four petitioners met at shopping malls, newsstands, parking lots. They shrugged and shook their heads in camaraderie. "Only in Pennsylvania," they said of the freakish blizzard. April in Bingham.

"We oughta write a song," Merrilee Dobbs shouted to Daphne. "*April in Bingham,*" she sang, making it up as she went along,

" *—chilblains we got some*
Blizzards and snowstorms cover the ground
April in Bingham
Long Johns, we bought some
Citizen actions abound —"

She had a bright, high voice that carried well. Mall employees alighting from car pool cars looked up, surprised, then smiled at the unself-conscious recital.

We should write some good songs for this campaign, Daphne thought, *We'll get a piano or keyboard or a band and make some music —something stirring and memorable. We need it for the first big public event, whatever it's going to be.*

Hal wanted an old-fashioned speech-in-the-park sort of

gathering for the first summer event, with notices posted all over the district, people gathering to hear and see the candidate. From a bunting-draped platform as well as on TV sets, Bingham Countians could hear him tell of this belief in his country, his belief in America.

Would Hal be drowned out, pushed aside?

Would smarmy celebrity cleavage and mindless sports matches continue to distract attention from the capsizing country —America going down for the third time?

Or would the Citizen Action plea reach the disillusioned and the disenfranchised?

Polls have been taken that said twenty-five percent of the population live at or below poverty level, Daphne recalled, *but I think the percentage is higher. How can the middle class continue their cliché-ridden lives? — grocery shopping, housecleaning, refrigerator defrosting, birthdays, weddings, religious holidays, class reunions, school board meetings, Kiwanis, Rotary —and not ask themselves if it all could abruptly end or they could devolve, regress into a life of 15th Century serfs sweeping out the feudal lords' fast-food restaurants?*

Daphne tightened her muffler around her throat and pulled her knit hat down to meet it. Cutting snow-swirled wind sliced through her wool slacks and long-johns, numbed her leather-gloved fingers. Clipboard at the ready, she approached a few individuals entering the mall. There were mixed reactions:

"No, I ain't registered to vote. Why should I? Whadya mean — Citizen Action? Are ya Democrats or Republicans? Whadya stand for? I ain't signin' nothin'!"

"Listen, Doll, *nobody's* incorruptible. I'm not interested. Politicians are all alike." This from a burly, vigorous-looking unemployed steel worker.

But he reconsidered. "Burgess snookered us. The Democrats are no better. A third party, huh? Gimme that thing, I'll sign."

Or "Why should I sign yer petition? It won't make no difference in *my* life. I was let go after twenty-eight years of service to my company, an' where'd I end up at? No pension, no savings left. I'm on welfare. That's where."

Or "Yeah, why not? It can't be no worse than what we've had. A bunch of crooks been bleeding the state, the country. Yunz won't be no worse. Maybe *yunz'll* do some good." Another signature.

Ink ran and signatures and addresses smudged and blurred in the wet snowfall.

This is madness. We're all mad, crazed, Daphne thought as she slipped into the entrance of the mall. *I can defrost in here for a minute.*

"You people got to get out of here," said a voice behind her. It was the Mall Association manager, an enormous man. "Merchants are havin' a hard enough time in this depressed community without you people blockin' the doorways and botherin' customers." He stood glaring down at Daphne.

"There *are* no customers in here," she pointed out. "I just wanted to get warm for a few minutes, for Pete's sake."

"G'wan, g'wan, stay outa here." The man and his ugly scowl blended surrealistically with grinning cardboard jesters flanking the pinball game-court entrance behind him. Three black teenagers in tattered army surplus camouflage attire began to play the pinball machines. Raucous electronic laughter floated toward the deserted mall commons area where the fountains were suddenly turned on. The glowing jets sprang up forty feet, depositing mist on the surrounding polished terrazzo paving squares. It was Versailles gardens come to Bingham County.

"*Please release me,*" a country-and-western group advised nasally via the PA system.

Salesclerks uncovered their cases and desultorily set out their wares: plastic trinkets, tacky polyester blouses, tiny eighteen-dollar jars of Miracle Nite Creme. A gift-kitsch counter featured an open bible-clock of porcelain with an ethereal Jesus face in its center. Minute hands radiated from Jesus' nose; black clock numerals wreathed his face.

At the opposite end of the commons, Daphne could see Merrilee and Harriet talking to the Mall Association man. He stomped off and the two women walked out of the mall.

Outside in the blizzard again, Daphne approached a stocky blond man.

"Are you a registered voter, sir?" Her Establishment hair, clothing and demeanor caught people off-guard.

"Yeah, yeah. I guess I'll sign." He blinked his white-lashed eyes rapidly as, very laboriously, he wrote "Whitey Banyar." He handed back the clipboard.

"I need your full address also, sir —"

"Nah. Nah. Ya got muh name. That's enough," Whitey Banyar winked.

Suddenly Hal rounded the corner and approached. "I've got some free time, until four," he told Daphne, then he shook hands with Whitey Banyar.

"So you're da candidate?" Whitey didn't stand still at all; he did a sort of graceful, crouching dance, hopping from one foot to the other.

Hal described the CitAct position. The dancing Whitey crouched lower and growled, "Are ya gonna *do* all that stuff ya said?"

When Hal said he was going to try his best, Whitey jabbed the air with massive fists.

"Well, ya better, see? I'm givin' her my name and address an I'll be watchin' ya, and if ya don't do it, I'm comin' to D.C., and we're gonna put onna gloves and duke it out."

"Fair enough, Whitey," Hal replied. After the man took the clipboard and finished his entry, they shook hands, and Whitey danced away.

Hal and Daphne worked the Mall entrance for three hours. Twice they slipped inside to warm up and twice Mall guards admonished them. When the wan sunlight faded altogether, the intense cold became unbearable. They had filled three-quarters of their petition sheets and had registered over half the signers.

They stopped for coffee and then stationed themselves in front of the newsstand with the unemployed Walker brothers, Harry and Phil. Each had obtained five signatures in as many hours.

"This is murder," Harry said. "How are we gonna get eight thousand signatures? It's impossible, man." He pulled up the collar of his shabby, denim jacket. At home, he and Phil had a third of a loaf of bread and a can of spaghetti to try to get along on until the end of the week when they could eat a meal at their married sister's home.

"I know how you feel," Hal apologized. "The two established political parties finish their petitioning in a few days —like highwaymen: 'Your signature or your job —.' That's all there is to it. They can afford to hire petitioners too. Believe me, I wish the party could pay you guys."

A well-dressed woman pulled up, parked her Lincoln and ran into the newsstand for her *New York Times*. When she ran back out, Daphne stepped forward, "Would you please sign my petition?"

The woman turned briefly and looked at Daphne with revulsion. "I most certainly will *not*." She spat out the words.

"Wow. Where does the hate come from?" Phil Walker watched the shiny Lincoln turn the corner. "Person like that should love everybody. With *that* car and *those* clothes. But she seems mad at the world."

They split up again, into groups of two, and worked for two more penetratingly cold hours. Then some of the group met at Hal's apartment to compare notes. Among the six petitioners, they had fewer than two hundred names.

Merrilee sipped the sherry that Hal handed her. "I only got one in ten to sign. I stood out at the super market entrance since early this morning, and I only have thirty names. We ought to go door-to-door, Hal."

"And your sheet's one of the best," Harry said. "Boy, this seems impossible to me." He rubbed his raw-looking red wrists.

"We should hit some of the supermarkets around Doncaster and Fitler and Palmer counties on welfare check day," Hal said. "That's the day I'm sure you could fill up a sheet quickly. Going door-to-door takes about ten times as much time as what we're doing. I've tried that. It doesn't work. People won't let men petitioners in their homes — they're scared. And it can be dangerous for a lone woman petitioner."

"We're just not going to make it if we have to register every other person," Merrilee said, "That slows everything down."

"Hal, it's true," Daphne said, as the sherry began to warm her. "It's just incredible. The ones most hurt by this dehumanizing administration are the ones who don't register, don't vote, and just plain don't care. It baffles me that they can be so ignorant of government, of their constitutional rights."

"That's what apathy does. It almost destroys their will to live," Hal said as he poured the last of the sherry all around.

"I wonder if the American revolutionaries were this apathetic?" Merrilee said as she swilled down her sherry and looked over to the bottle for more.

"The Minute Men, the Bunker Hill Gang, Paul Revere, George Washington, Tom Paine —everything I've read about that period indicates they had real passion and conviction for their cause. How could they have won the revolution without it? They had such — such — *chutzpa*, to go head-to-head against the British. We could sure use some of that today."

Hal's teenagers, Celeste and Pete, wandered through the cramped disorderly living room toward the kitchen. Both were pale and thin but seemed healthy enough, for all Hal worried about them.

Hal introduced the children to the petitioners. Daphne found herself wishing the others would leave so that she and Hal and the children could talk.

Merrilee put on her coat, and the others prepared to leave. Daphne felt conspicuous, so she, too, departed. Hal's eyes met hers as they said goodnight.

Driving home past the Copper Bottom, her sherry-warmed hands and feet comfortable for the first time in about fourteen hours, Daphne remembered a more pervasive, deeper warmth.

I wonder if this feeling is what D.H. Lawrence tried to describe when he wrote about Lady Chatterley —about Connie? she thought. *Was D.H. Lawrence Connie?* she wondered. *When Connie secretly visits Mellors' cottage in the woods, and when she kneels down by the chicken coop and exclaims over the baby chick, and Mellors is turned on by this. To him it's evidence of some instinctive, maternal, eternal, infernal* —Daphne's word — *femininity. A mindless drive to reproduce, like a cat, or a dog, or a rabbit.*

Daphne drove past the CorBlimey, whose lighted plastic sign announced, "Flaming Pizza Special 3.50," and the CorBlimey's Thought for the Day: "A virtuous woman is a crown to her husband."

What about a virtuous man? she wondered. *Clifford was a virtuous man —impotent, an invalid, and all Lady Chatterly ever did, the airhead, was push hubby around in his wheelchair while servants, behind the potted palms, saw to their every need. Connie didn't have a thought in her head but getting screwed. She and Mellors were nothing more than fucking machines.*

D.H. Lawrence was a jerk, Daphne mused. *He asked nothing more of womankind than a body to poke into, a mindless collection of parts, a thing. The parts can reproduce, instinctively, and there is no need at all for a woman to think, to have thoughts of conscious reasoning, ideas. For him, there must be no sharing of intellects, no blending. If Connie had brought that sort of excitement —intellectual energy —to Mellors, it would have been a turn-off for him. She would no longer have been desireable to him —not feminine.*

Daphne remembered the horror she felt when she heard her own father announce that if a woman had a hysterectomy, she was no longer a complete woman.

"She would be," he had said, "a thing; not a woman."

They had been discussing, rather embarrassedly, a neighbor —a very bright, kind, beautiful woman who had undergone a hysterectomy. Daphne's mother, misanthropic, obese, unloving, but in possession of all the requisite organs, had glanced at Daphne then, and an unspoken acknowledgement, a pledge of enmity, had passed between mother and daughter.

I think too much, Daphne concluded, unlocking her back door. *That's the reason, at age thirty-eight, I'm childless, single, and going to bed alone.* She switched on the kitchen light. *But I am also free, independent, full of talent, plans, goals, health — and, yes —desire for Hal Renshaw. I have said it.*

She unwound her muffler and looked at herself in the hall trumeau mirror.

There's time enough to get acquainted, she told herself. *Time enough.*

Chapter Fourteen

"All right, Congressman, move in a little closer to her. Don't have to ask you *twice*, huh? Ha Ha Ha."

The false joviality of the photographer from *The Bingham County Observer* annoyed Drew Burgess, but it wouldn't hurt, he thought, to be photographed with Miss Dialysis and her Royal Kort. Granted it was a little tacky; hadn't Ernest Hartley said that the Dialysis Kween and her Kort were all great lays? With all the attention paid to politicians' liaisons and the cheap Televangelist scandals, Drew had to watch his ass.

Still, Alma had always said "Don't worry too much about scandals. Start worrying when they don't pay any attention to you at all."

Posing like this was for a good cause —good causes —his and the hospital's. The five shapely young women appeared at benefit dinners, shopping malls and on TV to raise money for Bingham County Hospital's Kidney Korner.

Drew's own wife, Bronwen, had raised over fifty thousand dollars this year for the hospital's OB-Gyn department by giving guided tours of their replicated 18th Century home. Dr. Hartley himself —the Chief of the OB-Gyn Department —had personally sent a thank-you note. After all, Drew reasoned, it just made the Doctor's "plant," his "factory," that much more lucrative. More of this sort of publicity couldn't hurt.

Drew slipped his arm through Miss Dialysis's smooth, tanned arm and edged closer. Her hair, he observed, smelled like taffy apples. She was, as the guys at prep school used to say, "Built like a brick shit-house." It was time to trot out a joke.

"Looks like you ate gunpowder for breakfast — " Drew addressed one of the Kidney Korner Kort. "Your hair came out in bangs."

The goosefleshed women tittered and tugged at the back of their swimsuits. (Drew's office temperature was about sixty degrees.) The swimsuits were minuscule scraps of elastic laced together with several strings at hips and breasts. Miss Dialysis herself was clad in what appeared to be two sequin-covered paper cups and a matching six-inch-wide diaper. A cardboard crown bore the name "Kidney Korner Kween."

When she was not the Kween, Miss Dialysis dressed as "Nurse Funbuns" and, in a translucent body suit and a white spandex mini-uniform and starched cap, delivered telegrams to corporate offices. She visited executives on their birthdays to present scrolls chiding them and warning of the dangers of overwork and " —that dread disease, Lackanookie."

"That's it, that's it," burbled the photographer. "That was a beaut. Now, girls, turn slightly sideways, look at the Congressman, suck in yer gut, get a little lift to the boobs, gimme some nice cleavage, lick yer lips and —now —a —great —big —smile. EEEEEEEEE-ha!" The flash went off.

The photo opportunity completed, Drew said "Thank you, ladies," and turned to the week-at-a-glance calendar posted on the wall beside his desk —actually an Eighteenth Century rent collector's table. Bronwen had assembled antique furnishings which gave his nondescript office the distinctive look of a combination sitting room/library. Drew's Jack Russell terrier prints were neatly arranged along one wall. Behind his desk was the *pièce de résistance,* a fine engraving entitled, "Taking the Scent," showing Lord Salisbury as Master of the Hunt. Drew's secretary, Adele Nicholson, sat in an outer alcove at a black lacquered escritoire centered on a crimson Turkey-work carpet.

Drew noticed that the calendar showed a debate scheduled at Tri-County Community College the following Monday, the first event of the campaign. He and Ed Krock would be joined by that third party guy, Renshaw, the professor from State. Pretty cut-and-dried kind of thing. The debates and various public appearances, except for the TV appearances —Drew liked the excitement of TV —were boring, actually. But he had an all-purpose speech and a set of stock answers for all of the usual questions. The dim-bulb steel workers would nail him about jobs; Krock was *non compos mentis* and harped continually —futilely —about jobs, jobs, jobs for steel workers. But Krock *did* have the Democratic endorsement and he had plenty of money at his disposal. He would bear watching in that regard. Drew realized that his people would have to round up a lot of money for TV spots before the primary, and a real blitz in September and October, and maybe a spot ad here and there through the summer.

The primary was no real worry to Drew. No other Republican had declared; incumbents *always* won the primary, and went on to win the general election too, Drew reassured himself. He had spent his first two years in office preparing to win the next election.

The third-party guy would just be a joke. He definitely was not top-drawer; Harvard and State were worlds apart. But someone had told Drew that Renshaw's position paper had some cockamamie idea about putting a ceiling on Congressional salaries and imposing term limits. In any head-to-head it would be better to ignore this area altogether —not give it air-time —so it would never even become an issue.

Renshaw would probably take a few votes away from Krock, Drew told himself, so it wouldn't be all that bad. The main thing was to get good financial backing, even if he had to cash some of the bonds his mother left him. That might be tricky —those bonds were supposed to ensure Stephanie's never wanting for anything, ever, in her lifetime. Still, he could hardly be expected to touch a penny of the cash he had sunk into the money market. An investment in his success was the best security, anyway.

Gotta get those TV spots, he vowed. They can make you or break you. I need some traditional shots —nostalgia —strolling down our tree-lined Briarwood streets, reminding the voters of those easy, graceful days of privilege. People respect that. People will vote for a dream —a return to comfort and gracious living. They want to look away from sordid, social conflict and enjoy life.

Drew made a note to have his aide, Tim Rhodes, get down to the Bingham Borough Building in the morning to take care of questions about Social Security for his constituents, and Medicare, Veterans' Affairs —Tim handled all that. Now Drew had to drop off the Mercedes for an oil change while he had a fitting at his tailor's; TV always picked up on any sartorial carelessness. He leafed through a copy of *GQ* while he ate the ham-and-cheese sandwich Adele brought him.

If the oil change were finished by two he could make it to the Realtor's to sign papers for the parcel of land he was purchasing — the two lots adjoining the expensive acreage he already owned. He aimed to move his horses closer to home.

The Realtor also had arranged for Drew to see two apartment buildings that were up for Sheriff's auction. Drew had coached Tim about attending auctions. Then, after a short visit at home Drew would head back to the Capital. Bronwen wanted him to watch Stephanie swim in the Special Ed pool, but there would hardly be time to go over the fund-raiser plans.

Life with Bronwen was serious business. She had always been almost completely humorless, even in their dating days. But she was very pretty and extremely social, and she was devoted to Stephanie, and their home was a showplace; she was the perfect wife for a politician, even if her body wasn't that great. He couldn't remember the last time they'd slept together. When Bronwen had gotten a "tummy-tuck" after Stephanie's birth, Drew had asked the plastic surgeon about a derriere-lift and breast implants, and had recommended this surgery to Bronwen, but she wasn't interested; she didn't seem to care if she turned him on or not.

Drew wanted Bronwen to be sure to have the Bösendorfer delivered before the fund-raisers. Seventy thousand for a piano was a little rich for his blood, but they needed it in the living room, and it might as well be the best. There was always someone at every rally who could play the thing.

Tim had told Drew that people were laughing about a tape Renshaw's supporters were playing in malls and flea markets, referring to the two real parties as "Jumbo and the Jackass."

The idea of a third party materializing from almost nowhere was disquieting to Drew Burgess. He knew the Republicans and Democrats played footsie most of the time. But that's the way they wanted it. That way, everything was under control. Just Jumbo and the Jackass. A third party just stirred up trouble; it might upset the apple-cart —and derail the gravy train, he added ruefully.

When Drew was State Senator, Citizen Action groups were just starting to make a few waves in the eastern part of the state and a few midwestern states, and making a lot of noise on the West Coast. They were generally dismissed as another one of those nutty, populist groups. Nobody paid much attention to them, then. The Pennsylvania State Legislature kept the election laws plenty stringent, and a few radicals like Renshaw sputtered for a while, then petered out from lack of workers, time, and money.

But this Tenth District group had managed to get ballot status. Drew had seen them petitioning all over the district. Somebody said they had a booth at the auto show and they were registering people there. This was a development that could mess things up. They might take votes away from him, from Drew Burgess —not from Ed Krock. It *could* give Krock the edge.

Steelworkers had their backs up, and they actually believed Krock would bring jobs to Bingham County. He, Drew Burgess, could lose. It *could* happen. And he no longer had Alma to spur him on.

It was Alma, his mother —Drew used to call her Alma Mater —who had gotten him into the State Legislature by paying for five ballot boxes to be opened for recount. That way, he had just skinned by, and it had only cost the feisty Alma twenty-five thousand dollars. She had always pushed and maneuvered him, and after his father died it became her full-time occupation.

Alma was not at all the way her name sounded; she should have been a "Hattie" or a "Sadie." She always was able to see the main chance and then take off and manipulate people to get whatever she had set her sights on.

Manipulate men, that is. In those days women had very little influence of their own in the world. In her youth, she had been a prototype flapper, into heavy drinking and petting and embarrassing her parents — as if she'd posed for John Held Junior's original illustration. A splendid horsewoman, Alma could get a horse to jump almost anything and had revived the Briarwood Hunt when it languished after World War II.

Alma was so thrilled when Drew won for State Senate that she got sloshed and threw a three-day champagne bash that shocked even the hard-drinking Briarwoodians. When Drew ran for Congress and won, again just skinning by, he thought Alma probably did the Charleston in her grave. She'd be doing some pretty macabre bumps and grinds if he didn't get re-elected this time.

CHAPTER FIFTEEN

Five enormous cardboard crates sat on the loading dock at Designs For Living under half an inch of wet snow. Debbie Fentress brushed off their tops and spread sheets of plastic over them, then went inside to phone Robb Mulvaney again. It was his job to get the crates into the receiving room and unpacked, and he was late for the third straight day.

The crates contained upholstered furniture for the Krock installation Daphne had scheduled for Thursday, Friday and Saturday. Debbie had come in to work three Saturdays in a row. She could see that Daphne was getting crabbier by the day, from petitioning, on top of her workload. The Krock party was coming up Sunday, and the paper hangers had only a week to get a month's work done. The carpenters were so far behind schedule the mirror people had to work until midnight for three days. They charged overtime for that, and Debbie's vacation bonus would be affected because of it.

"Are you gonna get your ass over here, Robb? Fuck your bran loaves! Leave them in the oven and get over here."

Debbie slammed down the phone.

Robb marketed health foods on the side under the name, "Yoga Robb's Regulators." His health foods, his church activities and his camping trips definitely interfered with progress at Daphne's shop. Robb was obnoxiously "saved" and a fervent follower of Brimmie Krock and his Church of Christ Rising; he spoke in tongues and was sickeningly sanctimonious. Debbie knew he had found out she was sleeping with Bradley Hoffmeir.

Debbie wished James wasn't on sick leave. Maybe he *was* gay —all the neat guys she knew always seemed to turn out to be gay —but James really knew how to work, and baking soda wasn't falling out of his armpits, and what a sense of humor! Sometimes he made Debbie laugh until she was nearly sick. The Krock job would be a lot further along if James hadn't left.

Bobbye Krock had wanted quite a few alterations made on her house. She did not like the fancy imitation Villa d'Este interior, and Daphne couldn't talk her out of rearranging most of

125

the first floor. However, an excellent design was worked out, a contractor was hired —a friend of Ed Krock's, of course —walls were ripped out, and the Krocks were ripped off. Though he was a fairly skilled remodeler, the contractor was macho, sexist and crooked. He sneered at Daphne's ideas, and when the cost overruns exceeded his estimates, they were blamed on Daphne's design.

But Bobbye liked Daphne's idea for a skylighted cathedral ceiling for the rather dark kitchen, with a solarium and loft-office across one end, reached by an iron spiral stairway. The kitchen, a one-story "L" to the dining room, made this idea feasible, but Daphne was sorry she had suggested it. It was at least three months' work crammed into a few weeks.

Then Bobbye *really* got carried away. In the living room, she wanted —and was getting — a six-person Jacuzzi on a huge, curved, diagonal, raised platform; it opened into the living room from what had been an adjacent library. In front of the platform, behind a curved, tambour-mirrored bar, Daphne was having workmen hang eight mirrored folding doors which could be opened to reveal the ceramic-tiled, sybaritic hot-tub splendor. A hand-painted Rocky Mountains mural on the wall behind the Jacuzzi set the theme for the entire main floor —a mixture of Art Deco and Native American motifs.

The lighting plan had kept three expert electricians cursing into the night for ten days. Cerise and blue neon tubing outlined the curved bar canopy and the living room ceiling's perimeter as well as the large bay window. A low seating-platform/banquette was built into the bay and continued along a twenty-foot wall to the Italian Renaissance fireplace. The fifty huge toss pillows for this seating platform had thrown Daphne's workroom into a frenzy.

Furnishings yet to be installed were the slouchy, overstuffed, white couches and chairs and the thick, off-white Berber carpet and the white slubbed linen wall-coverings and clusters of giant cactus plants in chrome tubs. Tropheé arrangements of Hopi arrows and war bonnets and Kachina dolls would decorate one large wall.

At the windows would be hung mirrored vertical louvered blinds —Bobbye's dream ever since her first visit to Daphne's shop. These rooms were a planet away from the black- and red-flocked walls of the CorBlimey Steakhouse and Lounge. But it was what Bobbye wanted, and " —she's damn well gonna get what she wants," Daphne told Debbie. "It'll jar the be-Jesus out of Briarwood."

Ed Krock's basement hideaway was his own project. Daphne was relieved not to have to deal with Ed. To further disassociate herself from his plastic paneling and imitation leather, she had suggested that a plaque be displayed designating Ed as the room's creator, an idea that he enthusiastically carried out.

He had eight black vinyl recliner chairs arranged in a semicircle before a forty-inch TV. An eighteen-foot, tufted red and black vinyl bar dispensed shots and beers. Ed's personal arsenal of firearms —enough to outfit several infantry platoons — menaced guests from tall cases flanking the huge lavastone fireplace. Over the rugged oak mantel a leaping swordfish sawed at fake ceiling beams. Red- and gold-flocked wallpaper shed a feverish glow over everything. Ed had succeeded in recreating every Bingham Countian's dream game room: a duplication of the Mole People's underground environment that his family had admired when he was a child, but never could afford.

Only Ed's Democratic Committee, his select friends, and his NRA cronies would be admitted to his lurid bailiwick. Ed said Bobbye's left-wing Commie queers with their homo whirlpool and their pansy mixed drinks could stay upstairs.

Ed even had a basement bedroom featuring a seven-foot circular bed with a mirrored canopy tilted over it like a coffin lid. The bedroom had its own TV and stereo equipment and a mini-refrigerator. He wouldn't have to see Bobbye at all if he used the side entrance. But what use were the mirrors and stereo if he couldn't get Bobbye to come down there?

Maybe he *had* yelled too much about her staying out of his glorious hang-out.

Bobbye had been refusing to put on her Victor of Vegas outfit, and she said he was so snotty about her Jacuzzi that he wasn't going to get to put so much as his big toe in it. They had had a pretty bad fight about the decorating.

CHAPTER SIXTEEN

"Who's somebody? Who's somebody?" The stooped, elderly man shook with rage. He had told Hal and Daphne that he didn't vote because he couldn't get to the polls. Daphne had suggested that surely somebody could take him there. His shouted response belied his fragile appearance. His caretaker — she appeared to be his daughter —peered out at him from inside the supermarket.

"There's no somebody!" he shouted again. "I can't handle it!" He limped into the supermarket before Daphne could tell him that she, personally, would see that he got to the polling place. He reminded her of her own arthritis-ridden father.

Citizen Action petitioners were more than five hundred signatures short of their goal. Less than one week remained before the deadline, and they also were short three workers: Merrilee, Phil and Harry had the flu. Barry Spiegel, Harriet, and even Ellen petitioned every day, but Harriet obtained very few signatures. Her aggressive approach seemed to alarm rather than persuade.

Ellen, on the other hand, had a WASP establishment air of gentility that won potential signers' confidence before she spoke. At first she carried her ghetto blaster with her, and her song, "Money Talks," attracted attention. But after the batteries fizzled out, she continued to do well with her unthreatening pleasantness. Hal had promised to get new batteries for the blaster.

Ellen was always short of money. Her children's needs were endless. The big 1880s farmhouse that she and her husband, Larry —a Vietnam veteran —had bought after his discharge had a huge mortgage, a leaky roof and antique plumbing. House repairs were a constant financial drain.

Ellen's furniture refinishing supplemented their income a little. Larry's salary as district manager for PennWheat Bakery was barely enough to support four people, let alone eight. But getting through the petitioning and *still* managing the housework, grocery shopping and furniture-refinishing convinced Ellen that she could handle another job, part-time, despite her mother's jeers about keeping up appearances (which mandated a stay-at-home mother).

Ellen had begun to feel more positive and assertive. Learning how to petition had given her confidence. Other women CitAct members had said the same thing, had expressed the pleasure they experienced with activism, with speaking out — some for the first time in their lives —and with taking an active part in the world where they had been spectators all their lives.

Today, to revitalize their technique, the petitioners swapped assignments, Barry and Harriet working the Doncaster Flea Market, and Ellen and Daphne at the Newsstand. Still, it was very slow-going. Hal frequently had to return to his office at the college. He was deeply concerned as they neared the deadline. A drive to recruit more petitioners at this late date was not the answer; they would be too inexperienced.

He had recruited two of the pickets at the supermarket —two of the thirty workers who had been fired and replaced by employees who would work part-time for minimum wage and no benefits. Hal could hardly afford to pay the pickets fifty cents a signature; however, in ten days they had scarcely filled three petition sheets. They said shoppers acted as if pickets were invisible.

"What's it to *them* we were replaced — just let go and replaced with desperate slobs who'll work for minimum? Nobody cares. My wife and kids had to go back to her folks in Ohio. Fred, over there, lost his house. It was a dump, but it was *his*. But who cares? Man, in this country it's every man for himself! The last thing anybody wants to hear is some nut jabberin' about changin' the system."

The pickets took Hal's money gratefully enough but were reluctant to continue what was, to them, a humiliating act of begging for a lost cause.

Hal had car payments and dentist's bills and rent to meet. He could hire no more petitioners.

The biting cold continued, the snow changing to a penetrating drizzle. State electoral laws limiting petitioning to this short period of often inclement weather were an effective deterrent to dissenters, Harriet concluded. It only made her more determined. She had finally gotten one sheet nearly filled but it was growing dark, and soon the flea market would close.

A young woman approached pushing a baby in a stroller. A plastic dish drainer and some curtain rods were jammed in the stroller behind the red-faced baby in a virulent pink snow suit. The woman's hair was frizzled in the style of the latest soap opera heroine, her face distorted with painted-on eyebrows, fake eyelashes, a glistening fuchsia mouth drawn over her naturally thin lips. The eyes that squinted at Harriet behind bright turquoise eye shadow were frightened eyes.

Harriet stepped forward, "Excuse me, are you a registered voter, Ma'am?" The woman stared straight ahead and tried to pass. Her pink polyester hooded jacket, open at the neck, showed a high ruffled pink collar with pearl buttons. She wore pearl earrings. Her tight blue jeans made her buttocks look like a plaster casting. *Jesus,* Harriet thought, *She's tricked out like this for a flea market?*

"Will you please sign my petition?" Harriet persisted. "I'd really appreciate it. If you're not registered to vote, I can register you now. You'll be helping a good cause. The Citizen Action Party is running Dr. Renshaw —from State University, you know —for U.S. Congress, and the law requires over eight thousand signatures — we're a third party, you know. We oppose the nuclear arms race and corporations moving south —where there's no unions and labor's cheaper. We oppose Sheriff's sales of unemployed people's homes — our party will fight these dehumanizing things." Harriet took a deep breath. The frizzle-haired woman looked simultaneously terrified and contemptuous. "I don't think so. I have to ask my husband." She was not moving away, however. She stood squinting at Harriet.

"It's not a vote," Harriet continued. "Your signature will enable a concerned person to get on the ballot and maybe be heard in Congress —will enable an honest, decent person to represent those of us who are being ripped off by the syst —"

"I don't think so," the woman muttered as she pushed the stroller around Harriet. The baby twisted around in her seat and stared up at her mother. Pink mittens hung on strings from the child's jacket sleeves.

Good grief, thought Harriet, *the kid's nails are polished.* The baby's hands, like little red-tipped stars, waved in the humid air.

The woman minced down the aisle with tiny steps, her terrified eyes staring straight ahead. Harriet saw Barry watching. Something made Harriet persist. *This woman brought a child into the world,* she told herself. *She's gotten herself up to look like a hooker. What's in her head —if anything? What's to become of that poor child? What if there's a nuclear war? Has she given that one single thought?*

Harriet had seen hundreds of such women at malls and flea markets. They moved trancelike through the aisles fingering plastic bowls, old curtains, sleazy silk blouses just as all over America, in exclusive department stores and boutiques, their upper-economic-class counterparts examined Andrea Cassotti furs and suits and four-hundred-dollar Swiss food processors.

Harriet caught up with the woman and walked alongside her.

"The CitAct Party's in favor of a national health plan. Did you know that the United States is the only industrialized country in the world, besides South Africa, without a national health plan? Our party will fight this undemocratic system and bring about vital change, particularly working to change the unfair electoral laws —the restrictions that make it difficult for citizens even to vote, to exercise our rights. Why should we be oppressed with unfair voting laws, ma'am? We need your signature. I can register —"

"I have to ask my husband!" The woman walked faster. Several flea market shoppers stared. Harriet's cheeks were burning as she hurried along beside the woman and thrust her clipboard toward her.

"Don't you want to participate in the democratic process?" she demanded.

"I don't think so," the woman snapped.

Fury rose within Harriet. "You don't think so? You don't *think* so? Well, you'd *better* think so. What kind of world will there be for your baby to grow up in? Will there even *be* a world? Ma'am, you'd better start thinking. You'd *better* start!" She heard her own voice rising.

"I'm gonna tell my *husband!*" The woman stuck out her lower lip petulantly and whined like a five-year-old. She rushed up the aisle and into the crowd.

Harriet walked back to Barry, who was cajoling a dejected shopper. He had one sheet three-quarters full. He licked his chapped lips and managed a smile when he saw Harriet.

"You sure deserve an 'A' for effort," he commented.

"Oh shit." Harriet lit a cigarette. "Did you get a load of Miss Teen Bingham? There are so many bimbos out there, and they're *all* reproducing. Those women lurch through their airbrained lives in their lip gloss and cheerleader boots, questioning nothing, looking forward only to being screwed, then raising more cheerleaders or more macho males. They have no identity at all. TV, the movies, even their own parents trivialize women a thousand times a day in a thousand different ways. TV can do it in a split second. Ever watch those women in those TV rock music shows —those dancers?"

"You mean the Solid Gold Buttocks show?" Barry lit his pipe, grinning. "Yeah, sure, I watch it. Normal guys are just gonna do it, Harriet. Do you think we look at all that T and A and say, 'OOOh lookee —those women appear to be trivial'?"

Harriet shook her head. "And you're supposed to be educated — one of the cognoscenti! You're all alike! Steel worker, ditch digger, college professor, corporation president. You're all alike."

"Just because we like women's asses?"

"Why do I even try to reason with you?" Harriet turned away, tears of frustration dimming her depressing view of shuffling shoppers.

From the end of the aisle a familiar, pink-coated figure

approached with tiny steps, pushing a familiar pink blob. Stomping beside her was a massive muscular man straight out of a "pumping iron" ad. His clenched fists alerted Barry.

"*Now* look what you've gone and done, Harriet. Here she comes with 'Big Daddy.' I'm the one who's gonna get punched out. What did you say to her, anyway?"

The bizarre triumvirate kept coming.

"Oh boy, oh boy, he looks mad, Harriet, oh boy — " Barry's pudgy five-foot-seven looked pudgier than ever. Miss Teen Bingham smirked triumphantly.

"Oh boy. Here it comes," Barry muttered.

"Oh, shut up, Barry."

Harriet stepped, tall and imperious, into the aisle in the path of the three.

"Did you wish to speak to me?" She switched her gleaming, auburn braid like a tail. Without missing a step, and looking straight ahead, the duo and their nail-polish-bedecked baby silently veered around Harriet and down the aisle to the exit.

Barry sighed with relief. "Hooo-boy!"

"You were plenty worried, Barry."

"Not with you to protect me." He re-lit his pipe. "What's a nice Jewish girl doing in a place like this? For all my overbearing, macho, educated judgement I honestly can't figure that one out, Harriet. You could have had it all: steady Jewish doctor husband —or a root canal man. Las Vegas vacations. Fur coats. Big house in Briarwood. The three esses: Security, Shopping, Sex."

"Oh, what can I expect of a man who, when he goes to religious services, first thanks Yahwe that he wasn't born a woman?"

"I don't go to religious services."

"Well, all your fucking male ancestors did, and they all felt the same way you do about women — the Woman-As-Pussy philosophy."

"Harriet, if that were true, I wouldn't let you play in my

quintette, and I wouldn't take your political activism seriously."

"Barry, you *need* a violin in the group, and I'm the only one you can find who's good enough. You tolerate my playing in *spite* of my gender. And it's not *your* quintette; it's a cooperative effort, as all chamber music was intended to be. As for taking me seriously, you know I'm as well-educated as you are —you know it and —"

"I *like* educated pussy," Barry interrupted.

"*Shalom* to you too, Barry. *Mazel Tov.*"

Harriet blinked back tears of rage and approached one of the few remaining shoppers, an elderly woman whose frayed coat was held together in front with a safety pin.

"Are you a registered voter, Ma'am?" Harriet did her best to speak calmly and appear reasonable.

Chapter Seventeen

Ellen Kirschner shoved aside fifteen dozen hot dogs and buns in her crowded freezer to make room for two six-pound packages of ground beef.

Without hamburger and peanut butter, she asked herself, *how could I turn out meals day after day?*

Her children had healthy appetites. They drank more than ten gallons of milk each week.

Meals, laundry, packing school lunches, her furniture refinishing business, and her work at the Shelter made Ellen's days blur together. And now she also was responsible for the CitAct petition drive victory celebration. Hal had assured her that she would be reimbursed, and she knew she could believe him. She was charmed, as were all of the other Party members, by Hal Renshaw's sincerity, his earnestness.

Ellen's husband's bitterness was a marked contrast to Hal's idealism. Larry sneered at the human rights premise of the CitAct Party platform and, so far, had refused to attend meetings, pointing out cynically that it was a "bleeding heart lip-service" party and would never get off the ground because "nobody really gives a shit about anybody else. Only money talks."

Ellen's jump-boogie piano composition, "Money Talks," was a concession to Larry's negativity, but party members had made of the song a positive political statement.

Hal was on his way to Harrisburg at this moment, to deliver over eight thousand hard-won signatures. Petitioners had worked to the very last hour. If the names were not challenged, Hal was indeed assured a chance to run for Congress on the Citizen Action Party ticket.

Maybe a celebration was a little premature, Ellen thought, even if it had been her idea. But now it was a *fait accompli.* She had called all the CitAct members about the celebration, and most were planning to attend it and were bringing potential new members; she counted two hundred twenty-five.

Word has travelled, she realized. *In a very short time, CitAct Party membership will have tripled!*

It was proof that what was, to Ellen, a complacent, mean-spirited community might have some humanity, some heart, after all. It was wonderfully encouraging.

Increasingly discouraging, however, were Larry's problems, his depression and nightmares about Vietnam, his "spells," as Ellen's mother called them. Larry's troubles, his unpredictability, had alienated his family from normal Bingham middle class activities: church suppers, PTA events, Bingham High sports events, Bitsy Balls, the Gessler Museum Women's Committee activities with the Briarwood women in their expensive clothes mingling with anxious Bingham matrons at Museum Teas. All of this sort of thing enraged Larry.

Larry's unremitting anger carried over even into his sleep. He would go to work, then come home and drink and watch TV sports matches and Vietnam videotapes. What semblance of family life they had was maintained tenuously by Ellen. Ellen's narcissistic widowed mother, Mrs. Ames, nagged Ellen from the sidelines about keeping up appearances, finagling Bitsy Bids for Kitty and Kelly, trying to meet Briarwoodians socially, avoiding all mention of anything that was Not Nice — Vietnam and feminism were at the top of *that* list — but offering little assistance, emotional, financial or otherwise. In fact, Ellen regarded her mother as a seventh child.

After being pregnant for nearly one-fourth of her marriage, Ellen found that she and the Women's Movement had gravitated inexorably toward each other. Having never had a sister, and with a mother who disliked women —Mrs. Ames even hated the Kirschners' female dog —Ellen had found the heady feeling of sisterhood, early in the movement, intoxicating. Joining NOW, participating in the consciousness-raising sessions, and the spirited, exciting marches for Title Nine and the ERA, the International Women's Year, starting the Sojourner Shelter with Harriet and Daphne and Allison and the others all made her feel infinitely more alive than housework had ever done. Although she loved Larry and her children, and the home she and Larry had created, she had never thought she really mattered much in the world or in their lives. For the first time in her life, Ellen felt that, through feminism, she had found a voice.

Ellen's older children, along with their father, regarded feminism with barely tolerant contempt. Her eldest daughter, Kitty, sarcastically picked up on such feminist side-issues as whether or not women should remove body hair or wear make-up. It gave Kitty a springboard for maternal defiance. She stopped shaving the dark hair on her legs and armpits and, smirking, wore only shorts and sleeveless blouses and kept her hands on her hips for an entire summer.

Undaunted, Ellen continued to learn and grow, her feminist associations and her reading leading her to more and more insight.

Ellen's mother, in her WASP horror of the Women's Movement and of Kitty's "underarm birds' nests," as she called them, and her granddaughters' "not sitting with their knees together," kept the already raucous household in a furor.

Today, as Ellen waded through piles of clothing and toys to make the beds in Karl's, Kirk's, Kitty's and Kelly and Kathy's bedrooms, she remembered with regret her and Larry's decision to give five of their six children alliterative names. It was such a WASP, middle class thing to do; it exploited the children.

Ellen and Larry had allowed Mrs. Ames to wear them down about the children's names. She liked, particularly, the Presbyterian-sounding "Kirk." When, in defiance, they had named the sixth child Mark, there had been Mrs. Ames' hurt feelings and long silences to deal with.

It was plain that she didn't like Mark. *Because of his name?* Ellen asked herself, dismayed.

Her mother catered to Larry, though; she preferred men to women, or to children. She loved Larry's being big and muscular and thought his name, Lawrence Earl Kirschner IV, impressive. She couldn't get it through her teased-at-the-beauty-shop-every-week bubble hairdo that such dynastic pretensions embarrassed Ellen. Larry sometimes even received mail with the salutation "Dear Mr. IV."

The Raunch Factor

Ellen flung her beloved double-wedding-ring quilt over her and Larry's old Victorian bed. She picked up his pillow and pressed it against her face and tried to concentrate on the early happy days when they were first married, before he was a patriot, before he went to Vietnam. Memories of their laughter and passion, their delight in each others' bodies were what barely held them together now. Now, during many nights Larry leaped to his feet and stood on this same bed in a deep, savage, terrified sleep and shouted at the enemy in his dreams. When Ellen would awaken him, he often would punch her. With sweat pouring, he would pummel and curse her. One set of bruises would barely be healed when he would have another nightmare and inflict a new batch.

Larry had what was being called "Vietnam Delayed Stress Syndrome." Ellen heard about it at the Women's Shelter Coalition meetings, and several Sojourner Shelter residents described their husbands' similar behavior. The phenomenon was being reported throughout the United States and was cited as a cause of incredible suffering of many Vietnam veterans, sometimes unendurable suffering. Larry knew of numerous veterans' suicides, and the number was growing.

Larry kept in touch with other Green Berets, some of whom, surprisingly to Ellen, had made the Army their career.

"It gets in their blood," he had told Ellen. "In spite of the killing, the fucking blowing up and burning people up, it's still irresistible to a lot of them. Some guys told me it was the only time they really felt alive. Death makes them feel alive!"

Larry subjected himself to reliving his war experiences by watching old Vietnam newsreel videos and TV movies. It was as if he immersed himself in the horror again to try to emerge cleansed, somehow purified. "I have to do it! I have to do it!" he told Ellen. At his insistence, they went to a theater in the city to see the latest first-run Vietnam War movie of another wrenching, questioning, brutal reenactment of past savagery. Larry had sat staring at the film in silent tears. Around the theater sobs could be heard. When Ellen could stand it no longer, she groped her way up the aisle to the lobby and glimpsed in the audience, lighted by the screens ghastly glow, eight or ten men (and a few women), their agonized faces bathed in tears.

It must stop, it must stop —the wars —must stop. Ellen's incoherent thoughts had raced as she stood in the lobby, stuffing her mouth with Milk Duds. Then she realized, with horror, that she was thinking of the soldiers in the film —our side and the enemy's —stuffing the genitals of the dead soldiers into their dead mouths.

At the same time, thoughts of her children crowded into this grisly hell. She thought of Karl and Kirk and, now, baby Mark —their chubby toddlers' arms and legs, their babyish protruding little bellies, their squealing joy in their baths in the big lion's claw-footed tub. Mark, as an infant, had so adored his bath that Ellen had to wear, back-to-front, a plastic raincoat for his nightly leg-kicking ritual. Sometimes neighbor children asked to watch, and their delighted giggles mingled with the steam and warm soapy baby smell. Plastic ferryboats and old kitchen colanders — their "rain pans" the children called them — littered the bathroom. How could these same exquisite little boy bodies, that she had carried with such love within her own body, grow into the coarse male killing machines of the movie?

Ellen could not think beyond a movie of Vietnam. To fathom the war's reality was beyond her most intense imaginings. Newsreels, actual film footage of actual killing, she processed out of her brain, closed her eyes and blocked it out. Larry told her of his repeated participation in the ruthless wiping out of civilians.

"They would hang onto the choppers, onto our feet, when they found out their village was gonna be napalmed —try to climb in the chopper —and we'd take off with them hanging on. What we had to do to them made My Lai look like kids playing cops and robbers. Over and over we shot unarmed civilians — little kids, mothers and babies, old, old men. We had to, Ellen. It was that or be court-martialled."

Larry had received a battlefield citation and thereafter had the responsibility of ordering others as well as himself to carry out the madness over and over.

I'd rather my sons would die young than to mature and have to kill every living thing in a war, Ellen told herself wildly. *Why can't we and the enemy just make films of war —and then show them to each other in comfortable theaters while we eat JuJubes? At the end, one side or the other could win. Then we'd all go home to warm beds. If the men —the world leaders —felt more anger and grievances or the need for more power nagging at the insides again —they could make another film and act out, with actors, the rapes and torture in realistic color with blood capsules —get it all out of their systems.*

But no, they want it for real. These crazed men need the actual, the real thing — real killing, real maiming, real disembowelling and attendant, assorted mutilation.

It has to be real for them or it's no good, she realized.

There would be no stopping it. *Why, they even talk about Land War, Terrorist War, Nuclear War —variety in war, for God's sake!*

Ellen had sat, that night, on a plastic covered bench in the orange and royal blue theater lobby, waiting for Larry. The actors' agonized screams and death gurgles, the blasting guns ("They can fire a hundred bullets a minute," Larry told her) searched out and found her ears. Killing would always search her out, she mourned.

At last, in a burst of patriarchal timpani and French horn movie music schmaltz, the debacle ended. The gray-faced audience straggled blinking, embarrassed, two by two, out into the lobby. Some of the red-eyed men stared straight ahead, tears unstaunched. Ellen hadn't realized there were so many Vietnam veterans living in the region. *But then, that war —that hell went on for ten years,* she reminded herself. Her own husband probably was being driven insane by it. But the wasted, wrecked lives, the broken-spirited left-overs from that war simply didn't seem to interest anyone very much.

Ellen looked up from Larry's pillow, startled. Something

had hit her knee. It was the frayed, saliva-frothed tennis ball of Barkly, the family dog. She wanted to play "toss and fetch." Again, she dropped the ball on Ellen's knee and grinned and panted her happiness. It was eleven-thirty. It was car pool day and time to pick up Mark and the other nursery school children.

"Come on, puppy," Ellen threw the sticky ball down the steep back stairs. Barkly scrambled and rolled down after it, cushioned by her thick Border Collie winter coat. After putting on her own thin winter coat, Ellen tossed the ball once more — this time into the fenced back yard.

She backed her old VW around the lilac bush and set out to collect Mark and four squealing four- and five-year-olds. Mark, at three and a half, was accepted into nursery school because he was toilet trained. *Were Vietnamese children toilet trained?* Ellen asked herself. *In a nuclear war, toilet training won't matter.* Sometimes her thoughts ganged up and raced around her brain making her dizzy.

She ate a stale doughnut out of a box she kept in the glove compartment. Soon the piping cries of little Dwight, the Pentecostal minister's son, would fill the small car as he jostled and whined in the back seat and warned his sweaty schoolmates that "The devil's gonna take ya t'hell if you don't gimmee them M an' Ms!" And beruffled little Sharon, her thin bare legs blue-white with cold, her silky hair frizzed into a straw-like "perm," would chatter about her Mommy and Daddy's fights. Fights because "Mommy has to wash clothes in the cold basement an' her feet get wet an' it makes her sick when she gets her period." They were such *old* children!

Once, when the VW had slid into a snowdrift and Ellen rocked the car back and forth for five minutes, Dwight led prayers, intoning, "Lord, don't let the devil git us," and the children all cheered when the car chugged back onto the road.

They'll all survive this life, Ellen told herself. Her hands itched from furniture refinishing chemicals, hands that could play piano jazz and blues but which now were bruised from Larry's latest pummeling. Her feet were numb because the VW heater didn't work, had never worked, and she felt the telltale vaginal warmth that signaled her menstrual flow. Three periods in one month; it was, as Dr. Hartley had chortled, probably endometriosis. Tonight while she did a two-hour clean-up after another Hamburger dinner and then did two loads of laundry, then nagged the children to bed, a seething Larry would again plant himself in front of the TV, ready for his nightly, personal disembowelling by the Vietnam war.

We will survive this life. We will survive this life. Ellen stuffed another powdered sugar-covered doughnut into her mouth. *We will all survive this life.*

Chapter Eighteen

Hal ran his fingers through his hair and hurried across the parking lot to the Odd Fellows' Hall. He counted fourteen cars —most of them what Mrs. Helbrun would call "jalopies." *No elitist parking lot, this,* he observed.

Excitement banished Hal's fatigue. He had driven all through the previous night to Harrisburg in a rented car —his own ailing car's performance was too uncertain to risk —filed his petitions in the morning, and then driven back, turned in the car, and put in the remainder of the day at the college.

He had had one very bad moment at the capitol when he was told that twenty-five of his petition sheets were filled out incorrectly and therefore were disqualified. He had, in haste written the name of the county where the district should have been filled-in. He felt defeated — wiped out by a silly technicality. Finally thwarted by bureaucracy.

A Philadelphia Citizen Action Party member had shown Hal how to cut out the petition errors and staple new, correctly written sections in their place —cutting the new sections from some blank petition forms he had, luckily, in his brief case —a permissible correction. The petitions were then accepted.

Citizen Action petitioners from the Tenth District had obtained five hundred more signatures than necessary; if some sheets had errors, the extras surely would cover them. But it was close. They would soon be on the ballot. Hal felt, rather foolishly, like leaping into the air.

Inside the noisy hall someone had hung a Citizen Action Party banner up front. It had bright orange hand-lettering on white, and a smiling Old Sol sun face wearing a tricorn hat —the jaunty logo that Philadelphia CitAct party members had designed six years before. Ellen's song, now boogieing out of the PA system was as jaunty and catchy as the logo. One of the Sojourner Shelter residents, Ann Brill, had a fine blues voice and had made a tape with Ellen. Ann belted out the CitAct Party message with Ellen's classic blues boogie piano back-up.

The chorus came first:

145

The Raunch Factor

A Congressman must show
The better way to go,
No dollar sign
Should underline
That he depends on dough
He must have resistance —Money talks —
To PAC groups' assistance —Money talks —
No one owns Hal Renshaw
Let Hal Renshaw talk

Then came the Delta blues-style bridge with a syncopated
chord after the words "choice" and "voice":

Do we really have a choice? BLAM
Is the buck the only voice? BLAM
I can't believe Democracy means money says
who's slave or free
Our country is a glory —Money talks —
Is the buck the only story? Money talks
Renshaw is the answer —
Let Hal Renshaw talk

Ted Mather was setting up folding chairs. He turned up at
meetings but had done no petitioning. He had a carpentry job to
finish, he said. Rumor had it that Ted had left town during most
of the petitioning. Well, no matter; he was here now, in all his
behemothry, big-toothed, red-faced, grinning at the women. He
introduced a young couple to Hal: Don and Mary Alice Franz.
"Two new recruits, Hal." Ted laughed his snuffling laugh. The
Franzes, also red-faced, shook Hal's hand limply.

The hall was filling up. An odor of grilling hot dogs floated
over the disinfectant that wafted from the men's room. A third,
faint odor —marijuana —alerted Hal briefly. *Is pot that essential
to them?* he asked himself.

Daphne and Harriet rushed over to him, waving and smiling.
Hal felt something catch in his chest —his heart? —at the sight of
Daphne. They had scarcely had time to talk during the
petitioning, and she had called her office repeatedly, and often
had to go back and work there for hours at a time. He noticed
dark circles around her eyes. In fact many of the petitioning crew

were sunken-eyed. They were a loyal group; they had stuck with him and really had worked. Hal was moist-eyed as he happily accepted the two women's hugs. Getting into bed at home, the following morning, he remembered how slim Daphne's waist felt within the circle of his arm.

Some CitAct members were dancing —gyrating and waving their arms and wiggling their shoulders. Touch dancing had not yet come back strong, as it would in another year, and besides, there was almost a sixties' *déjà vu* about this crowd.

Allison DeVries introduced two more new members to Hal, and Ellen Kirschner waved as she came out of the kitchen carrying trays of hot dog buns. Hal noticed that, miraculously, she had gotten her skeptical husband, Larry, to come to the meeting. Phil and Harry Walker were helping him haul a keg of beer to a corner. More new members were being introduced. A line formed by the beer keg as Larry pumped it up.

Somehow, the CitAct Party's minuscule treasury would pay for this celebration. Felicia Haselas, the party's new treasurer, had assured Hal that they could afford it. But his future expenses —meals, gas, car repairs for trips throughout the district for debates and TV appearances —would have to come out of his own threadbare pocket.

Yes, he said to himself, *money talks. It swings elections, controls everyone, decides the fate of the entire world. And I'm flying in the face of this immutable fact.*

Hal was expected to say a few words, of course. He looked out at the nearly-filled hall and saw flushed, lively, eager faces. Many had taken pains to dress up a bit — there were a few neckties and even a telltale mothball odor from seldom-worn sports coats and three-piece suits. Hal felt all eyes upon him. Everyone's enthusiasm, their spirit, their hope, their decency flowed out to him, washing over him. He held out his arms and, clearing his throat, said, "You're —you're all wonderful to work so hard for the party and to come out to celebrate our victory tonight. We're gonna be on the ballot! The CitAct Party will be in the history books and on the map and it is *your* doing. As Ted says, we're gonna kick some ass, cut some inroads into the bureaucracy, the elected dictatorship. All the isms — racism, sexism, ageism, fascism — are in trouble.

"Jumbo and the Jackass — just two sides of the same coin — are in for a big surprise! Corporate America look out!"

There were cheers, applause, whistles.

Hal went on, his face glowing, his deep expressive voice enthusiastic as he described the Citizen Action Party's ideal world where a national health plan assured that good medical care was available to all, where minorities — economic, racial, political " —our mothers, sisters, wives, daughters are a political minority, for Pete's sake," he admonished — could find self-respect and a living wage. Where the steel industry's colonializing would be stopped so they could no longer take their banking and manufacturing to low-wage areas overseas and then profit hugely by selling their products back to the United States — back to their own country!

He told of the shame of the mad, paranoid, crazed, negative militarism which, under the guise of "defense spending" produced the smallest number of jobs of any national enterprise and caused desperately-needed education and health programs to be cut. He told of the need to rebuild the infrastructure —reduced military spending could fund such rebuilding, creating thousands of jobs and new self-respect among angry, despondent "have-nots," thus helping to reduce drug-dependency and crime. "It can work, friends. It can work!"

While Hal spoke, Daphne stood at the back of the hall and watched members' reactions and expressions. Hal's voice carried beautifully wherever he spoke. He had the natural ability to project it seemingly without an effort. Almost everyone looked hopeful and expectant.

What a contrast to the first meeting, Daphne said to herself. Tonight there was very little of the "being cool" attitude so characteristic of laid-back twenty- and thirty-year-olds of the eighties; these people were genuinely moved, and they weren't afraid to show it.

Only three faces in the hall were relatively expressionless: Ted Mather and the Franzes, although Ted rarely was without his toothy grin. The three sat to one side together with Merrilee Dobbs and Allison DeVries. Ted sporadically laughed his silly giggle. Daphne surmised, *I guess the Franzes need time to get acquainted.* The unmistakable odor of marijuana drifted past. *Pot,* she thought. *That's pot. Someone must be smoking in the kitchen.* No smoking of any kind was the rule at the Oddfellows hall, and pot was tacky —at a political meeting! After all, it *is* illegal. Daphne made a mental note to take it up later with Hal.

Hal was telling a joke. Everyone laughed. Daphne had missed the joke but knew that Hal's wit was non-hostile, and he could be genuinely funny without resorting to obscenity, racism, sexism or ethnic slurs. Barry Spiegel often acted as a foil —a straight man —to Hal's Scholarly Leader, deflating any pedantry that Hal might drift into. *On the whole,* Daphne observed to herself, *Hal has never taken up residency in any of Academia's ivory towers.* A boring pedagogue he was not. His idealism, his fundamental simplicity made his human rights platform seem natural and logical, not outlandish or radical, even though the Tenth District's two-sided-coin politics hadn't addressed human rights issues since the 1860s, if ever.

The need for reform, for a return to concern for the quality of life for all —not just a monied, white male elite —became dynamic, valid and real with Hal's vision. In fact, "Return to Concern with Renshaw for Congress" would become the bright orange and white poster and bumper sticker message for the CitAct campaign.

And Hal knew how to put that vision into words. Without unctuous tricks, he made his followers know that a better world could happen, *would* happen, if they all worked together. There was electricity in the air.

I am witnessing a phenomenon that does not occur often throughout the history of the world, Daphne realized, wonderingly. *I shall never forget this moment.* Months later, in a climate poles apart from this collective decency, she would recall desperately, again and again, this magical moment.

Hal was building now, descriptions of his ideal world. "Why," he asked, "should we have to accept an unconstitutional shadow government — in which we citizens have no say? A government that ships arms and American soldiers, the CIA, the NSA, the FBI —are they any different from Russia's KGB? —to torture and kill hundreds of thousands of defenseless peasants just to protect the interests of some huge American corporation —the American Fruit Company in Guatemala, for example?"

He went on, "If we have a voice in Congress —*one* voice —a voice that cuts through all the PAC groups, cuts through the frantic I-want-to-be re-elected mentalities, that cuts through the worship of money, there can be a whole new vitality in America, and —"

"And we're gonna legalize marijuana, folks!" Ted called out, laughing his snuffling laugh.

The spell was broken. Someone turned on rock music and lines again formed at the hot dog table and beer keg. Something nudged Daphne's subconscious for a fleeting moment, *That voice —that voice.* Debbie handed her a hot dog.

Hal moved through the throng, grinning and slapping shoulders, shaking a few hands. Excitement hung in the air, still, as it must have done when Thomas Paine entreated broken, disheartened American Revolutionary soldiers — the Sunshine Patriots —to keep on fighting in those "times that try men's souls"; as it must have done when abolitionists led slaves through trap doors into basement escape routes; as it must have done in the late nineteenth and early twentieth centuries when a few outraged, brave women denounced child labor to the English Parliament and the American Senate.

Hal wanted to hold onto this moment; he would have liked a few more minutes with this rapt, receptive group. He loved them and wanted to thank them again and again —to let them know that he realized how much they had sacrificed by petitioning, by going out day after day in the bitter cold and cheerfully contributing what little money they had. He knew some of them even had become ill. His own throat was sore, and he had an earache. He saw Daphne beckoning to him.

"You were terrific." She handed him a hot dog in a bun.

"I know you like mustard —"

How does she know I like mustard? Hal wondered.

He bit into the sandwich, and it tasted marvelous. Someone handed him a plastic mug of beer. Music blared. On the dance floor Harriet and Barry were doing a comical shimmy while Robb Mulvaney conducted Debbie Fentriss through a very stiff cha cha cha. Mrs. Helbrun, in tee shirt and flowered "Jams," moonwalked with Phil Walker. Merrilee Dobbs and some of the Sojourner Shelter staff seemed to be hitting it off at a table in the back. Celeste and Pete Renshaw appeared to be enjoying themselves in a silly mambo-like gigue-step.

Everywhere Hal saw, happily, "his people" mingling in relaxed conviviality. Ted and the new couple, the Franzes, sat watching but not talking much.

That new couple seems withdrawn, Hal remarked to himself. *They're probably up against it financially.*

He was acutely attuned to and in sympathy with those in the district who had been severely hurt by the mill closings, and the resulting depressed economy.

Someone dimmed the lights and lit the candle stumps that stood in bottles on the tables. Smiling-faced oranges wearing paper tricorns were CitAct centerpieces —Ellen's handiwork. Hal sat with Daphne, and they finished their beer. His earache throbbed, reminding him that he hadn't slept for thirty-six hours. He felt Daphne's warmth against him. A few people began to leave, and the clean-up committee was horsing around in the kitchen. "I'll give you a ride home," Hal told Daphne, knowing she had come to the meeting with Harriet.

They rode to Daphne's in companionable silence and exhaustion. Hal walked up the icy walk to Daphne's door with her and looked so haggard and sick that she invited him in. She lit a paraffin log.

"You sit by the fire. I'm going to make you a hot rum

toddy. I have some 151 proof rum,'' Daphne directed. Hal sank gratefully into the deep, soft sofa cushions. Bowls of narcissus filled the room with vivid fragrance, and in a moment, the feeble fire glowed cheerfully in the little fireplace.

Daphne bustled about in the kitchen and soon brought Hal a hot sweet cinnamon-flavored drink in a big mug. He gulped it down and felt a delicious bliss begin to move from his toes up his shins, over his knees and on up, across his torso into his jaws and skull, and the next thing he knew, Daphne was shaking him.

"Hal, it's four A.M." She shook him again, gently. She had covered him with an afghan.

"Oh my God, Mrs. Helbrun." He tried to sit up. His sore throat and earache had worsened. He pulled at the knot of his tie and finger-combed his hair.

"Mrs. Helbrun's staying with Pete and Celeste, and I have to call her." He lurched to the phone. Daphne watched him. He looked ghastly, with sunken feverish eyes, and his skin had a yellow tinge. He walked unsteadily back to the sofa.

"I patched things up. She's going to sleep on the couch until I get there." Daphne touched his shoulder lightly.

"You look awful"

"You don't look so great yourself, my little chickadee," he answered in a W.C. Fields comic voice.

Whenever we have a chance for something personal, some intimacy, he retreats into comic routines, thought Daphne.

"Well," she said, "I had planned to seduce you, to celebrate." She adjusted her pale peach peignoir significantly.

"Ohh. I'm sorry. I'm really sorry." Hal rolled forward and slid his arm around Daphne's silken waist. With the other hand he untied the peignoir; his face was slipping down into the lace covering her breasts. *This is it,* she thought, *This is it.* She felt hot all over. She had known it would be good, but nothing like *this.* Moisture seemed to seep from her every orifice. She slid lower on the couch and happily started to open her legs.

She felt Hal's dead weight, and then she heard it. A snore. He was snoring.

He was snoring still, under the afghan, when, at eight A.M. Daphne closed the sitting room shutters, and, leaving the coffee maker on, prepared to leave for her office. He looked pitiful there on the sofa. She saw his soiled, rumpled old Alligator raincoat. His leg projected from beneath the afghan; the foot and ankle attached to the wrinkled pantleg could have been part of a scarecrow except for the pathetic inch or two of pale, hairy ankle revealed by the drooping, black sock. His shoelace dangled.

A spring-like warmth grazed Daphne's cheeks as she walked to her little garage at the end of her back yard. Crocuses were poking up alongside the end of the garage. *They're doing the only pushing that's going on around here,* she observed wryly. The nighbors would be buzzing about Hal's car being parked out front.

CHAPTER NINETEEN

"But that's what split receptacles cost, Mrs. Krock. You asked for stuff that wasn't contracted for." The contractor tried to placate Bobbye while the disgusted electricians packed up their tools, their dimmers and cable and switch boxes and stomped out to their van.

"I wanted them dimmers and extra outlets, but not at that price. Everything was supposed to be included in your contract. And they were supposed to be metal switch boxes, not plastic. I never agreed to no extra charges. I'll get someone to finish this for a fair price, after my husband's fund-raiser."

"But you got to have lights in your living room dontcha, for your party? Every outlet had to be moved because of the built-in couch. Ya don't have no juice yet —no electrical current."

"I'll figure something out." Bobbye spun around and marched out of the open front door, nearly colliding with two window-shade installers. Daphne and Robb stumbled behind them carrying five pillow-filled plastic bags.

"What happened? What's the matter?" Daphne called after Bobbye. "What? What the heck?" The electricians slammed their van door and drove off. And it wasn't even lunch time.

The frantic countdown before Ed's fund-raiser was making Daphne wish she had gone into some other profession. Painters were finishing window trim with fast-drying paint, keeping one window ahead of the window shade people; the paper hangers alternated between the kitchen and the Jacuzzi area; as drywall people and carpenters and painters and tile setters finished one area, the wall covering went up in another. Then a plumbing adjustment sent the paper-hangers back to the loft over the kitchen for a while. Pasted, taped-edged strips of suede-cloth had to be gingerly passed up the spiral stairs.

In the living room, the carpet people rolled out thick pale wool Berber carpet on the heels of the tack strip installers, while the caterers stepped over them going in the kitchen door. Meanwhile Daphne's scheduling and careful planning and order-of-work went out the window.

155

Robb was unpacking the huge linen sofa pillows and lining them up on the long custom built padded banquette. Daphne ran outside just as Bobbye pulled out. "Wait, wait!" She wove around workmen's cars to get to the departing Cadillac —as mad as Ed was at Bobbye, he still let her drive his car.

"The electrical work ran a thousand dollars over," Bobbye sniffed to Daphne. "I can't pay that much. Ed won't pay it. He'll be home tonight. He was already *pissed* that you petitioned for Renshaw, Ed's opponent! and mad about the delays and the mess —and he got his basement hangout done over two weeks ago. There isn't any electric current in the living room at all, Daphne. We can't use the track lights or the lamps. We got running water in the Jacuzzi and the toilet, we got six-foot tall cactuses, Kachina dolls and Indian war bonnets, but no electricity! People are paying a hundred dollars apiece to come to this party and we got no *lights,"* she wailed.

Perspiration made the white hair at her temples coil up like little pasta springs.

"We could run extension cords in from the kitchen, Bobbye!"

"And have them wires snakin' up the walls to the track lights? No way!"

"Well, everything's so light in there, so reflective, with the mirrored window blinds and your glass tables, we'll put some of those little oil lamps around the room and a big fire in the fireplace and —"

"There's no fucking chimney! It isn't finished! My God, Daphne, you know they had to change the chimney when they put the other flue in for my loft stove —it's *your* design."

"Oh, you're right. I forgot. Well, we could put a Swedish fire in the fireplace, for atmosphere —"

"What's a Swedish fire?"

"We line up those little oil lamps in tiers on bricks, in the fireplace opening. You don't need a flue for that. It's a fantastic effect —very dramatic, a Scandinavian idea, something really different. Palmer's have them in the downtown store. They may have them in the mall, too. Go and get about forty lamps and extra oil and —"

"I can't —I'm supposed to be in court in a half-hour. I can't come to the board meeting tonight either, and I just don't see how I can give a fund-raiser party tomorrow. All this hoo-rah for nothing! A chance for me to make Briarwood sit up and take notice, for once, and it's shot to hell. Daphne, I used to do *housework* for some of these women." She gestured toward the ostentatious houses down the road, and began to cry.

"Oh Bobbye, don't cry. Go on to the court house. I'll send Robb to get the lamps. I'll help you tonight. We'll pull it off — you'll see."

Bobbye seemed mollified. "You're a good friend," she blubbered, blotting her mascara.

Robb Mulvaney twitched impatiently while receiving Daphne's detailed instructions —instructions she would regret long, long after the party. She noticed the gold cross and chain Robb was wearing. She had forbidden his wearing his wooden cross. He quipped flippantly, "No one said anything about a *gold* cross," when she admonished him again.

He knows he's got me over a barrel, she thought, *—that I can't get another trained person at this critical time.*

She licked her dry lips and watched sweating caterers carry another crate to the kitchen. The weather was warming up. A hot sun was out full force.

"This is an order, Robb. Take off that cross. It's unprofessional. We have a lot of good Jewish clients —even some Atheists. Get over to Palmer's and get those lamps, and the extra oil. That's vital. Have them here no later than six, tonight."

"I only have two hours," Robb whined. "Debbie and I planned to go camping, since the weather warmed up. We're leaving today at three."

"I didn't say you two could leave early today!" Daphne was aghast. "This weekend is critical. We have all the wall decorations to install!"

"I guess I forgot. We have our plans made. We're all

packed and everything —"

"You're behaving like a real shit, Robb. You're needed today! Deb's packing all the accessories for this job. She'll never be done by three." She felt like twisting his silly, skinny neck. *When did this office romance begin?* she wondered to herself. *After this job, he's gonna get canned so fast —*

She was so angry with Robb that the paper-hangers' announcement that they had run out of suede-cloth —"three strips are defective" —didn't faze her even though she knew their own smeared paste had ruined the strips. Never again would Daphne attempt to jam six months of work into six weeks. Robb's smart-ass attitude, as though he were doing her a favor just by coming to work —by doing the work at *all* —"He's a real *jerk*" —she said out loud —was so enraging that she clasped her hands tightly to prevent their shaking.

She had felt a vague, underlying, indefinable fear when Robb had protested her banning his crosses. His high-pitched whining and wheedling — undeniably irritating — was more sinister than she wanted to admit. Her heart thudding, she turned back to her desk, to orders and accounting and other business at hand.

CHAPTER TWENTY

The eight new members of the Sojourner Shelter's Board of Directors looked innocuous enough. Ostensibly chosen in accordance with women's shelter coalition funding requirements to represent a broad sampling of community residents and interests, everyone knew they had first been lobbied by Traci to assess their manipulability.

Daphne glanced around the hot, humid room. They were meeting in Traci's *soignée* office, furnished with everything but an air conditioner. There had been a fracas about who would get office fans and who would get air conditioners for the coming hot Pennsylvania summer — though there had been no money for either.

Traci had not yet arrived. Daphne noticed a new Oriental rug in front of Traci's desk. It set off the newly-finished oak floor. Ora Shaeffer's son, Thaddeus, had done over the floor in exchange for Traci's counseling his sixteen-year-old daughter, Marva, the unmarried mother of his grandson; the counseling was to build up Marva's self-esteem and motivation, Traci said, so she wouldn't lie around all day eating caramel corn and watching TV while Ora took care of the baby.

Some deal, Daphne thought, *Ora's so sick after the stroke she had after Traci fired her that she needs someone to take care of* her. *What could Traci —who hates blacks, women and children —teach any bewildered black sixteen-year-old child-mother?*

Realizing that such thoughts were not contributing to a positive outlook with which to begin the new shelter organization, Daphne turned her attention to the board members as they were announced. Felicia and other staff members and volunteers took seats in the back. Harriet was busy signing in a new client in the check-in office.

Allison, chairperson and ninth member of the board —*Where was Traci?* —first introduced Hal, who looked tired, but nodded and smiled nicely. *That wondrous smile,* thought Daphne. His press conference and campaign appearances had been keeping them apart. She had not caught his eye when she arrived at the

159

meeting tonight. She would have to leave early and work most of the night and couldn't meet him after the meeting and go somewhere and hug him, and kiss him, wrap her arms, her body around him, John Wayne, W.C. Fields, raincoat, and all, to bring him to life, to make him understand the human need for personal passion, for intimacy —make him realize that they were as vital as intellectual passion. *Do we have any future at all together, Hal and I?* she asked herself.

Agnes Harrison, a modest-appearing attorney, was introduced next. She smiled coolly. *A good connection,* thought Daphne. *The Shelter constantly has court dealings. But then, there might be a conflict of interest if a board member —* Her thought broke off. Two housewives were next: Elizabeth Heckman and Mildred Babich-Pacelli. Daphne mentally chalked up another hyphenated name. *I wonder if they're at all conscious of the significance of those trendy hyphens? Well, at least it might be the beginning of heightened, new assertiveness. It's terrific,* she decided.

Daphne had heard that Elizabeth, "Liz" Heckman, a plump thirty-five- to forty-year-old, was a mover and shaker type with an unassailable reputation. *Hardly sounds like tractability,* Daphne thought. A formerly-affluent divorced mother of two, "Liz" was now making a home for her family in a shabby neighborhood and was gaining community recognition, and her name had been linked with Hal from time to time.

What could he possibly see in her? Daphne wondered. *But here I am, acting just as the system decrees —trying to discredit another woman, a potential rival — another human being, by picking apart her physical appearance, making a list —first, her face: not memorable (and mousey hair), her body: too thick through the middle (Daphne was thinking of her own tiny waist), legs: terrible. She has no ankles to speak of. She's just kind of shapeless. But she seems bright and earnest. Maybe she's truly concerned about oppressed people, is a caring person. She could interest Hal intellectually, certainly, with her reputed conscientiousness and activism. Could I do what she's doing?*

Raise two children alone, without a husband? I doubt it. Daphne faced up to the fact that her own sensual temperament and ego probably would always prevent her from living her life as selflessly as a Liz Heckman.

Next, Allison introduced (rather obsequiously, Daphne thought) Dr. Kamala Gupta, a general practitioner from Kinkaid. Darkly beautiful, her gleaming scarf-tied black hair and hot-pink silk blouse setting off her flawless creamy-tan skin, she would have been conspicuous in any gathering. More and more Asian professionals were settling in Bingham County.

"They come here for training," Harriet had said, "and then can you blame them if they don't want to back home to inoculate trachoma victims, after getting a look at the open gold mine M.D.s have here in the U.S.?"

Daphne had heard that Dr. Gupta was married to gynecologist Jahawrwalal, "Jerry," Gupta. There were no hyphens in *that* marriage.

Also from the medical community was Carla Campagna, R.N., a big rosy-faced smiling woman. To Daphne none of these people appeared maneuverable.

Next, a blushing Allison introduced the Reverend Earl Roy Krock, Ed Krock's older brother and known around Bingham as "Brimstone," or "Brimmie." His leadership and money-raising expertise had been extolled by the pious and "saved" Robb Mulvaney. When Brimmie stood up and bowed, a gold cross and chain glinted against his brown turtleneck sweater. Daphne knew that Allison and several other staff members had wanted Brimmie to open the meeting with a prayer. The other staff members voted them down.

Last to be introduced was Allan Snellenburg, a middle-aged Gregory Peckish business man from Doncaster. *Rather attractive,* Daphne thought.

But *where* was Traci?

There was something calculated about her absence. She liked to make an entrance. Allison had been instructed to go ahead without Traci if she was late. Two afternoons a week Traci did marriage counseling at the shelter —Domestic Court channeled many counseling referrals directly to her — and individual counseling sessions later, at home, all on a fee basis. Two other afternoons a week she taught at the Community College, and she had replaced shelter CR with required weekly lecture sessions — she called them group-therapy, though they were actually punitive mini-courts for censuring the hapless battered shelterees' understandably erratic behavior.

Requests by Shelterees for Harriet's CR were ignored.

Traci also was arranging a trip for herself, Allison and Felicia to inspect a southern women's center. "It's near that Hilton Head resort," Allison had chattered gleefully to Daphne and Harriet and Bobbye. "We can party almost for free!"

The new board members and the staff were shuffling about now, in preparation for the business meeting. They fanned themselves with shelter reports and brought forth notebooks, while outside, a rainstorm shook the seventy-year-old locust trees surrounding the handsome old shelter building. Faint shouts — which were forbidden by written Traci-edict — from the two floors above were the only evidence that five children and eight women were in shelter.

Traci ran a tight ship, but kept clear of shelter residents and their children. Allison had been thrilled to be named chairperson of the board —"Only, Traci won't say 'chairperson,'" Allison explained. "She says it makes us sound like NOWies. *You* know, too grass roots and all."

Daphne thought, *But we are grass roots! Without NOWies — those years we gave to that organization, this shelter and Traci and Allison's jobs wouldn't exist.*

The symbiosis between Allison and Traci grew stronger every day; Allison was being counseled by Traci and accompanied her to Coalition meetings. In Allison, Traci had a sycophant who reported to her daily about all that occurred at the Shelter. No one had as yet met the "Bloom" on the other end of Traci's hyphen.

The vestibule door banged; Traci, wearing a black and white

polka dot raincoat stuck her head in the office doorway. "Hi, everyone."

All conversation stopped. She elicited gasps, still, wherever she went, with her mantrap fifties pointed uplifted boobs, platinum hair, the Marilyn Monroe polka dots, skin-tight sweaters, the unmistakable knee-snapping strut, the breathy baby voice.

Daphne was incredulous that this aberration could have occurred, that this caricature of a woman now controlled their once splendidly democratic organization, their brainchild, the child of their hearts. But it *had* happened. It *was* a reality. What once had been one small, desperately-needed protesting voice from one grubby hotel room had grown to a dignified, forceful demand emanating from a no-nonsense, albeit slum house, a demand for independence for all women, and was receiving government recognition and sustenance, but *now* was rapidly becoming a chi chi ladies' club, simpering in a toney, brick edifice in one of Bingham's best all-white neighborhoods. And by some paradox, by some irony, a clone of one of America's most famous symbols of male-defined female dependency had control of it. If this board of directors chickened out, Traci would end up owning the whole enterprise.

CHAPTER TWENTY-ONE

Daphne's bloody fingers gripped the cliff wall. Beneath her feet she could feel the rock ledge; above, the glowing, red eyes of the Navajos seemed to pierce her. She knew that her nakedness, her weakness, her obvious vulnerability doomed her. Darkness was everywhere, yet she felt the sun's heat on her back. She was slipping, slipping. She grabbed for another handhold but slipped again, crying out shrilly. She screamed and screamed and began to fall, fall, fall, fall.

The telephone rang two more times before Daphne, bathed in sweat and shaking free of the dream, rolled over in bed and answered it.

"Hello, Daphne. I still haven't ate that juicy pussy of yours."

Peabrain was back again, pathetic, sex-befogged and ungrammatical as ever. Too groggy for her usual raucous rejoinder, Daphne slammed down the receiver.

It was six o'clock and the pale hint of morning light was barely discernible through the pouring rain. She lay half-awake, the nagging thought a flag in her brain, *That voice — who? There's something I recog —*

The clock radio buzzed her fully awake. She had had only four hours of disturbed sleep. Much work remained to be done at Bobbye's. Daphne could not let her down today.

The window people had agreed to stay on the job the night before —for a price, of course —and she had spent most of her time up on a ladder, rigging the many hooks and wires needed to hang the feathered war bonnet, arrows, beribboned lances and Kachina dolls that South West Wind, Inc., had shipped at the last minute. An exquisite three-dimensional tapestry resulted, accenting the wall above the long, suede banquette. On the couch, fifty feather-patterned chintz pillows were arranged to form over twenty feet of casual but dramatic seating. Robb had managed to get forty-five Swedish oil lamps, and the Svenska Hemsloid shop had delivered them —but not the oil —at six o'clock.

165

Bobbye said she thought the special oil was in the garage.
Gus Quip, wooed away from the housing compound's
employ to trim the Krock hedges, said he would have the lamps
filled and ready on time.

What gods of our fate could have foretold that the special
lamp-oil, in its special Svenska Hemsloid earthenware jugs,
would actually be miles away in Robb's car trunk? There it was
totally forgotten, as Robb and Debbie fashioned frayed-twig tooth
brushes and ate Robb's dried Survival Mix deep in the dense
forest of Bearcat Park.

Should Gus Quip have known what the jugs of kerosene in
the Krock garage were for? Kerosene was certainly never
intended for Svenska Hemsloid lamps.

A little after midnight, Ellen had come in with selected tapes
for Bobbye to play throughout the event the following day.

"All the greats, Bobbye! Joe Pass, Stan Getz, Gilberto —if
you *must* have rock, here are some of my Weather Report tapes
—guard them with your life —and here's Pat Metheny —he's
very new —and here are some groups that play fusion. The
Brazilian tapes are very 'up,' that classy rhythm sets a mood —
they'll be good at the beginning of the party, when everyone's
arriving. Later you can play Ella and the Cole Porter things —I
wrote out a program for you —and then you can wind down with
the more intimate guitar tapes when everyone is sitting around,
having coffee and talking and —" Bobbye threw her arms around
Ellen.

"You're such a sweetie to do this for me!" Her face
gleamed with sweat in the glare of the contractor's three trouble
lights —the only illumination in the living room, except for the
red and blue neon tubing. The idea of NRA members,
steelworkers, union stalwarts, the Democratic Committee
"winding down, having coffee and talking," to the dulcet riffs
of Joe Pass or Cole Porter's elegant wit might have seemed like
a reasonable scenario to Bobbye then, when the restoration of
order in her dream-home was proceeding well, but a kindly fog
dimmed her brain to any further speculation, a fog she was soon

to look back upon and yearn for, again and again.

Daphne finished the wall decoration placement as the four paper-hangers trooped out with their thermos bottles and promises to finish hanging the Adrian Horowitz canvas batik panels in the foyer in the morning. The expensive, brilliantly colored panels had delighted Bobbye when Daphne first proposed them. A natural connoisseur, Bobbye invariably gravitated toward the loveliest, most original of the many furnishings Daphne proposed for the house.

The house was a smashing success —so smashing that it filled Daphne's heart to overflowing. She felt that magic, that "high," that leap of the mind and spirit that artists feel, and that energy-burst they use to banish fatigue, to eschew drugs indefinitely —sometimes even food for long periods —and can translate into ever more and more creativity.

They shoved furniture and the huge cactus plants into place; then, for hours, they arranged painstakingly upon the glass and chrome dining table dozens of small terra cotta pots of cacti clustered about a long, flat basket of Daphne's own forced amaryllis bulbs, now in flaming maturity. Beneath the plants, on the polished glass table top, they arranged a wavy bed of sand and pebbles into a wonderful textured sculpture running the sparkling length of the long table.

Herb Haselas and his CorBlimey Caterers, busily setting up even as Daphne departed at one A.M., complied with Bobbye's menu requests for hot hors d'oeuvres, light seafood salads, biscuits, cheese, fruit and *petits-fours*. And there was champagne to sip with it all. A Southwestern repast with "tacos and that stuff," wouldn't be classy enough, according to Bobbye.

Not particularly Southwestern but definitely Western Pennsylvania was Ed's menu for downstairs: ravioli with tomato sauce, hot *hot* chili, pigs-in-blankets, sandwiches of fried jumbo, kielbasa with sauerkraut, baked macaroni and cheese, lime jello marshmallow salad, pickles, nut rolls and butterscotch ice cream pecan balls, all to be washed down with limitless shots and beers.

Daphne's bones and muscles cried out, albeit futilely, as she

pulled on jeans and a shirt and stuffed aching feet into boots —
summer sandals would not have seemed inappropriate. The hot,
humid morning was indeed another crazy Pennsylvania
meteorological quirk. "I promised Bobbye," she groaned, "I
promised Bobbye."

She jumped as the phone jangled again. A warning shot
through her. But it was Hal's voice.

"Sorry to call you so early, but I called three times last
night and got no answer —even after one A.M. I was worried."

"You were worried?"

"Well, yes. Sure. I know, I know, you're the independent
artist, self-defined, fearless. I *know* all that but, well, do I *believe*
it? You're sort of controversial, you know. Your sort attracts
trouble."

"What sort of trouble does my sort attract?"

"Well, all kinds of stuff could happen to a bachelor girl."

Daphne gasped. Not *that* garbage again!

"Bachelor girl, Hal? Bachelor girl? Why is it that, just when
you make me feel that there's a sane creative plan for humanity
developing out there, and I am getting to know a gentle,
educated, braintrust guy with a valid life plan and a lot of no-
strings-attached straightforward sexiness, you come up with this
nineteen fifties *Redbook Magazine* cliché?"

"Oh, Sorry." He was stunned, and elated, at her assessment
of him.

"Shit," Daphne mumbled.

"It is that bad?"

"Yes. Shit. Yes."

"*Oh.*"

"My God, is that all you can say, Hal? 'Oh'? Is 'O' all you
can say? I've read *The Story of O*. Do you know what the 'O'
stands for?"

"No."

"It stands for zero. *Zero*. Nothing. *Zilch*. *Naught* in
England, *null* in Germany, and you can look it up for Italy,
Spain, France et cetera."

"Oh. Er —*excuse* that, excuse that. Forget I said it. Things really are bad. Much worse than I thought, evidently. Did you have a bad night?" he asked. "Something pretty awful must have happened."

"Yes. I'm tired and discouraged, I'm not awake, and things are ganging up. Things are getting very awful, and I got another one of those phone calls."

"An obscene call?"

"Yes."

"The same guy? You're sure?"

"Yes."

"Oh."

She screamed, *"DON'T SAY THAT TO ME AGAIN, HAL!"*

"I'm coming over. I'm no good to you at all jabbering into this plastic mouthpiece. Daphne, shall I come over?"

"If you have to ask, you shouldn't come over."

"Stay there." Click.

She put Ravel's "Introduction and Allegro for Harp and Flute" on the turntable, lay down, and promptly fell into a deep sleep, this time sans Navajos.

Daphne would never stop reconstructing this morning in her mind. For the rest of her life, she would think about how she had opened her persona, her essence, to Hal that day. He had appeared at her door in that useless, dripping raincoat. She realized that the Kovals across the street would be peering through their Venetian blinds —at six A.M. on Sunday, yet. And she had let him into her house as she let him into her brain and her being, and held him there ever afterward.

"I want you, yourself, Hal, for me, myself, Daphne. No J.P. Sousa, no John Wayne, no Congressional candidate, no W.C. Fields, just you."

She was kissing him, peeling off that wretched raincoat, running her hands over his silky hair, his face, down his chest and over his belly and penis, the condition of which dispelled for all time any question she had ever had about different degrees of limpness. All such questions were dispelled. They. Push. Were.

Push. Dispelled. Push.

How had her underpants disappeared so quickly? She stopped kissing him and looked down at her wide-apart thighs. Her knees seemed miles up in the air.

"Don't you want me?" She raised herself on her elbows.

"Jesus. Yes. Can't you tell? Lie down."

"Well, I want to hear about it." She pulled herself up again. "About how you feel. All of it. Your feelings. What you want from me." She felt weariness and Hal's body rolling up her legs, over her thighs and deliciously into her again. Her head and heart were pounding but her eyes were heavier than she ever knew they could be. He grasped her thighs gently and lifted her and slid his hands under her buttocks. He looked into her eyes.

"Be quiet." Push.

"No." Push.

"Yes." Push.

"No. Why?" Push.

"Because you talk too much." Push. "You always talk too much." Push. He pressed his face into her breasts. The stubble of his chin was rasping, even painful, but after a moment she couldn't feel it. Delicious love and sleep were overtaking her, and she welcomed them, and slept.

He was shaking her. "Daphne, Daph —"

"What time is it."

"Eight o'clock. Eight A.M. And I'm being selfish. I want you to wake up, that's all."

"Is it possible —could I have fallen asleep. Was I asleep — while fucking?"

"Fraid so, my girl. About two hours. But you didn't drift off until I had had my way with you. Don't you remember?"

"We did it for two hours? While I was asleep?"

She didn't wait for an answer.

"Well, at least now it's quid pro quo, Hal. Can you forgive me —ever?"

He laughed. "I may. I owed you, after all, but don't you remember anything? How *was* it?"

"How was it for you?"

"I asked you first."

"It was, well —" she drew a deep breath, "a marvel of nature. A Mozart symphony. Something I never experienced before. Can I —should I hope to experience it again? Can such moments happen more than once?" She pushed her straight black hair back from her forehead and looked up into Hal's eyes. He seemed vulnerable without his glasses.

"We will," Hal said, "we shall —I feel just the way you do. It was a first for me. In fact, as I used to say as a child, about wondrous things —ice cream, candy, burnt sugar cake with caramel icing, Christmas morning, rice pudding with raisins —it felt like *more —more —more* straightforward, no-strings-attached sex." He slipped his hand under the blanket and across her belly.

"I have to be at Bobbye's in a half-hour. I didn't finish everything at the house last night —"

"Just enough time," he said as he slid the blanket down from her lovely chest. One breast popped out. He unzipped his fly. She sat up quickly.

"It takes twenty minutes to get there, Hal. I *want* to, I *want* to, but I promised Bobbye!" She rolled over and got out of the bed and stood up with the sheet wrapped around her. "I'm not trying to be coy. I just *must* get dressed and go. Please don't be hurt or feel that I'm being abrupt. Please."

"It *is* abrupt. I didn't have any sleep last night, and I didn't sleep after our —our fuck, either. I just watched *you* sleeping. Just lay there astonished. Well, it *is* abrupt." He tucked in his shirttail.

"What were you doing up all night?"

"I was at Barry's —at Spiegel's. We were mapping strategy for the debate. We had a few drinks. I had taken the kids to Doreen's after the Shelter board meeting, to stay through Tuesday. Then I went to Barry's."

"What were you doing about five-thirty A.M. —just before you called me?" Daphne asked. She managed to dress inside the sheet without exposing much of herself. Hal wasn't entirely conscious of it, at first, but she was doing a wonderful reverse strip-tease, also unconsciously. He was aware of his pants starting to bulge. He sat down.

"You mean about quarter *to* five?"

"Yes." She was getting into her tee shirt and underpants and skirt, showing just fleeting glimpses of skin.

Those pornographers have it all wrong, he thought, *everything should be reversed. They should begin naked, then put it on. It's amazing!*

"About quarter to five I was taking notes. Barry was talking and I took notes. Why?"

He caught glimpses: first a nipple, then black pubic hair. He thought, *God damn! I never paid much attention to porn —to erotica —before —*

"Did Barry go out of the room —leave, at all, around that time?"

"Oh, gee. Let's see. I think he might have gone to the bathroom about then. He had had quite a few beers. He —"

"Does he dislike women, Hal? Do you think he likes women, or has sex hang-ups, uh —gets off on weird stuff at all?"

"Ye Gods, to use one of Barry's expressions. No, heck — no. I don't think so. He seems to be very sexually well-adjusted, considering he's been divorced for so long. If he gets any sex, it's not at his place —he'd have to go out for it because three of his younger kids are living with him. His 'ex' has the other two. He's that old-fashioned that he wouldn't do any overnights or anything with his kids around. Why? Why do you ask?"

"Oh, just wondered. I think he's rather sexist. He says things that surprise me, for such an educated, supposedly liberal sort of guy."

"Yeah, yeah." Hal was annoyed that his pants still were tight in the crotch, binding, pulling tantalizingly as Daphne rolled tights up over her smooth legs while still sheet-draped to the waist.

He realized, in exasperation, *When she's fully dressed and*

got her coat on, I'll probably come all over the place. —*That's Renshaw, always beyond the pale, ever the iconoclast* —
He went on talking.

"Barry can be quite obtuse about feminism, about letting go of the old attitudes. He can be annoying. But I think he likes women, Daphne. I think he has the hots for Harriet. I think he's hot for her lately. *That* could be *real* hot." Hal crossed and uncrossed his legs.

"Harriet never said anything about him to me. I think she finds him more than annoying, Hal. Really a shit, if you want to know."

Daphne pulled her denim skirt up to her waist over sheer pantyhose, as the sheet slipped to the floor. The pantyhose almost but not quite obliterated the V of her crotch. Now she was fully covered with a loose shirt and was pulling on her boots, and Hal was in such a turgid state that he turned his back and tried to fix his attention on her gold clock.

"That's a nice clock," he offered lamely.

"I have a good eye. I don't buy expensive antiques. I only buy sleepers." She was brushing her hair, bending forward toward the mirror. Hal turned slightly to watch her. Her very small waist swelled spectacularly into her very full hips and derriere, even with the covering of the loose shirt.

Jesus, he thought, *What's happening to me?*

Doreen never did *this* to him. She was always dieting and was skinny to the point of anorexia. Her thighs were like two sticks and her ribs showed. She had been the second sexual encounter of his life, the first having been an unsatisfactory coupling in the back seat of a car at age seventeen. He couldn't remember the girl. After a few more short-lived, rather pallid relationships, Doreen had reappeared in his life, and they had drifted into marriage.

He sat down again, now, legs pressed together. *I'll change the subject,* he thought desperately, but he was reaching the point of no return. It was humiliating —

"Will you be coming —er, when are you coming? back, I

mean. Soon?''

Her waist seemed even smaller viewed from the front. Nothing else was visible but the swell of both calves above her short boots.

Hal thought, *Those legs —disappearing up into those thighs —into that —*

Daphne put on a big cotton sweater.

Here it comes, he thought. *Here it comes —never in my life has my control just left me and —*

She tied a silk scarf over her hair, her back to him, as the orgasm swelled over his crotch and the wet warmth slipped back toward his buttocks. He gasped at the force and pleasure of it. He grabbed for a magazine and plopped it over his lap.

"You all right?" she asked, rushing toward the door to the hall. "I'll be back at noon. We have to be out by then. Everything starts at two. Bobbye's a *wreck*. Ed came in late last night. He doesn't speak to me at all he's so mad about my working for your campaign. Why don't you get some Zs —be my guest —I'll tell you all about it when I get back. Please, please forgive me." She blew him a kiss and ran down the stairs.

Hal stood up cautiously and started to take off his pants. *Jeans should dry in four hours,* he reasoned. *Or, I can wash'em and put'em in her dryer.* •

Midnight found Daphne and Hal slumbering happily in each other's arms, a sheet their only covering, the phone off the hook. The bedroom windows were open wide to catch what few breezes were stirring in the unseasonal eighty-five-degree weather that was establishing a Bingham County record for late April. A tray beside the bed bore two empty champagne bottles, two crystal wine flutes and remnants of crabmeat salad, biscuits and a dozen *petits-fours*, a still-life worthy of a Chardin or a Vermeer.

Earlier that morning, as Daphne packed up to head for home, Bobbye had hugged her. "Take them, *take* them!" she insisted, as she filled Daphne's arms with chilled champagne and party viands, " —you really came through. Everything looks phenomenal! I don't know *how* to thank you."

CorBlimey caterers were lining up champagne flutes on the mirrored bar as Daphne said a weary goodbye. Now, her dream —she was floating in a delicious, pain-free limbo, intermittently touching down to a heavenly, warm vaginal throb — ended abruptly when, a long way off, thunder sounded. The thunder continued. It seemed to be getting closer. It shook the whole house. In an instant she was fully awake. Someone was pounding on her front door. Hal poked her shoulder.

"I don't know *who* it is, Hal." She threw on her kimono.

"I have no idea. But don't worry, no one knows you're here, with your car parked in back. Just stay put."

She ran down the stairs to the front door, switched on the outside lantern and peered through the sidelight. It was Harriet. She was wearing her best silk shirt and velvet jeans. Daphne flung open the door.

"Thank heavens you're here, Daphne. I tried to reach you for the last two hours but all I got was a busy signal."

Daphne stared. Harriet's face and hands, even her clothes, were a sooty gray-black. She had whitish circles around her mouth and eyes —like a red-haired Al Jolson.

"I just came from Bobbye's —from the party. I wanted to

tell you myself; I had to prepare you, and not have you find out later —"

"Find out *what?* What, Harriet? *What?*" Daphne grabbed her by the shoulders. "Was there a fire? Was it a fire?"

"No. No, not exactly. No, there was no fire. Sit down. Calm down."

"Not *exactly?* Omigod. Omigod, Harriet, what *happened?*"

"Be calm. I'm telling. I'm telling." Harriet drew a deep breath. "Well, Bobbye said we could sort of drift in about eight —Felicia, Ellen, Melba Cochran and Lorene and I —and sort of mingle, at the party, and no one would notice. We certainly weren't going to donate any hundred bucks apiece to Ed Krock's campaign! We aren't supposed to do anything political, according to Traci, because we work for an agency, and we're 'Hatched' —you know, our Women's Shelter jobs come under the Hatch Act. But we went anyway. Oh, there was a terrific turnout. Lots of people from other agencies —you'd think they'd be 'Hatched' too, wouldn't you? There were Community Chest, Helping Hand, Association of Regional Educators, EPA people, loads of Democratic stalwarts —all that were missing were the JayCees. With their whoopee-cushion mentalities, they're perfect Krock supporters, but they're all Republicans. There were no Bitsys either. They're the mainstay of the Republican Party, with all those pickles up their asses — Anyway, I'll bet there were over two hundred. Wow! The contributions he got!

"Everybody on the main floor —mostly Bobbye's group — were partying nicely." Harriet lit a cigarette and went on, "boogieing, eating —the house looked sensational, Daph. Then they started getting a little high on the champagne. There was plenty of *that,* but the buffet was on the light side. I smelled some pot, but I didn't see anyone doing coke —I was in the powder room a lot, because of the champagne, but there was never anyone in there doing coke —"

Daphne entreated, "Oh, Harriet, I can't stand this —"

"OK, OK." Harriet started to snicker. "I didn't go downstairs to Ed's rec-room-playroom-bailiwick, but Felicia and

Ellen did. they said he had a huge buffet —terrific chili —and there were National Rifle Association guys and Ed's Democratic Party handlers —the ones who tell him what to do and say, and that Miss Dialysis —can't remember her name, and her Kidney Korner Kort, from the hospital benefit thing. And a lot of the upstairs people started to go down to try Ed's buffet."

Harriet drew another deep breath and tried to re-light her cigarette.

"My *God*, Harriet, go *on!*" Daphne was ashen-faced.

"Anyway, it was looking pretty successful. Ed's music was *very* loud. Upstairs, Bobbye had some really classy jazz going and even some k.d.lang and Patsy Cline —very eclectic. Ed broke her Holly Near records last year. But anyways, down in his 'den,' Ed was playing that Floyd Taggert 'Honey Baby Geetar Rock' album over and over, louder and louder, and the rec-room crowd was getting pretty sloshed —I guess you could say really *krocked,* and that's when the Commissioners left," she laughed. " —And, Lord, was it *hot!* The air conditioning didn't work, for some reason.

"It got even hotter upstairs," Harriet continued, "because, after dark, Bobbye lit a whole lot of little oil lamps, and in that room off the living room —the Jacuzzi room —she had filled the Jacuzzi and had candles floating all over the water in little wooden saucer things. She said the electricity was messed up."

Daphne nodded impatiently.

" —and there were just these low-wick flames and these glowing candles everywhere. It was *so* dramatic! You know — with the mirrors and glass tables —but it sure was *hot!*" She started laughing again.

"Then everything began to get out of hand. Everyone started to come upstairs from Ed's rec-room-den with their fried jumbo sandwiches and chili and they poked around in Bobbye's fancy buffet. The sandpile in the middle of her table got spread all over."

Daphne gasped. Harriet went on.

" — and they were swilling down the champagne, and

Bobbye was frantic."

"The next thing you know somebody pushed Ed in the Jacuzzi, then Miss Dialysis jumped in and then a couple NRA guys jumped in too —they had stripped down to their shorts —" Harriet stopped and hooted loudly and wiped her Al Jolson-mask eyes, then went on.

"That Jacuzzi is huge, and deep. Everyone by that time was screaming with laughter, Daphne. It was turning into a real bacchanal, with Krock down to his shorts by this time, too, feeling up Kween Dialysis, and guys were singing at the tops of their lungs, and they turned on those showers on the two poles on the corners of the Jacuzzi —you know —like those hand-held showers —"

Daphne nodded, frozen-faced.

" — and they sprayed water around and sang 'April Showers' and 'Singin' in the Rain,' and two union guys —I think it was Steve Papich and Terry Lanahan —got the Indian feather bonnet and lances off the wall and put them on and waved the lances around and were doing a rain dance around the Jacuzzi, and in that red and blue neon light, it looked like the Venusberg orgy scene from 'Tannhauser,' for Pete's sake — oh, Lordy Lordy." Harriet howled and rocked back and forth, wiping her eyes.

Daphne shuddered and buried her face in her hands.

"That's when I began to notice everything dulling down — turning grayish-black —the walls, the floor, the couches, the chairs, the ceiling, people's faces, their clothes. The sparkle was gone, all the mirrors were disappearing —"

"Some of the guys turned out the kitchen light and carried oil lamps in there and tried to get the Kidney Korner bimbos up the spiral stairs into that loft room, when one of the guys — Howard Beasley from the Doncaster Helping Hand —he was in his jockey shorts —fell down the stairs into a big cactus plant. People said you could hear him yell clear out on Interstate Seventy-five." Harriet erupted in a huge guffaw.

"Just about that time, Ed and two EPA guys got into a fight

in the front hall —real fisticuffs! What happened was that Ed accused Frank DeAngelo —you know, that gorgeous Frank, God what a hunk —he has a Ph.D. in anthropology beside his MSW, you know — well, Ed, in his underwear, of course, yells at Frank, 'I happen to know you take expensive jazz piano lessons and trout fly-tying classes on agency time with agency funds,' and Frank —'' Harriet whooped again, "Frank tries to keep it light, although he is *very* drunk, and he draws himself up and says it is a lie and says, ' —in regard to the jazz piano lessons — I am an autodidact' —and then Ed says he knew it all along —he knew Frank was a disgusting *pre*vert, a lousy scumbag commie fag, and then Frank socks him right into that big cactus by the stairway, and another EPA guy jumped on Ed, who was really yelling, and then Ed vomited —all over those handpainted wall panel things —that canvas wallpaper. I think it was then that the woman next door must have called the police. I saw her standing out in her yard."

Daphne groaned, "Mrs. Hartley. Oh, God. Mrs. Hartley."

Harriet was shaking with laughter. "Anyway, things began to deteriorate after that. The NRA president vomited into the sandpile on the dining room table. People were screaming and jumping in and out of the Jacuzzi, spraying the sprays. The music was blaring, the Kidney Korner Kween and court were naked to waist —one of them was *starkers* —and I'll answer your question before you ask it —no, none of the guys were starkers —they didn't take off their shorts —phallic imperialism reigned! One guy was in a closet with Miss Dialysis, yelling about getting some nookie, and all of a sudden the kitchen light went on. The police had arrived.

"Guests pushed their way into the kitchen —they all looked pretty much like me —all covered with blackish film. All except the ones who had been in the Jacuzzi —they were sickly white from the waist down —

"The police were uncomfortable when they saw Ed. They hemmed and hawed and shone their flashlight around the living room —everything in there is gray-black —and they laughed apologetically and joked around with Ed. Boy, were they embarrassed, and Ed pulled himself together and must have given the high sign about Miss Dialysis' group because they just sort of disappeared, and things began to simmer down.

"Fern Slagle and Melba and Lorene and I tried to clean up the vomit, but Bobbye went to her bedroom in tears. She wouldn't speak to me. Some of the guests tried to find her to tell her what a good time they had, to thank her —Christ, think of the dry-cleaning bills she'll have —but she wouldn't come out of her room. She's devastated!" Harriet lit another cigarette.

"It must have been some defect in those oil lamps. The oil didn't burn properly, or something," Harriet said.

Daphne sat in mute horror.

A car door slammed. Someone was running up the walk. The front door was kicked open with a crash. Broken window glass fragments tinkled onto the ceramic tile floor. It was Bobbye. Her clothes gray-black, soaked and dishevelled, her formerly white, curly hair now hanging in gray-streaked strings, her small kitten face soot-smeared and distorted with rage, she stood in the living room doorway, chest heaving, and glared at Daphne and spat out the words.

"You! You did it on purpose!"

THE RAUNCH FACTOR

Book II

CHAPTER TWENTY-THREE

The CitAct members riding in Ellen's chugging old VW to the State College debate viewed the glorious, cloudless Pennsylvania afternoon as a favorable augury. Hal would more than hold his own today, they were certain.

Merrilee Dobbs, wearing an orange and white "Renshaw For Congress" tee-shirt, gave identical silk-screened tee-shirts to the others along with miniature orange felt tricorn hats that she had made. Lorene Wilton slapped the little hat on top of her brownish-black dreadlocks, snapping it on its elastic band.

"Dobbs," she laughed, "this elastic under my chin makes me look like what Whitie thinks all us pore Blacks look like — like Jocko the monkey in them old movies."

She snapped the hat again, jabbering and chattering and scratching while the others groaned. Lorene's growing political savvy and natural comedic insight delighted CitAct members, but her Atrocity-Of-The-Week satires on racism were becoming known in certain circles — such as the super-conservative Bingham NAACP —who were not amused.

Allison DeVries yanked the rear-view mirror and peered at herself, arranging her carrot-colored hair around the rakish tricorn; meanwhile Felicia Haselas and Ann Brill struggled out of their blouses and into CitAct tee-shirts, while Lorene held her jacket over the left side window for privacy. A PennWheat Bakery Truck passed their car slowly on the right, the driver leering and waving. Lorene gave him the finger, something she would not have done a year before.

"Ellen, your husband just drove by and got a free show," Felicia yelled. Taking off her blouse in a car out on the highway was something *she* would not have done a year before, either.

"Please excuse it," Ellen said, " —you don't know what I went through to get him to take the afternoon off and come to this debate. Any freebies he can get may cheer him up. He's more depressed than ever, these days, since he heard PennWheat may be closing down their plants. If they do, I really don't know *what* we'll do —" she broke off, as if to push the thought from her mind.

Inside the rapidly filling auditorium Daphne, Phil and Harry Walker and Barry Spiegel saved seats for other CitAct members. They would form a volunteer claque to cheer and encourage Hal. Luckily, Daphne had been able to leave her shop in the competent hands of James McInnes, who had at last returned to work and was helping to restore order after the *Götterdämmerung* of the Krock fund-raiser party.

Debbie Fentriss and Robb Mulvaney were into their second week of lying face-down in their respective beds in their respective apartments, with compresses on their respective ulcerated buttocks, having contracted poison ivy rashes in Bearcat State Park.

Yoga Robb's Camping Credo permitted no food other than his Natural Dried Fruit Survival Mix and his Regulator Bran Bread, and what turned out to be Camp Diarrhoea, pitched on approximately one acre of dried poison ivy leaves, featured none of the amenities Robb scorned, such as toilet paper.

Robb also was treating additional complications: joblessness and painful facial contusions, as a result of Debbie's having slashed his jaw with several frayed-twig tooth brushes.

Robb's pallid excuses for not delivering the Svenska lamp oil to the Krocks' were the last straw for Daphne. Now she was in very big financial trouble. Bobbye, enraged at Daphne after the fund-raiser debacle —cars had slowly passed the Krock house, drivers gawking, for more than a week afterward —had emerged from three days' seclusion and, in a suit against Daphne, was retaining Sojourner Shelter board member, Attorney Agnes Harrison.

Hurrying through the auditorium vestibule, Ellen noticed a uniformed guard in "Mountie" hat and Sam Browne belt standing at semi-attention surveying the crowd. Reportedly employed by Drew Burgess, he was present at all of Burgess's large public gatherings. Ellen observed the gunbelt of the plump, knock-kneed guard, slung low on his hips, the two bulging holsters obscenely flanking his large, shapely buttocks. *A guard?* Ellen thought. *Two guns? Three-fifty-seven magnums? Why?* Her scalp prickled. *In this college building we will have a discussion about government, about human rights. Why does there have to be a guard —with two guns?*

She felt the familiar jarring inside her head and shook slightly to clear her thoughts as she pushed her way down the aisle towards the front seats where Daphne and Barry were waving.

The candidates walked on stage now: first Hal, then Krock, then Burgess, and took seats at a long table draped in yellow where they looked out at the audience impassively. Daphne was glad to see a microphone at each place, as well as individual pitchers of water and tumblers, along with a neatly-lettered name plaques. She knew Hal could send his voice resonating into almost any-sized crowd, but he had begun to experience occasional hoarseness and a sore throat.

Daphne saw Hal's eyes sweeping the auditorium. Now he spotted her and smiled. She felt blood rushing to her face as she waved. At the same time she felt the pressure of Barry Spiegel's shoulder against hers. And his leg —what *was* he doing with his leg? He was —could she be *imagining?*

Five students were walking out on stage now. They took seats at a table of their own, set at an angle opposite the candidates' table. There were cutout letters pinned to their table cover spelling out "Congressional Debate At State." Paper daisies were pinned on either side of this message, and, as a sort of after-thought, a few pots of geraniums flanked both tables.

Dan Weldon, Professor of Political Science and today's debate moderator, approached the lectern at the side of the stage. Daphne twisted around in her seat and was elated to see the auditorium seats filled and rows of standees at the back. Students were still pushing into the vestibule and lining the side aisles.

Who said the young were all shop-till-you-drop air-heads? Daphne asked herself. Ordinarily the students would have been out goofing off and sun-bathing and washing their cars on such a beautiful spring day. They had chosen, instead, to come here. Student attendance at political debates was never required by the College, but Barry Spiegel had made attendance an optional assignment.

Dan Weldon cleaned and adjusted his glasses as the audience quieted down. He was a distinguished-looking man, fortyish, broad-faced, and slightly-built with rather long, straight, streaky dark-blond hair which sloped over one eye. He tossed this shock of hair frequently as he spoke. Instead of looking silly or gimmicky, the gesture served to further distinguish him; he was widely impersonated on campus, usually with affection.

Weldon's controlled façade concealed a raging passion for reform politics that he rarely revealed. He was not yet tenured in a super-conservative college; his obligations toward three children and a discontented beautiful wife prevented his true thoughts from ever being known.

He now addressed the audience:

"In the Eighteenth Century, Thomas Paine, one of the heroes of the American Revolution, wrote in his brilliant essay 'Rights of Man,' and I quote:

> Reason and Ignorance, the opposite to each other, influence the great bulk of mankind. If either of these can be rendered sufficiently extensive in a country, the machinery of government goes easily on. Reason obeys itself: Ignorance submits to whatever is dictated to it.

"End of quote."

He adjusted his glasses, tossed back his hair and went on. "Our form of government —that men have fought and died for —is examined at regular intervals, and, among other tests, it is tested through the scrutiny of its leaders and would-be leaders at the time of election.

"Although no political parties are mentioned in our nation's Constitution, their invention was inevitable; even Thomas Paine foresaw this inevitability. As an Englishman and an adopted American, he saw the insufficiencies of England's Magna Carta —the document that perpetuated monarchy and serfdom. Paine staked his hope —even his life —on the new, free, young country that was to become the United States of America.

"Today, in one of the few major tests of excellence or lack of excellence of established leaders and potential leaders, three candidates for a seat in the Congress of the United States —the land of Tom Paine's dream —will present their arguments for or against issues of great importance to us as citizens and of importance to them if they are to wisely lead and represent us."

Again he tossed back his hair.

"Questions were compiled by Political Science students of this University and by members of the Student Governments. A minute-and-a-half time-limit will be observed for each candidate's answer. Our time-keeper today is Doctor Gertrude Pemberton, a member of this university's Department of History. She will signal with her bell when your time is up, gentlemen.

"At the close of the prepared-question period the audience is invited to question the candidates in a open time period. Debate winners will be determined by audience applause.

Let the debate begin."

The first question asked by the designated Poly-Sci student concerned the future of steel production in Bingham County and was addressed to the incumbent, Drew Burgess, whose jaw had sprung open even before the question was completed.

"Steel production, at this point in time," he recited, "is impacted by industries moving out of the area. My belief *vis-à-vis* Bingham County unemployment is that, by and large, we need federally-funded help reactivating performance motivation programs, if you will, for steel workers, plus getting behind awntrapranoors to get the county back on its feet *vis-à-vis* the present economic slump —er —that is, work stoppage.

"Irregardless of unemployment," Burgess droned, "in terms of Bingham County, jobs will not basically be affected, *per se*, if we kick a field-goal with retraining programs, and I believe teamwork will impact basically on each and every Bingham County individual at this point in time and —"

Re-Training? thought Daphne. *Re-Training to do what? Repair doctors' cars? Computers?*

Burgess "vis-à-vised" and "per se'ed" his way through his one minute and thirty seconds, and then, like a wind-up toy, subsided, his jaw snapping shut.

Ed Krock's response to the steelworkers' jobs question was predictable. He was in favor of "jobs, jobs, jobs — and hopefully, food onna table. An' I will do everything in my pawr to bring back jobs to The tenth Distric'," he pledged as he smoothed back his already-glued-in-place nineteen-fifties duck tail coiffure —part Elvis, part Friar Tuck —and went on.

"I believe Bing-Ham will hopefully come back strong inna job sweepstakes. Over the years I've established reeport with the steel workers and, as the old adagio says, 'It's a doggy-dog world-an' then you take yer foreign imports are the first target, basically, on the playing field an' my eight years pitching at home base in the the State Legislature where I used my voting pawr to insure that every senior citizen in the Tenth Distric' would get a discount on their orthopedic shoe inserts an' I —"

Dr. Pemberton's bell ended Ed's peroration, confusing him. He grinned blankly and sat back in his chair.

Well, thought Daphne, *that's Ignorance. Now let's hear Reason.*

Hal's succinct summation of Corporate America's greedy plan of abandonment of workers through tax write-offs for plant closures or moves overseas or to Mexico was a miracle of clarity, albeit grim, after the preceding rhetoric. His positing of the idea that steel workers themselves consider taking over the operation of their mills within their Constitutional right of

Eminent Domain — "Gayleton Steel did it, and last year they made over a million dollars' profit —" —elicited whistles and cheers.

There were also audible "Whatareya — a communist?" mutterings from the Krock camp.

Daphne stared at the candidates in disbelief, thinking, *Burgess is up there in a thousand-dollar suit, yet he's a hundred miles away at some sheriff sale. Krock can't even wave bye-bye by himself. This is all some kind of joke. They rattle off and jabber this nonsense that's an insult to these students —to all their constituents. What can be in voters' minds when they have had to cast a vote for either of these two ludicrous poseurs?*

Hal had actually been worried about holding his own against Burgess. He had said, "After all, Daphne, he *is* an Ivy-League grad, and he *is* the incumbent —".

But it was laughable, embarrassingly so, to have to watch this decent idealist —this incorruptible man, sitting on the same platform with these joke-people.

Question followed question, delivered in the student panel members' grave, though often barely audible, monotones: Bingham County's possible nuclear and hospital waste storage dump on Blake Casting Company Property, nuclear freeze issues, foreclosure laws, the national deficit, arms production, foreign policy; the students' questions were remarkably astute.

When abortion issues were raised, Ed's *Deus Ex Machina* was to excuse himself for a restroom break, thus disrupting the line of questioning. This device became know as Ed's Potty Parry.

Hal's credibility as a speaker, as a wit, as a humanitarian, together with his quick intelligence, invigorated the audience. Their foot-stomping, cheering response each time he spoke left no question as to who was winning this debate.

Drew Burgess was inscrutable, although his eyes darted about nervously as he droned his memorized spiel with its pop-culture "if you wills" and peppering of trendy, Anglophiliac pronunciation: "few-tyle", "miss-syle" and so on.

Daphne marvelled that this foppish, preppy cypher of a man could ever have won any office, in any election, any time anywhere. He was an over-tailored testimony to the unfathomable workings of the political machine —and to Alma Mater's shrewd ballot-box purchase.

The formal debate questions and summations having been completed, the audience question period began. A question about gun control —*de rigueur* at any political gathering in this hotbed of ardent machismo —revived a rather crestfallen Ed Krock, who recited, passionately, the NRA creed: "Th' ony way you'll get muh gun away from me is ta take it outta muh cold, dead hand," which was met with some scattered applause as well as jeers and booing.

Warming to his first applause-getter of the afternoon, Ed grinned and lurched on, his tiny deep-set eyes glistening as he maundered, righteously, NRA platitudes about the Constitutional right to bear arms and of his dedication to forays "with muh Dad an' muh uncles an' muh brothers" into Bearcat State Park's annual orgies of wildlife butchering — one of Bingham manhood's *rites de passage.*

"An' its muh right as a cit-zen —muh patriotic duty —" Ed quavered on, "in muh defense o' muh home an' fam-ly an' —"

Here Hal cut in, laughing, "There's something Freudian about it, though, you know, Ed —"

"Wha —?" Ed, dumbfounded, turned in his chair toward Hal, "whadjasay, Mel?"

"Well, you know what Freud said —" Hal persisted.

"Who?"

"Freud. Sigmund Freud. In his concept of the human psyche —the subconscious."

"Wha —What —" Ed jabbed his finger into the top of his collar and grinned weakly.

"It's a long time since I got outa college —" Ed said. "I don't —uh —wha —"

Ed had spent exactly two semesters in an Indiana Bible College on a softball scholarship thirty-plus years before.

The audience buzzed with titters and guffaws.

"You recall Freud's Theory, Ed, that many men subconsciously feel that a gun is a penis substitute," Hal explained.

Ed's face reddened deeply as he crinkled his tiny eyes into another grin. The audience roared as he tugged at his collar, and Hal reached over and patted Ed's shoulder benevolently.

In their front seats, the nearly hysterical CitAct claque applauded wildly. Drew Burgess, unable to suppress a grin, threw back his head and gave a thin, sarcastic whinny. Hal had won the day.

Ed, struggling for composure, could only gaze at the audience, his round tonsured head tilted benignly, like a drunken monk.

The audience was screaming, now. The debate was breaking up. A group of standees in the back chanted, "Hal's our pal . . . vote for Hal . . . Hal's our pal . . . vote for Hal —" and began a snake-dance around the vestibule.

Dan Weldon leaned over the microphone, "All right. All right. Let's keep it down. Keep it down," he said with a small smile. "Let's go on —let's continue to have questions from the audience —"

The debate was being broadcast over a number of small radio stations whose signals nevertheless reached all of Western Pennsylvania and parts of the two adjoining states, West Virginia and Ohio. For Dan Weldon to lose control, for the conservative radio audience to have heard Hal's "penis" remark on the air, would not reflect well on the college. Weldon was on dangerous enough ground just mentioning that purported deist, Thomas Paine; never mind the sick, perversion-citing double-entendre rap and rock and roll lyrics that assaulted this same radio audience from the same radio stations, hourly, day and night; for someone to say the word "penis" out loud in the context of a college debate —well, it was —well, it looked bad.

Dan Weldon held up both arms and said sternly, "All right, let's proceed."

The laughter began to subside. A few more ecstatic shrieks sounded from the back, and then the delighted, relaxed audience settled into that euphoria that only shared hilarity can produce. They resumed whole-hearted participation in what a Professor Emeritus later told Hal was " —one of the best events ever seen at the college."

Hal was declared winner of the debate amid wild applause.

The snake-dance formed again and wove down to the stage, dancers chanted the Hal's-our-pal chant, hitched the laughing Hal onto the line and danced him back up the aisle to the vestibule and down the front steps and across the lawn.

CHAPTER TWENTY-FOUR

"Shoot-out at State," *The Bingham Observer* called the debate the next day. In a second page story with a big photograph in which all three candidates were barely recognizable, Hal was reported the easy winner.

City papers gave the story lower-front-page space but only one city article had a picture: a murky, head-on shot in which the three candidates, gargoyle-like, mouths open, stared into space, reminding Daphne of the drain-spout sculptures of Chartres Cathedral in her college textbook, *Art In The Western World*. She didn't mention this to Hal.

The major six o'clock TV news channels each gave less than thirty-second coverage. CitAct members, jammed into Hal's tiny living room to watch, switched channels so much that nobody really saw anything. But Hal was clearly pleased. It was a great campaign send-off.

The next morning when Daphne arrived at her shop, she was surprised to find Merrilee packing up her typewriter and cleaning out her desk.

"I can't be campaign manager anymore. My parents are really pissed. They heard the debate on the radio. They heard Hal talking about Krock's dick. They said I can't have anymore to do with the Party —that Hal has a filthy mouth. That he's a dirty-minded *socialist*."

"But — Merrilee — " Daphne was laughing in spite of herself.

Now who could they get for campaign manager? she wondered. *All of the big events are just starting.*

"You're twenty-two years old. Do you have to do everything they say? Hal —a filthy mouth? Hal?" She started laughing again.

"I live at home —their home —and they won't pay my car insurance, and I certainly can't pay it. I'm unemployed, and I'm up shit creek without a car." Merrilee was about to cry.

"They control you in this way?"

"They control me in this way."

"I'm really sorry, Merrilee. See what you can do. I know you can't just pick a job off a tree, not in this county —"

Daphne watched as Merrilee trudged across the parking lot to her car, then turned to matters at hand.

She turned on her phone answering machine for the previous night's messages. She had forgotten to check her home answering machine. The first message was a crabby Mrs. Hartley squawking, "The dining room drapes and 'vay-lances' need adjusting, Daphne, and the library shutter color doesn't match the walls. Call me."

Daphne sighed. She had carefully explained before ordering the shutters that louvers created shadows, and that when they were closed they caused colors to appear slightly deeper.

The next call was a hang-up, then another hang-up, then *his* voice. It was Peabrain.

"Hello, sexy Daphne with the very very hairy pussy. Ha Ha — That's a pome," he confided, unctuous and idiotic. "I called to see if you want to go fishing. My rod would make you reel! If you would have stayed home we could have went —"

Daphne snapped off the machine. She *knew* that voice, and yet she *didn't* know it. It was Everyjerk. Was it the U.P.S. man? Could it be Barry Spiegel? *Could* it be?

Barry could change his voice completely at will. His hilarious imitation of Ed Krock's debate performance had CitAct members weak with laughter that night at Hal's *aprés-debate* party. Could it be that plumbing contractor who talked in an insinuating tone about sink traps and PVC pipes and kept edging closer and closer when they went over bathroom drawings —the oaf that grinned insolently whenever the word "bidet" came up? She ran into these cretins, these two-hundred-pound little boys, fairly often.

She started to erase the messages but stopped. Maybe Debbie would recognize the caller. But Debbie was still at home with her ulcerated rear-end. When James came, maybe *he* could place that voice. James could pick up on things —nuances —in social situations —visual and auditory clues that escaped other people. She heard James now, unlocking the front door of the shop.

"Hi, pal," he called, waving his can of diet Pepsi and limping slightly as he sauntered through the Country Boutique and across the aisle of Eighteenth Century Accessory vignettes to Daphne's office. He was so stylish, so beautiful, that involuntarily, she drew a deep breath. The beige pleated nineteen thirties' linen slacks he had found at Thrift Village for five dollars were knowingly insouciant with his three-dollar nineteen twenties' pleated-front tuxedo shirt, the stiff collar long gone, the round, open neck now showing off his tan throat.

James had a perpetual tan. It was his natural color and had nothing to do with tanning salons or the men's cosmetic "vibrancers" that in winter made many Bingham males' faces into weird, pale-orange masks. He was very tall. Were he not so tall, he could have been Nijinski in his faun costume, or the boy-king, Tutankhamen, or the beautiful Narcissus reflected in his lily pool —the image of the Margaret Evans Price Art Deco illustration in Daphne's prized book of Greek myths from the nineteen thirties.

James bent down from Mount Olympus and laid a cluster of lilacs on Daphne's desk.

"Ohhh . . . gorgeous." She crushed the moist, sensuous blooms to her face, breathing in their Victorian fragrance.

"You know all my weaknesses, don't you, James. Maybe my weaknesses are my strengths, huh? How's the foot?"

"Tolerable. Barely tolerable."

"I really appreciate your coming back to work, James. I don't know what I would have done —I just feel guilty that —"

He waved his hand in dismissal and lit his after-Pepsi cigarette.

"Listen to this." She hit the replay button and turned on Peabrain's message.

"Oh, Christ," James said, disgustedly.

"What do you think? Recognize it?" She played it again.

"I've been getting one every month for the past six or seven months. Now they're on the increase."

James sat and thought for a few seconds.

"I haven't a clue, Daphne. Not a clue. But there's something familiar —something —it's —it's —but you ought to report it to the phone company."

"Yes, but changing to an unlisted number would wreck my business. That was my last hope. If you can't identify him, nobody can."

She handed him the lilacs and took an antique buttermilk crock down from her bookshelf.

"Put these in water for me, will you? And then round up all the Hartley upholstery fabrics and get them ready for the afternoon U.P.S. pick-up. Farley's are ready to cover the chairs and sofas. Don't forget to pin an arrow on each patterned fabric to show which way is up. There's a work-order and a fabric cutting with each package. That house has to be ready for the fund-raiser party Mrs. Hartley's throwing for Drew Burgess."

"God, will I be glad when Debbie's ass heals up," James groaned as he limped to the receiving room to do Debbie's job — a job he hated. He even *limped* gracefully, Daphne realized.

She turned on the stereo and P.A. remote, and salsa jazz rhythms pulsated lightly throughout the shop, making her forget temporarily that she had resolved to call the telephone company and get a wire tap on her phone, but subliminally she knew that what had begun as feelings of revulsion and disgust were now turning into fear.

CHAPTER TWENTY-FIVE

"Fuck!" muttered Karl Kirschner as he dragged the ladder through the hydrangea bushes. "Fuck, fuck, fuck!" Dirty water ran down his arms and dripped from his elbows. It was an unseasonably hot and humid day.

Ellen, watching Karl through the kitchen screen door, hoped that Mark and Kathy, who were making missile nose cones and dead G.I.s in the sandbox, couldn't hear him.

Not that this word was any news to *them*. They could spell them all, and they did so, often. They spelled out forbidden words in the supermarket, the drug store, at Ellen's mother's home and next door at the Reverend Earl Roy (Brimstone) Krock's house.

"Are you changing the water often enough, Karl? It looks dirty to me. And you have to put ammonia in the water to get the windows clean, Karl."

Karl mimicked his mother in falsetto, "ye hev-tew-put ammone-ya in th'-water to git the windows clean, Kar-ruhl," climbed down the ladder and yanked the hose through the lilies-of-the-valley. Jonquil buds lay with broken-off blooms along the length of the old house's west side, where Karl had washed five windows. He had at least fourteen to go: inside and out on the first floor and then inside only on the second and third floors.

A graduation trip to Colorado, every Bingham High graduate's idea of El Dorado, was to be Karl's reward for getting though high school and helping with the spring cleaning. Through the winter Ellen had saved five hundred dollars toward Karl's Hegira. Maybe "Exodus" was a better word; so far fifteen of Karl's class mates had Colorado trips planned.

Ellen looked up from the dried beans she was picking over for chili. She could hear the sound of Karl's harmonica coming from the direction of the front porch. He was playing —expertly —his jazz version of *Tenderly*.

Suddenly fourteen-year-old DuWayne Krock's face appeared in the window over the sink. He and Ellen stared at each other. He held a dripping sponge in his hand and smiled tentatively.

Ellen smiled back, then walked into the living room where Larry sat in a darkened corner with the curtains closed, watching a Vietnam newsreel on the VCR.

"That bastard, Westmoreland," he growled.

It was Saturday morning and Larry had already had four beers; he had had plenty the night before. Ellen was desperate for help with the children. Larry scarcely spoke to them and was particularly uncommunicative with Karl.

"Will you tell Karl to get back to work on the windows, please, Larry?" she said. "He's pulling a Tom Sawyer routine and now he's talked DuWayne into washing them. Then he went out on the porch and he's playing his harmonica. The Krocks don't even want DuWayne coming over here at *all*. Karl and I have an agreement about the windows —"

Larry leapt up from his recliner chair. Immediately Ellen regretted that she had said anything. Through the window she could make out what appeared to be Karl flying across the porch and down the front steps, with Larry close behind. Then DuWayne crossed her field of vision, running across the Krock driveway, past Brimmie's Cadillac and up the steps to his own back porch, where he stood peering at the Kirschners' through the trellis.

Karl was shouting. Ellen ran to the kitchen window and saw Larry push him against the side of the house. The ladder fell over, throwing the bucket into a lilac bush. Dirty water splashed out on Larry as he broke off one of the dried lower branches of the lilac and swatted Karl with it. It snapped in two, and Karl ran laughing to the garage, jumped on his bicycle, and sped across the lawn to the street.

Larry ran toward the VW, but Ellen reached it first; she got in and locked the doors.

"I'm gonna break these goddam windows, Ellen," he shouted. "Get out or I'll break the windows!"

How could this distorted mask of rage be the thrilling, virile person she had fallen in love with so long ago?

Ellen knew he meant what he said, and got out of the car.

"Let him go, Larry, let him *go*."

Larry was already gunning the capricious motor; the car started and stalled.

"Goddamit." He accelerated again, and again it stalled. "All I know, Ellen —all I know is —he's gonna get it."

Larry jumped out and strode up the walk and into the kitchen. A moment later he came out again, carrying an empty beer case. He got into the Penn Wheat truck. He was breaking his own rule about using the company vehicle only for company business.

Larry roared past Ellen's mother as she pulled up to the curb in front. She parked and undulated slowly up the path to the house, walking the way she was brought up to be: prim, reserved, with shoulders back but adding a decided twitch to her behind. She was that most doleful of societal aberrations: a WASP Princess.

"Larry's putting on weight," she said to Ellen. "And you could stand to *lose* some. But he has a big frame and can take the extra weight. Is he going to the *beer* place *this* early?"

Mrs. Ames sat down at the big, cluttered kitchen table, cleared a place for her purse and studied Ellen's face to see if she had been crying. Ellen decided not to tell her *again* not to put her purse —which had been on the floor of every department store lunch counter and rest room in Western Pennsylvania —on the table where they ate their meals.

"He's taking some beer to the Citizen Action meeting, tonight," Ellen said, quickly dumping the breakfast grapefruit halves on top of six empty beer cans in the garbage can under the sink. "We're serving chili dogs and beer after the meeting."

"Alice Parker told me about the radio broadcast —about what was, uh, said on the radio. I was appalled. Saying a word like that, well...your father would be spinning in his grave if he knew. And you from a good solid-citizen Republican family too —getting involved with crude people —tasteless people. And all those darkies too. I know you go around with darkies. And that Women's League! I don't know how you —"

199

Ellen had never been able to get her mother to understand the difference between the League of Women Voters and the Feminist Movement.

"Mother, will you *please* skip the Bingham Civic Club speech? It's not crude to want a less corrupt, less violent world for my kids. I don't tell *you* what to do. You can hang out with those useless Bitsy snobs to Kingdom Come, and do I run them down —do I tell *you* that *I'm* appalled? I don't try to run you life!"

"Well, you just *did* run them down. Just now. Right now. And other times you let me know, all right. *You* have your ways. A certain tone. A facial expression. Bitsy and Bitsy Junior are my link with a gracious way of life with privilege and security that I lost when Dad passed away."

"My God. why didn't you just commit suttee —throw yourself in Dad's grave, like women used to do in India? You talk as if your life ended when Dad died. Like *he* was your entire existence and there was nothing left after —"

"I am *appalled* that you would say such a thing to me, Ellen —"

The phone rang. "If that's Tyson," Mrs. Ames said nervously, tell him I went to the hairdresser. He knows I was stopping here first. He gets bossy. Checks on my every move." She picked up her purse and started to the door. With Ellen's back to her, she stopped and glanced quickly under the sink at the beer cans under the grapefruit rinds.

"Hello, Tyson," Ellen said to her mother's boyfriend of eight years. "Mother's gone to the hair dresser's."

"Tyson Tightass," Kelly, Karl and Kitty called him. None of the Kirschners had seen him without a coat and tie in all those eight years, but Mrs. Ames had coyly hinted that he took them off "on occasion." The idea of her prudish, anorexic mother and the perfectly-groomed, colorless Republican Tyson W. Tylass, CPA, engaging in oral sex or locked and rocking in some hot genital coupling in Mrs. Ames' menopause-blue bedroom —she actually kept her girlhood taffeta-gowned bed-doll on the bed —

made Ellen feel simultaneously hilarious and nauseated.

Ellen climbed wearily up the steep back stairs to try to awaken Kitty and Kirk. Nineteen-year-old Kelly had been getting herself up every morning in the freshman dorm of State University's main campus. It would be her first and last year there if Penn Wheat folded, Ellen realized.

She glanced in at Kelly's neatly-made bed where Barkley lay proprietarily stretched out, sleeping, with all four paws aligned and her head on a small heart-shaped pillow on which Kelly had embroidered "Never Complain, Never Explain," after reading that the actress Barbara Hershey had such an embroidered pillow. Ellen had read the same pillow story about the actress, Elizabeth Taylor, and Mrs. Ames said she had read it in the forties about Joan Crawford.

Karl had not yet washed Kelly's windows. Their old white organdy curtains, bought second-hand years before, had taken Ellen one full day to iron, their crisp spray-starched ruffles filling her with anticipation of the joy Kelly would feel when she came home from the fourth grade to find them.

Ellen remembered that day: Valentine's Day, Kelly's birthday. Larry was in Vietnam for his second tour of duty then —on the organdy curtain day.

Ellen's thoughts tumbled about in the sickening juxtaposition of their adorable children —their sweet voices, their breakfast chatter, their innocence —and the many flashbacks Larry told her about: machine-gunning of old women as they tried to climb into helicopters, old men, young mothers with infants, eight-year-olds, five-years-olds, eleven-year-olds — "Mom, I *love* my curtains!" —Ellen had wanted to write a love letter to her children on those starched ruffles! —Larry had said the faces of the Vietnamese were just bloody pulp, bloody pulp!

In Kitty's room the windows had center ovals of fairly clean glass but in all four corners the dirty spandrel-like blotches made Ellen wish that Karl had left them unwashed altogether. She let Kitty sleep on.

Karl's and Kirk's windows were worse even than Kitty's.

The TV was on and Kirk was snoring, his mouth open. Ellen looked around the room at Karl's jazz tapes neatly stacked in numerous matched Plexiglass cabinets. Occasionally, he used to play his harmonica with her, and they would make a tape, but he had to be in exactly the right mood and even then he had an air of boredom and condescension that made her want to slap him. Together they sounded as good as Bill Evans and Toots Theilmans. Their jazz waltz version of "Tenderly" made Ellen glow, yet she couldn't bear to play it now, either the tape *or* on her piano.

Ellen knew Karl wanted her to be more "cool" and "laid back." Didn't these kids realize that their denial of feeling could betray them —that the moment might be gone forever, that there might be another war? There might be terrible killings and violence demanded of them, and the chance to make a jazz recording might be gone forever. Didn't they *realize?* They might have to be soldiers and shoot children in the face.

Ellen wondered where her first-born son was now. No doubt he was at a friend's house. She knew Karl; he would stay away. How would their home seem without him, without his adolescent exuberance, without his music?

The YMCA meeting room was filled when Larry and Ellen arrived at the CitAct fund-raising planning session. Rallies and picnics were good morale and membership builders, Hal said.

Membership now stood at over seven hundred; turnout for this meeting was astonishing. Soon a bigger meeting place would be needed.

Ellen noticed the odor of marijuana. It seemed to come, as usual, from the corner where the Franzes and Ted Mather were sitting. Allison DeVries — defying Traci's mandate about Sojourner Shelter employees' non-involvement in politics —sat beside Ted. She was giggling quite a bit. Up front, newcomers were shaking hands with Hal.

The pot odor at meetings was a disturbing element. The

The Raunch Factor

Citizen Action Party was attracting the young, it was true, but many older people also were attracted to the party platform with its urgent advocacy of a national health plan and its inspiring messages against ageism. A drug linkage with their new growing political party was the last thing they needed.

"Do you smell pot?" Larry whispered to Ellen. She nodded as they took seats. Daphne was giving a short treasurer's report. There was little money to keep track of. Canvassing for funds was not the CitAct way, Hal explained to the new members. TV and newspaper ads, the expenses of his trips and of printing fliers, and the hundreds of campaign signs they would need in autumn, would have to come from voluntary contributions. In a society where millions were spent for political campaigns, a third party had to nickel-and-dime it all the way.

Throughout the meeting Hal's good humored and enthusiastic answers to questions, his explanation of CitAct Party goals and direction were interrupted regularly by Ted Mather's silly giggle. It was picked up by the Franzes, and even Allison tittered until Daphne glared at her.

When Hal, somewhat weary, sat down behind the table he had been using as a lectern, Ted called out, "Don't lecture from the chair, Hal. I thought this was a democratic group."

A few members laughed. Hal shrugged and grinned. He looked tired and cold. They were having a long spell of November-like weather, in true Pennsylvania style.

Ellen saw Merrilee come in a side door. She sat down beside Allison.

She must have worked things out with her parents, Daphne surmised, pulling her sweater closer around her shoulders.

The group agreed unanimously to a July Fourth speech and a picnic in the Bingham Town Square and to have baked-potato booths at all the fairs and festivals in the District throughout the summer. Members quickly volunteered for this work. Merrilee agree to continue as campaign manager and would turn out the monthly newsletter from Allison's apartment where she was now staying.

What kind of liaison can that *be?* Daphne thought. *They're both cozying up to Ted.*

"The next debate will be at the Briarwood High School, sponsored by the League of Women Voters," Hal announced.

"I was not invited, of course, but when I saw *The Bingham Observer* article, I immediately called the League president and demanded, and was granted, equal time; of course they know we would picket the debate otherwise."

Hal got into the meat of his speech. "Briarwood is in the Tenth District due to Drew Burgess's gerrymandering maneuver when he was a State Legislator. He manipulated to annex this traditionally Republican stronghold. These votes are what got him elected to Congress by a very slim margin in what had been the Democratic-dominated Tenth District. That year Democrat ward heelers must have slipped up. They weren't out strong-arming members to vote or alert about patrolling the polls on election day. Ward heelers, you know, are paid or otherwise rewarded by the party to harass the faithful and see that their party stays in power. Members vote the party slate or find themselves without jobs, or worse. Some Democratic Party heads rolled the year Burgess won. So you see what we're up against. It's money and manipulation. It has very little to do with the democratic process. CitAct power must come from our idealism and our numbers. That's all we have."

"But, Hal," Ted called out, "where's our unity? I mean from state to state? If we're gonna kick ass, we should know what the West Coast is doing. In California they don't even call themselves CitActs. They're the Green Futurists."

"I know what you mean, Ted," Hal answered. "Reform movements like ours seem fragmented. Groups start up here and there, but as we grow —and CitAct is growing fast, very fast, here and in Philadelphia and in New England —we can definitely look forward to getting a few of our candidates elected to state offices. In off-year elections we can run candidates for local row offices and gradually —through our tenacity and numbers, join with other states and win out over money and machine strong-arming and we'll —"

"Hal," Ted interrupted, "Hal. Hal. This all *sounds* good but can we justify going into other states? There are Green Future people in Maryland who organized and worked as Green Futurists. They won't want to lose their identity. They'll never join us. It's useless to work for that goal."

"Well, I *never* say 'never.' We're meeting with Brian Maharis next week when he stops off in Bingham on his way to the Green Future convention in San Francisco," Hal said. "You can stop by Daphne's house then, and meet him. He has quite a different view from yours. I think you'll find that he wants to work together with us from state to state in our shared idealism, our *very* similar platforms and —"

"Does he share the idea that we should legalize pot?" Ted interrupted again, and giggled his maniacal giggle. The group of new members in the front row looked uncomfortable. They were members in their fifties who had come from the part of the Tenth District which extended into Kincaid County —had come in a chartered bus and were eager to work to get active members in that economically distressed area. They even had a Black lawyer who was interested in running on the CitAct ticket for State Supreme Court.

Shut up, Ted. Shut up, Daphne said to herself.

She turned around and stared at him. He stared insolently back at her.

Time was running out for the "Y" meeting room. Larry pumped up the beer barrel, and Ellen began setting out the chili dogs. She could see that they were going to run out of refreshments.

"This party growth is phenomenal," Ellen said to Daphne. "And it's all due to Hal. Even Larry's taking an interest. I just hope we can tone Ted down or phase him out somehow."

CHAPTER TWENTY-SIX

"I'll be getting a Bavarian enema any minute, now, Daphne. So I can't stay on the phone long. The doctor put me in the hospital for my chronicle colitis. Boy! do I hate these Bavarian enemas," Mrs. Hartley complained. Her hospitalization for barium tests was occurring at the same time as the completion of her furnishings installation.

Daphne giddily envisioned the "Bavarian" treatment: a yodelling, lederhosen-clad gastroenterologist schuhplattling around Mrs. H's bed, while aproned, blond-braided, Teutonic nurses, singing "hi-lee hi-low" prepared a floral-garlanded enema can.

"Don't worry," Daphne soothed, "We'll get everything done. Debbie's back to work now and everything's moving along. Don't *worry*, Mrs. H."

"Well, I don't know," she answered querulously, " —after all that trouble with the Krocks and all —by the way —did them scones come in? The ones for the front room?"

"Yes. Yes," Daphne assured her. The crimson-walled, twenty-four-by-thirty-six-foot living room —or drawing room, or great room — might be an ode, a paean to the finest English Georgian sensibility. Its over-door split pediments, white crewel-embroidered draperies, Oriental rugs, brass chandeliers, gleaming plank floors and chintz-covered chairs and sofas were a hymn to eighteenth century grace, balance and proportion, but to Mrs. Hartley, it was still "the front room." Her simple Western Pennsylvania row-house origins kept puncturing her pretensions.

"Was that the nouveau-riche biche again?" James laughed.

"Oh, she's not so bad, James —she's just 'out of it,'" Daphne said.

They were wrapping blue and white Chinese porcelain lamps for the Hartley master bedroom. ("It's the 'Master Bedroom,'" Mrs. H. had insisted, "not the 'Owner's Bedroom.'")

Mrs. Hartley seemed to want to participate actively in her

own subjugation!

Debbie marked and stacked boxes and took them to the loading dock. She was still walking cautiously. To sit, she had to use an inflatable rubber doughnut-shaped cushion. They had spent days packing and loading the Hartley furnishings.

"We'll need two flat dollies for this installation, Daphne," James said.

"Well," she shrugged, "that lets out me and Debbie."

Debbie and James groaned at this uncharacteristic sexist witticism, but it was like old times again. They were joking together again. Debbie was getting her head straightened out at last, and, except for Mrs. Hartley's endless telephoning, the completion of the Mellors Lane house was imminent and had been relatively pain-free. Besides, Mrs. Burgess was so organized there was no doubt that the party would be a breeze.

Not that it was pleasant seeing Bobbye coming and going next door. She stuck her short nose up every time she saw Daphne.

A letter to Daphne from Attorney Agnes Harrison had set forth Bobbye's demands: The woodwork was to be repainted, the furniture recovered, wall coverings and carpet replaced, a new glass table top installed in the dining room. The total cost would exceed ten thousand, wholesale, and no combination of placating letters and phone calls would ever soften Bobbye's heart. Daphne's hopes of splitting the costs with her had died when a second legal missive arrived, designating Designs for Living as solely responsible, even though Bobbye and Ed's guests had turned the home into a scene from the movie *Animal House.*

Whenever she thought about Robb Mulvaney, Daphne's fingers curled. She could *feel* his skinny neck with its knobby Adam's apple and its gold cross and chain.

The burden of added expenses loomed within Daphne's thoughts —even in her dreams —and she found herself becoming deeply depressed for perhaps the first time in her life since her parents' death.

Her shop's walk-in traffic sales were slow but steady,

D.J.Muns-Blancato

always had been, but her long-term custom-design projects, though also steady, were not enough. Maybe she would have to bid on that MHMR job. She would have to find additional work, somehow, and soon.

"Nineteen thousand dollars for a station wagon?" Carla Campagna asked at the meeting of the Sojourner Shelter Board of Directors. From now on these were closed-to-all-but-board-members-and-director-meetings, a Traci-Edict that had been moved and seconded so fast that dissenters heard only a blur of voices.

First on the agenda was the station wagon Traci had selected, "for Shelter use," from a number of bids. The bid was by no means the lowest —in fact, it was the highest. Traci said that changing the specifications to include automatic transmission and car phone " —immm-pacted on my selection."

There was money to pay for it. Shelter funding was steady, and —no doubt about it —in Bingham County the entertainment value of Traci, combined with Bobbye's rape and child molestation lectures and programs, was resulting in increased contributions to the shelter.

Allison asked for a motion to buy the baby-blue vehicle. It was quickly seconded, and Traci got her way. It would be delivered the next day. Her Porsche could and would stay in her garage indefinitely.

The next Shelter business to be dealt with was a scheduled visit to a women's shelter in Las Vegas.

" —in Las Vegas?" Harriet had asked when she found out she would be working two double shifts while Traci and Allison were gone.

"Why not?" Allison had said. Harriet did not mention that worry about her son Norm's impending operation was causing her sleeplessness night after night. The all-expenses-paid trip was approved, and Allison moved on to the next item on the agenda.

Hal, in repeated attempts to get the floor, wanted to bring

up the dismantling of the Shelter child care program. Mothers in the shelter could no longer set up education arrangements or job interviews, and, as CR had not been reinstated, the women and children spent their long, hopeless days watching TV soap operas while they waited for their AFDC and food stamps. When discharged, after the three-week limit was up, most of the women went back to their abusive situations out of economic desperation.

Allison ignored Hal and announced the next issue: "Banishment." Shelterees whom Traci deemed guilty of rule infractions could be banished from the facility for an indefinite period.

Notification occurred indirectly —Traci no longer had any direct contact with the shelterees —through curt messages in the day-book: an entire page would bear only the date and the huge, angry, scrawled punitive order: "As of this date Leona (or Patty, or Kim, or Jennifer) is forbidden to enter the Shelter premises FOREVER. (signed) T.B.B."

Liz Heckman, Carla Campagna, and Hal protested the banishment ruling. Even the previously very quiet physician, Kamala Gupta, now spoke out against this cruel, shunning action.

"The forbidden person cannot defend herself. It seems to defeat the whole purpose of the Shelter —"

"Yes," Hal added, "The basic premise that the Shelter is a haven, a place that holds out hope —that —"

The other board members quickly voted down the dissenters. Item after item on the agenda were disposed of in this manner. Allison barrelled through the list, and Traci won every issue with scarcely a pouty-lipped murmur.

Walking out to the new off-street parking lot after the meeting, Hal, Liz, Carla, and Dr. Gupta talked together. Hal could see Traci and Allison watching them from the back vestibule.

"I have a very uneasy feeling about this agency," Liz said.

"I know what you mean." Carla was frowning. Kamala

turned toward her.

"You're an R.N., aren't you? I want to speak very frankly. I'm going to have to resign from this board. It is too dangerous for my career for me to be associated with this woman. Executive Director or not, she is unbalanced, she is not normal. Her paranoia and constant manipulation —what she is doing with the other board members —all these actions are self-serving. All are abnormal. If you want some day again to work in the medical community —you are teaching now, in the city?" Carla nodded, and Kamala went on, " —if you some day wish to return to hospital work, your association with this agency will not be good for your professional record. It would look bad for you —uh — work bad against you."

They stopped by Hal's old Buick. Liz turned to Carla, then to Kamala. "She's right. You're right, I think, Kamala, but if we lose the two of you, our power, our input to try to guide this Shelter, is diminished even more. But I can see why you feel strongly about it."

"I have, I have given much thought." Kamala Gupta's blue-black hair gleamed even in the faint twilight of the leaf-shadowed parking lot. "My psychiatric residency, before I decided to go to pathology, was at Menninger Clinic. There was a classic paranoiac —a woman —permanently institutionalized there, near the clinic. All of the medical residents studied her. She did nothing but chart arrivals and departures of ocean-going vessels all day long, every day, using huge, graph-like schedule sheets which hung on every available space in her room. She stopped only to sleep. Her charts were based on once-active nineteen twenties' steamships. The arrivals and so on —the schedules — all were her fantasy. She had to believe that she had complete control over everything, everybody. Any disruption of her control of her charts would cause wild, suicidal crises. Her disease's etiology — we know today that it is a chemical imbalance of the brain, but it was not then known —no doubt was similar to this Traci Bilsen-Bloom's disorder. I believe Traci Bilsen-Bloom is profoundly neurotic — not schizophrenic, perhaps —but a schizoaffective bi-polar treatable disorder."

"Good heavens," Hal exclaimed. "That's awful. Such a waste!"

"Yes, it is very sad. A wasted intelligence. A bad condition —but it might respond to medication," Kamala explained. "Individuals with this disorder often are attracted to hospital work, or to public agencies —to work of this type, where there are opportunities to gain tight control."

"It's dangerous," Liz said. "Tax payers are being bilked, duped; we're all being used. We should stick it out, try to effect some change, get Traci fired —she should get into treatment — and we should find a more suitable Executive Director. You should stay on, Kamala, for a while longer, at least. You're not resigning, are you, Hal?" Hal shook his head.

"I cannot stay on. My mind is made firm —uh —up-ward," Kamala said. "I come from just a middle-class family. My people are Parsis —Zoroastrians. We all have worked hard. Parsi women especially must guard everything about our careers. I have my child. My husband and I have careful plans."

"Do you worship —uh —is the Parsi deity Ahura Mazda, then?" Hal tried to speak as the Academic, not the Imperious Interrogator.

"In such a tradition we cannot say any longer 'worship.' We cannot say there is a *darshan* except in tradition observed. I am a scientist. Our families —my husband and mine —we have tried to uphold a tradition which served our ancestors well. Mazda is a god of light; a good god —uh —" Kamala searched for words, "I am not comfortable talking about the religion of my ancestors."

"Oh, of course. Of course," Hal said solicitously.

"You really think I should resign?" Carla asked. "What do the rest of you think?"

"I do," Dr. Gupta said. "Knowing the medical community, I have to say that I do think so."

The others were silent. Finally Liz Heckman spoke:

"It must be your own decision, Carla."

"She's right," Hal said. "How can we tell you what to do? But the doctor makes an important point. You're an R.N., you're divorced, every move you make is vital because you're picking up the tab. No one else is around to pick up the tab," Hal leaned forward slightly, " —or is there someone?" he smiled.

"No. Hell, no. There's no one. I see now that I'll have to kiss the Shelter goodbye. It was a beautiful concept. I was so proud to be associated with it! My name is on the list on the official stationery, 'Carla Campagna, R.N.' Hell, I think it looks terrific. I *believe* in this shelter. If you knew how I grew up, the brutal, macho crap my mother had to endure! My father wrecked my mother's life, and *my* childhood, and my sister's! This Shelter, when it was first organized, was a wonderful thing. There were consciousness raising sessions, then day care, then they got this beautiful house, they even got Dottie Davis, an R.N. friend of mine, which fulfilled state requirements for twenty-four-hour child care, and we had dynamic black women and there was even talk about a bank just for women — a women's *bank!* Oh God." Carla's tears spilled over, now. "Do you see what's happening here? Blacks are taboo. CR is taboo. A whole wonderful plan for women of this county — a large group of women need it —has all been for nothing."

"It can't have been for nothing." Liz insisted. "We can make every minute we gave count for something."

"Are you resigning too?" Carla asked Liz.

"I meant to say that we can make every minute *you* gave count," said Liz. "I'm going to try to stay on longer, see if we can do something, but it's a risk, probably, to *my* career plans too. I don't have anyone picking up the tab either." She glanced at Hal.

Carla wiped her eyes. "I'm sorry for losing control. I *never* do this. It was just —just so important to me. Traci was so cold, so remote and unapproachable, from the beginning. My son even donated his time and hauled truckloads of furniture from a Doncaster household sale —enough to furnish the whole third floor —and Traci stood right there by the stairs, and when he and his buddy came back down from hauling those heavy dressers and things, Traci didn't say one word of thanks —no 'We appreciate it': nothing."

"She cares nothing for that. She cares only for what affects only herself. Also, she cannot laugh or make jokes. Such individuals are profoundly humorless," Kamala explained. "She will never make any effort except to manipulate what she perceives to be —to be —what the British call 'the Main Chance' —for only herself. It is her sickness. And now, goodnight. I have been happy to meet you all. Now tired old Auntie must go home," Kamala giggled. "I must rest before I begin work at midnight at the hospital."

As he drove out of the parking lot, Hal could see Allison and Traci talking to Brimmie Krock on the back steps.

It had been reported that Brimmie was being counselled by Traci. Now she would be able to manipulate *him* as well as the others. Hal marvelled at the skill with which she gained the confidence of strategic individuals within the agency. Hal had noticed at board meetings how the Reverend Krock ogled her movie star boobs. When Traci walked in or out with that knee-snapping Marilyn Monroe strut, Brimmie watched her every move.

CHAPTER TWENTY-SEVEN

"Doctor Renshaw, you know I could get sacked for using college facilities for political purposes," Mrs. Helbrun gasped as she hoisted stacks of paper from her car onto the hand-truck on Daphne's shop dock. "It took me two hours to run off these flyers after the office closed."

Hal thought she was more likely to be suspect for her auburn Afro, stirrup pants, high-heeled boots and big-shouldered purple shirt. The conservative History Department was still abuzz about the infamous Debate at State broadcast, and Mrs. Helbrun's outfits seemed to grow more *au courant* with each new scandal of Hal's.

"Two hours' use? Two hours' use of a machine that faculty members use constantly?" Hal asked, "For Little League schedules, garage sales, church notices? This, too, is a good cause, don't forget."

They pushed the loaded hand-truck into the receiving room.

"Daphne's expecting you to drop off this shop key at her house on your way home."

Hal handed Mrs. Helbrun the key, then went inside and groped for the light switch. "I have to pick up Celeste and Pete."

"Hi there." A male voice spoke out of the darkness. Hal jumped, his heart pounding.

"Hi ya, Daphne, baby." The voice continued. It was the answering machine.

"How's that luscious pussy? I could have went for some of that political pussy tonight, you cunt, but I guess you like the candidate's dick better, right? You don't know what yer missin', cunt. Yer missin' a great big one. Maybe I better come over an' show ya —" The machine beeped off.

"Sweet Jesus!" Mrs. Helbrun snorted, "What was *that?*"

"I don't know. Daphne keeps getting these calls."

"How revolting! Why doesn't she notify the phone company? He sounds dangerous."

"I'm going to play it again," Hal said, "to hear that voice again. It reminds me of —"

215

"Spare me, Doctor, spare me. I'll drop off the key. Just let me get out of here before you play it again, Sam." She hurried to her car.

"I'm crazy aboutcha, Bebby," Fred MacMurray said to Barbara Stanwyk.

Debbie and James and Daphne were in Daphne's little sitting room watching *Double Indemnity,* again, on *Late Nite Oldies,* their favorite channel.

"Kiss me, Wooltuh," Barbara Stanwyk said, and Fred MacMurray —Walter, in the wonderful film noir mystery —*did* kiss her.

James' loud, braying laugh and Debbie's cascading nasal giggle made Daphne feel hopeful. Things couldn't be too bad; she and her staff were organized and getting along together again.

Setting down her Scotch and water, Debbie turned to James with pouty lips. "Kiss me, Wooltuh," she commanded grabbing him around the neck. They scuffled on the couch and fell to the floor shrieking.

It was wonderful to have drinks together and to unwind. They had worked all day on the Hartley house. The major rooms would be completed for the fund-raiser, but two guest rooms would have to be off-limits; their quilted bedspreads and crocheted canopy nets would not be ready on time. Mrs. Hartley was irate and every day her telephone nagging became worse. She was going to be discharged from the hospital and would soon be under foot again.

There were additional problems caused by her idea of getting Gus Quip — the Factotem of Mellors Lane — to dress in Eighteenth Century livery à la Williamsburg, in blue satin coat and knee breeches, immaculate white lace jabot and powdered wig, and serve as the fund-raising party's butler, footman and major-domo. The Hartleys had attended several parties in Virginia and Grosse Pointe where their hosts got their staff — mostly Blacks —to dress this way for social events on the estates. It was rumored that some staffs were required to dress every day in this garb.

Gus Quip not only was not Black, but he also chewed tobacco, was not willing to wear anything but his own "overhauls," and was threatening to quit altogether.

The Hartleys were planning to costume Fern Slagle — "unfortunately, White" —and Melba Cochran and Lorene Wilton —"good and Black" —on loan from the Burgesses, as washerwomen in "mammy-turbans" and aprons and neckerchiefs. The washer-women would be attractions in the authentic replication of Mount Vernon's Eighteenth Century wash house that had been erected for the Hartley laundry room. The three women were to preside picturesquely over kettles which would hang over a roaring fire in the huge, open fireplace, and would stir the "laundry" in a kettle that actually contained exquisitely wrapped favors to be handed out to each guest: sterling silver candle snuffers for the ladies; cigar nippers for the men.

More than twenty thousand dollars had been spent for antique laundry benches, wooden wash tubs, sad irons and pressing tables, a "hired man's bed" for the rustic beamed-ceiling wash house; plus old baskets, brass and copper kettles and wooden and iron tools and museum-quality artifacts. Mrs. Hartley did not want her home to take a back seat to the Burgess estate. Her guests would tour "Hartfeld" and realize the refinement, detailing and innumerable features, and remember and savor its charm and the ease of bygone days.

Two clever octagonal out-buildings even had been built at the back of the knot gardens —homage to the two-seaters of the goddess Cloaca —but which were actually air-conditioned *salles aux poudres* with the latest plumbing and amenities. Cartouches over their doors bore, in graceful calligraphy with gold-illuminated capitals, the inscriptions, "Mesdames" and "Messieurs" which, according to Gus Quip —long on history and short on decorum as ever —"looked as if LaFayette had just went in and took a crap."

When Mrs. Hartley had outlined her plan to Gus, he squirted a mighty sluice of tobacco juice on one of the landscaper's rolls of sod and said slowly, "A *lotta money*. You'll hafta come up with a *lotta money* to get me in a suit like that. A *lotta* money."

There was a knock at Daphne's kitchen door. It was Merrilee carrying an enormous box of sausage for the CitAct Speech in the Park booth. "There are more boxes in my car. Can you freeze some of them?" she said. "Ellen is freezing some too. They had a special on them so I got them ahead, through the CorBlimey. They accepted my check. CitAct owes me a hundred and twenty dollars, Daphne, or my check will bounce. I'm broke."

Merrilee's impulsive acts were well-meant but annoying, but she *had* gotten a job as a CorBlimey waitress and she *was* paying her car insurance on her own. Daphne wrote out a check without comment, and Debbie and James carried in the prematurely purchased sausage.

"Ellen got a piano-playing job at the CorBlimey," Merrilee reported, settling down in the sitting room with a vodka and tonic. "Her husband got laid off. Tonight was her first night. Herb Haselas had been looking for a pianist to compete with the Copper Bottom. They have that organist, you know. Ellen sounded great. If you *like* all those Cole Porter and George Gershwin songs —and Jerome Kern —she plays Jerome Kern too. There were three couples there tonight that knew all the words. They had a real sing-along. Imagine!"

"I can imagine it," James said. "They're great songs, great lyrics. They're sure a lot better than a lot of rock lyrics, with their 'Fuck me, fuck me, fuck me, c'mon an' fuck me' etcetera."

"Since when were you bored with 'fuck me, fuck me,' etcetera?" Merrilee and James were catalysts for each other. She resented the fact that James was gay. Daphne, knowing this talk would lead to trouble, changed the subject.

"The Briarwood League of Women Voters' debate is tomorrow. Hal will be in it —if he can talk, that is. He has a sore throat and a cough. I hope you can be there, Merrilee. I'm going with Hal."

"If my car will hold up. It needs new ball joints." Merrilee smirked at James.

Daphne, realizing that Merrilee was just going to become increasingly ribald, announced, "Time to close up shop." She had a stomachache which was steadily worsening.

On the way to Briarwood in a cold gloomy rain the following day, Hal's throat began to bleed. He was coughing up blood into a tissue when, almost at the same moment, Daphne doubled up with intense stomach cramps and chills.

"We've got to stop somewhere," she gasped. Hal nodded and coughed again, raucously, as he pulled into the Porky's Diner parking lot.

"I coughed all night," he said. "I just can't get rid of this cough." He wiped blood from his lips.

Daphne moaned and huddled against the car door.

"Did you ever have this bleeding before, Hal?"

"Yes. It's happened a couple of times over the years. It's caused by irritated capillaries or something. What about you? Is it some kind of stress reaction or what?" he said irritably.

"This is some kind of flu, Hal! It's the flu."

Hal's vasectomy reassured her on one point. She added, "We both know I'm not *pregnant*. What'll we do Hal? What're we going to do?" Another ghastly pang shot through her mid-section. The burning and aching were increasing. Hal's car heater didn't work. No sense asking him to turn *it* on.

An immense, tee-shirted belly emerged from the Diner's back door.

"There's Porky," Hal gurgled.

"Do you *know* him?"

"No."

"Well, how do you know it's Porky then?"

"I just know."

"Well, how do you *know?*"

"This is his diner, isn't it? Hal insisted. He gurgled and spit again.

"That doesn't mean anything. That man could be anyone —

219

an employee —the dishwasher. You said you don't *know* Porky."

"I just *KNOW* godammit." Hal coughed up more blood. "This whole conversation's ridiculous," he said between coughs. *Her reactions are erratic. She's nuts!* he thought.

"See —" Daphne said, "he's dumping the garbage. It's an employee." Her stomach pains were agonizing. She turned to Hal and repeated, "See —it's an employee. I told you —that's not Porky. You just can't make an assumption. That's some other...."

"I don't give a flying fuck *WHO* it is, Daphne! I have to *do* something. We've both gone mad. I'm going to look for a motel," Hal shouted, spinning his wheels.

He careened down the highway. Daphne sobbed. There was blood on the collar of Hal's white shirt.

In spite of her searing, burning abdominal pain, Daphne became aware of their having passed four so-called "Adult Video and Novelty" stores; four pornography purveyors in less than eight miles! *Why? Why?* she wondered. The area they were driving through was a Christian stronghold; the home of the state's oldest fundamentalist college, founded by reformed sects of already reformed Presbyterians. There were four private Christian grade schools and high schools as well.

Is the sex-as-sin fundamentalist Christian obsession a possible cause of society's —men's (for they control society) warped view of womankind —a reaction perhaps to religious prudery? Does it stem from early Aristotelian, Augustinian, Knox-Calvinist flight-from-worldliness? Or is it just that Christians in general (WASPS in particular) are bonkers about fucking?" she mused.

*It could **hardly** be as healthy as that —normal eroticism — the porn shops' products dehumanize women,* Daphne tried to reason it out. *And that's not erotic, it's sadistic. Maybe some day I'll begin to understand it,* she thought, obscene phone calls not far from her mind. Eluding her reasoning process entirely was male religionists' fear of the power of female sexuality.

Another sharp abdominal pang claimed her attention. Hal pulled into the first motel he came to. A large sign said "Loaves and Fishes." A lower sign bore the admonition "Absolutely No Filling of Coolers From The Ice Machine."

"Oh God, I think this is Brimmie Krock's place. The motel his church owns. We can't go in here. We don't have any luggage. We —We —"

"We'll just *have* to," Daphne sobbed. "Go in and register as Mr. and Mrs.! Mr. and Mrs. *BILGE* for all I care!" She howled, wrapping her arms around her mid-section.

"I'm freezing!"

"But what about luggage? We have no suitcases. It'll look like some cheap —"

"Just *GO*" she wailed. "Then you can sit out on the porch by the door. We'll go in the room separately. That way one of us will always be outside, in full view."

Hal gave a great hockering, quacking noise and spit into a bloody tissue.

"I believe I am in dire need of medical attention, Daphne."

"Christ," she squealed, "can't you ever say something simply and to the point? Can't you just say 'I need a fucking doctor'?"

"I *do* need a fucking doctor!" His bubbly cough again cut him off.

"Go and register, and I'll get ice from that machine, and you can hold it on your throat. Oww-w I can't stand this!" She rocked back and forth.

She's gone berserk, Hal thought as he walked shakily into the Loaves and Fishes lobby. A very wide, very bald-headed clerk with very long auburn sideburns looked him over and pushed the registry toward him. In desperation Hal wrote "Harold Renshaw and associate. He gulped and wiped his lips.

"My throat is bleeding," he said to the clerk.

"Praise Je-*HEE*-sus."

"My associate is ill. She wants to lie down. And I need a doctor. We're on our way to Briarwood High School, to a debate."

"Praise The Lord."

On the wall behind the Jesus-praising clerk hung a large sign

221

with Day-Glo orange plastic letters which said
     "BFFLE TWAB MACOL BEZOX"
     Want to Know What this Means?
     Look It Up in Your Bible. Only The
     Bible Knows
     It was one of Brimmie Krock's patented "Jiffy Tongue"
signs marketed by his rapidly expanding Pentecostacraft
company. His signs, plastic-covered *Expurgated* Bibles and
gewgaws were popular in Bingham, Kincaid and Truschel
counties as well as throughout the Midwestern Bible Belt.
Brimmie showcased the devices through the Loaves and Fishes
chain and at airports and shopping malls throughout the U.S.
     Walking unsteadily to the door, Hal said to the clerk, "I
must give this key to my associate."
     "Praise God," said Sideburns, but he was openly leering.
     The whole world has gone mad, Hal thought. Daphne was
packing ice into her make-up bag.
     "Here," she moaned, zipping the bag shut. "Sit out here
and put this on your throat. I'm going in and get in the bathtub."
She handed Hal the dripping bag.
     "Don't take your clothes off, for God's sake, we have
another half-hour's drive —"
     "Do you want me to get in the tub fully clothed, you jerk?"
She was wild with pain. Hal was incredulous. She was
actually going to do it, he realized. Was going to get in the
bathtub! She jabbed the key into the lock.
     "But I want to call a doctor —" Hal croaked. "I need to
use the phone." Another coughing spasm shook him.
     "Well, stay out here till I get some relief. Then I'll come
out and you can go in."
     The bleeding stopped almost immediately. Hal sat back in
the uncomfortable metal chair and sighed. Ice water seeped
through the make-up bag onto his shirt front. He'd have to deal
with Daphne's crazed behavior later —wouldn't think about it
now.
     He took off his shirt and, shivering, poured some of the ice
water onto his blood-stained collar and dabbed at his chin. He

could see Sideburns watching him.

Some nut with his shirt off in this freezing weather, the clerk seemed to be thinking.

Several couples — with luggage — checked out of their rooms. Three businessmen came out of the restaurant chewing toothpicks. In the restaurant window the big blue neon fish sign in the shape of the early Christian symbol cast an unearthly glow on nearby diners who solemnly masticated the restaurant's single offering: deep-fried turbot on sesame buns with one of three secret recipe sauces: P.G.P. (Praise God Pimento), H.T.R. (Holy Trinity Relish with three different kinds of watermelon and cucumber pickle), or C.C.C. (Chastity Chow Chow). For five dollars diners could, on their way out, pick up a bottle of any of the sauces from the large display by the cash register. P.G.P. and H.T.R. sauce came in plastic church-shaped containers with screw-off dispenser-steeples. C.C.C. sauce bottles were in the shape of a medievally-gowned pneumatic female torso wearing a chastity belt with a brass-toned plastic lock and a key that you turned to open the flip-top lid. The fact that the chastity belt was on the outside of the dress didn't seem to be deterring sales.

The hot water rose as Daphne, gasping with relief, sank as low as possible in the tiny tub, her knees raised high and her feet propped on the faucets. Water lapped at her chin. Only two days before, she had been in this same position when she and Hal tried out some Kama Sutra positions in her bedroom. Holding the book in one hand, he had so studiously arranged her limbs and his that Daphne had burst out laughing, ruining the mood. Hal had told her to " —try to control your levity," and added that he'd bet Liz Heckman wouldn't laugh during sex, and the idea of Liz Heckman contorted into Kama Sutra love positions struck Daphne as so hilarious that Hal had given up in disgust.

Now he was pounding on the motel door. All Daphne could do was to think, over and over, *Blessed relief. Blessed relief.* She sank deeper into the steaming water. The pounding continued.

I could just stay here, she thought. *He could go on alone, and I could just stay here in comfort, free of all my damn problems, free of his crises, his bleeding throat, his unmanageable kids.*

Pete and Celeste had turned out to be self-centered whiners —not the witty, fun-loving companions she had expected.

I could just forget it all: Bobbye's law suit, the Sojourner Shelter nightmare, Mrs. Hartley, trying to meet deadlines —forget it all!

And yet —and yet —how many people ran for Congress? Really fought the fight? Had the courage to make the climb at all? Faced the insurmountable obstacles, and with *no money* — just moxie, when everyone knew that money alone, the power that it bought, determined the fate of the whole world? How many men were this idealistic, had this much verve, nerve, audacity? To go on and persevere and believe and persist in the face of the ridiculous odds? How many men? Or women? And Hal was making headway, steadily gaining adherents; a busload of new CitAct members from Truschel County was to meet them at the Blake Gymnasium.

About now, Daphne speculated. *They'll be there about now!*

She climbed out of the tub.

"I'm coming —I'm coming —give me a minute," she shouted.

CHAPTER TWENTY-EIGHT

The two-million-dollar Georgian-style High School gymnasium was Leonard Blake's gift to the wealthy community of Briarwood. A greater need for such an endowment for Kincaid or Truschel or Bingham County school districts concerned Blake not at all. He wanted the Blake name to be associated with clean-cut, rich WASP athletes and all that they signified: old, established, rich, Republican Tory values; winning the game, carrying the ball; the best in well-kept homes, lawns, cars and women.

In Briarwood Leonard Blake and Drew Burgess and their party stalwarts felt comfortably at home. Hal saw them now, circulating familiarly through the debate crowd, shaking hands, slapping shoulders and effusively hailing their well-met fellows. Burgess's guard with the three-fifty-seven magnums was nowhere to be seen. Ed Krock's handlers had sent in his place his aide, Allan Cope. Cope's baggy, rusty-brown, three-piece suit contrasted conspicuously with the trendy Bwana Land attire of the League of Women Voters members and their Bill Blass-cologned husbands who made up the majority of the audience and panel of on-stage officials.

"Even Krock's handlers know better than to let him rush in where I —fearing or not —am about to tread," Hal said, *sotto voce* to Daphne.

"Piece o'cake, Hal," she said. "Let'em have it today, Demosthenes. Give 'em both barrels!"

Hal grimaced. "Unfortunate metaphor, M'dear." He started down the aisle to the stage before Daphne could tell him to straighten his tie. She noticed, also, that he could have used a hair trim. Most of the League husbands sported Ollie North clips.

The CitAct chartered bus had discharged its fifty or so new members who now filed resolutely through the Georgian doorway. Daphne had recognized other CitAct members' shabby cars in the parking lot. They skulked there among Mercedeses and Cadillacs and Porsches and Jaguars like renegade old Methodist aunts and uncles at a relative's Episcopalian wedding.

Here and there in the crowd an orange spot —a tee shirt, or

a tricorn —lifted Hal's spirits. CitAct members had little to give but they gave it with such *brio* that Hal was sure that their enthusiasm was responsible for much of the Party's rapid growth. A jazz combo already had volunteered for the July 4th Speech in the Park picnic. And James McInnis and Debbie Fentriss were silk-screening signs and bumper stickers, thus saving the Party several thousand dollars. The vivid orange banner, "Return to Concern, Renshaw for Congress," was showing up on cars all over the tri-county area.

Hal felt exuberant now; he felt good. His throat pain had abated, the blood stains on his shirt were barely discernable, and he was ready to do battle again. The argument, the panic and sickness that threatened their trip to the debate were nearly forgotten. *We're only human*, he reassured himself.

In the back of his mind, however, a growing awareness of Ted Mather's marijuana obsession, his constant disruption of meetings nagged at Hal's consciousness. Dissenting political voices —and a reforming third party certainly was a dissenting voice — invariably attracted eccentrics; it was inevitable. Eccentrics — kooks — had followed Eugene Debs, Norman Thomas, Adlai Stevenson, Eugene McCarthy, George McGovern, Barry Commoner. Dissenter candidates of the two established parties as well as third parties always had some loony hangers-on, and the parties tried to "contain" them. But Ted was going too far. He would have to be confronted at the first opportunity. It was impossible to go on containing him, and he was influencing others.

The candidates were seated now at their microphone-equipped table. There were no name-plaques or water pitchers or glasses. League members, all young-looking and expensively slender, trotted up and down the aisles, prettily attending to last-minute details and collecting index cards with audience questions.

The League Ladies had added feminine touches to their snappy khaki poplin Bwana Land shoulder-tabbed British shirts, Daphne observed, by means of pale pink or violet —perfectly awful with the mustard-toned khaki — ruffly collared under-blouses or chiffon scarves and pearl ropes. *They can't get along without the reassurance of those fluffy-ruffles.*

She often contemplated, wonderingly, women's addiction to ruffles and pastel-colored femininity statements. Nice, maybe, occasionally, but *perpetually?* Were they *that* unsure of their sexuality?

The audience was settling down. The League president, Muffy Palmer, smiling shyly, stepped to the lectern, and with barely-audible sorority-girl sibilance —a combination of Jackie Kennedy, Katherine Hepburn, and, Daphne realized with a jolt, Traci Bilsen-Bloom; or was it Marilyn Monroe? —explained the debate format. There was to be a one and a half-minute time limit, like the Debate at State, but questions would be on cards from the audience — *that means the League controls the questions,* Hal realized —and Muffy closed her introduction by saying, "I want to remind you all about the game tonight on TV, which I know none of us wants to miss, so let's try to wind everything up by eight-thirty. Thank you."

She did a sort of fanny-twitching *pas de bourée* back to her seat and the debate began.

Whether by some unspoken *droit de seigneur* or by League directive, Drew Burgess, without benefit or name plaque or other introduction, simply began speaking first.

He chortled his way through a Good Old Boy Isn't-It-Great-To-Be-Among-Our-Own-Kind —Rich-Republicans? —joviality-session.

It had nothing to do with the first question in the debate, which Mopsy Brewster read from a card: "When are nuclear arms corporations going to be taxed commensurately for their huge profits from so-called 'defense' production? If elected, would you propose or vote for such a tax?"

Drew took additional time to start his answer, for which the Timekeeper, Troozie Trowbridge allowed him more than three minutes before she signalled by tapping the first seven notes of "Yankee Doodle" on a toy xylophone.

Drew's predictable answer was, "Being against all government interference in business, I would not propose or vote for such a tax."

Hal spoke next, prefacing his succinct affirmation of a corporate profit tax with a denunciation of American males' sports obsession:

"If a modicum of that mania, that energy, were directed to this country's government, we, as a country, would not be on the way to becoming — no pun intended — fair game for a dictatorship à la nineteen thirties' Germany —" which evoked gasps and scattered applause.

By Daphne's count, the Yankee Doodle bell sounded a full ten seconds before Hal's time was up. This was, plain and simple, supposed to be Drew Burgess Day.

Allen Cope's answer to the first question, a halting mumbling reiteration of Democratic Party cant, would have surprised no one had it been audible, and his attempts to shoot his knuckle-length cuffs and do the Democrat Centurion Swagger were more pathetic than debonair. The handful of embarrassed Democrats in the audience made a show of studying their mimeographed, League hand-out pamphlets and covered-dish-dinner notices. Tim's performance was worse than if the Democrat candidate had been a total "No-Show."

What the hell —Hal told himself, *The Republican Party Glee Club is going to take over this farce. About all the League Ladies are doing is just going through motions —although that first question was obviously a CitAct card —and Gidget-Goes-Political has complete control of that fucking xylophone. I'm going to pull out all the stops,* he resolved. *Why the hell not?*

Questions that followed dealt with many Briarwood Yuppie issues such as education: "Will you support the voucher system?"

Burgess said, "Our God-fearing founding fathers' views vis à vis school prayer mandate it in terms of Christian principles and I, by and large, will support it at this point in time."

Hal answered, "In spite of its shortcomings, I could not, in good conscience underwrite the dismantling of our entire public education system, which a voucher plan surely would do."

Allen responded, "Christian right to mphf umck splm school prer mkffr is, in additon to lmsx mph."

Other Yuppie concerns: "Welfare loafers are draining our tax base and are a threat to the American Way. Please comment, and "Would you advocate the death penalty for homosexuals as an AIDS deterrent? Is quarantining AIDS victims in Antarctica a viable alternative?" and "Will you vote to eliminate a tax on stock dividends, thus encouraging investors, thereby creating greater employment?"

These pressing concerns and the questioners' proposed solutions —all masterpieces of over-simplification —made up the bulk of the questions, most showing evidence of League Ladies' none-too-subtle editorialization. But, no matter; even though many CitAct questions were sifted out, Hal's barbed answers became increasingly ironic, his caustic analogies more squarely on the mark; he was clearly enjoying himself. He was hitting his stride.

Daphne could see the League Ladies responding to the irresistible Renshaw smile, his attractive — magnetic, really — guilelessness and openness, his virile wit. *Why don't men realize,* Daphne wondered, *that a non-hostile brain —intellectuality that doesn't deny emotion —is sexy?*

She watched the Leaguers' unfolding amazement at the Renshaw brand of undisguised honesty. It was the antithesis of the American Male Take Charge/Power-and-Rigidity mode.

"Sheee-IT." *as Lorene would say,* Daphne gloated gleefully. *They're seeing real eroticism and don't know what hit them; can't help themselves. They all thought they married Macho: Credit Card Macho in a one-hundred-percent-cotton safari coat; the ultimate in stock-portfolio-sex. They've complied with grouse-hunting, LaCrosse-playing Mr. Man's rules. League Ladies come across with Little Girl submission between embroidered Porthault wedding sheets, dutifully to conceive the requisite Republican male dynastic successor (among other promised, nay, **guaranteed** fulfillments) and they do it all in WASP, Designer Good Taste and have found that it stinks; that it's boring.*

But here, today, Daphne summed up to herself, *they know there is something unmistakably, profoundly different, something more, something indefinable, some wonderful thing. What these*

*women are experiencing at this debate is not eliciting their
compliance, it is eliciting their genuine, individual positive
response. Their lives are male-dominated; rich-male-money-
centered, in spite of their dowry-mandated expensive educations;
but they are discovering that Hal's mind, and his ideas, whatever
they are — they're not certain — makes stocks and bonds, the
Hunt, the Club, Shopping, deadly, deadly dull.*

League Ladies know, Daphne realized, *that here today
they're glimpsing another planet, a world of which they might
have gotten a daring hint at Bryn Mawr or Vassar or Bennington
—if they weren't Home Ec majors —in their required reading of
Rousseau, Voltaire, Racine, Moliere, Toqueville: from their
assignments in* Volpone *or* Tartuffe *or in writing themes on the
Mesdames de Stael and de Sevigné. They might have gotten some
vague inkling of that other world, that clitoris-twanging planet.
Dressed in their WASP Princess sweaters and stone-washed
jeans, they have leafed dutifully through their college assignments
on Maryanne George Eliot Evans and Aurore Georges Sand
Dupin, and glimpsed that new planet.*

Today the League Ladies were recognizing, perhaps for the
first time in their lives, the ultimate aphrodisiac —the world of
ideas.

What do the League Ladies know from sex? Daphne asked
herself. Sex was all they had, yet they had nothing at all: the
same, boring copulation over and over. They *fled* from
controversy — one doctor's wife, in a very controlled yet
revelatory statement to Daphne as they planned her living room
sofas, had whispered, "after *all* — I'm running away from
ugliness —"

For League Ladies to question Establishment, Republican
motives and goals, to analyze an elitist society's limitations or
their endless Getting and Spending was as unthinkable as it would
be if they openly took a blue-collar-class lover or drove a
Chevette or a VW or worked outside the home — had jobs,
careers. What did it profit them to improve ghetto housing or
street people's lives —people who had no homes at all?

"None of that stuff is any fault of *mine*," one lawyer's wife had told Daphne.

These women had no social conscience, no driving motivation, no passionate *anything*. They had only sex, and they didn't even protest when their resulting motherhood was described as "instinctive."

"What do these ladies know from sex?" Daphne laughed to herself, " — *Mozart-symphony-rice-pudding-with-raisins-Christmas-morning-colored-lights sex?"*

She had seen them slipping furtively into the Briarwood Galleria Mall's Penelope's Shame Boutique to buy trendy, Presbyterian garter-belts and wired push-up bras for themselves; had seen them making voyeuristic purchases for their eleven and twelve-year-old Bitsy Junior daughters, of high-cut-leg bikini underpants, into which packages they tucked, voyeuristically, pubic area depilatory kits.

"What do they know," Daphne grinned, " — *with their depilatory-kit sex?"*

Hal was speaking again. Something was happening throughout the audience. League Lady monitors at the end of each row of seats were gesturing frantically to each other. Hal was talking about nineteen thirties Germany again. A deep, quavering, matriarchal answering voice boomed out from a back-row seat:

"Muckraking is not the answer —has no place in a political meeting. We'll have no muckraking here, sir —comparing our country's president to Adolf Hitler is not to be tolerated."

It was an exaggeratedly-cultivated patrician, *grande dame* voice.

Daphne turned around and saw that the speaker looked exactly as her voice *sounded* —silver hair, massive bosom in an ancient gray crêpe dress; she was someone's very rich widowed mother and grandmother, alert, afraid, yet determined to protect the family inheritance.

Where do *they get those crêpe dresses and how do they grow those chests?* Daphne wondered.

"I'll make the comparison if necessary, Madam, and it *is* necessary," Hal interrupted. He stood up and stepped from behind the candidates' table and walked quickly to the edge of the stage and stared out at the astonished audience, his eyes and ideas blazing. He looked absolutely marvelous.

"This is my country, and I love it, and I have the right —the responsibility —to protest its imminent destruction; the right to speak out against the mockery that's being made of my country's Constitution." He raised his fist, "I *will* speak out. I *will* protest and let anyone *try* to stop me, to deny my Constitutional right of dissent, my right to speak —"

League Ladies were running toward the stage. Everything was happening so fast that Daphne saw only a blur.

Two enormous men in business suits, and an equally gigantic woman in a pink, stretch-jersey pants-suit were striding down the aisle to the stage.

"What'll we do? What'll we *do,* Muffy?" League Ladies whimpered to one another. Some members and their husbands had begun to climb the steps to the stage. Hal went on:

"The unmistakable parallel is before us, to be seen plainly. The warning is sounding its knell; a replay of Hitler's Germany could unfold tomorrow —even now *is* unfolding, ominously. Throughout the world we —*we* are the Ugly Americans! shall we turn back the clock to that despicable time of jingoistic imperialism? Are we going to continue to regress to —"

"Omigod, omigod, Troozie, we've *got* to do something." The League Ladies were wringing their hands. The two Business Suits and the Pink Pants Suit were surrounding Hal. Daphne recognized the three. They were a former Bingham undertaker and his wife and son who had "made it" back in the heyday of steel with their overpriced, ostentatious ethnic funerals, and then had moved to Briarwood to partake of the Good Life therein, to "knob-knob," as Pink Pants Suit had been heard to describe their new life, "with the Big Time hoi polloi."

Each more than six feet tall, the three of them bent over Hal now, holding their arms rigidly at their sides, clenching and unclenching their fists.

"Are we to understand," the undertaker shouted, "did I hear you compare the president of the United States to Adolf

Hitler?''

"You're goddam right I did," cried Hal unflinchingly.

Daphne said to herself idiotically, *"I doubt if I have ever seen a larger stomach or buttocks —certainly not encased in pink."*

Phil and Harry Walker, with a third man, all wearing CitAct tee shirts, were mounting the stage steps.

It's Whitie Banyar! Daphne realized, the ex-boxer from Truschel County who had wanted to "put on the gloves and duke it out" with Hal if he didn't keep campaign promises.

Now Whitie was crouching and feinting, dancing around the three behemoths. Phil and Harry stepped between Hal and the red-faced triumvirate. Photographers' flash bulbs went off.

Video crews from two TV channels were taping the scenario.

Drew Burgess and Alan Cope were pressed back into the gray velour backdrop curtain, forgotten.

"Adolf Hitler? Did you say Adolf *Hitler"* the undertaker wheezed apoplectically.

"You're *goddamn right* I did," Hal asserted again.

League President, Muffy Palmer turned to Daphne and hissed, "I saw you come in with him. I *saw* you. *You* do something!"

"I'll do something." Daphne walked quickly to the stage where Whitie, his superbly muscled frame menacing, was still feinting, as Harry and Phil closed off Hal almost entirely from his irate accusers.

She pulled Hal's coat and said, "Let's go, Hal. These three are gonna punch you out."

"We're civilized?" Pink Pants Suit screamed, *"We're civilized!"*

Hal sang out, "Three million people living on the streets in this, the richest country in the world. That's civilized! Millions living at poverty level, and thirty percent of them are children! that's civilized, all right, sure, that's civilized," he said disgustedly. "You people want to dismantle what few social programs are left and call yourselves civilized —"

"Hal, come on." Daphne started up the ramp to the back door behind the stage.

Phil and Harry walked with Hal to the ramp.

Whitie darted and crouched, still in a replay of that blizzard-cursed petitioning day when they all had first met. Then he too turned and followed, and they walked out to the parking lot.

Hal was laughing. "Wow! What a denouement!" he chuckled.

"You were wonderful!" Daphne held his hand.

"Way ta go, Hal," said Harry.

"You guys came just in time," Daphne turned toward Phil and Harry, then greeted Whitie and introduced him.

"They knew better than to lay a hand on me," Hal said, laughing again. "The whole thing was wonderful, wonderful!" He wiped his eyes. Other CitAct members rushed over to him. They all decided to go to the Holiday Inn and splurge on pizza and beer, to celebrate.

Hal, still laughing, tried to get his car started, but the motor didn't turn over at all. It was dead. After repeated tries he ran over and asked the driver of the chartered bus to wait while Whitie, a mechanic, took a look at the motor.

"Distributor coil leads are cut," Whitie said. "It didn't break, it was cut." He showed Hal the snipper marks.

Hal and Daphne rode the bus home after they all had pizza. Now there would be the added expense of having the car towed all the way back to Bingham or a Briarwood garage. Luckily, the insurance would cover part of it. Politicians slashing tires or disabling vehicles was not unheard of, of course, but a cut wire to the distributor coil, inside the cap? It seemed more sinister, somehow, than slashed tires. But on the bus they sang and laughed all the way home.

CHAPTER TWENTY-NINE

The Mental Health and Mental Retardation office of Glenview State Hospital was in the building where Tad Shaeffer's Special Education classes were held. The ugly old stone ziggaurat had been a tuberculosis sanitorium from the turn of the century into the nineteen thirties. Its long south-facing enclosed porches were the areas that Daphne planned to bid on. Harriet and Norm were standing in the murky entrance hall. Norm was wearing a helmet and was very pale, thin and hollow-eyed. He scarcely spoke to Daphne.

"It's our pal, Daphne, Norm. Can't you say 'Hi'?"

Harriet's eyes were dull. Her wonderful hair had even lost its healthy glint.

"Hi, Norm, my man. How's the back-stroke coming along?" Daphne offered.

To Harriet, she explained, "I'm here to be interviewed for the sun porches project. They want to start mainstreaming some of these residents, and they want parlors fixed up where social encounters can take place. Dating and things —so that individuals who've been institutionalized all their lives can get the feeling — uh —feel less institutionalized in social situations —"

Harriet was staring.

Daphne thought, *I sound like I'm presenting a paper at a meeting. Harriet's eyes. What's the matter with her eyes?*

"Sounds good. Hope you get the job. You sure could use it, right?"

"That's the understatement of the year, Harriet," Daphne tried to continue in a bantering tone.

Norm lurched listlessly out of the building; he was dragging one leg. Harriet and Daphne watched him for a few moments.

"He's much worse, Daphne. I don't think he even knew you. Don't be upset. He's been having seizures. The operation didn't help. He gets wild and he won't eat, and his sight seems to be impaired. Tad says it's impossible to keep track of him, to be responsible for him, for his exercising and everything. He's out of the swim program altogether —he and Stephanie Burgess were the top swimmers. I don't know what to do. If he can't come to Special Ed every day, how can I keep working? He'd die if he couldn't live at home with me." The words came tumbling out.

"Daphne, he's my little boy. He's my adorable boy." Harriet fell against Daphne and sobbed, then recovered herself and stood up straight. "God knows *you* don't need this, Daph."

Daphne was about to say something loving, but fearing to sound sentimental, changed her mind. She shook Harriet's shoulder.

"Don't give up, pal. Where there's life, there's hope, Harriet. You have us, your friends. Always know that."

The two friends avoided the obligatory hug. It seemed out of place, too tragic.

"Right! Good luck on the job."

Harriet turned abruptly and walked out of the building.

At that moment two spiky dried-out sansevieria plants by the door become imprinted into Daphne's mind forever; forever after that day she would hate sansevieria plants.

She walked down a long hallway. Painters were putting a coat of cheerful cerulean blue over the khaki-colored walls.

Khaki is a color that came out of the Boer War, Daphne mused to herself, *but it sounds like it came from the British Raj —sounds like an Indian word —Hindi, maybe —*

She felt Harriet's words. Words, words. Words on the answering machine. Words everywhere. Harriet was hurting. Her words, "My adorable boy."

Adorable boy.

Norm was Harriet's adorable boy.

His father had vanished after Norm was born.

Harriet had no one.

I'm really starting to lose it, Daphne thought.

The MHMR office, with its many up-to-date computers and high-tech furnishings, was deserted.

Now what? Daphne wondered as she sat down in a hideous bright orange fiberglass rocking chair, a left-over from some architectural firm's nineteen sixties renovation.

Several men walked by, bouncing elastic-strung rubber balls on wooden paddles.

Two young women in shapeless dresses skipped into the office, then skipped out again.

A creature hobbled into the office on stilt-like heels three and a half-inches high.

"M'ulpy? Jawapntmnt?"

With its inch and a half magenta talons, the creature stabbed at files stacked on the desk.

How does it put on its clothing? Daphne wondered.

The creature squinted at Daphne from beneath a sticky-looking glob of black hair. Daphne explained the purpose of her visit. The creature nodded. Enormous jet-beaded hoop earrings swung against its hollow pimply rouged cheeks. The neckline of its crotch-length, purple jersey cocktail dress appeared to be split to its navel. It began composing its features to speak again. Daphne leaned forward.

"Dunahll Bsadadrnksheen," it said.

"Pardon me?"

"Dunahll bsadadrnsksheen!" the creature shouted.

It grabbed an emery board from a jar full of peacock feathers and rasped savagely at its talons.

Then it bent toward a huge computer console. Two sallow, dumpling-like lumps lolled about in the low neck of its garment. They may have been breasts.

It began to type.

"Down the hall." It's saying *"Down the hall,"* Daphne reasoned.

She could see people filing through a doorway near a soft-drink machine. A rather short pleasant-faced, bearded man stepped out of the doorway, smiled at her and held out his hand.

"Nick Dellavalle. You're the decorator?"

"Yes, I'm Daphne Singleton, the designer."

"Oops. Designer. I guess I goofed."

"No big deal." Daphne smiled.

"Come on in. We're having the Convivial Spaces discussion today."

"I'm glad I found you, Nick. The —uh —person in the office does not appear to speak English, and —"

"Oh, you mean Wanda. Wanda in Administration. She's Dr. Arlington's —that's the director's —girlfriend. She takes some getting used to."

Nick directed Daphne to a seat. A semi-circle of folding chairs was arranged in the gymnasium-like space.

Why is it that every major event in my life seems to take place on a folding chair? Daphne wondered.

Nick spoke first.

"I want to thank you all for coming today. This is a big planning day. I know you all have busy schedules, so we'll get right down to business —"

A young woman of twenty —maybe twenty-two —nubile and beautiful with glossy brown hair and glowing, rosy skin, slouched through the ring of chairs and over to Nick and put her arms around his neck. Her shabby skirt brushed her ankles.

"I love you, Nick," she said, nuzzling his cheek. Nick's face reddened as he gently removed her arms from around his neck.

"O.K., Elaine," he said, "you go out to the playground now, O.K.? They're gonna play jacks at the picnic area, today, and have races. You wanta be in a race? Go ahead now."

"All right, Nick." She ambled listlessly across the gymnasium. All eyes followed the lovely willowy form.

A psychologist and a psychiatrist next recited the specifications for equipping the glassed-in porches in which the retarded adults could socialize, have dates, experience less institutional living and even have sexual encounters.

"A few of the parlor seating areas should be somewhat private, to permit some intimacy," the psychologist said.

Daphne took notes.

"Sex areas," she wrote.

Then the psychiatrist spoke directly to her.

"Nix on any red flocked wallpaper or velvet couches, though," he snickered.

The others exchanged glances.

Did this man actually think Daphne was going to propose tasteless, brothel-like furnishings such as that? Was this place going to be Glenview State Bordello? Daphne was astonished at the insensitivity of his remark —of the very idea.

After a long period during which nurses, aides, orderlies and other staff offered suggestions and outlined needs and restrictions — no glass topped tables, metal lamps only, vinyl covered *everything,* pictures bolted to the walls, no throw-rugs —"We just want your average homey look" —the meeting was closed.

Daphne prepared to measure the huge spaces but noticed a group of seven or eight young retarded adult men lined up at the porch doorway. "They want to shake hands with you," Nick explained. "Don't let it bother you." Daphne got along well with Norm, of course, but he was only twelve years old. These were men.

"Well," she said, "should I shake hands?"

Nick looked surprised.

"Sure," he said.

"I just wanted to understand what your policy is here, in regard to —" Daphne began.

"I think you'll find that they're pretty much just a human bunch of nice, polite guys. They knew you were coming. They're just excited about the new mainstreaming idea. They're wearing ties, you'll notice, and have taken pains with their hair. Just think of them as fellow humans —"

He strode away.

Was he being sarcastic? Maybe she had spent too much time around Traci, and Allison, and all those Mrs. Hartley types. Maybe she was losing touch.

Daphne got out her measuring tape, then shook hands all the way down the line. The group followed her through every step of the measuring of the first porch, and turned the corner with her, and followed as she measured the second sixty-foot-long space. They took turns holding the end of the tape where she told them to stand on it.

There was some shoving and jostling.

"Dummy!" they called each other.

After handshakes all around again she said good-bye to the smiling well-mannered group and drove back to her office, mulling over the day's events. The hospital residents had seemed bright and a good bit more civilized than some of the administrators.

The funding available for the hospital project had to be expended before the end of the fiscal year —six weeks off —and payment was to be made only after the furnishings were installed. It was a very tight budget and time frame.

She had seen no other bidders. Maybe they had come on another day. She hoped she had a chance at the job; it was a lot of work to do on speculation, but she had to at least try.

CHAPTER THIRTY

The Shelter was cleaned and ready for the Open House. Traci was off to Las Vegas with Allison on the board-approved inspection tour of innovations in women's shelters and centers. The responsibility for the Open House was left to Harriet, Daphne and Ellen. This authority consisted of one scrawled, socio-speak dictum in the Daybook: "A disordered value-base implements dichotomous retrenchment motivation, impacting negatively upon the community as significant other."

Recruited by Harriet to help with the event, Lorene read Traci's Sanskrit aloud and said, "Translated, she sayin' 'you cats better scrub hell outa this joint while we at Caesar's Palace or I'll whup yo-all's ass'."

They all walked through the Shelter, checking on last minute details. A neat, hand-lettered sign on Traci's locked office door, tacked below her brass name plate and Chief Executive Director plaque, announced:

Behind this door is someone who cares.

"Bullshit!" Harriet snorted, ripping down the sign and rattling the door knob. "Tax payers ought to get a look at this cushy office."

She tried Allison's skeleton keys in the lock. The sixth try opened the door. Harriet swung it open wide — *"Voila!"* she crowed as they all stared in at the shimmering penthouse decor.

Allison's door to her tidy office stood open, as did Bobbye's; her office was neat and efficient-looking but *sans* Bobbye. *Damn it*, Daphne said to herself, *in spite of all that's happened, I still miss her.*

The PineSol fumes gradually dissipated; punch bowls, cracker trays and cookie plate after cookie plate were set in place, and flowers were arranged on the tables, but there was no sign of the Women's Club volunteer committee who were responsible for the fruit and cheese.

The last member of the Shelter Board Open House Committee to arrive, Hal stationed himself at his assigned location by the front door as visitors began to pull into the parking lot. They entered the Shelter hesitantly, in twos and threes, and peered with great interest into the offices and parlor, then climbed to the upper floors, where residents and their children stared back as frankly as they were stared at.

The general demeanor of most of the visitors —all women except for several male church leaders — was that of the genuinely concerned. When Hal or Harriet sensed curiosity verging on the prurient or the sensational, such as giggling comments about "the inmates," references to "the battered ladies," or remarks such as "Is this where the raped ladies smoke pot?" such remarks were swiftly dealt with:

"When a woman comes here, often with broken jaw or teeth, bruised in body and spirit, drugs usually are the furthest thing from her mind," the visitors were told calmly.

"The injured woman —somebody's mother, wife, sister, daughter — is seeking safety —a refuge. She is dealing with profoundly traumatic experiences that we try our best to alleviate. We offer her temporary security as well as more long-term solutions to her problems."

Carla Campagna and Liz Heckman were less diplomatic, responding to flippant comments by saying, "Isn't that a trivializing view of women's despair? Violence against women is a serious matter. The Sojourner Shelter is not a ladies' club, no matter what you might have heard."

The Open House drew carload after carload of visitors. For whatever reason —response to titillating media accounts of rapes, or talk-show guests' accounts of childhood molestation or just word-of-mouth about the Shelter — it was evident that public awareness was growing; Bingham Countians certainly were being educated and informed. That could only be to the good, Harriet, Hal and Daphne decided. Their efforts would not be lost after all; their long struggle *had* accomplished something.

Not as encouraging, however, was the Midfield Township Women's Club fruit-and-cheese committee of eight who finally filed into the Shelter parlor wearing elaborate, low-cut cocktail dresses and high-heeled "slides" — what James wryly called

"Fuck-me shoes," —and bearing a small slab of brick cheese and one platter of apple slices. They had brought along their heavily-made-up teenaged daughters who stood along the parlor walls and watched nervously as their mothers cut up the pound-and-a-half of brick cheese and, with a spoon, dribbled lemon juice on the apple slices. Each committee member performed one task, as directed by the Committee-Head: "Okay, Betty, now the knife. Okay, Ginny, get your lemon juice ready. That's it, Rachel, hand the spoon to Chris," and so on. They had brought no plate for the cheese, so a runner had to be dispatched to the Shelter kitchen upstairs for a platter.

Talking about it later that night with Hal in her living room, her rare collector's recording of Debussy's *Iberia Suite* playing softly, Daphne agreed that the cheese ladies certainly were a far cry from the Pankhurst or the Grimké sisters.

"The Pankhursts they definitely are *not*, I concur; at that rate women *still* wouldn't have the vote."

"I tried to draw out a couple of the teenagers," Hal said, "to get their impression of the Shelter, to see what their perceptions are, and they haven't a clue as to what the Sojourner Shelter is about or what their mothers were doing with that cheese. To those future bimbos, it was some vague club event they were forced to attend, like those Gessler Museum teas where they hand out popcorn balls to poor, Black —I guess that's redundant —kids. Today one of the daughters, the one with all the blonde, frizzed-up hair —that huge mass of hair —started to 'come on' to me, for Pete's sake!"

"Oh, I know. I know. They think that's what they're *supposed* to do. You saw what kind of role models those kids have. How are they ever going to mature into self-defined assertive women —women who know exactly who they are, and won't be made into dupes to any male —who can be women who will hold public office, women who will have equal responsibility in making a decision as to who's going to wage nuclear war or *not* wage nuclear war, if it takes eight of them to get a piece of cheese sliced? And showing up dressed like B-Girls besides. It's so disheartening that I'm embarrassed and ashamed for them."

"Speaking of embarrassed and ashamed, I hate to say 'I told you so,' but —"

"Well, don't say it, then, Hal. Don't say it!"

"I feel that it's important to remind you of a conversation we had last March or April, just after we met, during which you said that the Ilse Koch type of woman, the female counterpart of male Nazi S.S. types, is 'one in a couple of million,' I believe you said."

"Was it when we were at the Copper Bottom, that night after your Thomas Jefferson Talk? Our first date, so-to-speak?"

"Yes. That night. Pre-Traci Bilson-Bloom."

"I see what this is leading up to. *Touché mon ami, mon amour.* It's Traci-as-the-Ilse-Koch-person we discussed that night. I see your point, Hal. Maybe Traci's a one-in-a-million woman too —as I so steadfastly contended Ilse Koch was. I appreciate your not having thrown it up to me before this. But you're sort of thrashing me while I'm down, now, aren't you? I told you before that I weep sometimes — out of discouragement and frustration about these disasters — about what's happening to Allison —about Ora's stroke —brought on by Traci's action I'm almost certain —about the methodical dismantling of our terrific shelter programs — about the joke-people who make up the Shelter Board majority. I cry, that's what. I cry that there should *be* such women!"

"Don't cry. Good heavens. Don't cry, please. That won't help. Oh, Christ! Don't cry. Come here." He held out his hand.

"Oh. Oh. Oh. 'Dwate Big Mans sees any sign of emotion —tears —if any slobbering begins —it's time to call the police. Call the police, then, Hal. I'm crying."

"I didn't mean to bring you to this —not to tears."

"Well, if you say some stinking, patronizing thing, I will hate you."

"It's a worn-out line, but you're *so* cute when you're outraged."

The gin and tonic she hurled splashed onto his forehead and

glasses and ran onto his shirt front. He took off his glasses and cleaned them, then wiped his face.

"I'll whistle 'On The Mall' or 'El Capitán' or even 'Colonel Bogey's March,'" he placated.

"Oh, shut up," she sobbed.

"Do you want to fuck?"

"Yes," she blubbered.

They walked up the narrow stairway with their arms around each other.

After the Shelter Open House, Ellen drove to the Doncaster CorBlimey Steak House and Lounge. "Newly-Remodelled," the garish sign out front had said for over eleven years. She was going to be late again. Gino, the owner, would snarl as he always did, even if it was just a few minutes past nine.

Gino wanted to snag late-dinner business from The Bingham Blue Barn Players' audience. Ellen had been hired for a hundred dollars a night plus tips, to play the piano on weekends from nine P.M. until one A.M., starting with the after-dinner-liqueur crowd from the next-to-the-last dinner seating. The patrons sipped their Bailey's Irish Cream or their Peach Schnapps or Kahlua at the long bar, or seated at the little deuce tables scattered around the piano, while Rita, the bartender, kept the thimblefuls of liqueur flowing. At five dollars a thimble, Gino could clear a quick couple of hundred from the bar alone in that brief interval before the Blue Barn disgorged its ravenous audience.

At ten o'clock, Ellen was scheduled to take a break. When the next wave of patrons pushed and shoved their way in, the bar would quickly become jammed, and the last of the Schnapps crowd would leave, while Rita began expertly slinging mixed drink orders for the next dinner seating.

Gino watched Rita carefully, for she was a cocaine addict. When bartending pressure increased —Gino was too cheap to hire an extra bartender for weekends —Rita would slip behind the piano and around the corner to the Ladies' Room for a snort, during which time Gino would sneak her tips into the cash register. After about two minutes he would go and bang on the Ladies' Room door and shout, "Are you gonna come out of that goddam can, or *not?*"

Ellen had been instructed to swing into very loud Oscar Peterson-type stride pieces when Gino started his banging and yelling. The regulars were accustomed to this nightly routine, which Gino, being somewhat deaf himself, thought no one else could hear.

The CorBlimey Front-of-the-House, with the bowing, fawning Gino, its dim lighting, many mirrors, red and black and gold amalgam of nautical-English-pub-in-a-medieval-castle kitsch decor, its dining room's starched white napery, overloaded table tops with tinkling-ice-in-crystal, its excessive air conditioning, gave new meaning to the expression "diametric opposite" when compared to the Back-of-the-House. There, manager and recently-appointed chef, Herb Haselas, ran something like the slave-ship scene in *Ben Hur.*

At frequent wait-staff meetings, in a spirit of avuncular *bonhomie* and morale-boosting camaraderie, he would wave in the air a sheaf of job applications and threaten, "See these? These are from applicants who'd give their tits and their balls to have your job, so think about it the next time you fags and cunts are plannin' to come in late or start draggin' your asses."

The CorBlimey dinner menu was not extensive. Chef Haselas's interesting but over-priced entrees weeded out all but Bingham's and Briarwood's most affluent diners, almost all of whom, when sated with "Castle Coc au Vin" or "Jouster's Special Trencher of Boeuf Steak," were generous tippers.

Elwood, the muscular and conceited cross-eyed *sous chef,* only slightly more convivial than Herb, expected to engage in behind-the-walk-in-cooler carnal knowledge with every waitress. At regular intervals, loud whoops and shrieks and the sound of slapped flesh punctuated the kitchen clatter.

The skinny tattooed *plongeur,* Rudy, the soul of the Back-of-the-House, hopped and darted, Shiva-like, before his altar of stainless steel sinks, brandishing his scrapers and whirring, rotating brushes. His fairly frequent hung-over absences spelled misery to the wait-staff who then would have to wash glasses and silverware in between serving their orders. Their sacred mission was to Not Aggravate Or Cross Rudy. They brought him fudge and Toll House cookies and brownies in the hope that sugar binges would supplant his alcohol cravings.

"Now all I need is a woe-man," the celibate Rudy would chuckle, and "woe" was what womankind meant to Rudy.

Though she spent her fifteen-minute breaks amid the cacophony of the Back-of-the-House, Ellen's main territory was the Front-of-the-House. Playing jazz and blues entirely by ear enabled her to comply with most patrons' requests, once they realized that she did not play top-forty pop pieces. She "seeded" her large brandy-snifter tip-collector with six or eight one-dollar bills and several fives, for inspiration, on the advice of Harletta Hoskins, one of the friendliest of the CorBlimey waitresses.

Ellen's audience represented a fairly well-mannered age range, mid-thirties through sixties. They requested music ranging from the ragtime of the eighteen eighties and nineties to the standards of the nineteen thirties and forties: Cole Porter, Gershwin, Berlin, Jerome Kern, Errol Garner, Harold Arlen and on through the fifties show tunes, the sixties and the Beatles, Peter, Paul and Mary, Carol King, Burt Bacherach. It was a wide range.

Ellen interjected a few ethnic pieces —"Funiculi, Funicula," or another occasional Tarentella —if she sensed a fairly large group of ethnic diners, and played some light opera as well as Mancini and LeGrand movie themes.

Her tips varied. They could be as much as seventy-five dollars or as little as five, depending on the weather, the general mood, and the size of the crowd.

The inevitable "mellow" patron's request for pizza joint sing-along "Irish Eyes are Smiling" or "MacNamara's Band" she deflected graciously with her Rafe Vaughn-Williams-inspired "Danny Boy" or "Green Sleeves." Her arrangement of "Days of Wine and Roses" with a Chopin Nocturne introduction was surprisingly popular considering this was not a clientele oriented to classical music.

Request for the pop-piece "Feelings" and other pieces that Ellen personally disliked increased at holidays to the extent that she finally lettered and propped by the snifter a small card that said

> *Song Rates*
> "Feelings" $50.00
> "Memories" (from "Cats")$75.00

Well-liquored businessmen became indignant when they read the sign, their sense of humor diminishing in inverse ratio to time spent drinking at the bar, and waiting, voraciously hungry, for a table in the dining room. Ellen could see that, in addition to being a tremendous appetite stimulant, alcohol also could be a depressant.

Once when a patron unsteadily approached the piano and asked, blearily, "Do you know 'What I Did For Love'?" and Ellen had jovially replied, "No, what *did* you do for love?" he reached into the brandy snifter, retrieved his five-dollar-bill and went and sulked alone in his booth, and no apology would placate him. He left, finally, scowling, without ordering dinner.

This brought Gino running. "Whatsa mat'? Whatsa mat'? Dijou smart-mouth Mr. Devane? Watch your smart-mouthin'!"

Gino's mafia and bookie cronies were to receive special, deferential treatment and certain of them even ate and drank "for free." The staff were supposed to know this. Harletta Hoskins was the most well-versed on The Code. She helped Ellen to learn to whom to cater for the best tips and how to avoid Gino's wrath.

Sometimes there were problems with women patrons. One young woman, the wife of a much older Gino-crony, took an intense dislike to Ellen. The woman's once-handsome, former-musical-comedy-performer husband, still in possession of a very fine tenor-baritone voice, chatted occasionally with Ellen about music and requested opera arias and show-tunes from time to time. He would nod and smile when she played "La Donna é Mobile" or "Una Furtiva Lagrima," or "Nessun Dorma."

One night, while she played a *Fiddler on The Roof* medley, the singer quickly left his booth and went and stood by the piano and sang, spontaneously, marvelously, "If I Were a Rich Man," thrilling the other diners —and Ellen.

The singer's wife, in her red Joan Collins-style puff-shouldered jumpsuit, glared, enraged, at Ellen from the cave-like tufted red vinyl booth, her white face gleaming like a red-mouthed disembodied head. Thereafter the couple chose a table far from the piano, and the singer avoided Ellen.

What a pity, Ellen thought, as she looked at herself reflected in the mirrored wall opposite the piano, seeing her short-cropped brown hair, her heavy eyebrows, her home-made silver-sequinned blouse that ill suited her pudgy cheeks. *She's much more beautiful than I, and he seems very attentive to her and their little son, yet the man's obvious passion for music is a threat to her. Instead of sharing that passion with him, she feels insecure and transfers her rage to me.*

Watching the couple across the dining room Ellen felt — uncharacteristically in the midst of a music performance —a stab of sorrow. She contemplated what had happened: The kind of innocent, joyous communication that she had had with the aging singer —through the music alone —was one of the most rare and sublime of human experiences: the honest giving and melding of art forms, all other personal considerations forgotten. Yet the unmusical often were mystified, confused, misled by the phenomenon, were suspicious of it; instead of speaking to them, the music closed them off.

"Just ignore it, Hon," Harletta said, "They're not important to Gino —well, *she's* not. There won't be no trouble."

Ellen started now to play, softly, dreamily, a meandering Bill Evans-style medley, beginning with Michele Le Grand's "Noelle's Theme" and ending with "Tenderly." She thought about Karl, his harmonica, his exuberant, whistling, rhythmic presence in their home —gone now.

Karl had returned home once after he fled on his bicycle that day —Ellen called it the Spilled Water Day —had packed his duffle bag, gotten his money and departed for Colorado without saying goodbye to his father. They had received one post card:

Am odd-jobbing it Don't worry Mom am eating right Hi
to Kitty, Kelly, Kirk, Kathy and Mark.

First to leave had been Kitty. She would be staying the summer at the College, where she had found a job. Now Karl. Even though Larry was adjusting to being laid-off, was less depressed and talked to her more often, Ellen felt acutely, with bone-deep aching, the absence of her children. These wrenching separations were a part of motherhood that society glossed over, ignored. Was some dog or cat or sheep or goat or bird "instinct" supposed to get children conceived, born and loved, and was the same mandated, atavistic process supposed to sever them from their mother painlessly, instinctively, like the plastic wraps from sweetrolls or a loaf of bread?

Harletta bent down and handed Ellen a ten-dollar bill. "Wow, Hon, look what that couple by the mirrored wall sent over. They want to know if you know a piece called 'Lush Life.'"

Ellen smiled at the couple, who were new to the CorBlimey, and nodded, held up the ten and mouthed "Thank you," tucked the money into the brandy snifter, and began the Billy Strayhorn classic, "Lush Life," one of her all-time jazz favorites.

CHAPTER THIRTY-ONE

"If I can't have them brioches, then I don't want no carriages at all," Mrs. Hartley said petulantly. Romantic rides to parties in barouches were increasingly popular with affluent Bingham countians.

It was her first day home from the hospital, and Edith Hartley was completing phone call number five to Daphne. Someone else had pre-empted the carriages she wanted, and all she could have get was a pair of stage coaches, and she thought they would be hot and closed-in.

Ellen soothed her: "Just think —it'll be a coach-and-four — so romantic-looking — really classic — and you can leave the windows open."

"Well, I suppose that's true. But the carriages only have two horses apiece, and the invitations already have a brioche printed on them. And them washerwomen aren't working out for the wash house.

"I can get Fern and Melba for seventy-five each, but that Lorene —well, that darkie doesn't know her *place*, I can tell *you!* I offered her a hundred, and *she* said *no* amount of money would get *her* to put on those '*effing*' —she actually said the 'F' word —slave costumes. Can you imagine! What awful language! I offered her a hundred, and when I offered to pay those two darkie youngsters of hers to open my poodroosie doors, out in the garden, don'tcha know, Lorene said she'd see me in East Hell, first. If that's not an uppity darkie, I don't know what *is!*"

Goodbye Civil Rights, hello Jim Crow, thought Daphne as she finally hung up, after agreeing to talk to Lorene again. She was even going to try to get Lorene's nephew, Nelson, to be an extra footman.

Gus Quip's fee for "gettin' trussed up like a real dude" reportedly was in the neighborhood of three hundred, plus a week's paid vacation at Epcot Center during which he would stay at the Hartley's Florida condo for free.

The Hartley house was shaping up, but the last minute details were overwhelming. The paper-hanging was incomplete.

251

There were draperies to be hung. The catering was a nightmare. Loaves and Fishes cuisine was too common and " —I've never even been to the CorBlimey," Bronwen Burgess said. The whole project was too close to being a replay of the Krock disaster for comfort.

And Daphne's Glenview Hospital drawings were suffering. Her other jobs had to be turned over to James, and his overtime pay wiped out most of the profit.

Bobbye wanted "reparations" made on her house, and Hal needed campaign help. It was overwhelming. Daphne was not sleeping well, and could not eat anything but yogurt.

The last of the carpet of emerald green sod was being rolled onto the side terrace as she drove up the curving entrance driveway to "Hartfeld" the following day. Amazing changes had taken place in the landscape. Five mature trees stood to the left of the driveway, and six more to the right, beautifully interspersed with dogwood and small evergreens where the week before there had been an empty brown field. More velvet green swaths completed the front and right lawn areas.

Daphne drove through the beautiful antique arched-top wrought-iron gate whose doors stood open, supported by handsome stone pillars. Once the sod had taken hold, sections of iron fence would be installed, stretching forty feet or so on either side of the pillars, defining the elegant brick and stone house with its white pillars and cornices. Gus Quip, on loan from the Burgesses, was directing the landscape architect's design, even to the shallow walls of the English-style haha surrounding the property like a dry moat to control the flock of sheep the Hartleys had ordered.

Now all they need is Marie Antoinette Hartley in a dairy-maid's get-up and a bunch of milk cans grouped around a fake barn, thought Daphne.

. She could see the small sheep barn under construction across the adjoining back field. The dome of the Krock's garden belvedere could be seen to the left.

Walking out of the front entrance doorway and onto the

252

planter-box-lined brick entrance terrace was an unfamiliar shapely woman. She pointed to one of the white-painted Versailles-style planter boxes. Three nurserymen heaved a dirt-balled mature dwarf maple tree into it. Daphne parked her car and walked toward the front door.

"Hi-dee-hi," said the woman. It was Edith Hartley! She looked about thirty-five pounds lighter.

"Hardly knew me, huh?" she smirked. "I lost over twenty-five pounds in the hospital, but I'm so short, you'd think it was more."

"I honestly wouldn't have known you!" Daphne stared. "You look terrific!" she said, truthfully.

They walked into the foyer. In the curving stairwell, working on a scaffold, paperhangers slid the edge of a panel of lovely Chinese scenic wallpaper to the ceiling. Its hand-painted pastel flowers grew down the wall as the pasted panel unfolded and was skillfully brushed into place. Wallcoverings were among the wonders of the design profession; Daphne never ceased to be amazed at paper hangers' sleight-of-hand transformation.

She turned to Mrs. Hartley, "They promised to have this area completed by the end of the day."

"Oh, that's good. It's beautiful," Edith said; her speech was somewhat slurred and she seemed subdued. She had a swollen, bruised lower lip that her heavy make-up did not completely conceal. She drew her collar up around her chin, "Doctor's here, in the library. He wants to talk to you."

Daphne studied her client. She looked shapely and youthful in body, but what had happened to her face?

"Yowza, yowza, yowza, young lady." Doctor Hartley did not take his eyes from Daphne's chest as he shook her proffered hand.

"What I want to know-dee-oh-doe is whether your painters are going to show up here tomorrow or do we get a new crew — croop-a-doop?"

"They are finishing the last of the interior doors in the paint shop, Doctor, and all of the other wood work in the house is

253

completed. Two more paperhangers will come in to complete the dining room tomorrow. When they finish, all of the doors will be installed at once."

"Door trim sure looks unfinished to me."

"They have been given a three-coat stripped-pine-effect finish," Daphne explained.

"You okayed the plan, Ernest —the lighter finish shows off them decorator folds better —"

Dr. Hartley turned and stared at his wife. "Well, well, well," he interrupted, "Goddamit to Hell. That's a pome, Edith."

Without another word he turned and walked out of the room. Fear nudged at Daphne. What was it? Was it that voice?

Walking together to the car, Daphne asked Edith Hartley, "What's the highest you'll go for Lorene?"

"One-fifty. Twenty-five each for the pickaninnies."

"I'll talk to Lorene."

"I should never have insisted on doing the fund-raiser," Edith said.

"Well, it's more politic for someone else to do it than if the candidate's wife were to put on the party, don't you think? You're gonna be O.K. You never planned on being sick."

"No, I didn't."

"It *has* been a big job to undertake, but everything's shaping up."

"Yes." Edith Hartley looked more pensive than silly, now that the authority of her weight —most of it had been through her torso —was gone. She had a waistline now, and shapely breasts.

"Yes," she murmured. "I buttered my bread and now I'm lying in it."

She's smarter than she lets on, Daphne thought as she pulled into Stop And Spend to stock up on yogurt. *But the doctor must be an alkie. Or he's just cracking up. His voice is too deep to be Peabrain. But the nuttiness —the off-the-wall cracks —it* could *be.*

The June sun beat down. The air was very humid, though strangely clear. Steel mill pollution, once claimed by the EPA as its chief concern, was now being replaced by water and soil contamination from the region's electronic and chemical manufacturers, and who-knows-what nuclear and hospital-waste pollution?

Inside the freezing Stop and Spend, Daphne started filling her cart with a six-pack of diet Pepsi for James, who was working late on the hospital drawings. She saw Ellen at the end of the aisle, at the hamburger counter. Kathy hung from the back of the child seat where Mark sat, thus unbalancing the cart and tipping the front end upward. Ellen's eyes were dark-circled. Pounding Muzak proclaimed "You do something to me!" over the din of the frosty cool super market.

"I've been trying to reach you," Ellen said. "Have you heard the news? Allison's back. *Without* Traci. They weren't due in town for three more days. She just left Traci in some bar and flew back here. Said she's had enough. Traci wanted to hang around the hotel pool and different bars all the time, and she was picking up men *and* women, and doing coke and other drugs and...."

"Woo, slow down, slow down. What about touring the women's centers and shelters out there."

"Oh, they didn't ever get to *that,* Allison said."

Ellen lifted Mark down to the floor.

"Where is she now?"

"Allison? She's at her office. No one's heard from Traci."

"Holy Toledo. *Now* what? Drugs? Drinking? Sex? Maybe now some attention will be paid, Ellen. Maybe now there's hope for a —"

It was at this moment, while they were stuck in the long checkout line, that Kathy and Mark began to run in circles by the cigarette and candy shelves loudly chanting, spelling out "B-S-T-R-D! B-S-T-R-D! S-H-I-T! F-U-C-K-! F-U-C-K!" and grabbing Reese's Peanut Butter Cups and loading M and Ms packages into the cart while they ran through their gamut of swear-word spelling. Daphne moved over to the Express line.

"Got to get back to my office, Ellen, I'll call you." She walked out of the store with Mark's "poop poop poop" — shouted at the top of his lungs —resounding over the Muzak. *How* do *women live through that period of their lives?* Daphne wondered. Ellen's patience, and her unflagging hope were astonishing.

The phone was ringing when Daphne unlocked her kitchen door. She answered it with foreboding. But it was Hal.

"Can you pick me up? I've had an accident." He sounded out-of-breath. "I couldn't steer the car at all! It just veered off the road, barely missing two cars. I side-swiped another car and hit a pole. Remember Porky's Diner? I'm calling from there. I think my car's totalled, but *I'm* O.K."

When Daphne was about a mile from Porky's Diner, she saw the tow truck and Hal's car. The car door had a huge dent and broken window. "It's the tie-rod," Hal said. "The tie-rod was sawn almost clear through. Then when I was this far out of town it just let go and —"

"Yer lucky you wasn't killed —" the tow truck man said. "Wasn't you the one with the distributor coil trouble? Somebody don't *like* you, Buddy."

Driving back to Bingham, Daphne said, "Somebody *don't* like you, all right, Buddy. What'll we *do?*"

"I'm lucky to be living within walking distance of the college. Now I'll have to find another car, fast. I'm supposed to be on statewide on the PBIX Network Wednesday. At least the public broadcast people recognize third parties."

Daphne put her hand on his knee. "I'm sorry, Hal —sorry you're having this trouble. We're so lucky you're not hurt."

"Well, dammit *you* could have been in that car too —in the smashed-up passenger seat —killed! Killed!"

"Do you feel like giving up? Chucking it all?"

"Yes. For the first time. Yes."

"Really? Truly?"

"Really."

They rode in silence for a while. Then he spoke again. "Dion Simms —the Black lawyer who agreed to run for State Supreme Court on the CitAct ticket —called me last night. He wants to withdraw. Changed his mind! He said he was out petitioning with some of the Truschel people, at the Grange fair —the annual spring agricultural fair they have —where they display the old steam tractors, you know —there was a *huge* turn-out to that fair.!"

Daphne nodded and he went on. "And Ted Mather and those Franzes —Don and Mary Alice —were running the CitAct baked-potato booth, and Ted —I find this *strange* —Ted evidently was talking to the sheriff there, and several deputies and told them that the CitAct Party is *serious* about legalizing pot —that *this* is one of our *missions,* for God's sake. The sheriff told Dion about Ted's *saying* this! Then, later, Ted was actually smoking a joint, in the booth. Dion saw it. He's disgusted, he told me, and definitely quitting.

"Do you believe it? I mean, that Ted talked to the sheriff?"

"Why would Dion lie? He really *wanted* to run. He had a good chance to win, and he has a strong following in the district."

"Maybe the sheriff lied. They think it's all just nutty third party stuff."

"Yes, but losing Dion! It's a serious set-back." Hal put his hand over his eyes. "That lousy Mather. My patience is about worn thin."

"You're going to have to have it out with Ted. This can't go on, Hal. You've worked too hard, and you've risked too much."

"I know. I know. I hate the arguing. It's negative. Negative. when those busloads show up for meetings —I hate to let them down with that negative bickering. I'm always on the defensive."

"But it's *worse* not to fight back, don't you think? To appear to be so laid-back that you're ineffectual?"

"You're right. I'm going to confront him at the meeting

tomorrow. Dan Weldon's coming. The Poly Sci Department at the college represented at a CitAct meeting! A wonderful chance to have an intelligent discussion so beneficial and informative for members and I'll have to be so damned defensive-appearing —"

"You can't let Ted just plough you under like that —without a fight!"

"I know, you're right. You *are* right." Hal reached over and patted Daphne's knee. "Drop me off at Barry Spiegel's, will you? Do you mind?"

"Don't tell me your kids are cooking their own dinner tonight?"

"No, they're going over to eat on campus, at Food For Thought."

"Oh, well. I *thought* it was just too good to be true!" Daphne said sarcastically.

"Let's not get into a fight, O.K.? No bickering?"

"Gonna look at porno-films tonight with Barry? Bet he's into necrophilia and wants you to flip through his back issues of *Snappy Mortician Magazine.*"

"*Where* do you *get* these ideas, Daphne? He *is* my adviser, you know. A very smart man. Very smart and politically astute, believe *me!*"

"Well, somehow I just don't trust him." Daphne squeezed his hand.

Hal jumped out of the car at Barry's and ran up the walk.

CHAPTER THIRTY-TWO

When Daphne stopped at her office to see how James was progressing with the Glenview Hospital drawings, she found that he had completed them and had departed.

The drawings were beautiful — crisp and clear and professional-looking. Floor plans of the sixty-foot-long porches drawn to one-quarter-inch scale, with the wall elevations, necessitated large illustration boards but were impressive and easy to read, and should help in getting her bid accepted.

She had worked within the budget limits, and by shopping and searching, had found a few manufacturers who could supply sturdy, close-out-priced couches and chairs very fast. Lamps and tables were harder to track down, but she was gradually rounding up sources for them.

The phone rang. She started to shut off the answering machine, then changed her mind and waited through four rings. Sure enough, the oily slime seeped out.

"Hi ya, Daphne. I wish what I got was up your twat. That's another pome, cunt. How about suckin' my —" She snapped the dial to "off." She couldn't stand it, just couldn't *stand* it.

She waited a few moments, then looked up Barry Spiegel's number and called it. Barry answered, and she tried to sound matter-of-fact as she asked for Hal.

"Have you and Barry been in the same room together since I dropped you off there?"

"Yes, sure. What's the m —"

"Nothing. Nothing. I can't go into it. Just answer 'yes' or 'no'! Has Barry left the room *at any time* —did he leave just a minute or so ago? This is very important."

"No. No. As you know, I just got here. I just got some news. Barry's been telling me that Merrilee Dobbs —who's in one of his classes —told him that Allison deVries suddenly appeared back in town from Las Vegas —minus Traci. She said it was all sex-and-drugs-and-rock-'n-roll with Traci and —"

"I know. I heard. I was too upset about your accident to tell you. I'll talk to you later."

"Are you O.K., Daphne?"

"Yes. I'm all right. I just figured something out, that's all, and it's cleared up some important questions. Something that's been bothering me. I can't tell you anything more than that, just now."

"Well. All right. I'll talk to you later." Hal hung up.

So, it wasn't Barry. She could eliminate *him*. He wouldn't be likely to take the trouble to rig up a cassette and set a timer or anything complicated. Obscene phone-callers got their perverse kicks from live conversations or the idea of someone listening to them talking. Peabrain had made a live call and it couldn't have been Barry. It was a tremendous relief. She wanted to like Barry. Hal thought highly of him. But then *who* was making those calls?

The six o'clock rays of sunlight slanting in the shop windows —which always made the colors of her petunia-filled planters look so unusually intense —reminded Daphne that it would be twilight by the time she reached home. She was beginning to dislike entering her house —her own *home* —after dark. She wished she had a dog. A big dog.

These nightclubs have everything. You'd never know you were in a desert.

If I take another Percodan along with the rest of this Mai Tai, I can stay high for another couple of hours. Maybe. Probably not quite that long. Not as long as with nose-candy. Allison's been in the Ladies' Room more that fifteen minutes. I'll just pop in this pill, like so, before she gets back.

The two guys at the bar that are lookin' me over aren't bad. They're both really staring. Not that that's unusual. It's probably the tits, and the yellow hair, of course. They can't see my ass or my legs. Now they're takin' a seat at a table over there. Guess they want to check out everything else I've got. Too bad I can't sit at the bar. I'd be mobbed. But at the bar it's always great! I put one foot on the bar rail and one on the floor with a glimpse of thigh and it's like saying, "wanta look? No pants! Wanta get *a look up there?'' Then they start speculating about whether the collar and cuffs match. How many times have I heard **that** one?*

Well, you two dicks, the collar and cuffs do match. If you're muff-divers, you'll be happy to know there's a juicy lemon-yellow pussy available —matches the collar all right, all right, all right. Wow, right now I feel like taking on about five guys. The three at the bar and the other two down at the end table that just came in.

But I'll settle for the two at the table. I like their crotch bulges, and they seem to be quite interested in my bulges. I'll just cross and uncross my legs a couple of times for immm-pact. They're lookin', they're lookin'! Look, Guys, titties! Great big tits. Hey, you dicks! If they come over, I'll let them have a feel.

But where in the fuck is Allison? What a dud she is on a trip! Hardly touches a drink. Wouldn't even get high on pot, let alone the good stuff I stockpiled for this trip. And if she'd half-way showed any interest, she could have got that guy that was comin' on to her last night at the Fast Lane Lounge. Then, with his buddy, we could have done a real foursome. They looked like they'd be good for more than a half-hour —plenty young, plenty of stamina. Wow, the heavy metal group that played there was dynamite! The group playing here today is cool too.

"Another Mai Tai, Miss?"

"Yeah. Yeah. I'll have another one."

*Why not have another one? Why not? Why not? This is living, isn't it? And I don't have a worry in the world about Allison. With the stuff I have on her in her file, the stuff she's told me, she can't make a **move** in any direction, any time —ever.*

I gotta count the money before she comes back, but those guys might get away.

They're talkin'. They ordered more drinks. Bet they're not gonna leave their drinks. I'll just count the money down inside my purse. I've got a bundle under these rubbers. Seven hundred, eight hundred, one thousand, and two more hundred dollar-bills. Getting low. We've blown three thousand in less than four days. But I forgot —Allison spent six-fifty in Penelope's Shame to get those four Spandex outfits for me. So that means twenty-three

hundred and fifty in less than four days. I can't write a check.
Too risky. And I don't want to Quaalude and Percodan it the rest
of this trip. Wish I'd saved some of the good stuff. I'd better call
Earl Roy. I'll get a phone brought to the table.

"Miss! Miss!"

"Hello, Loaves and Fishes and Pentecostacraft. The
Reverend Krock speaking."

"Hello, Earl Roy."

"Je-*hee*-sus. Where *are* you? I thought you were in Las
Vegas."

"I am. I thought I'd check in with you. The internal-
external integrative visogeneric needs in a patient-therapist
disposition immm-pacts on any societal deprivation model that
our mind-exploration motivation might undergo, Earl Roy. You
and I both know you're a child-molester."

"Um. Well."

"It *is* immm-pacting on you, isn't it? You and I have been
oriented towards a non-social object with affective significance."

"I can't *talk* to you now!"

"I need three thousand more, Earl Roy. Wire it to the same
address as before. I have to pay the car rental place, and I'm
staying at a very classy hotel, and I don't want to utilize my Gold
Card at this point in time."

"God a-mighty! I already sent you two thousand! This is a
shake-down. It's sinful. It's blackmail."

"Earl Roy. You are in a non-decisional situation. Don't
forget the things I know —the information I have in your file.
Wire the cash to the same address as before. Goodbye."

Where is Allison? If I give them the nod, those guys'll come
over. I'm gonna go ahead and leave with them. She can just go
back to the room and fuck herself. Here comes the one now. But
I like the other one's pants better.

"Mind a little comp'ny, Blondie?"

"I thought you'd never ask. How about your friend? Doesn't
he feel sociable?"

"He could be persuaded. Buy you a drink?"

"No thanks, I've still got one."

God! Those eyes! If I turn sideways my left boob will just touch his arm. Good. Good. His pal's coming over, now. What a bulge! If he sits close my right boob will be on his arm. Now that's power! Although Earl Roy is mighty inspiring. I'll bet he was sweating when we talked on the phone. I love it! Earl Roy knows I know. I've got him by the balls and by the dick. He knows what he told me, and he knows it'll cost him plenty. Especially what he told me about the two eight-year-old girls and the whipped cream! God I love it! Nobody dares to make a move without my permission.

"Aren't you guys gonna ask me what my sign is?"

Yes, Guys, they're big. Real big tits. Big ones.

"We was gonna ask you, Blondie, do the collar an' cuffs match?"

CHAPTER THIRTY-THREE

"About twenty members from Truschel County got up and walked out, and Dion Simms didn't show at all. They all had petitioned for Simms to run for State Supreme Court judge, were really gung-ho," Hal said morosely. He had met Ellen and Daphne, and they walked together into the Shelter to await Allison. News about Traci had travelled fast, and news of the CitAct upheaval was circulating too!

"How many attended the meeting?" Daphne asked.

"About seventy-five. It started out well. Dan Weldon gave a talk about what an incredibly positive thing it was to have a progressive, reforming, third political party in such a conservative district. Then I tried to outline what we'll do at the 4th of July picnic, but Ted made the discussion almost impossible. He kept interrupting in that maddening way, saying 'Hal-Hal-Hal" over and over and dragging in confusing issues like the Green Futurist group in California, and he and Don and Mary Alice Franz were plainly stoned, and so were Merrilee Dobbs and Ann Brill. I'm afraid I yelled at Ted. Then the Franzes and Merrilee and Ann, and Phil and Harry Walker, too, said they couldn't take the constant bickering at meetings and they walked out. They were all good, loyal supporters and workers, Daphne! And Ted just kept up that *giggling*. He's been out of work longer than anyone else! He stands to gain if the Party makes gains! I wanted him to run for a row office next year —or maybe for sheriff, but he keeps undermining us."

"Oh, Hal," Ellen commiserated. "You've put up with him so long, and you've been so patient."

"Dan Weldon is ambivalent. I can see that. Ted's had me on the defensive for the last three or four meetings, and last night it got worse. I met Ted head-on, for the first time, and it just so happened that Weldon attended *that* particular meeting. He asked me why I had such a dictatorial attitude. *Dictatorial!* I trusted Ted all this time —even let him draft the Party by-laws!"

"Ted should have been confronted —challenged —months ago, Hal," Daphne said.

"I know. I know. But at last night's meeting I let my anger show. I lost control, with Weldon there! Of all the times to blow up! Now how can I get the Truschel County people back? And losing Simms' candidacy is a real set-back."

"You still have an active, loyal following," Ellen said. "You've done a terrific job, and with the debates yet to come — the TV appearances make a showing. Don't get discouraged."

"It's plenty discouraging to have my car tampered with, to lose vital supporters, to see the credibility the party has achieved just being chipped away systematically — there's almost something methodical about it —and by a bunch of pot-heads!"

"Remember the trouble we had in our anti-nuke group, Daphne?" Ellen stopped in the middle of the old brick walk leading to the shelter back entrance. "Ted did the same crazy things. He would stand up, stoned on pot, and make disjointed, incoherent speeches, and *The Observer* would quote him, and it made us all sound like we were some kind of Jim Jones group — a bunch of nuts or something. He never had a steady job back then, either. we couldn't figure out how he got along. He never did seem to have any steady work."

"I remember, Ellen. I remember it. Over three hundred people in that anti-nuke group. Three hundred!"

"What ever happened to the Movement? I was still in Phillie in seventy-seven," Hal said.

"It just broke up," Daphne said slowly, "Just gradually folded," the truth of what had happened dawning on her, breaking through the mist of that time a decade ago; it seemed as if half a century had passed.

On the back steps of the Shelter two white teenagers in tight cut-off jeans sat talking to a Black teenager. Ellen, Daphne and Hal had to pick their way around the three girls to get to the back door.

A record number of women and their children were in shelter, three of them Black. With Traci gone, Harriet welcomed any Blacks that called in for help.

Daphne heard snatches of the teens' pidgin-English; their

dialogue was timeless, universal, color-blind: "So he goes — 'Hey, I like your hair!' an' I go, like 'Yeah?' and he goes, like, 'Do you ever go to the Legion Hall dances?' an' I'm, like, 'Yeah, sometimes. Do *you*?' an', like, we're walkin' along together an' his buddy, like bumps into him an' then I'm, like — " Their giggles followed the group into the back hall of the shelter.

Harriet looked ghastly, her once rosy, merry face a gray mask. Norm was hospitalized and being fed intravenously, his prognosis not good. Running the Shelter almost single-handedly had reduced Harriet to a near stupor. It was quickly decided that Allison and Felicia would take over for her, and she could go and stay at Norm's bedside.

"I couldn't take Traci's craziness any more," Allison said when she arrived at the Shelter office, purplish circles around her eyes showing darkly despite her deep suntan.

"It had to come out sooner or later. She's ripping everybody off. You can't *believe* some of the things she did! She thinks I'll never reveal her true, sicko identity —her real nature —because of the things she knows about me, things I told her during counselling, during weak moments. This is the way she gets control of people. She said that, with the information she put in my file, I can never get another job *anywhere* —and I'd have to be her lackey, her stooge, *forever!* Forever controlled by her. Well, boy! This is one woman she had pegged *all wrong!*"

Allison's account of Traci's double life stunned the astonished but jubilant group. Now it remained only to see that the board of directors was informed and to begin the machinery of locating a new CEO. But they were to learn that they underestimated Traci. Again they had not gauged accurately the single-minded, self-obsessed, self-preserving power of her manipulative genius.

They realized, now, that they had underestimated Allison too. Her courageous breaking away filled Daphne with pride and the rare feeling of triumph of spirit that so few women experience personally, or are privileged to witness in another woman, in a world geared to dispiriting women at almost every turn —at every attempt they make at personhood. Daphne and Ellen and Felicia —and Hal, too —were nearly speechless with admiration and relief!

CHAPTER THIRTY-FOUR

After the meeting at the Shelter with Allison and the others, Ellen drove to the CorBlimey and played her regular Friday night gig. Tips had been good for several weekends; she'd be able to meet her car payment. She thought of the irony of the situation: only three more payments, but the VW needed a new windshield, transmission work, new muffler and two new tires!

Ellen had agreed to give Harletta Hoskins a ride home after the CorBlimey closed, because Harletta's son, her adored Russell, was using his mother's car for the evening. The two women rode in silence, exhausted, past one completely closed steelmill, then another partially closed-down steel fabricating plant, then past the Penn Wheat Bakery complex which once had sent its yeasty fragrance over a radius of miles and now was completely dark.

"I owe ya, Hon, for doin' me this favor," Harletta said.

"I'm not keeping score, Harletta. You've helped *me* out more than once. I still wouldn't have known who took that twenty out of my brandy-snifter if you hadn't seen Gino —hadn't been wise to him and told me."

"He's a real asshole, Ellen. Cheap asshole."

"He didn't say one word when I told him he'd been seen taking it. Just took a twenty out of the register and handed it to me. Didn't even deny it! He's all smiles when the Bingham Bitsies traipse in there. He's the Grand Old Man, then, with that kiss-ass smile," Ellen said.

"Did you know that the Congressman's wife has a reservation for tomorrow night, her and Hartley's wife?"

"Drew Burgess's wife made a reservation?"

"Yeah. They'll be at one of my tables. I'm supposed to give them the royal treatment. Gino's been coaching Rita for days. Doesn't want any of her off-the-wall cracks. He wants everything just right so he'll get the job catering Mrs. Hartley's political party she's throwing for Burgess."

"I'd like to get the piano playing job for *that* party."

"I heard from Leonard —er —Mr. Blake that a group from

the symphony's gonna play."
"Oh. Ex*cuse me!*" Ellen laughed.

Larry was still up. Ellen could see through the front window
the eerie bluish glow from the TV. She doubted that he was
waiting up companionably for her. He was finishing off a case of
beer and watching more Vietnam videos. He seldom conversed
with her, as yet. Still, he had been having fewer and fewer flash-
back episodes and had a better attitude about being laid off. Now
that her bruises had healed Ellen could wear her off-the-shoulder,
short-sleeved dresses to play at the CorBlimey. She attributed the
amazing changes in Larry partly to the therapy group he had
joined at the VA Hospital as well as to CitAct activities which
Ellen had urged him to participate in. Next, he had to tackle the
beer problem; he was a beer alcoholic, no two ways about it.
   Ellen stood in the middle of the kitchen now, and surveyed
the carnage: Hamburger and peanut butter globs ran down over
the counter fronts; chocolate syrup, ketchup and jelly rivulets
bordered the counter tops while on the floor in front of the
refrigerator more raw hamburger lumps sat in pools of oil. Wads
and crusts of bread and toast were strewn over every flat surface.
An opened-out gallon container of strawberry ice cream crept
across floor towards the living room as Barkley licked it clean,
a pink snail-trail marking the route. Barkley wagged her tail in
greeting but did not look up from her joyful task.
   Ellen felt like crying, but exhaustion made such a reaction
seem to be not worth the effort. She was too wound-up, still, to
sleep. She decided to try to talk to Larry as in their dim past
they had talked together, had talked over everything that
happened in their family, when all that happened had been
exciting, important news to both of them. Larry was sorting
through a collection of new video tapes as Ellen hesitantly
broached the subject of the evening's activities. Instead of leaving
Kelly responsible for the two youngest children, Larry had been
getting them bathed and into bed on Ellen's CorBlimey nights,

and Kelly had a boyfriend and went on dates on week-ends. It seemed almost as if they were a normal family.

"I nearly threw a dame out of the house tonight," Larry growled. Ellen felt her stomach and throat contracting; the old violence seemed very close to the surface.

"That Mrs. Beldige, or Belbrid, from down the street. You know, the big yellow brick house on the corner."

"You mean Mrs. Belbridge? The dentist's wife?"

"Yeah. She was going door-to-door with a petition. She said she wanted me to sign it saying I'm in favor of taking any listing of the 'subversive' category —like the section about communism —out of the high school's *Encyclopedia Britannica* and out of the library's encyclopedia too —wants to cut those pages out that explain about the Communist Party or Marxism any of that — censorship, in other words."

"What did you say? Were you —were you rude?"

"Well, I was pretty much to the point. That shrapnel in my left leg was getting me tonight, hurting extra bad. Her nicey-nice whining really got me too. She seemed to think I'd grab the pen and sign because I'm a Vietnam veteran, or something. Kept mentioning my 'war experience,' as she called it. What the hell *that* had to do with censorship I couldn't —can't —connect with. I tried to tell her it's unconstitutional, first of all; against the first amendment because — because — well, who's to censor the censors —where will it end? Maybe something *she* wants to say will be censored next if we allowed it to begin now."

"What did she say *then?*"

"She said this is different; that there are always exceptions! so when I told her I wouldn't sign due to my principles —my belief that suppression of all knowledge could only perpetuate more suppression and ignorance, she started to get mad. So then I told her about coming into the airport, wearing my uniform after my last tour of duty, and a woman came over to me and screamed that I had killed her son. I told the Beldige dame this incident was due to ignorance —the public's lack of information about their own country and, as the last thing I wanted to do was to have any dealing with suppression of information, I'd appreciate it if she'd get her ignorance the hell off my porch."

"Oh, God."

"Was I rude?"

"Yes. You know it, too. Couldn't you just have explained your views calmly? Maybe you could have dissuaded her from her censorship mission."

"I seriously doubt it. She was pretty self-righteous and know-it-all. She just stomped off the porch without saying another word."

"Now it'll be all over the neighborhood that we're Communists, or pro-Communist. You may have done nearly three tours in Vietnam, but it'll become construed some other way that you said that we're pro-communist —the exact opposite of what you tried to convey. Dear Heaven, Larry, this community is reactionary!"

"I saw her petition sheet. She had lots of signatures. Old LaVerne Hot Pussy Krock, next door, *she* signed it."

"Oh, Larry. That sounds so awful! So sexist!"

"Listen, since I was laid off —since I've been around the house more, LaVerne's been out in her yard with her ass hangin' out of some of the skimpiest outfits I ever saw. She's always lookin' over here."

"Well, if you see her doing that —always looking over here —you must be looking over *there* plenty."

"How can I help it? Kathy and Mark go over there every chance they get. DuWayne has all kinds of games and gadgets and a miniature golf course he's setting up. I have to watch them. Fifteen is too old for Kathy and Mark.

"The Reverend Krocks have a lot of money for extras," Daphne replied. "DuWayne says God sends it. And you're right about the age gap. Last week DuWayne painted pubic and armpit hair and big red nipples and penises on the Schaunecy's classic garden statues. They had to call one of those masonry-cleaning companies. You should lock our gate, Larry, and entertain our kids so they won't want to go over there."

"Ha! As if *that* would keep them from going over there. They're crazy about DuWayne. Incidentally, your mother stopped in tonight. She brought the gallon of ice cream. But, as usual, it was just complain, complain, complain. She didn't like Kelly going out on a date —or her wearing jeans —complained about how Kathy and Kelly won't go to Bitsy meetings, and they won't sit like ladies with their knees tight together an' their ankles crossed. Your mother, by the way, looks terrible. She wouldn't take off her dark glasses. If I didn't know better, I'd say she looked like she had a shiner —a black eye."

"Maybe she did," Ellen offered. "Tyson is capable of it. He's very controlling and domineering. Lately he's been getting worse. He wants marriage. She does too —but not to *him*. He could be a problem." Ellen went back into the kitchen, jubilant that she and Larry had actually had a conversation, a real discussion! She'd worry about her mother tomorrow.

She threw away the ice cream carton and Pepsi bottles, taking note of the seven empty beer cans in the trash can. She picked up the fetid dishcloth and began to dig at the dried ketchup on the table top. Ketchup was even stuck between the rungs of the chair backs.

"Ellen —C'mere. C'mere right away!" Larry was calling. His voice commanded, the way it had sounded when he had found Kirk lying beside his bike out on the front sidewalk the summer before, with a broken arm. Something about his command now made Ellen drop the dishcloth and run into the living room.

Larry was leaning forward, intently watching a video tape of some men loading boxes on an unmarked C-130 transport plane. In the background were palm trees, tropical-looking bushes, low-eaved sheds or houses in an unfamiliar architectural style —Maybe Haitian or Bermudian? The Florida Keys? The camera went in for a close-up. The men's faces were very clear. They were big muscular men wearing civilian clothing.

"There! There! See the guy on the right? With the striped tee shirt and the Rolex?" Larry exclaimed.

The camera backed away again. The scene became distant, as though the photographer might be concealed and was using a telephoto lens. Larry rewound the tape and played it again, stopping it at the very clear close-up. Ellen stared at the tee-shirted man. His face was in an almost full-front view.

"It's Ted Mather," she said.

"Yea, it's Mather, all right. No mistakin' that physique or that mug. Poor, unemployed Ted with a five thousand dollar watch!"

"What *is* this? Where'd you get this video?"

"A guy in my therapy group loaned it to me. It was smuggled out of Nicaragua by a buddy of his who managed to get a job piloting a plane for the National Security Agency. Those boxes the guys are loading on that C-130 all contain cocaine, and there's another tape, he said, showing them *unloading* boxes of arms: M-16 rifles, M-60 machine guns and Lase rocket-launchers."

Larry sorted through a pile of tapes on the coffee table.

"Here it is. The tapes are numbered and dated sequentially, in the order that they loaded the drugs and would take off and then when they would come back and unpack the arms. This all occurred less than three months ago."

He shoved the tape into the VCR. The same setting appeared: silhouetted palmettos, the same, sandy-looking landing strip and distant buildings. The men unloaded larger boxes this time. Some of the people looked different. However, the zoom-in for the close-up revealed Ted Mather in the group. He wore a well-tailored short-sleeved shirt this time, and shorts and a billed cap, and the gleaming Rolex. Larry stopped the film and studied the close-up.

"I'll be god damned!" he said. He started the tape again. The men were prying open the boxes, lifting out the rifles, smiling and laughing, aiming them and sighting them. To Ellen they looked like a bunch of enormous little boys. Ted was talking and laughing —probably that silly, maddening giggle.

The scene became distant again, showing box after box

being unloaded, pried open, checked by a man with a clipboard, then loaded onto motorized carts, which were driven behind a cement block building at the edge of the landing strip and then disappeared behind it, then reappeared, empty, a few minutes later apparently, although a time-jump-shot showed the return trip.

"Remember, during the petitioning? Mather said he had to leave town for a job interview? He leaves town at regular intervals, doesn't he? Says he has to deal with his depression because of being unemployed, by camping out at a place his brother owns. I guess that's to explain why he always comes back with a deep suntan — even in February. Man! Were we dumb! The bastard's a National Security agent."

"I can't believe this — it's too melodramatic — too corny." Ellen sank into an armchair and glared at the TV screen. "Are you going to play the other tape?"

"It's just more of the same, according to the labels. Loading drugs and flying to the U.S. then returning and unloading arms —U.S. arms, for the Contras. Isn't that terrific? A secret war in Nicaragua financed by drug sales to our own U.S. of A., and who knows how many millions siphoned off? But yes, I'm gonna run through the other tape. Sure. Here I am, trying to figure out how we're gonna come up with a mortgage payment, I've got shrapnel permanently burning my legs and my butt, and no job, after nearly three full tours of duty in that Vietnam hell, and Ted Mather's having a fun time making big bucks from drug sales and busting up Third Parties. Pretty slick, Ellen. That's pretty slick."

"Our own government. Our *own* government!" Ellen said, dazed and incredulous. "What about our right to dissent? Our Constitution guarantees the right to dissent. What about the First Amendment? Freedom of speech? The CitAct party members are exercising our right to assemble, our right to speak. We as citizens have that constituional right! I've got to call Hal!" Ellen started towards the phone.

"At a quarter after three in the morning?"

275

"He's got to be told!"

"It won't do any good to call him before morning. He needs to be clear-headed, to think clearly."

"I guess you're right. But think, Larry, we have proof! These tapes could be used in court to prove Ted has misrepresented himself. Hal —the CitAct Party could sue the government." Ellen went from window to window closing the curtains.

"I'm nervous about having those tapes in the house!" Larry said. "And incidentally, it's against the law to sue the U.S. Government, kiddo."

They ran the remaining minutes of film. Ted Mather participated in most of the loading and unloading; was absent from only a few of the scenes. He looked well-fed, expensively clothed, healthy and successful. "That God damned shit," Larry muttered over and over.

Ellen sat sipping a Pepsi, her mind racing, the truth of what happened, the corruption unfolding, opening like some terrible, lurid poisonous plant.

"It's hard to know what to do next. What should we do next, Larry?"

"I think we should get copies made of these tapes. But we should lay low. Hal should be told, of course, but we shouldn't act in haste. The whole thing must be thought out carefully. Don't even tell your pal, Singleton. No one except Hal."

CHAPTER THIRTY-FIVE

"So that's pretty much the size of it. Those eighty beds from Volker Institute will fill the entire area. Administration prioritized these cases. The Social Spaces plan had to be shelved — back-burnered at this point in time." The Volker Institute spokesman recited this announcement matter-of-factly to the Glenview State staff members and Daphne, who all slumped in their folding chairs.

Nick DellaValle glanced at Daphne as did the psychiatrist who, a few minutes before, had commended her on her proposed design for the porch furnishings. All her work had been for nothing. Weeks of measuring, telephoning, visiting showroom after showroom, wasted; hours spent on beautiful drawings, all lost. Her work had come to nothing because the state institute for severely retarded adults had an eighty-patient overflow and had chosen not to announce this until weeks after the fact; through a bureaucratic oversight they had simply failed to notify Glenview State.

There was no further discussion. The psychiatrist declared the meeting adjourned, and everyone rose simultaneously and walked out of the gymnasium. No one spoke to Daphne except Nick, who shrugged and said, sheepishly, "Gee. Sorry. That's the way things go around here sometimes."

Daphne shifted the three large illustration boards under her arm and gathered her carrying case full of samples, and her shoulder bag, then turned to Nick.

"Nearly a hundred lives are profoundly altered — mine included."

"Oh? I thought this was par-for-the-course for the decorating —er —*design* world; bidding and all that."

"I'm a working stiff —just like any other professional, but I've been able to avoid doing much design work on speculation. M.D.s don't work on speculation. *You* don't. Now, what will become of the mainstreaming plan for retarded adults?"

"I expect that eventually they'll mainstream them all anyway without any humane, uh —luxury measures —like Social Spaces;

they'll just plop them down in group homes to sink or swim. You'll be seeing the irate letters to the editor about zoning the homes, etcetera. Endless, hopeless bureaucracy. At least your work's creative. It's always something different isn't it? No two jobs alike?''

"I do a lot residential work; selling sofas and chairs and draperies to rich, self-centered women can be repetitive and boring rather than creative, even though it takes my superior design ability to achieve a beautiful finished effect. After a while, though, a sensitive designer starts to look beyond dollars and cents, starts asking herself 'sooo — is this living room really going to make the world a better place?' The world beyond this rich, doctor's wife, or this lawyer's or corporate leader's wife and family?''

"That seems to be a commendable attitude," Nick said, as they walked toward the entrance, " — but we're all bound by economic need. Idealism doesn't buy many groceries." He was chummier than he had been at their last meeting.

Five or six of the hand-shakers awaited Daphne at the door, smiling, hair combed and, again, sporting neckties. "There's your fan club," Nick said.

"Do you think you'd like to go out sometime?" he blurted suddenly. "I'm a classical music-lover. I like the Symphony in the Park Summer series and the German lieder recitals in the winter."

"I don't have much time — " Daphne began, but re-thinking her attitude, added, "I'm a music-lover too —classical, mainly —and maybe we *could* do something some time." Nick waved goodbye as she began the handshake line-up.

Why did I say that to him? she wondered. *I don't want to go out with him. I have Hal. My life has all it needs, now.* She realized that she had not questioned their relationship —hers and Hal's — until this moment. They had never once discussed marriage.

On the way to the parking lot she passed the Special Ed building. Faint shouts from within reminded her of her encounter with Harriet and Norm the day of the first Social Spaces interview. Now Norm was in very guarded condition. Out of curiosity she decided to go in and look around the building after stowing the now-useless drawings and sample boards in her car trunk.

The almost Eurostyle building with its big, bright atrium-like inner court was a new addition to one of the retarded adults' dormitories —taken over and funded as part of the Special Ed complex. A hand-painted three-story mural in the atrium lined the entire play area, part of which was ceramic tiled and another part carpeted with green astro-turf.

Brightly colored upholstered railing bumpers for wheelchairs throughout cheerfully painted hallways and classrooms were a pleasant visual shock after the retarded adults' dismal building interiors. Youngsters on their stomachs on flat carts and seated in motorized wheelchairs rolled past her. Others with heavy leg braces rolled about and played on the soft astro-turf. It was a fifty-fifty mix of White and Black kids, from what Daphne could see.

In the pool and gymnasium area cheap rock music echoed, hollow and discordant, throughout the big, open spaces, but was humanized somewhat by the children's happy-sounding shouts. Was rock music *all* they could find as a background for children's activity areas *everywhere?* Daphne had often wondered at the invariably low quality of music used for such activities.

Mothers and aides sat in the bleachers watching the swimming lesson while others in the gym superised as children on floor mats and in wheelchairs did aerobic and calisthenic exercises.

The slender Black swimming instructor with a dancer's well-muscled body must be therapist Thaddeus Shaeffer, Ora's son — poor sick Ora's pride and joy. He was reportedly living with the outspoken, very beautiful Audrey Hopper, a one-time Sojourner Shelter client and CR group member. Had Audrey ended up in shelter the time she had a broken nose and multiple wounds because of Thaddeus? Was he the father of Audrey's baby?

Thaddeus was bringing the swim lesson to a close. Mothers helped their children out of the pool and dried them with large towels. Thaddeus was conferring with one of the mothers —she had almost perfect classic features and straight, blunt-cut light-blond hair held behind her ears with gold barrettes — as she helped her daughter into a sweat suit and towel-dried her hair. Daphne sat on a bench and waited. She decided to introduce herself to Thaddeus.

The swim group filed out, and she said to him, "Mr. Shaeffer?"

He nodded and said, expressionlessly, "Right."

"I work —used to work —with your mother at the Sojourner Shelter." He continued to fish rubber balls out of the pool and didn't seem inclined to shake hands so she didn't offer hers.

"That right?" he said, still expressionless.

Thumping, thwacking, pounding rock percussion tore through the air around them. A whining, almost animal-call electric guitar howled a phrase. Over and over the crazy-making non-music caterwauled the phrase; it was anti-music.

"How is your mother doing?" Daphne had to shout.

"Not good. Doin' very poorly, in fact. Whatever went down at that ladies' group has sure got her in a very bad way."

Daphne thought, *Good heavens. He must think I'm one of Traci's stooges.*

She bent down towards Thaddeus as he coiled a long rope. "She's one of my most cherished people. I think she considers me a friend —uh, is she able to get along on her own? I'll admit I haven't kept in touch, other than cards and notes. When you see her next will you give her my love? I'm Daphne Singleton."

He stood up and stared at Daphne with such naked disgust that for a moment she was at a loss for words.

"She can't hardly do anythin' her own self," he said in an Uncle Tom voice. "My sisters and me, we take turns at gettin' her to the rehab center but her progress is slow. She spend part of each day in *bed*. My daughter stayin' with her."

He turned as if to go, curtly dismissing Daphne by the

action.   She said quickly, "I hope you don't think I'm in any way connected with the current CEO or her board of directors. I am one of the Shelter founders, together with your mother and three others."

"Yeah. She *say* she was you-all's Black token," he answered sarcastically, smiling slightly. At least it *was* a smile. They walked toward the doorway sign that said "To Lockers."

"This building is lovely." She looked around, smiling but trying not to burble or chatter. "The architecture and the bright, cheery furnishings all help the children's morale — and the instructors' morale too, I would imagine." Thaddeus nodded but made no comment. Thwack thwack thwack went the non-music.

"Uh, how is the music selected? Is it always this type? Like what's playing right now?"

"A couple of us, we put in requisitions and the tapes are sent to us. We trade back and forth with the adult administration office. Wanda, in the office, and me — we pretty much select them. She picked what's playing today. I like more fusion, new wave and jazz, for the kids." He was speaking like the Step n' Fetchit character of nineteen thirties movies.

The creature in the office! That explained it.

"You think we oughta have different music or somethin'? Funny you should happen to bring it up today. The lady I was just talkin' to by the pool, Representative Burgess's wife, Stephanie's mom, she was complainin' about it." So *that* was Bronwen Burgess!

"What does she think you should play?"

"She wants more classical. But this isn't ballet class y' know. That's what I told *her,* too. She just want less funky stuff."

"I guess I'd have to say I'm with *her,*" Daphne said. "I've met Wanda, in administration. I think that's all I've got to say on *that* subject." She laughed.

Again Thaddeus smiled his caustic smile. "Look. Many of these kids are from welfare homes. This place is a palace compared to the holes some of them live in. You wouldn't believe some of the life situations they've come out of: dope-peddler parents, hookers for mothers. Before they're seven or eight a lot of them have seen every hardened criminal trick there is. Do you think hearing Prokofiev ballet music matters in lives like that? Or Glück? Or Khatcheturian?" He had dropped his Step n' Fetchit accent altogether.

"You know that music?" Daphne asked, amazed.

"I'm a dancer first —ballet and every other kind —then I'm a physical therapist after that."

"I think Prokofiev —and Katcheturian —and Glück —would be marvelous for these kids. *Any* kids! It's music that's full of life and quality and makes you rise to it instead of pulling you down to it —like Wanda's mating calls."

Thaddeus laughed in spite of himself. "What about Third World music? The jive you're talkin' about is what Carmichael —Stokely, that is — not Hoagie —calls 'White-western-world-liberal-arts-and-humanities values.' There's nothing Ethiopian or Masai or Kikuyu about it. What about Black kids' values? Are they supposed to be exposed to nothing but White values?"

"Well, no, of course not. There are whole worlds of great stuff to choose from: Benin chants, Bob Marley reggae, Jamaican dub poets Mutabaruka, Linton, Kwesi Johnson, and 'Miss Lou' Bennett as well as African inspired Gospel music, Richie Havens, Miriam Makeba, Odetta, and there's Cajun Zydeco, and Oriental, East Indian as well as Native American, and music from Central and Latin America, and Bluegrass —it just doesn't quit!"

"You make a pretty good argument," he said, "but I'll level with you. I was prepared to not like you."

"I could tell."

"Sho'nuf?" he said, straight-faced.

They both laughed, and Daphne found herself wondering how this obviously caring man could have battered Audrey Hopper —could have inflicted such injuries. Her lover's name was not discussed due to the strict confidentiality of CR sessions.

Thaddeus accompanied Daphne to the door.

"Do you know how Norm Hoffmann's doing?" he asked.

"He's in the hospital. He's not doing well at all."

Thaddeus shook his head. "We miss him. And Harriet too. She cheered up this place as much as that rainbow and sun face up there." He glanced up at the gymnasium mural; an enormous rainbow, above which Old Sol grinned, was an arc extending from the gym entrance doors to the pool area entrance, a distance of over fifty feet.

"She's a very talented dancer, did you know that?" Thaddeus went on, "I know she has an M.S.W., but she's also very gifted in musical expression. Sometimes she leads the kids' aerobic motion studies I worked out, and they love her."

"Yes, I know she's versatile; she's a fine violinist too. She's having a very bad time now, with Norm so sick." Daphne gave a little wave, "Nice to have met you, Thaddeus."

He smiled. "Same here," he said.

CHAPTER THIRTY-SIX

Neither Claudio Arrau playing Chopin nor a vodka and tonic, sipped in her cozy sitting room, could lift Daphne's spirits. More than three full weeks of research and drawings, as well as James' overtime pay for Glenview State work, were irretrievably gone. This fact was so depressing that it seemed an affront to Arrau and to Chopin. She turned off the stereo and switched on the TV. Three animated toilets harmonized a ditty about bowl deodorants, lifting their lids in unison and sliding around in a sort of dance; on another channel three women squealed in orgasmic ecstacy over their husbands' white athletic socks. On the public broadcasting channel there were never-before-photographed mating tree frogs.

She switched off the TV and picked up *The Observer*. A Melvin Township man rated a front page story about how he made his own bowling ball polish, and a Kincaid group called Precious Pink Feet fought abortion —White women's abortions only; PPF were racist anti-abortionists — and were stringing rosary beads and selling them to raise money to print brochures, and they rated three columns *and* a picture. The sports section alone rated twelve pages.

She stuffed the newspaper in her kindling basket and walked about the small room; bills were piled on her writing table along with another letter from Bobbye's attorney. It was enough to sour her completely on what she once had perceived as an ideal, exciting dream-career. To be creative, self-employed, self-sufficient, was what she had wanted above all else; to be the exact opposite of her indolent, unimaginative, unloving mother. But such a life exacted a terrible price.

In the kitchen she switched on the lamp over her pine table, took a plate of melon and lettuce from the refrigerator, then switched on the air conditioner. She took a favorite majolica bowl from the corner cupboard. She heard a thud.

At first she thought she must have pushed or jostled a pitcher from the top of her corner cupboard and it had fallen behind the cupboard. The she realized that the noise was too loud and there were two separate sounds of breaking glass and two thuds. Quickly it became clear that the sounds were not in the kitchen at all, but had come from the living room. Without thinking, she ran to the blue-walled living room where she had left the ceiling track lights on.

Something had come in through the bottom sash glass of one front window and the top sash glass of the other window. There were large irregular holes in the glass of both windows from which jagged cracks radiated.

On the opposite side of the room, on the pine board floor lay two iron balls about two and a half to three inches in diameter.

Cannon balls? Should she drop to the floor, she wondered. Would there be more shots fired?

Daphne ran back to the kitchen, turned out the light and dialed the Bingham Police number. Only then did she realize fear. She began to shake. With all of her lights out, it would be more difficult for someone to see window locations from outside, she reasoned. She continued to shake as her thoughts raced.

There were houses lining both sides of her two-lane street. She was on good terms with her neighbors, although they all usually kept pretty much to themselves. There were a few young families and some elderly retirees who would wave pleasantly to one another as they went to and from work or shovelled snow or trimmed hedges; artillery crews they were not. It must have been someone driving past.

She wanted to look out toward the front, to assess any possibility of a loitering truck or car. She decided to run upstairs. There she could survey the whole street, and as her house sat up on a sort of rise from the sidewalk, only some kind of bazooka or gun could shoot anything into her second story windows.

Crawling across the front bedroom floor she realized she had been thinking so hard that she had stopped shaking, but now the jangling phone triggered more violent tremors. Should she let it ring?

Dear Heaven, she thought, *I can't take any more of*

PeaBrain's sleaze. After five rings she answered it. It was Hal.
"Oh —Hello," he said, his voice tight and funny-sounding.
"I've got to talk to you —at your place. It can't be on the phone."
The police car's light was flashing in front of the house, now.
"Yes, Yes. Come over now," she said. "Come right away. Someone, something shot two cannon balls through my living room windows. The police just arrived."

"Whatever propelled it —a gun of some sort or a good pitching arm, it had to have real force to go acrosst the room like that." Two of Bingham's three-man police force speculated on the episode.
"Someone got some kinda grudge against ya?" one of the officers asked Daphne.
"Not any more than the average business person might occasionally encounter. But actually, there's just no logical explanation that I can come up with," she answered.
"There's kooks ever'wheres nowadays," the officer ventured. "They'd just as soon pop ya off as they'd look at cha."
"But iron *balls* like that! What if I'd been sitting in the line of fire —there by the fireplace?" Daphne shuddered.
"You was lucky."
"Well, what's going to happen next? I don't feel safe here in what I thought was a pretty tame neighborhood."
"We'll take these here balls and check 'em out. See if we can trace where they come from. Then we'll patrol your street ever' half hour for a few nights. Okay? If I was you, I'd keep to the back of the house for a while. Stay out of the front rooms for the next coupla weeks. Okay? Don't worry, Hon, we'll be watchin' this street."
If she hadn't been suspicious of the officer beforehand, after the gratuitous "Hon," Daphne felt subliminal alarm.

They departed but not without giving her arm a squeeze and offering one more "Hon."

"I don't know how to say it, Daph, I just feel responsible!" Hal said, as they drank a bottle of ale in the kitchen. Daphne couldn't eat her dinner.

"It's getting out of control. The situation is bizarre, of course, the idea of Mather's being employed to break up the CitAct Party — employed by our own government — the government of the country I love, whose integrity I'm trying to uphold —to restore, before it's too late! We have a fucking KGB, here in our own country!"

"Then you don't think Ted's an agent?"

"I didn't say that! Of *course* I think he's an agent — is misrepresenting himself, posing as perpetually unemployed and near indigent. The puzzle pieces all fit. His manipulation of the Franzes, Merrilee Dobbs, Phil and Harry Walker, Ann Brill, the anti-nuke group bust-up, your NOW group. The NOW group never got very far, did they?"

"No. The whole feisty, pioneering, grass-roots quality of our early NOW group fizzled out and turned into a ladies' club type of thing. Now they're just the Democratic Party Ladies's Auxiliary. The don't run candidates for office, don't *do* anything. They *did* come out, brave and noble, for *Mondale* in one presidential election! Big deal!"

"We have the tapes that show Ted's duplicity. But the fact remains, what right has our government to prevent a third party from having a voice? We have a Constitutional right to dissent," Hal said.

"There's no doubt that our CitAct Party power is growing. Membership has steadily increased and even the media can no longer block us out, because of the debates —media exposure is becoming impossible to prevent. But prevent it they will! One way or another out own United States KGB is going to close us down!"

"I find it so hard to believe, to *comprehend* our country doing such a thing, taking such an action when it so clearly states in our Constitution that —" Daphne began.

"I'm deeply concerned for your safety, Daphne. Deeply concerned. When I see what happened here tonight — for a violent act such as this to have happened to *you* — and you wouldn't even be involved if I hadn't broken my word to Ellen and Larry, I'm ashamed to say. They didn't want me to tell even you —about the tapes, I mean. But I *had* to, just *had* to."

"Thank you for confiding in me, Hal. I think you did the best thing. It's best that I know. Especially now, after tonight."

CHAPTER THIRTY-SEVEN

"Do your nipples get stiff when ya go in there?" Elwood, the sous chef, sneered at Merrilee Dobbs as she emerged from the walk-in cooler carrying two frozen Cointreau cream cheesecakes.

"Up yours, Elwood." Merrilee muttered. There was a run on the frozen cheesecake tonight at the CorBlimey. After they ran out of chilled zabaglione —which none of the wait staff could pronounce —they called it "Jabloney" —the cheesecakes were the only cold dessert left other than plain old ice-cream.

The first two dinner seatings had been hectic; there were many finicky yuppie deuces who spent about fifteen minutes each, vacillating about the wine list, even putting on an act about wanting to "talk to your sommellier," sniffing the cork, sending bottles back —a lot of would-be corporate executives trying to impress their dates.

And in the Back of the House, Rudy clearly was drunk. He had been nipping since early afternoon and was getting mean, and glassware was piling up —crowding over onto the work spaces where the wait staff were supposed to garnish their orders before whisking them to the dining room. A tray of little saw-toothed-edged orange-baskets of sticky orange sauce for the Roast Duck Special got knocked to the floor and Chef Herb Haselas was a barely-controlled mass of rage. Gino had told him they'd better get the Burgess party catering job, or else —"or else something incredible would happen to his balls," Harletta had told Ellen. "I wouldn't even *repeat* it, Hon. Not even to you!"

Gino's bookie crowd seemed to out *en masse* tonight. About ten of the men sat in a row at the bar dressed identically in Mafia cliché pastel silk or jersey tailored shirts open nearly to the waist with the requisite gold chains glinting and peeping out from so many hairy chests that Ellen told Harletta that it "looks like a Fuller Brush convention out there."

Bookie wives and girlfriends circulated throughout the bar area, easily identifiable by their high-fashion leather clothing which they seemed to favor all year around —mini skirts and

291

hand-painted sequinned jackets, drop-dead strapless tops worn with soap-opera-trollop coiffures. Everything they ever were or ever would be —and some of the women had strikingly beautiful facial features —seemed to show like a map or chart on their vacuous, expressionless faces under their elaborate makeup.

They rarely smiled as they chattered to each other about their latest acquisitions and activities: clothes, cars, jewelry, sets of leather luggage, shopping, the racetrack, Las Vegas. Around their men, however, they scarcely ever *stopped* smiling. They had no inkling that they were stereotypes. They all displayed the trappings of their monetary success — their wealth that they schemed and gambled and daily risked everything for —yet from their vapid conversation it was immediately evident that their cultural lives were profoundly impoverished.

These women, and the bookies, made a conspicuous ritual of ignoring Ellen, the music, the piano, even to the extent of standing in groups of three or four immediately beside the piano and shouting at one another over the music. One particular member of the group, a Mrs. Palumbo, herself a bookie —not just a groupie —was older and tougher-looking than the others, with rigidly set bleached, yellow-dyed hair and black leather pants so tight that she 'had to take tiny steps. The other bookie groupies showed her some deference, as did the wait staff. She was a big tipper, simultaneously patronizing and condescending to the waiters.

Mrs. Palumbo once had gone so far as to dump out the contents of her purse on the grand piano's closed lid (while Ellen was playing) and proceeded to shake out the handbag onto the polished wood. Then she replaced the contents, one-by-one, throwing bits of paper and other flotsam and jetsam onto the floor and kicking it under the piano, a gesture of such undisguised contempt and crudity that Ellen was fascinated rather than angered or insulted. Where did all the contempt come from?

No doubt it came from fear, Harriet and Daphne had suggested, when Ellen told them about the incident.

"You're clearly not working there in a subservient capacity,

like the waiters. You are getting by on talent —a woman getting
by on talent can be scary to bimbos like that. You have earning
power. And there are symbols, you know —the jar of money
sitting there, no male escort or obvious 'provider' hovering
nearby. They sense that you're not dependent as they are."

"Their actions are so obvious that they're more intriguing
than anything else," Ellen went on. "Being in that situation
makes me feel as if I'm in a time warp. It's as if the Women's
Movement —our massive, powerful shift into the future —never
occurred at all, and except for their leather outfits, those women
could all be what were so euphemistically called 'Ladies of the
Evening' back in the eighteen eighties! When I'm playing the
CorBlimey I'm in another historical period altogether!"

Ellen could see and feel the tension building tonight. Rita
had been to the Ladies' Room twice for cocaine snorts and now
was jabbering and chattering like a chimpanzee as she scampered
back and forth behind the bar. She was so short her head barely
showed above it.

As luck would have it, a thirty-ish couple were to celebrate
their one-month's wedding anniversary tonight. The husband had
talked to Ellen the Saturday before about playing Their Song,
"Evergreen" at a signal from him, at which time Rita was to
serve flutes of chilled champagne. This choreography seemed
simple enough, given the frequency of such celebrations at the
CorBlimey, but Rita hadn't remembered the instructions and
hastily rammed a bottle of champagne into the freezer when Ellen
reminded her.

"I'll play 'As Time Goes By' when they come in," Ellen
instructed her. "That's your first cue. Let them get settled a few
minutes at the bar. Then I'll play 'Evergreen.'" She ran through
the introduction. "You know, the Barbara Streisand song —that's
the main cue to serve the bubbly —"

Rita shot down to the end of the bar with three more
highballs and small talk for the open-to-the-waist bookies —"If
ya like my ass in *these* pants, ya oughta see me in my *white*
pants!" —then ran back to Ellen. "Yeah, Ellen. Yeah. Yeah,"

she laughed, "I'll be ready. I'll be listenin'." The throng from the Blue Barn had begun to drift in.

How could the Blue Barn show be over already? The well-dressed theater aficionados always looked forward to their leisurely late dinner. But the second dinner seating was not moving along at all; some tables were just now being served their entrees! Gino was doing a nervous little dance-like shuffle and going in and out of the swinging door to the kitchen.

The bar was filling up fast. Rita's inane chatter grew more shrill. Now she was chirping cheerfully about "when my boyfriend was in organized crime — " to the bookies who guffawed and brayed like characters out of *The Satyricon*, their brutal arrogance increasing with each piña colada.

A dreamy-eyed couple floated in and shyly took the last two bar seats. It was the anniversary pair. Alerted, Ellen rambled around the piano with some jazz *arpeggios*, waiting to catch the husband's eye. He was nuzzling his smiling bride's cheek, kissing her ear and whispering. Then he turned to Ellen and nodded.

She began the first musical cue, "As Time Goes By." Rita ignored it; she didn't get out the champagne or the glasses. Ellen played the cue again and tried to get Rita's attention. Still no luck. Finally she got up, walked to the bar and whispered, "Serve the champagne to that couple!" and went back to the piano and began playing "Evergreen."

Rita yanked out the bottle of champagne, ripped out the cork with a loud, vulgar "thwunk!" slapped two champagne glasses down in front of the startled couple and poured the still-warm champagne to overflowing. As the misty-eyed pair, in their shared, very private moment, emotionally raised their dripping glasses in a toast, Ellen played the lovely *crescendo*, the almost operatic chords of Their Song, and at that moment Rita thrust her zany Pulcinella face between the newly-weds and yapped "I've got plastic hair bands in every keller there is — red, green, purple, yella, pink, oreenge —you name it, I got it —"

Ellen realized that she could forget about that ten dollars

for her brandy snifter.

At that moment Gino disappeared into the kitchen again. Heads moved rapidly back and forth in the tiny window of the swinging door indicating an altercation.

In the Front of the House, "Mrs. Drew Burgess's party" entered the vestibule and walked into the bar area. Ellen recognized Bronwen from Daphne's description — the striking straight blonde hair, the perfect features etcetera. There was no Gino to seat the growing line-up of patrons, no Harletta, and no tables available in the dining room anyway, though the wait staff shot in and out of the kitchen in an increasingly frenzied tempo.

Six or seven couples were now lined up behind the Burgess party. Ellen recognized Mrs. Dr. Hartley, although she had become so svelte and shapely as to be almost *un*recognizable, but she *was* the wife of Ellen's obstetrician, after all, and it was the same rather oriental-looking round face. She was wearing a long red plaid prairie dress. Mrs. Burgess was in a Khaki Bwana Land Shops Special with shoulder tabs, bone buttons, full skirt and wide leather belt.

Ellen finished "Witchcraft" — This seemed to be a Cy Coleman sort of mixed crowd —and segued into "Deep Night," albeit from an earlier period in music history. The hairy chest line-up at the bar had not budged. Their raucous laughter grew louder and louder. The deuces around the piano were nearly filled, and the air conditioning was turned up so high that, in the dining room, women diners, shrouded head and shoulders in wool stoles and shawls, looked like laundry piles from which glasses or forks intermittently projected and withdrew.

"Overheated people don't eat worth shit," Gino was always saying.

Mrs. Burgess walked to the bar with great dignity —she had a strikingly graceful presence —and quietly addressed Rita who began to look around frantically. *Where* was Gino?

"Do younse have a reservation?" Rita's nasal, cocaine whine carried very clearly above the bar din and the music. She ran from behind the bar to the dining room, then skittered back again. She was supposed to give "The Burgess Party" special consideration.

"There aren't no empty tables in there but —" She glanced quickly around the bar area, then waved her hand toward the one remaining deuce table, "Oh —what the fuck —sit over there."

Bronwen Burgess recoiled as if struck in the face, but gamely picked her way through the crowd, Mrs. Hartley following. Dutifully they took their seats as Rita threw a tablecloth on the table, propped two special peak-folded CorBlimey napkins crookedly before them and shoved menus under their noses. "Bone Appetitty," she chirped and sprinted back to the bar.

Patrons now were standing three-deep at the bar, but inexplicably, unfathomably, Rita ran to the vestibule and out the front door. Ellen realized that the Porsche cruising past the entrance was Rita's coke connection.

Now Bronwen Burgess got up and disappeared into the Ladies' Room. A few moments later, Gino, scarlet-faced, out-of-breath and pop-eyed, appeared in the dining room doorway and, aghast at the sight of the crowded, untended bar, stomped to the Ladies' Room and pounded on the door, shouting, "Are you gonna come outa that goddam can or *not?*"

Whether Mrs. Burgess went out the Ladies' Room window was a matter of conjecture for some time. But when finally she *did* emerge, white-faced, twenty minutes later, and crept to her seat, the bar chatter had diminished by only a few decibels. But Mrs. Hartley had ordered for them both and their *nouvelle cuisine* appetizers miraculously had arrived, and Rita was back on duty behind the bar.

Between the bar jam-up and growing kitchen discord the frantic Gino jettisoned his Sicilian Uriah Heep act and began herding the standees to one side saying, "Make room, make room, let them people past ya, c'mon, step lively." In the Back of the House he exhorted Chef Haselas and the staff to "Move 'em out! We got to get the food the fuck *out* there!"

Rudy lay insensible on a pile of flattened plastic take-out

cartons, having been flattened himself by Elwood, while Merrilee and the busboy took over the dishwashing. They were making a very small dent in the huge stacks of glassware and silverware, while the pots and pans piled up.

By concentrating on the Burgess Table, Chef Haselas placated Gino; some calm was restored: two beautiful CorBlimey special entrees, Gadzooks *Gamberi con Risotto* with all the proper garnishes, went out to their table via a very nervous but proud Harletta together with a complimentary bottle of House Burgundy.

But the moment was short-lived. They all had underestimated Rudy, who, reviving, stepped with drunken dignity into the middle of the kitchen, turned around, pulled down his pants and mooned the staff. Then, with surprising agility, he sprinted to the doorway between the dining room and the bar where all could see, pulled his pants down again and mooned all the diners, then ran out to the street, with Gino, Elwood and two busboys in pursuit.

CHAPTER THIRTY-EIGHT

The Screamer's cries rang in Debbie's ears. Holding the phone at arm's length she gestured frantically for James to pick it up in the office, out of ear-shot of the three Yuppie Moms who were browsing in Designs for Living's aisles.

In taking over many of Daphne's clients while she completed the Hartley work, James had inherited The Screamer along with other slipcover, re-upholstery, drapery, wallpaper and carpet clients. Over the years, Daphne executed fairly lucrative work for the very temperamental Screamer "for the money" because, after all, business expenses had to be met, but as James put it, "We all pay a high price to get our price."

There was no such thing as a discussion with The Screamer, only her one-way screeching complaints. Once when she had been making her usual demands for immediate service, and the slipcover people could not deliver sofa and chair covers "this very day," The Screamer wrapped a threatening note around a rock with string and threw it in the shop door at Debbie, who was sitting at her little reception desk. An alcoholic —and a very rich one —The Screamer surfaced from time to time, adding even more tension to the design work which was tense and exacting to begin with.

In the front of the shop Debbie politely conducted the Yuppie Moms through the Eighteenth Century Accessories Gallery. Two enormous red-faced infants, probably about six months old but nearly the size of two-year-olds, each projected from a canvas sling hung around its mother's neck, causing both Moms to walk in a painful-looking semi-crouch.

The three-hundred dollar, hand-decorated Serengeti Slings were a hot item at Briarwood BwanaLand Junior Shops, along with seventy-five dollar suspenders for three-year-olds and two-hundred-dollar wooly haired, negro-faced Jolly Golly dolls that played a New York Philharmonic recording of Debussy's "The Golliwogs Cakewalk" on a concealed cassette whenever "Your toddler tweaks Golly's nose."

The third Yuppie Mom yanked the arm of her five-year-old —"Thank God Justin will be in school this time next year" —who weighed as much as Debbie weighed when she was in the eighth grade. The Mom took from her purse a large wooden spoon and brandished it in her child's face. "See this?" she shouted, "See this?"

Male Yuppie children most often seemed to have names beginning with "J" —Justin, Jeremy, Jarod, Jason; they were named for Gothic Novel heroes that ripped open the bodices of Romance heroines.

These time-clock-running-out, late-thirties Moms each had produced the requisite heir and were hating every minute of it as were their children. Even Debbie, a June-moon-spoon Romantic, was appalled.

Boy! she thought, *There's another argument for remaining childless.*

There was a loud Whack! and Justin was sent sprawling, then picked up and slammed onto a slender-legged Empire armchair and handed a Snickers bar. He snuffled and whimpered piteously and rubbed mucous on the beige damask chair seat and arm-pads; the sticky Snickers wrapper lay alongside the child's sweaty thigh. One of the slung infants began to howl. Its Mom shoved the infant's head under her magenta "Cancun '81" tee-shirt to breast-feed.

Debbie observed the straight-chopped jaw-length hair, held behind the ears with giant gold paper-clip barrettes, *de rigueur* with most of the Moms. *Poor things,* Debbie thought, *they all seem so miserable.*

"Oh God! Look at the time! Brad will kill me!" The Moms gathered up their purchases and, while Debbie wrapped and packed the brass candle sconces, Williamsburg Queen Anne cypher trivets, marble book-ends, a pair of petit point pillows, they rushed across the street to a newly-opened gourmet deli. There, for about forty to fifty dollars each, take-out dinners could be selected and quickly packed.

The Moms with their shrieking young returned to pick up their packages, which Debbie charge-carded, then tottered to their two sports cars and raced out of the parking lot, Justin, Jarod and Jeremy howling. Watching them, Debbie speculated that in a few years they'd all probably have new husbands, new places to shop, new children, new sports cars, new —platinum — paper-clip barrettes.

James and Debbie began to clean up after the onslaught. Water didn't do any good with the chocolate smudges. James got out the dust pan and broom for the broken little Favrile-type glass vase; Debbie got out the carbon tetrachloride. They both felt strangely depressed.

DelMonte Workrooms delivered the last of the Hartley draperies, cornices, valances, bed hangings and vanity skirts just as James closed up the shop; some complex installing work lay ahead.

Daphne had signed on to teach the Briarwood Art League's summer interior design course at the Gessler Museum and wouldn't be in until one the following day.

James found himself shouldering more and more of the shop responsibilities, and he found, also, that he didn't deal well with the added stress. He missed his lover, Kenny Savage, who had gone to Florida to try working in the newly-opened gay bar of a friend. A mutual friend, Lon McManus, had told James on the phone that Kenny had been seen a few times with "a great big guy." In fact, James was fairly certain Lon had telephoned from Florida just to drop that piece of news, even though it was interspersed with other gossip and news about the new bar and Gay Rights Movement activities in which Kenny had become involved.

James couldn't get the phone call out of his mind. Kenny was a sweet guy but naive; he could do some pretty dumb things; he needed looking-after. He was slightly built and relatively defenseless and so blond and angelic-looking that he seemed to attract guys everywhere he went. He certainly was mis-named, however. He was just a peaceable man who loved to party. Lon had told James that every other Florida guy seemed to be "fresh outa' the pen." God! Kenny and *jailbirds!* James had never wanted him to leave Bingham County.

The women assembled in the Gessler Museum classroom assigned to Daphne for her design course seemed to be generally humorless and rather grim. They had come in one by one and self-effacingly slipped into seats at the three long tables. Daphne checked off their names on the class roster as they entered. There were fourteen altogether, and they went around the tables and introduced themselves and, when urged by Daphne, gave embarrassed accounts of their reasons for signing up for the course: "We're building a house," and "I just always wanted to do it," or "It seems interesting." One very carefully-groomed young woman seemed to have come from the tennis court. She carried her silk scarf-tied tennis racket into class —as she would to every class thereafter —and announced in a whisper that she was "recovering from a divorce, and I want to get a fresh start."

Another young woman, the daughter of an inseparable mother-and-daughter team, Alfreda and Mrs. DeAngelo, who were to be the bane of Daphne's existence throughout the course with their cleaning-methods approach to design, said, "I haven't *any* talent at all for this, but my mother wanted me to drive her to the class."

Daphne welcomed everyone and explained that "everyone, absolutely everyone, has some degree of creativity." In the back of the room, Sugantha Govinda, the plump, sari-clad, caste-marked wife of a New Delhi-born Briarwood cardiologist, stridently boomed out, "Yess-but-some-haf-more-than-*oth*-therss!"

Seven of the women were building new houses. There was considerable disparity of income perceptible within the group, the seven home-builders being expensively dressed and — it developed over time —obviously well-travelled, though not at all informed in geography. They drove to class in big expensive cars.

The other seven were a mix: mostly housewives. All,

however, were abysmally uneducated, Daphne was to learn as the course progressed, and unacquainted with the most rudimentary knowledge of history, art, literature or literary references or even Pop cultural references.

All humor eluded them entirely. Irony, or satire, was a vast *terra incognita* to them. It was amazing to Daphne. She knew that nearly all of the women had children —conventional families with bread-winner husbands —they were part of that vanishing segment of the population — which the Republican Right mandated as the civilized world's Last Hope —and they had, then, brought children into the world, and seven of them had a great deal of money, and the others were comfortably-off, yet they all seemed to be retarded.

How could they possibly deal with The World, Daphne wondered. What did they talk about to their husbands? To their children? What did they *do* to pass the time? They certainly had much leisure time. She was to discover, as they solemnly took notes, gravely drew scale drawings, viewed silently the Metropolitan Museum slides, that with one exception, all of these women were either chronically depressed, frightened, simply not of normal intelligence, or were borderline psychotics. Chronic depression seemed to be the most logical diagnosis. It became her goal to *reach* these women, to stir them in some way, to strike some chord that their apathy had muffled or buried. It was uphill all the way. They were apparently passionless and unmotivated about everything.

The one exception in the group was Martha Iverson, a sweet-natured, pleasant woman who crafted careful drawings of her own home's furnishings —mostly terrible couches and chairs —which seemed to be her sole artistic interest. She drew "from life," as she said, more and more of the remarkable beautifully-shaded drawings in one and two-point perspective and brought them to class each week, but she cared little for other class assignments and did them half-heartedly. Her "taste notebook" was filled with "rain lamps," featuring oil-dripping wire shades that simulated rainfall, and gimcrackery from the back pages of her husband's *Field and Stream* and from Green Stamp catalogs. The principles of design completely eluded Martha. Daphne encouraged her to consider taking a fine arts course. "You should be painting and learning composition. You have a fine talent," Daphne told her.

The class reviewed slides of the Lascaux and Altamira cave drawings and Egypt's incredible art that came out of its immutable four-thousand years before Christ, and stunning slides of Oriental art recommended and sent by the Cleveland Museum. A suggestion of a bus trip to see this museum's splendid oriental collection elicited two raised hands. What did you have to do to bring these women to life? Could they ever be invigorated?

Yet they would show up dutifully at class each week, and they carefully completed each assignment, handing in magazine-clipped examples of Doric, Ionic, and Corinthian columns, egg and dart mouldings, broken pediments, triglyphs and metopes. Much of what Daphne taught was architecturally inspired. Yet none of this appeared to move the class in any way. They were not excited by anything.

When Daphne began the opaque projector section of the course and showed, from her own collection, some of the great interiors of the world, the famed designer Givenchy's Paris apartment caused a slight stir. There was in the apartment a six-foot-square coffee table, artfully stacked with marvelous art books, bibelots, *objets d'art*, candle-holders, sculpture —the table top in itself a work of art composed of works of art. Mrs. DeAngelo raised her hand when Daphne asked for comments, and said, "It makes me wanta go in the room and redd-up."

Every view of particularly fine chairs or sofas elicited Alfreda's nasal enquiry, "How wouldja clean sompthin' like that?"

Daphne thought of the passion, the vigor of the women in the Sojourner Shelter CR group. What set them so apart from the lassitude, the passivity of the design class group? Poverty? Hardship? Having to talk with a broken jaw wired together? Being repeatedly made to feel worthless, being Black in a relentlessly White supremacist culture? Or could it be a geographic, a regional phenomenon? All in the design class were from Briarwood. Perhaps it was something in the water they drank, or in the soil.

None of the other classes Daphne had taught had been like the Gessler Museum class. Township denizens had flocked to her Community College classes, and although there was almost always inordinate concern with cleaning methods, there was also laughter within the Community College group, good natured banter; there were humorous exchanges; there was enthusiasm and phone call after phone call at the end of the course to ask "When's the next course?"

Midway through the Gessler course Daphne brought to class some of her finest wall-covering books and fabric samples. They were set out on the tables, and a problem room plan was drawn on the blackboard and typical family needs and requirements listed for a class design project.

The women sat passively, with vacuous expressions, making no attempt to open the exciting, colorful wall-covering books or touch the one-of-a-kind sample fabrics. Daphne found herself saying to the women in desperation, "Grasp the cover of the wallpaper book between thumb and forefinger. With wrist rigid, raise the forearm from the elbow, propelling the outer cover into an upright position revealing the contents within."

They carried out these instructions solemnly, without a trace of humor or any apparent rancor. This response left Daphne ashamed at having resorted to sarcasm.

My God, she thought, *They're Zombie Wives!* This is what their husbands *want!*

She had stumbled onto a clue. It was all tied to money, and to these women's dependence upon their husbands to get money. They had to be what their husbands wanted —because of money. Their mothers' dependence, and their grandmothers' and great-grandmothers' before that —was because of money.

Didn't the men hate their dependence? Their women's depression, passivity and blunted affect? These women were intellectual zombies — often malevolently so — perhaps for generations. Such women rarely made the Overland Trail trek to Oregon and beyond. In the early nineteenth century those pioneer women had spirit and passion. Evidently Briarwood women had remained in the East for generations, according to intermittent genealogical accounts printed in *The County Observer*.

Their lives were a microcosm of the money/power malaise of the world — what it could do to men and women. Daphne would be relieved when the course was completed. But she was to be surprised at an unexpectedly passionate act that would result from her teaching the course: another Briarwood Enigma would be added to the zombie enigma.

CHAPTER THIRTY-NINE

Steve Vurokovich puttied the new panes of glass into Daphne's living room windows, having let himself in that morning to do the repair while she was teaching her design class.

The holes in the glass were fairly clean cut, Steve observed. The iron balls she told him about must have been shot or thrown with real force to make a hole like that, with that kind of radiating splintering. *Somebody must not like that lady,* he thought.

"Hi, Steve." Daphne tried to sound casual when she entered the room, but she was startled to see the contractor in her living room. They were old friends —and he had gotten into the house, of course, when he removed the glass from the outside —but it was just an example of how you can fool yourself into thinking your home is an impenetrable bastion.

"Oh, Hi, Daphne," Steve replied. "Is it lunchtime?"

"Yes. Just thought I'd check in to see how you're doing. How about a beer?" she called as she took some coleslaw and a tomato from the refrigerator.

"No, thanks. I never drink on the job."

Daphne believed him. Steve was a good, steady, conscientious worker whom she trusted. But still she felt uneasy about his being inside her house without having unlocked a door.

Steve packed his tool box, chatted about the cannon ball incident which, again, made Daphne uneasy, and gave her his bill which she paid; then he left. Through Daphne, Steve had gotten the lucrative contract for, and had expertly installed, the Hartley's new twelve-pane windows. Daphne noticed that he had billed her today for "materials only" for her window work. She was about to call him back and offer to pay the labor too, but she was too tired; she'd take it up with him another time.

She sat at her little pine kitchen table to eat her salad. The phone rang. Panic began to choke her, but she picked up the receiver. It was Harriet.

"Can you come?"

"Harriet, what *is* it? You sound awful!"

307

"I lost him. My Norm. He's gone. Norm's gone."

"God, Oh God." Daphne had to let the news sink in, to register. She had known that Norm's condition had worsened over the past few days, but not to the point of losing hope.

"Of course, I'll come. Where are you?"

"At the hospital. I can't stand to wait for you in the waiting room. I don't think I can drive. Come pick me up by the front entrance."

" —of course. I'll be there right away."

Harriet's braided, auburn hair was the first thing you noticed about her, usually. As Daphne wove slowly onto the long curving driveway to the hospital, she could pick out even at this distance that distinctive head, the graceful, long-legged stance, the narrow, cotton pants, the big full-sleeved top. Hospital visitors and personnel were opening their umbrellas on the way to the parking lot. A light rain had begun. Harriet could have been just another hospital visitor in dark glasses, waiting for a ride.

She ran to the car and got in quickly, reaching over to receive Daphne's cramped embrace.

"Don't talk to me," she said. "I can't talk yet. Drive to my place, will you?" She was dry-eyed, very controlled. The rain was heavier now, really coming down.

At the apartment she walked directly to the kitchen and got out a bottle of Pepsi, then put it back in the refrigerator and instead took a bottle of bourbon from the cupboard. She turned to Daphne.

"Go and shut the door to his bedroom, will you?"

When Daphne came back there were two glasses of bourbon poured.

"Just sit with me. Stay with me." she grasped Daphne's hand, pressing so hard that Daphne inadvertently winced.

"Oh, forgive me, Daph. What am I doing? Do I *know* what I'm doing? Harriet, do you *know* what you're doing? No, my girl, you do not know at *all* what you're doing," Harriet babbled. She raised her glass. "*Mazel tov.*"

"Does Ellen —have you told Ellen?"

"No one yet, except you." She gripped Daphne's hand again and drank the whiskey straight down.

"Harriet. Harriet. —Oh, Harriet —"

"Don't. I can't talk about it. Nothing. Nothing. No. Thing. I need time. Time. Time." She poured another glass of bourbon.

"How about if I try to reach Ellen —and Allison? I know Ellen's at home and Allison's at the Shelter. Felicia and the volunteers are there now, too. When did you last have anything to eat?"

"All right. Yes, call them. I ate yesterday. About six or seven last night. Try to get the others. Tell them to get me some fries and a quarter-pounder hamburger and a chocolate shake."

Daphne blanched, shocked. It had been Norm's favorite meal.

"Really? Can you eat that?"

"Yeah. Yeah."

Daphne pried loose her hand and dialled Ellen, then Allison.

Harriet walked, paced, back and forth in the little kitchen, into the dining area, into the living room, then back into the kitchen. Norm was everywhere: in his drawing of divers and swimmers taped to the refrigerator door, his Special Olympics mug in the dish drainer, his medicine bottles lined up next to the sink, his blue and gold zipper jacket hanging on the back of the desk chair, his fiberglass helmet on the desk, his bongo drums. They would have to be collected later and put into a closet, Daphne decided.

Pacing and drinking, Harriet insisted that Daphne drink her bourbon.

"Don't make me feel like a lush, Daph. I don't want drugs, tranquilizers. I just need some time!"

"It surely won't help matters if you get good and *sick* —" Daphne began.

"Nothing will help matters. Nothing. Everything is nothing. Sick. Not sick. Sloshed. Sober —what can it possibly matter?"

She had not shed a tear.

Back and forth, back and forth she paced. The rain on the

little window over the sink splattered loudly.

Daphne wondered, *Why is that damned rain so damned loud? Is it my imagination? It's loud! It's plenty damned loud.* She was worried that Harriet would be sick. Where *was* Ellen? How could Harriet keep everything bottled up this way? It wasn't like her to bottle up emotion.

Footsteps sounded on the stairs. Daphne ran to the door. It was Allison.

"She doesn't want to talk much," Daphne warned. "Just give her a hug. Keep it light."

"Light?" Allison said, incredulous.

They walked into the kitchen. Harriet turned and accepted Allison's embrace but resumed her pacing, then she stopped for a moment and took a glass out of the cupboard, poured some bourbon and handed it to Allison.

"You know I'm on the wag —" Allison started to say but was silenced by a look from Daphne.

The dutiful sips Allison took made Harriet laugh.

"Boy! You're *some* drunkard! Boy!" She bent over, cackling her familiar cackle. She was getting hysterical, Daphne feared, *and* drunk.

A knock at the door: It was Ellen, carrying a Burger King box. Daphne warned her about the situation.

"What do you think we should do?" Ellen said. "Doesn't she have a sister? In Mexico, or Guatemala or someplace? She lost her parents in the sixties. I don't think she's heard from Norm's father since right after he was born —"

"I'll have to get my car," Harriet said. "It's in the hospital parking lot. I have to go to Hirschbaum's tonight. To do the Last Act of Human Kindness. Norm's service is set for tomorrow night. I want it tomorrow, a memorial service for his friends. We have to call them. They may miss the newspaper announcement because it's the weekend."

"What? What do you have to do at Hirschbaum's?" Allison asked.

"It's the burial tradition. The Last Act of Human Kindness.

I wash him and put on the burial garments."

Harriet the intellectual, the iconoclast, was accepting the comfort of remembered family religious tradition.

Ellen drew in her breath in a little, gasping hiccough, tears filling her eyes. Daphne thought, in desperation, *Ellen's gonna mess up. Harriet seems to know what she's doing; the way she wants to get through this.* She motioned Ellen out to the hallway and told her of these thoughts.

Harriet finally sat down at the shaky chrome-legged dinette table on one of the two shaky chrome chairs, then got up again, went into the living room and returned with the desk chair and a fourth, folding chair. She sat down again and opened the Burger King packages. She ate a couple of fries. The others sat and watched as she tore open the foil packet of ketchup. She had had more than four glasses of bourbon. How did she keep from getting sick?

"He used to ask me why I named him 'Norm,' used to call himself 'Norman Abnormal.' I tried to explain to him that I named him after my father." She took a bite of the quarter-pounder but handed the chocolate shake to Ellen.

"I don't think I can handle this. You drink it. You like this stuff. You guys don't have anything to eat. Take some fries."

"We ate. We all ate already."

"He knew. He knew." Harriet went on. "He might not have been able to read and write so well, that twelve-year-old; he was no scholar, but he was perceptive! He didn't talk much, but there was very little that went on around him that he missed. Things others said. Little nuances. I never knew anyone who listened to music with more intensity."

She was finishing the hamburger. And the fries. She looked around the small space, at Norm's drawings on the refrigerator door, and through the doorway to the living room. She gave a little chuckle.

"Sometimes I thought those bongo drums were going to do me in. Can you imagine? I thought I'd like to have just one quiet evening sometime!" She chuckled again. "I guess I'm gonna have plenty of *them!*''

Ellen gasped another little gasp. Harriet rolled up the take-out containers and foil and stuffed them in the trash. "I have to get his things from the Special Ed locker. Come with me, huh? Then I can pick up my car."

They filed out onto the wet street with its rain-brightened buildings — mostly larger, older homes, remodeled into apartments — the wet gleam intensifying their general decrepitude. Two elderly apartment dwellers were walking their dogs, holding umbrellas over their pets: a poodle and a collie-German shepherd mix. Harriet had often referred to the neighborhood as "the dog poop capital of Bingham County."

Two young men in dirty denim jackets were attaching jumper cables to an old Chevy.

The street was a mix of students, young couples, retirees. The inevitable, desolate bundles of discards waited on the curb in front of the houses for street pick-up, proclaiming the ad hoc, transitory nature of their owners' lives. Faint strains of piano music floated down the street.

"A piano teacher lives in the corner house," Harriet explained. "She's terrific. Can play most of the Rachmaninov third Concerto and the Franck Sonata, Chopin Ballades. Lots of great stuff. Norm and I sit here on the porch sometimes, and listen."

Harriet's friends asked themselves what it could portend — that she had not shed one tear. It was plain that she was in a state of deep shock. Yet she *was* talking about him. It wasn't as though she refused to talk about Norm. But when the bourbon wore off, *then* what? It didn't seem wise, at this time, to go to the Special Ed building.

The Special Ed busses were lined up in the parking lot, chrome yellow, glistening in the heavy downpour. The four women huddled under umbrellas and were walking toward the gym as the doors opened and the wheelchair kids started down the ramps toward the busses, the usual two or three speed demons, in rain coats or capes and sou'westers, racing one

another, laughing and yelling. Following them were the spina-
bifida group, also in bright rain-slickers and hats, making their
slower, patiently determined way. Here and there a Kelly green,
blue or a red helmet bobbed.

Harriet stumbled and slumped and nearly fell. Daphne and
Allison supported her between them and entered the building
through a side door. The locker area was deserted and they sat
down on a long bench.

"Give me the key," Ellen said gently, after a few minutes.
"I'll get his things."

"No," Harriet said, "I want to do it."

She unlocked the locker door and filled her friends' arms
with her child's books, swim goggles, gym garb, sweat pants and
shirt; she untaped from the door the Olympics swimmer photos,
a photo of an unidentified pretty teenaged girl, a small mirror, a
classroom schedule. From the shelf she took a cassette tape. She
clasped it to her for a moment. Then she said, "This was his
favorite music of all, I think. It's *Der Rosenkavalier,* the Strauss
opera. It took months of saving for us to afford it —it cost forty
dollars. Norm loved the 'Presentation of the Rose' scene where
the doors burst open and Octavian, dressed all in white and
silver, presents the silver rose to Sophie. 'Play the silver music
again, Mom,' he would say. He never tired of hearing it. Norm
really was a romantic at heart. He loved the part when Octavian
and Sophie —both so young, just teenagers —sing of the wonder
of their love-at-first-sight meeting at the Rose Ceremony, and
Sophie smells the attar of roses perfume in the silver rose and
sings, ' —it is like having chords around one's heart.'

It goes like this: *'Ist wie ein Gruss vom Himmel / Ist hereits
zu start / ais dass mans ertragen kany / Zieht einen nach / als
lugen Strike um das Herz!'* It's so beautiful it's almost
untranslatable. I wish I could play it for you now."

They were walking past the gymnasium doorway. Thaddeus
Schaeffer, Norm's physio-therapist, came into the gym from the
pool area doorway at the opposite end. "Wait," Harriet said. She
walked into the gym and stood looking up at the giant rainbow

mural. Thaddeus, seeing her, smiled and waved and walked quickly to her. The others stood to the side by the bleachers, waiting.

She told him, then, and he stood looking at her, at her uncharacteristically slumped broad shoulders, her limp arms, her lowered auburn head, her ravelled-looking braid with its escaping, curly tendrils, her wrinkled shirt, and he put his arms around her, and they stood thus for a few moments as he wept with her.

He was looking now at the *Rosenkavalier* tape in his hand, turning it over and opening it. He nodded and disappeared into his office, and in a few moments the glorious, transcendent Richard Strauss music came flooding into the vast, empty, high-ceilinged space, filling the stillness where so recently Norm had laughed and shouted with his friends.

As the sublime "Silver Music" floated over them all — Norm's beloved "Silver Music" —Thaddeus held out his hand to Harriet.

An oboe called, a French horn answered.

Sophie begins to sing, "It is like a greeting from heaven / it is already too strong to be endured / It draws one as if there were chords around one's heart."

The exquisite, soprano voice scales an octave of incredible, tremulous purity as Thaddeus and Harriet begin to dance a slow, elegant Pavanne.

"Allein ich sterb is nicht," the unearthly beautiful soprano voice informs: "But I am not dying —*Das ist ja weit*—that is far away."

Harriet, her back arched, face upturned, eyes closed, tears streaming, is led by Thaddeus through a delicate arabesque, then hands joined, they step together in measured rhythm the ancient expression of grief and joy.

"Ist Zeit un Ewigheit in einem sel 'gen Augenblick —" The ecstatic voices of Sophie and Octavian blend as the French horn joins in counterpoint: "This is time and eternity in one, blessed moment —"

Arms outstretched, reaching upward, head thrown back, one knee bent, Harriet pivots slowly, surely, with every muscle tensed, toward the rainbow mural and the Old Sol sun face which once had smiled down upon her son.

Harriet danced for Norm; danced her grief, her love, her hope for herself; danced in memory of and in thanks for Norm, for his courage, his strength, the triumph of his life; danced with one who had loved and helped to care for and to teach him in that brief life. Harriet danced for her lost child.

CHAPTER FORTY

In the midst of Harriet's preparations for Norm's memorial service Traci appeared at the Shelter. Looking tanned and rested, she strode into her office (now air-conditioned) wearing turquoise silk coolie-pants, a golden oriental coat with black-silk-braid button loops, a wide-brimmed straw hat, also black, fancy spike-heeled sandals, and a Rolex wrist watch.

She took an antique ivory cigarette holder from her purse and, as she tapped a cigarette on her desk top, glared at Allison and Harriet. In the entry office Felicia filled out admission forms for two shabbily-dressed shelterees and their four, sweaty-looking children. Upstairs there were already seven new shelterees, two of them Black women, admitted in the last two days. It had been a frenetic weekend for Felicia and two volunteers.

"Clean out your desks," Traci ordered. "I want you out of your offices, out of this shelter, in twenty-four hours."

"Just like that?" Allison said.

"Just like that," Traci said breathily.

"You think you can *fire* us, after what's been going on — after what I witnessed, after your depraved *partying* and the *orgy* you told the board was an inspection and evaluation of a Nevada Women's Center. You think *you* can fire *us?*"

"It is within my power to hire or fire, in this organization. I have spoken with board members —the required majority —and they approved my decision. The confidentiality of my Las Vegas study cannot be breached. I am unassailable, unimpeachable. You are no longer employed here. Now get out of my office," Traci said, her lip-glossed mouth wetly forming each syllable, her enormous chest heaving.

"But Harriet just had —her son, Norm, just —you can't prove anything, that we committed any —"

"GET OUT!" Traci screamed.

"Come on." Harriet said, "Come on, Allison. This is useless." They went into Harriet's office.

Traci was using the "confidentiality ploy." Hiding all *her* sleaze behind "unbreachable confidentiality"! She had done it many times before. And she had a file on Allison containing "confessed" information about an abortion, a lesbian relationship, marijuana use — this occurred in high school — revelations that Traci would say later were *not* protected by the confidentiality between psychologist and client but were merely informal, friendly conversations —not counselling sessions at all —when Allison protested to the board of directors. "What about *my* confidentiality factor? What protects me?" Allison would ask them.

"Can't you see what she's doing? The injustice of it?"

"I know," Harriet said, simply, hopelessly.

"Oh Harriet. For you to have to have this happen —to go through this, at this time! We've got to get the board to listen! We'll call the Coalition. They should be told about what a *sleaze* she is! Do you know she was —oh —she," Allison continued with revulsion, " —she didn't inspect any women's center in Vegas! She came on to men in the motel, waitresses, me —she wanted me to put two steel ball bearings in my *vagina* and —"

Harriet winced and turned away.

"I'm sorry, Harriet. I'm sorry about all this shitty stuff — but it's the truth —"

An argument was going on in Traci's office. Then a door slammed. Bobbye ran across the hall to Harriet's office.

"I just got fired!" she exclaimed.

"So did we," Harriet said.

"Oh Harriet. What a thing to happen! I heard about Norm. Oh, I'm so sorry." Bobbye ran to Harriet and flung her arms around her neck.

Harriet was close to tears. They stood holding each other, but it was Bobbye who was crying.

Lorene Wilton suddenly appeared in the doorway, her baby, Tiffany, in her arms.

"What are you doing here, Lorene?" Allison asked, "I thought you were banished long ago. Did you know Traci's back? She's in her office!"

"I know. She call me this mornin'. Axt me to work today. Said you-all fired. She even say I could bring Tiffany for the day. I need the money, Allison." Lorene was reverting to her Butterfly McQueen routine — Prissy's dialect from the movie *Gone With The Wind*. It was a device she used, mainly in talking to Traci and others whom Lorene perceived to be racist.

"What strategy! Traci would even hire the Blacks she fired! She'd hire you back after firing you, Lorene, in order to get us out. You and Ora were the first fired when she first came here!" Harriet exclaimed.

Bobbye pointed out: "Yeah. She knows she has to keep this profitable place operating. We have over thirteen in shelter now, and I heard Felicia taking another call, just now. Traci won't dirty her hands — won't risk her designer outfit by having anything to do with the filthy *victims,* the unfortunate individuals this place was founded and funded for! But she knows that sheltering women keeps the money flowing. But what if a rape case comes in?"

"She'll fall back on volunteers. The very people you so carefully trained," Harriet said, "or she'll handle it herself. She likes all the juicy details of those rape cases!"

"Incredible!" Bobbye said. "She could carry it off. Run the place mostly with volunteers, and Felicia. The source of the money won't dry up — there'll still be the goose laying them golden eggs. And we join the ranks of the unemployed!"

Lorene nodded. "I know it. She a witch! But I need the hundred dollars she payin' me for today an' I might get some more work here. Tomorrow I got to dress up like a fuckin' slave an' be a washerwoman with Melba at that Congressman's party. I need the hundred and fifty dollar we each gettin' for that party. Miz Burgess payin' my niece and nephew to dress up like plantation niggers an' open an' shut her shithouse doors she got out back. —They AIR-CONDITIONED shithouses! Then my sister's other boy he gonna be a *house slave* at the party! We all doin' it for the money!" Lorene turned to Harriet. "Hey! How you doin', girl?"

"Rotten, Lorene."

Lorene handed Tiffany to Bobbye and went to Harriet, and they embraced silently for a few moments.

"Well," Allison said, "we have twenty-four hours. I can't believe there is no alternative, that nothing can be done and we're just being dumped from the Shelter that we founded and worked and *worked* for and she only lucked into. When she leaves tonight, let's barricade the doors and just keep her out; stall for time. Maybe some solution can be worked out."

"Stranger things have happened," Bobbye said. "Do you guys want to shut her ass out? Stall for time? Maybe get her the hell out of this shelter forever? Allison? Harriet? Lorene?"

"Do I *ever?*" Allison said.

"You're *ESKING?*" said Harriet in her best Yiddish accent.

"Is grits *groceries?*" said Lorene.

CHAPTER FORTY-ONE

"These things have been prying on my mind, Daphne, so that's why I called." Mrs. Hartley wanted a progress report nearly every hour. With her *soirée* only one day away, the countdown had begun for the increasingly anxious woman.

Her CorBlimey dinner experience, though unnerving — especially Rudy's moon-shot — convinced Edith and Bronwen Burgess that Chef Haselas's fashionable cuisine was the way to go for the "Coaches-and-Four-at-Five" fund-raiser.

"We gouged ourselves at the CorBlimey Saturday night," Mrs. Hartley had told Daphne.

A gourmet buffet menu had been contracted for with the understanding, of course, that "those awful men" (Rudy, the dishwasher, and Gino, the owner) and " — that appalling woman" (Rita, the bartender) would not be setting foot on the Hartley premises. But still disturbing was the women's realization that the CorBlimey waitress, Harletta Hoskins, was one of the invited guests to the party.

Also taxing Bronwen's *sang-froid* was Edith's insistence that the Consortium Antigua ancient instrument octette play such pieces as "Tumblin' Tumble Weed," "Wagon Wheels," and "Canadian Capers."

"Have you ever heard "Wagon Wheels" played by a viol da gamba, three viols, a sackbut, three recorders and a harpsichord, Drew?" Bronwen asked her husband contemptuously.

If it were up to Drew Burgess, they'd set the radio on the Easy Listening station and use the fourteen hundred dollars for a thirty-second TV spot for his campaign.

The Consortium had presented for approval these recommendations: works by Monteverdi, Gabrielli, Palestrina, Purcell, with some Vivaldi, Lully and Dowling "to liven things up," and Bronwen agreed to see to it that this program was adhered to.

James and DelMonte Studio's drapery installers stood ankle-deep in chintz. Scroll-edged upholstered cornices stood up-ended in a row in the spacious upstairs hallway. The last of the windows in four bedrooms would necessitate their working late, then returning at dawn and working all day. They would no doubt be escaping out the back door as guests came in the front.

Daphne and Debbie hung the last of the pictures. There were many reminders of the Krock's *Walpurgisnacht*. It was too close for comfort, again.

Near the breaking-point, Edith was hoarse from non-stop orders, questions, entreaties, phone calls. Gus Quip's knee breeches bagged in the seat and had to be run to the tailor's. Gus argued, too, about having to wear white stockings, and even suggested his one pair of black silk lodge socks, worn with black sock-garters, as an alternative. "And I never agreed to them buckled shoes in the first place —"

A week's cajoling had been necessary to get Gus to agree to the powdered wig. When he was reminded of the sum he was to be paid *and* a trip *and* a free condo, he argued that it was all a mistake and he expected to go to Epcot Center " —and all that other stuff," just for helping out with the coaches and horses, but he was not going to dress up, too. Loud fights ensued, the doctor had to be summoned from his office, Edith collapsed in tears, and another two hundred dollars changed hands before all was settled with Gus.

Melba, Lorene and Fern went through a dress-rehearsal without comment, Mrs. Hartley mistaking the two Black women's seething fury for passivity. LaVonda and Frankie " — my two poodrewzi kids,"did their bowing and curtseying with considerable charm. They were beautiful children, but so poor that the twenty-five dollars apiece, the lovely knot-garden, the flower-lined gravel paths, trees, seats and statuary, and the promise of a free party-meal besides, seemed to them a fantasy —an unbelievably wonderful dream. They annoyed Lorene by chattering happily and cooperating perfectly.

"I didn't axe you to like it so much," she muttered, snatching the white ribbon-trimmed cap from atop LaVonda's corn-rows.

The Raunch Factor

No one from CorBlimey Catering had yet appeared, but the bar had been set up in the library by Gus and the washerwomen, and many cases of liquor delivered. Rented metal tables were set up on the patio and side terraces. Tubs of geraniums, petunias and ivy accented the driveway and wide steps of the terrace, and flanked the French doors which opened onto the two back patios, and marked the brick walk leading to the large, graveled driveway where guests would disembark from the stagecoaches.

Mrs. Hartley had wanted speakers for the PA system installed at all four outside corners of the house, a suggestion at which Bronwen gagged. The Consortium could move outside after dark, she had maintained, and Edith sulked in her room a whole day about that —but to no avail. Bronwen won that round.

The services for Norm were held at the Hirschbaum Mortuary. Norm's Glenview Special Ed swim group, Harriet's Sojouner Shelter friends, including some loyal CR group graduates, were supportive. Even Ora managed to attend, with Thaddeus' assistance. Harriet's reunion with the sick Ora was both a sorrowful and a joyous one. Bronwen and Stephanie Burgess were the last to arrive, the first to depart, but their warm condolences were clearly heartening to Harriet, as were Barry Spiegel's and Hal's.

There was no music at the service other than the hauntingly lovely Kol Nidre, beautifully sung by Rabbi Levy whose Kaddish brought to Harriet's pale, drawn face an expression of peace and repose not seen in her before by Daphne. She spoke of it afterward to Hal as they drove to Ellen and Larry Kirschner's, where Hal was to see the video tapes. Bobbye and Allison had returned to the Shelter to clear out their desks.

"Harriet never talked about her family much —her parents and sister —to me," Daphne said. "I do know that she and her parents attended reformed Jewish services. Her grandparents were Orthodox. The service tonight affected her tremendously, I think. She seemed to gather strength from it. From that tradition of her childhood."

"I could see that," Hal agreed.

"I wonder what she'll do now. Her child gone. No job. Traci could even trot out some vindictive thing to prevent her getting work at another shelter —or *any* job. Just because Harriet was one of the original founders, had gained a following in her wonderful CR work —was a friend of Allison's!"

"When it comes to Traci, I have no comment, Daphne. I don't dare!"

"Oh, Hal." Daphne reached over and patted his knee. "I know. I know. I'm wiser now, but sadder. "

They parked in the Kirschner driveway and walked past Mark and Kathy's play-yard. In the center of the large toy-strewn sandbox was an expertly-modeled, near-life-size nude female torso, its mountainous breasts each tipped with a cherry tomato.

"Mark and Kathy do very advanced sculpture work," Hal observed to Ellen and Larry.

"That's DuWayne Krock's expertise. Our kids aren't allowed over there so he comes over here," Larry laughed. "It's a no-win situation. I wish he'd get a paper route or something."

"Well, you *could* have made short work of that sculpture with the *hose,* Larry," Ellen sniffed.

"It's supposed to rain again tonight," he said. They all sat down in the living room. The curtains were still closed.

After viewing the two video tapes, Hal sat in silence for a few moments.

"You do see, now, that I had to talk about this to Daphne, don't you?" Hal said. "I have spoken of it to no one else. The question is 'What do we do with this incredible information?' How do we fight a skilled agitator whose job —whose training — who is paid a large amount to do what he obviously has been expertly doing, to the CitAct Party? And in the employ of our own United States government! What do we do now? What can the Bill of Rights mean now if this sort of thing can happen —*is* happening to those of us who thought we had a guarantee of this freedom —who thought we actually lived in a democracy?"

"I don't know, Buddy," said Larry. "I don't know."

"Well, it's proof, isn't it?" said Ellen.

"Proof of what?" Hal asked.

"Proof that he has misrepresented himself, is passing himself off as someone entirely different from what's in these films. That he's claimed to have been unemployed for years, and just barely get along doing odd jobs. All these years he's had no visible means of support. And that's the Franzes' pose too, the 'unemployed' pose, I think. They work hand-in-glove with him. They're seldom ever apart. I think they're dupes. He uses them."

"Dupes, like us?" Daphne said ruefully.

"No, they're *in* on it. They have been right along. I think he pays them. And they're stoned a lot. I think he keeps them supplied with drugs —pot. Probably various drugs." Ellen said.

"I was so naive, so trusting," Hal said, "when Ted said he'd like to draw up our by-laws —he sounded so enthusiastic, really well-intentioned, as if he really wanted to be of help to the Party —I welcomed the suggestion, I saw it as an earnest effort, on his part, to be of help. Now, in going over those by-laws I can see all manner of loopholes. There are statements that are open to all kinds of interpretation. How could I have been so naive?" He put his face in his hands.

"You were just human, Hal," said Daphne, her brown eyes flashing, "just one person, doing all kinds of incredible things — your human rights platform, your desire to reform the system, to open up the undemocratic, incredibly restrictive ballot access — I should say 'non-access' — in this country. All have been questioned, shaken —are being taken apart and examined expertly by you, Hal!" Daphne said, her brown eyes still flashing. "You've bucked the system and were succeeding!"

"Yeah. You're doing such a good job of it, Buddy, our terrific government decided you have to be stopped! Stopped cold."

"There's the rub! All our work, for nothing. I had such plans. We could run people in the next election —it's an off-year, we could run people for row offices —and win some! I had the idea that Ted could run for Sheriff. He could *win!* People like the idea of a big, big guy for a sheriff candidate. Ted had it all. The promise — well, the *hint* of brains, the easy-going personality. The physique. Small town boy makes good!"

"Running for Sheriff? Him? That's small potatoes to him!" Larry laughed.

"Yeah. Heavens yes." Ellen added, "Knowing what we know now, almost any job would be small potatoes —a good joke. That sick giggle of his! How he must be laughing!"

"You *do* agree, though, that we ought to keep a low profile about this? Not confront him? Any more controversy could just cost us more members. They're staying away from meetings, walking out of meetings, there's trouble enough already," Larry said.

"Well, something in me is outraged! I want him stopped! I want the agitation to end. Why — we have a *KGB* in this country!" Hal almost shouted.

"Of course! We all want him out, Hal. That's natural. Your —brain-child, all your work, your energy, all that *petitioning!* It makes me boil to think about it. But what good can confrontation possibly do? Larry's right." Daphne said. "And yes, we *do* have a KGB —just like in Russia."

"My better judgement says you're right of course. All of you can think more objectively than I can right now." Hal answered.

The phone rang. "Who could *that* be, at midnight?"

Ellen went into the kitchen. She returned quickly.

"You're not going to believe this, Daphne, but your client, Mrs. Hartley —she's been raped! She's in the Bingham General Hospital! She called Bobbye —I guess they're neighbors —and Bobbye went and got her and drove her to the Emergency Room. The poor woman is pretty badly beaten up. Allison thought you would want to know."

CHAPTER FORTY-TWO

Daphne climbed the stairs to her bedroom, her thoughts whirling, jumbled, exhaustion causing some suspension of disbelief. How could it *be?* Edith Hartley, beaten, raped?

Edith's home and property had been swarming with workmen for weeks. She, Daphne, had subcontracted work with floor-finishing people, painters, window replacement people! They were all old, established firms who were bonded and trustworthy for years. There were never any thefts or accidents or "incidents," just good work. Could it have been one of the workmen? Maybe a landscaping person, hired temporarily. Maybe robbery was the motive; there was obviously money being spent — all that conspicuous consumption, the elaborate furnishings, the paintings.

The police would be called in, would be there by now, and so would Bobbye. Bobbye was an expert. She may have been fired, but she was on the scene doing the same, conscientious job she always did. Allison and Ellen had locked the Shelter against Traci. It had been decided that she would be kept out. They would barricade the doors if necessary, to gain time, to decide what action to take.

And the Burgess party! The fund-raiser! Surely they'd call it off! But how could they notify hundreds of people? The guests had paid five hundred dollars apiece! Most of those invited had accepted. Edith had gleefully told Daphne, there were very few "regrets." The money had been received. They would not let the news of the rape out to the papers. Now, surely they'd go ahead with the party. They'd simply *have* to!

"Can you talk at all?" Bobbye asked gently. "Or does it hurt too much? Your lip, I mean."

Edith Hartley, her upper lip swollen to triple its normal size, tried to sit up. Her swollen left eye gave her round, moon face an even more oriental aspect than usual. Her arms and throat were lacerated, and bruises like thumb prints or fingerprints lined her legs and ankles.

"We need to take some polaroid pictures now, and the nurse wants to get a vaginal smear, Mrs. Hartley. I know you're hurting, but it's essential if we're going to track down the man who did this to you."

Edith shook her head and moaned. "Nooooo hnlp. Nooooo, dneedatumlp!"

"You won't give your permission?"

She shook her head again and groaned. "Dneedatumlp."

"Do you *know* who did it?" Bobbye bent closer.

The nurse was standing by with a cotton swab.

"The officer's out there waiting to take your statement, but we must get this other work done first. You want to bring charges, don't you? Don't you want this man to be tracked down?" Bobbye insisted.

Mrs. Hartley propped herself on her elbow and looked into Bobbye's eyes. "I knyow who jdid it!" she said thickly.

"You *know* who it was? Did you —do you know the man?"

"Yedze."

"Do you know his name?" Bobbye was trying to remain calm.

"Ut waj myh huzhban!" Edith croaked.

"Your husband? The doctor? He beat you up, and raped you?"

"Yedze." She began to weep, rocking back and forth on the high examining table.

"Are you sure? You're absolutely sure?"

"Yedze, yedze!"

The curtain to the cubicle was pushed open and the resident physician entered. "Let's take a look at that lip." Ten stitches had been required to repair Edith Hartley's mouth. "Maybe tomorrow a plastic surgeon should take a look at this," the resident said.

"Mnotszdayun hur," Edith moaned.

Bobbye asked the resident, "Can she be discharged? Is it okay for her to go to the Sojourner Shelter after they've done taking her statement?'' She turned to Edith, ''Do you want me to take you to the Shelter —the women's shelter, you know?''

The resident nodded, gave Bobbye a prescription, and left the cubicle.

Edith nodded also and lay back on the table as sterile gauze was placed on her sutured lip. She reached for Bobbye's hand. ''Zjank you,'' she said weakly.

Before morning three more Bingham County women checked into the Sojourner Shelter: Felicia Haselas, Harletta Hoskins and Audrey Hopper. All had been severely battered.

Although she had driven herself to the Shelter, Felicia, obviously suffering from a broken nose, and possibly a broken jaw, was driven to the hospital Emergency Room by a volunteer, where a sworn statement was taken and officers were dispatched to arrest Herb Haselas.

Harletta's problems, though mainly dental —three of her upper teeth had been knocked out — and she had a possible broken rib, also were psychological. She had tried to break off a relationship with Leonard Blake who had administered the beating after an argument about the peculiar circumstances surrounding his wife's death.

''I can't take it no more,'' Harletta sobbed. ''It's a lucky thing Rutthell can get me in at the dental thchool clinic.'' She lay back as Ellen put a cold compress on her forehead. ''Thank God for you girlth,'' Harletta lisped as she wiped her eyes. Her elaborate hair-do was in disarray, but she had managed to tie an old flowered short wrapper from the Shelter's discard-box over her black CorBlimey waitress pants, creating a stylish ensemble.

Edith, Harletta and Audrey were in the Sojourner Shelter attic bedroom. Four single beds and a baby crib fit in a row in the sloping-eaved room. The Shelter was now filled to the capacity permitted by fire laws, except for three roll-away cots.

Audrey lay on her side, a compress on one eye. Bloody white gauze on her arms and on one leg contrasted with her dark smooth skin. Her close-cropped Afro-style hair showed her well-shaped head in spite of the slanting, stitched-together cut that sloped from her upper hairline back toward her left ear. She wore, defiantly, the little close-fitting purple-and-white woven skull-cap that had become a sort of signature —her costume, her style —complementing the colorful African blouses and dresses she loved. She had been treated at the hospital and then discharged, like the others. Only Felicia was detained for observation and x-rays.

Audrey's baby daughter, wearing only a Pampers diaper, slept in the crib, undisturbed by Edith Hartley's moans and sighs.

It was hot in the attic. The heavy rain of the previous two days, almost a record cloudburst, had not cooled the atmosphere, but only made the humid, murky night more sticky and oppressive.

Allison came puffing up the attic stairs with a large electric fan. "This might help a little," she said, plugging it in. "If the sun comes out in the morning we're done for!"

"Ahhrw," Edith groaned. "Ijht's sjwewtewrin hewr." She turned onto her side, thought better of it and rolled onto her back again. Her pain pill had not yet taken full effect, but she was aware, hazily, that an urgent happening of some sort was to occur soon, but she couldn't focus on it clearly enough to nail it down. She wished vaguely for a telephone, for some ice water; she should be talking to —talking to —flowered curtains were closing over her mind. She slept.

"As far as I can tell, Chef Haselas is not going to get out of jail for another twenty-four hours at least. His wife, who it turns out was pregnant, has had a miscarriage! With her other injuries and her sworn statement, they can legally keep him in jail and set very high bail. My husband has explained to me the legality of this so I thought you might know some of the CorBlimey Catering people. The owner —here Bronwen Burgess's voice shifted into frosted *hauteur* —that *Gino* person, doesn't know anything about the Hartley party menu, the preparation, nothing. But this party is going to go forward on schedule —just as if Dr. Hartley and his wife —that poor, dear soul —were here. No one's heard from *him* at all."

Daphne shifted the phone and sat up in bed. It was six A.M. Felicia —a miscarriage? In the hospital? Herb in jail? It was so confusing.

"Herb Haselas controls everything. He was never much for delegating things. Not ever," Daphne told Bronwen.

"Next in line would be the sous-chef. Maybe he can take over. I don't know his name, but the piano player there, Ellen Kirschner, would know. Why don't you call her?" Daphne gave Bronwen the phone number then took a cold shower and tried to wake up.

By seven-thirty the drapery-hanging crew were on the job, James had the fresh flowers allocated for three immense Flemish-style bouquets that Daphne had contracted for, and the last rolls of sod were being rolled into place on the west terrace. There were no caterers, still.

At ten o'clock heavy rain began again. "Great for the sod and the planters!" cheered the landscaping crew; not so good for Mellors Lane which led from the Burgess driveway to Hartley's entrance, and was bordered with deep, muddy ravines. The two stagecoaches had been delivered on a flat bed truck and were parked in the Burgess driveway. The eight horses were grazing in the Burgess pasture. Gus Quip, the major-domo, was to direct the liveried drivers, footmen and car-parking boys, as well as welcome the guests. Alas, Gus was clearly in over his head, a fact to be discovered all too late.

Good Lord! thought Bronwen as she hung up after her idiotic conversation with Elwood, the sous-chef, *There won't be any food! There's nothing prepared at all!* The vodka-campari aperitif to be served just before the dining room doors are dramatically flung open (revealing the stunning buffet supper set out on the table), all the hors d'oeuvres — walnuts in Parmesan butter, whipped mortadella canapés with chopped pepperoncini, little plum tomatoes stuffed with eggs, anchovies and capers; the grilled goat cheese in vine leaves; little fried eggplant slices, layered with a pesto of green olives and capers; zucchini boats stuffed with shrimp! Those were just the canapes, to be served on the hunt board in the gun room. And the buffet —the buffet to be set out on Edith Hartley's beautiful "Shippingdale" table in the gorgeous dining room with the stunning Zuber *Scenic America* mural — "just like the one in the White House," Edith had crowed to Bronwen. There was simply not going to *be* any sumptuous buffet supper after all! No *Teglia di Cozze,* the wonderful baked mussel dish with potatoes and fresh tomatoes, no *Torta di Spinaci,* and the veal for the *Polpettone di Vitell Farcito di Peperone Roso* wasn't even ground yet, that stupid Elwood said, and the special Italian celery for the dish —for which Bronwen had made a trip to the city — wasn't even cleaned!

"Practically nothing is done!" Bronwen went in search of Daphne. The sun had come out at last! But it was hot! Hotter than ever. Thank God for the Hartley central air!

As she rolled up her car windows and turned on her air conditioner, Daphne saw Bronwen running across the field, through the knot garden to the driveway. She was waving.

"Oh," she gasped to Daphne, "we've got to talk! Edith is sound asleep at the Women's Shelter. I talked to her twice and she's non-compos —just out of it. I don't know what to do next! No one knows where the Doctor is. Of course, there's an all-points bulletin out. Those stupid CorBlimey people haven't prepared a thing!" Daphne got out of her car and they walked into the Hartley kitchen.

"We can't serve Kentucky Fried Chicken! Or those stupid fish sandwiches from the Loaves and Fishes, although my husband loves them," Bronwen said morosely as she and Daphne had coffee in the Hartley breakfast room.

"Why *not* Kentucky Fried Chicken?" Daphne asked.

"These guests paid five hundred dollars apiece! It has to be a special menu and plenty of it. I had exquisite dishes worked out

—a northern Italian menu with very unusual hors d'oeuvres and about ten entrees and *all* to be served on special china, with beautiful crystal and silverware the CorBlimey was to supply. And desserts! There were to be five superb desserts served from a dessert cart —the washer women were to pull the buckboard wagon around for the desserts —"

They decided to try calling local restaurants to see if a buffet menu could be assembled quickly from the specialties of five or six of them. They would skip the hors d'oeuvres. An open bar with olives and fruit in mixed drinks might mollify the guests. Not a thought had been given to ordering plates, glasses or flatware.

CHAPTER FORTY-THREE

The baby-blue station wagon, the official Sojourner Shelter vehicle, now assumed to be Traci's "own," was parked in the Shelter parking lot.

Lo and behold, Traci's in it, Daphne observed. *I'll drive around the block and park on the street so they can let me in the front entrance without her knowing.*

"Friend or foe?" someone yelled when Daphne rang the doorbell. It was Allison's voice.

"It's *me,* Daphne. Let me in!"

Inside all was quiet. "They're all asleep. Everyone was up most of the night," Allison said, pulling the mini-blind apart to look out at the parking lot. "She's been out there since six this morning. She won't get past *me!"*

"I'm still in shock," Daphne looked around the parlor. Coloring books and toys were strewn about, a *Love Story* magazine lay on the tattered sofa. These evidences of human life were not permitted by Traci-edict, but there it was anyway — human life. How much longer could she be kept out of the Shelter? It was stifling in the parlor with the door closed. The small fan served only to stir the humidity.

Harriet and a volunteer, Marie Schwartz, were wrestling a roll-away bed into Traci's office.

"Marie has stuck by us and is a tremendous help," Allison said. "I've had four hours' sleep in the last thirty-six. Bobbye had to get some sleep so she went home. The other volunteer, Betsy Benton, is one of Traci's acolytes and won't 'man' the barricades, excuse the expression, so she left. We're running out of food. If Harriet or I leave, we can't be sure what the Shelterees will do. They're in pretty bad shape —some of them so despondent they're almost crazy. No telling what Traci might get them to do. We can't prevent their going out for food, though, and diapers —provisions —things like that."

Three roll-away beds in a row in Traci's office, visual blasphemy in those sacred precincts, stood opposite a baby's play-pen. To Daphne's unspoken question, Allison answered,

"It's too hot for the women in the attic. They're sweltering up there, and they're in pretty bad shape —hospital cases actually — but they wanted so much to come to the Shelter. What the heck, this is the only air-conditioned space in the building —Traci finally got it —so why not use it to help make them more comfortable?"

Marie Schwartz quickly tucked sheets on the three cots. Harletta, holding her hand over her mouth, came slowly down the hall from the stairway, carrying her pillow and her purse. "Thith purth ith all I have with me," she mumbled to no one in particular, " —and theeth panth and my shooth. Thath all I ethcaped with when the bathtard sharted to thmack me." Panda-like purple circles around Harletta's eyes were incongruously droll, but filled Daphne with sickening shame —almost nausea.

She was to feel, repeatedly, the same profound chagrin in the weeks to follow, during which she would teach the Briarwood Zombie Wives at her Gessler Museum classes. She would continue to ask the same question of herself, over and over: "How can they turn off their brains, relinquish every vestige of autonomy, pride, their personae —for money; to be reduced to being well-fed, walking corpses in designer shrouds? How?"

Daphne knew Harletta was a hard worker —waitressing was hard, physical work —but how could she have endured any contact at all with the exploitative, violent Leonard Blake? Was her self-esteem that shaky? Had he driven his wife, Lucille, to suicide? Harletta had had a liaison with him for many years. How could she let him use her all those years? And for what? Perks? An occasional payment on her car? Or clothes? Or an apartment in a slightly better neighborhood than she, alone, could have afforded? Harletta doted on her son, adored him; maybe she did it for him. Women would do amazing things sometimes, for their children.

Audrey Hopper limped down the hallway carrying her baby, her pillow, her purse, and the baby's diaper bag. Daphne knew her slightly from CR days at the Shelter. Audrey was considered outspoken, controversial.

"Hi, Audrey," she said, " —here let me take your pillow, and that bag —"

"Take *her*, will you?" Audrey nodded at the baby. "She heavy on my arm. I don't have a good arm. Got one good leg, but not much else," she grimaced as she lowered herself onto the bed, panting. Sinking dread and shame again filled Daphne, seeing the cut scalp, the bandaged arms. She felt shame for the whole human race.

She was astonished at the baby's weight, the solid-feeling chunkiness of the little body. She was about five months old. Her close-cut cap-like hair curled softly, was not yet divided into sections as Lorene's Tiffany's hair had been since babyhood. "What's her name?" Daphne asked.

"Kereema."

The infant began to squirm and whimper. She turned around and looked into Daphne's face, her little snub nose wrinkling, her face changing into an expression of dismay-fear. Had she seen, could she remember the violence done to her mother? The big, round eyes filled and she twisted toward her mother stretching her plump little arms and wiggling. Daphne thought the child smelled wonderful. She had held an infant on very few occasions in her lifetime —she came from a barren family, was the last of the line — but on those few occasions she was struck by the lovely infant fragrance; not powder, not soap — it wasn't identifiable like that —it was just different from an adult body, an indefinable deep sweetness, not just a superficial applied perfume substance. She didn't want to let the baby go.

"She's beautiful," she said simply, and handed her back to Audrey.

Mrs. Hartley shuffled down the hall as the others had, carrying her purse and her pillow. Daphne involuntarily cried out, "Oh! Oh, Edith!"

What was this grotesque mask? *This* had been the Mrs. Doctor Hartley she knew?

"Hay dah hay," Edith gave Daphne a ghastly, lop-sided smile with her lower lip. She was dragging one leg, moving very, very slowly.

"Let me help!"

Daphne rushed to her, took the pillow, and attempted to take Mrs. Hartley's arm.

"Owwww!"

Daphne jumped back. "Omigod, forgive me! I didn't mean to hurt you, Edith."

"Oh-ell, a few 'or 'ont 'ake 'uch difference." She sank groaning onto the remaining bed, then lay sideways and looked up at Daphne. "'Wing muh 'eet up, 'ill ya?" Daphne lifted the wretched woman's feet slowly onto the bed. She could hardly bear to look at the ruined face.

Marie Schwartz took Allison's place at the venetian blind in the parlor.

"She's still out there. Why don't you lie on the couch a while?" she said to Allison.

Harriet came in with two glasses of ice water and bent paper straws. "It's time for another pain pill. Who wants another pain pill? Edith gets one for sure; Harletta? Audrey?"

"I can't. Not unless she get one too," Audrey laughed, indicating baby Kareema.

"I'll watch her for a couple of hourths, Harletta said. "I'm not gonna take no pain pill. Give me her food and thinths and you get thum sthleep, thum relief."

"Her bottle upstairs in the Frigidare. She only eat cereal, an' apple sauce, in this here bag." Audrey sagged sideways, then swallowed her pill and lay down. She had, beneath the bruises and contusions, one of the most classically beautiful high-cheekboned faces Daphne had ever seen. Her delicate looking, almost too-thin body was nevertheless shapely, even in the drooping pajamas supplied her from the Shelter discard box. Could Thaddeus Shaeffer have done this thing to her? Not the Tad Shaeffer Daphne had met, had seen that day in the gym with Harriet. It could not have been Tad; was it the baby's father, then?

Thaddeus Shaeffer could not visit Audrey to be supportive

and to comfort her; the Shelter was not like the hospital. Here, men usually were not permitted past the outer vestibule.

Our civilization has come such a long way, has progressed so admirably, thought Daphne, —*that we need these sanctuaries to set women apart, to seal them off, to protect them from their benefactors.*

Allison had told Daphne that Dr. Hartley had mistreated his wife over a long period.

"When I asked her why she didn't come to the Shelter before this, for help, she said it was because of the 'astigmatism' connected with anyone who goes to a women's shelter. She felt shame."

That was Edith all right; she felt the "astigmatism." Again Daphne felt the searing dread, the sorrow —and anger —anger for the distortions of mind and body that the sick, sick system produced in men as well as in "their women" —the victims of "their" men's warped perceptions.

The Stop and Spend meat department was frosty and cool, even cooler than the rest of the super-cool store. Time spent here was a wonderful relief in summer.

Daphne consulted her list of items she had agreed to pick up for Shelterees. All had hot dogs on their lists along with baby food, Pampers, tampons, baby aspirin; a pathetic testimony to their vulnerable state of fecundity and hapless femaleness.

Ellen Kirschner rounded the corner at the end of the aisle and was headed for the hamburger department when she saw Daphne.

"Hi," she called, "Hal's around here somewhere. I saw him a little while ago, by the peanut butter."

She grabbed her usual five-pound packages of hamburger as Daphne brought her up-to-date on the Shelter situation. Mark, seated in the cart, started yelling "Poop Poop Poop" upon seeing Daphne.

" —So they're just sitting tight, now, with the place pretty well barricaded, it's under control for now. Traci's tried all three doors and hasn't left the parking lot yet. I'll keep in touch."

Daphne found Hal in "baked beans" and together they pushed their carts to the parking lot. He looked haggard and depressed.

"Let's get an after-dinner liqueur," she suggested, "and I'll cook a special dinner tonight. Something really different!" He nodded half-heartedly and they unloaded their groceries. His purchases were the unimaginative, dry cereal-crackers-coffee-milk-detergent-toilet paper supplies of an inveterate diner-out. His children, who were spending the summer with their mother, could barely pour a bowl of cereal on their own.

"I have another neat idea, Hal. Karen Schuyler's at Club Sappho tonight — you know, that lesbian comic. She's very politically astute and really funny. The show starts at 10:00."

Daphne was eager to help Hal pull out of his depression.

"Oh, thanks, but no, thanks. One or two scrotum jokes would be my limit and she tells them all evening, I've heard."

"Well, now you have an inkling how women feel, have felt since the beginning of time, with tits and ass jokes flying around them at all times."

"Yeah. Good point. But the women don't protest —they go right on posing for *Hustler* and your oft-referred-to necrophiliac mag *Spicey Mortician,* and shakin' it in those infernal beauty pageants and night clubs. Men won't permit themselves to be trivialized in this manner."

"Brainwashed, women are brainwashed!" Daphne insisted.

They walked across the heat-shimmering asphalt, past the CorBlimey "moat" over which a drawbridge led to the restaurant's brass-studded door. The battlements and crenellations of the imitation stone castle never looked more pathetic than they did now. Even the two tall square towers, the talk of the community when first built, today seemed even sillier and more childish than ever, as did the two fiberglass knights in armor flanking the door —like a poor man's Disneyland.

A leaping marlin —caught by Gino at some Florida Mafia

hideaway —which greeted CorBlimey patrons in the vestibule — along with other nautical collectibles: rope rigging, sextants, fish nets, ship wheels, portholes; this conflicting mixed metaphor decor and the excellent Italian peasant cuisine made Daphne smile. The patrons' lives were as garbled as the decor. How many deals were struck here? How many pay-offs — Machiavellian maneuvers? All revolving around power/money. Yet —how were corporate heads, agribiz, stock manipulators any different from Gino's Mafia shark and bookie cronies? And the medical profession with its huge PAC support of the AMA lobby —didn't they have their own "Cosa Nostrum"? How were they any different from the Mafia —just because they ostensibly operated within the law?

"What are you grinning like a Cheshire cat about *now?*" Hal said as they walked into the icy-cool liquor store. It was so early that the store was nearly deserted. In the rear, by the bottles of golden Attitude Adjuster Mix display stood Ted Mather and Don and Mary Alice Franz. Their almost-filled shopping carts held Harvey's Bristol Cream, Hazelnut liqueur, vodka, Chivas Regal. Daphne could see these items from where she and Hal stood.

"Hal," she squeezed his arm. "Don't look now. It's Ted and the Franzes. Just didn't want you to be startled —"

"I feel like punching him, Daphne."

"I know, the poor folks have such a hard time of it so they need plenty of alcohol for solace."

"They're looking this way. They see us."

"Just act natural. Remember our agreement. You can carry it off," she said.

The three were coming down the aisle, red-faced —there was always that facial flush like a heavy drinker's flush —like the alcoholics they obviously were —Ted giggling and snuffling, towering over Don and Mary Alice —over them all.

"Well, speak of the devil —" Ted was giggling harder than ever. It was clear, up close, that his cart held about two hundred dollars' worth of small-sized bottles of exotic liqueur.

"Hello, Ted," Hal managed to appear cordial. "Hello, Don. Hello, Mary Alice. What're ya up to?"

"No good. No good, Hal. You can be sure of that. Ha ha," Mary Alice snickered.

"Hi, Hal. Hello, Daphne." The Franzes nervously pushed their cart toward the check-out counter.

"Stocking up for the weekend, or what, Ted?"

"A buddy of my brother's is visiting him —wanted me to get him this stuff. And to think I could have went to the cabin this weekend —in exchange for painting his place, that is. But it looks like this weekend I *ain't* gonna *paint*. That's a pome. See ya at the Speech In the Park meeting —"

Abruptly Mather pushed his cart past Hal and Daphne and into the check-out lane. The Franzes already had departed. Daphne felt the hair prickle on the back of her scalp. Suddenly a chill crossed her neck and back.

She went quickly into a raspberry-cordial display area —a mock half-gazebo complete with trellis and carpenter's gothic jigsaw work, with painted foliage background —and the floor seemed to move beneath her. She held onto Hal's arm when he went to her. He looked questioningly into her eyes. Up front, the cash-register rang; at last Ted would be leaving.

"You did okay. Don't take it so hard," Hal said.

"Hal! Hal! It's Ted! Ted's the one. The one who's been making the obscene phone calls!"

She tried to whisper. She felt like throwing up. Ted was ambling out the door now, wheeling three full bags.

"How did you figure that out *now?* All of a sudden you just *know?*"

"Yes. Yes." She swallowed another wave of nausea. "It just hit me. Just now. Suddenly it's all clear. His grammar. He's very careful about grammar. I think that's why he talks relatively little. He has to be on guard at all times. Well, today he slipped. Just now. He let slip a stupid use of a participle. In the calls I get —in almost every single one —he messes up grammatically —especially any use of participles, as I said before, and that

342

phrase, 'That's a pome,' he said that in the last couple of calls. And his voice pitch —he speaks very high and whispery on the phone —well, he let that slip too, just now —that high tone is his normal voice. He forces the pitch somewhat in everyday conversation —at CitAct meetings —situations like that."

"Then you've solved it."

"Yes. I'm certain. And I'm certain that he realized what he did just now. That he *did* slip up. To think that I've known him for nearly ten years, yet never once suspected him!"

Again she felt as if she were going to vomit. Then it was Ted who had been making those revolting calls! And *he* knew that *she* knew!

CHAPTER FORTY-FOUR

Debbie and James pulled into the Designs For Living parking lot in the truck; Daphne, having arrived a few minutes earlier, was unloading her car. On the dock she stacked her picture-hanging kit, electric kit and small tool kits. The early afternoon June sun beat down on the concrete, amplifying the temperature far beyond the summer average of eighty-five degrees.

"Whoever said Western P-A has a temperate climate? I sure miss the Hartley air-conditioning," Debbie gasped as they hauled the ladders and drills from the truck to the cool receiving room.

"Well done. The Hartley job was *well done*. You guys rose to the demands of that installation and I'm proud of it —and of you!" Daphne said as they drooped into her small office. She turned on the air-conditioner and took three cans of beer out of the little Arctic-Aire refrigerator built into the long credenza behind her writing-table-desk.

"To Debbie and James. *Cent'anni!* May you live a hundred years!" Daphne raised her beer can in a toast. "Now, how quickly can you vacuum the whole shop and wash the front windows?" Their faces fell.

"Only kidding! We're closed for the rest of the day, so take the day off!"

Debbie looked sideways at James, "Wanta go swimming at Bingham Creek?" Her very unsubtle yearning after James was embarrassing to Daphne *and* to him.

"Uh, sorry," James explained, "I have three weeks' laundry to catch up on."

"Pretty feeble," Debbie whined. "Pretty feeble. You've crawled around six bedrooms with me for the last three days, Jamie. You'll have to come up with something better than that." James' golden tan colored into a deep red. He was acutely aware of her romantic, frankly sexual interest in him and, though he was accustomed to women's interest in him —he was accosted everywhere he went —bars, show rooms, clubs, on the street — Debbie's Unrequited-Love script was never ending and

increasingly unsettling. Now, if *Daphne* had the slightest interest
—had given the slightest indication —

Debbie slammed down her beer can on Daphne's desk and
ran out of the office.

"Oh, shit. I'm sorry, Daphne. Just when things were going
along a little better. We didn't have *one* on-the-job argument
doing the Hartley's installation," James said.

"Don't worry about it. She'll get over it. What do you hear
from Kenny these days?" Daphne said abruptly; she was aware
of James' loneliness for Kenny and of his worry concerning him.

"He writes or calls every couple of days. I'm thankful for
that. He likes the job at the Xanadu Bar, sent me some Polaroids
of a party some Tampa guys had last week. The menu must have
been phenomenal. You know Kenny —boy, can he eat, and never
gains an ounce! He said the desserts there are famous." James
dug in his breast pocket and extracted a packet of photographs.

"There's one picture I particularly wanted you to see." He
handed it to Daphne. It showed a gathering of stylishly dressed
handsome men, standing, glasses raised, around what appeared
to be a lavish spread of exotic-looking platters of food. In the
back of the group, one very tall, heavily muscled man grinned.
He fairly jumped out at Daphne. It was Ted Mather. It was a
very clear photograph.

"That look like Ted Mather to you?"

"Yes. I think it's Ted all right. When was this taken?"

"About a week ago, according to Kenny."

James said nothing to Daphne about the gossip concerning
Kenny being seen with "a real big new guy."

Ted at a Florida Gay bar? He *was* reportedly out of town
last week. Florida would be a logical stopping-off place for an
agent unobtrusively flying into some private —or even public —
airport, in an unmarked plane, from, say, Costa Rica. But why
would he be so casual about allowing himself to be
photographed? And in a Gay bar? Ted —Gay? Whom was he
stalking now? Tracking down? Maybe he had had a lot of
cocktails, was letting down his guard.

The Raunch Factor

As Alice-Through-The-Looking Glass said, "Curiouser and Curiouser," Daphne thought. She felt a skin-crawling burning on her neck. She couldn't mention any of the recent happenings to James, of course. "What do you make of it?" she asked him.

"Beats me. A friend of mine said he *thinks* he's seen Ted in a Gay bar here in the city. He sort of stands out, of course. But there were fairly low lights, the way they always have the lighting, and he couldn't be absolutely sure. I was really surprised."

"Did he ever come on to you, say, at CitAct meetings or anything? Not that this is any of my business, I guess, but, well, I don't understand him at all —his behavior at our meetings and fund-raisers. His Pot-head behavior is a real turn-off for many members. It's damaging to the party."

"I think the whole thing's an act. Like he has a script and is acting out a part."

So James suspected too! Where to from here?

"See if you can find out anything, from Kenny, about Ted. Don't mention a name. Just ask him 'Who's the guy in the back row in that picture' —or something like that —maybe we can find out an a.k.a. We're getting bogged down. Iron cannon balls being shot at my house —Hal's car tampered with —"

James did indeed want to question Kenny, but for different reasons.

They turned out the lights and air-conditioner and closed up shop. Daphne had hoped to check on Felicia at the hospital, but had promised Bronwen Burgess to make one final check-up at the Hartley's.

They were in a real bind for food for the affair. And they needed so darned *much* of everything. People would just get knee-walkin' drunk if all they served was that seemingly endless supply of alcohol. It would seem really tacky not to have plenty of special food. There was the CitAct Party sausage in her freezer and Ellen's. But that wouldn't be nearly enough. Daphne smiled. Imagine the Republicans being served hot sausage sandwiches! What a come-down. By now, Mrs. Burgess no doubt had rounded up a bunch of entrées they could set out on the table.

When she pulled into the Hartley's parking area the Consortium Musica octette members were getting out of their cars and carrying in their instruments and folding music stands. They had disappointed Bronwen when they told her they didn't have antique brass back-to-back music stands with candle holders on them. "Only our instruments and our music are antique," the Concert Master had said dryly.

An ethereal-looking gray-haired man carrying an odd-shaped trombone-type instrument went in the front doorway. "That must be the sackbut player," Daphne surmised.

Two octette members lifted a digital keyboard from the hatch of a Chevette. They could hardly be expected to pretty up the driveway with Mercedeses or Morgan sports cars. *Where's the antique harpsichord?* Daphne wondered.

It was clouding up and looking like rain again; the humidity was closing in. On the side terrace Fern and Melba and Lorene, all wearing blue jeans, spread pale pink circular cloths on the tables. Several landscaping people had been drafted to set up folding chairs. There was no sign of Gus Quip. Thunder rolled faintly from somewhere in the direction of the next pasture.

Bronwen Burgess in red-and-white poppy-print organza and dyed-to-match scarlet shoes and white embroidered hose —all stunning with her tow-colored WASP hair —teetered across the brick terrace and down the wide steps.

"Oh, you've no idea how terribly frustrating this is!" she called to Daphne. "Do you know that every restaurant I called has reneged on their promise —"

Inside the house there were sounds of recorders tuning up and the deep resonance of a cello-like instrument. Daphne paused, "Ah!" she breathed, "that's a viola da gamba. There's no sound like it in the world."

"Do you like baroque music?" Bronwen asked, brushing back blond strands from her glistening forehead. "The university music department wouldn't let us have the antique harpsichord for tonight, *also* at the last minute."

"Oh, yes! I could listen to baroque music by the hour. But, omigod, we've got to get back to the food —the food!" Daphne said. "Here's an idea —The Presto Presto Pesto Pizza —" She ran her finger down the page of the phone book,

"The *what?*"

"Presto Presto Pesto Pizza. 'One-half hour delivery or your order is free.'"

"Pizza?" Bronwen said wonderingly.

"Well, it says 'Pesto' too. Didn't your original menu have pesto dishes?"

The Consortium evidently had finished tuning up. Melancholy strains of the introduction to "Dido's Lament" from Purcell's opera, *Dido and Aeneas,* commanded attention with its elegant simplicity and sonority.

The octette's arresting sound was an ideal harmonic blend for the stately, early compositions; the almost creaky-sounding sackbut, the viol's vibrance, and the keyboard on its harpsichord setting played Dido's haunting song, sung to Aeneas after he has abandoned her.

> When I am laid, am laid in earth —
> May my wrongs create
> No trouble, no trouble
> Within thy breast.

Bronwen and Daphne sat for a few moments, transfixed.

"That's so lovely! I wish I could forget this entire hullabaloo —just send everybody home and sit and have some drinks and listen to this octette. My husband's so nervous and keyed-up, and Stephanie has been talking of nothing else — waiting for this day when she can 'help Daddy' with his campaign. She wanted a long dress and apron and cap, just like LaVonda and Fern and the others —"

Another thunder clap shook the house. It began to rain again.

"The tablecloths!" Bronwen gasped. "The girls are changing into their outfits in the washhouse! Where *is* that other little darkie —Nelson — the one that's to be an extra footman?"

"I'll help you," Daphne said.

They began to snatch up the pink linen cloths. Frankie, LaVonda and Stephanie, laughing and giggling, rounded the corner of the house at top speed, pelting one another with petunias. Ten-year-old Nelson, who, like Frankie, wore knee breeches, stockings, buckled shoes and full-sleeved shirt and a white peruke tilted over one ear, followed, shouting, "I'll wup yo-alls' asses," shaking an antique fly-whisk. The four children disappeared behind the two elegant "poodroozies" at the back of the knot-garden.

Tablecloths crushed in their arms, the two women fled back to the kitchen. Daphne looked back in time to see Gus Quip drive the tractor over the crest of the back pasture, holding an umbrella over his blue satin suit. A flock of eight Merino ewes and one splendid, curved-horned ram had arrived three days before, to Edith Hartley's delight, and were now installed in the pasture. The new small gambrel-roofed barn, not yet painted, but undeniably picturesque, stood in the protective bower of the hill that Gus now descended. It was a calendar scene of quaint bucolia.

Drew Burgess's Mercedes pulled into the parking area to the far side of the south terrace —an area deliberately planned by the landscape architect as an enticing, midway vista where a glimpse of five expensive cars could titillate at all times, from any direction, with the espaliered wall of the five-car garage providing a mellow brick and foliage background.

Burgess sprinted across the terrace and into the kitchen. He wore the *de rigueur* open-necked blue-and-white houndstooth-checked shirt, navy flannel blazer, chino trousers and loafers.

"Wow!" he said, "quel pluie dans la jardin!" (This rhymed with "well phooey hands lay carbin.")

"Drew Burgess," he announced in a nasal bray, as he shook Daphne's hand, while staring intently at her chest. "Found out anything about the eats, yet?"

"We're working on it, Drew," Bronwen said sourly.

"Get a bunch of Fritos and some onion dip and we'll just keep the wine and spirits flowing and nobody'll know the difference," he whinnied. Having spend the earlier part of the day on the golf course, he was now scarlet-faced and sweating.

"Everyone will be sick all over Edith's chintz couches," Bronwen scowled at him.

"Does that combo play anything else besides hymns? Jesus —don't they know something cheerful —you know, something *swinging?*" Drew complained.

"Even Edith agreed to an all-baroque program, Drew."

"Well, I'm gonna get a drink and then see if I can get'em to play 'ShaBoom ShaBoom.'" He whinnied again and went into the foyer where Gus was propping open the forty-two-inch-wide solid walnut front door. The first coachful of guests was due to arrive at any minute.

In the kitchen Bronwen blotted her make-up and patted her hair. "I'll be expected to make an appearance before long, but first I've got to call these damned Presto Pesto Pizza Pesto places. If they have six locations, surely they can supply us! But do you realize we never once thought about plates and glasses and flatware?"

"You won't need silverware," Daphne said.

"I guess not. But we should have plates and cups. About three hundred."

"Leave it to me," Daphne said. "I'll go and get some plastic ones."

She started down the long, wide, beautifully wallpapered foyer toward the front door where the first stage-coach load of six guests now entered. They murmured and laughed guardedly, the women fluffing up their rain-flattened coiffures.

Daphne was astonished at Gus's appearance. He looked quite presentable — even elegant. His feather-trimmed tricorn sat squarely on his peruke. He lifted the hat and swept it in a wide arc as Edith Hartley had coached him, and bowed low before the guests, one foot extended, as he wheezed, "Wel-come. Mind you don't trip over at-terr rug."

The guests entered the vast living room.

It is *gorgeous,* Daphne realized. Working so closely on its individual parts had obscured, for her, the finished whole, but as in all of her design work, that finished "whole" had flashed through her brain the first time she had ever seen the space, before she had begun any work on the room.

The women guests murmured and shook hands with Drew and mentally assessed the cost of the furnishings. The men haw-hawed loudly and shook hands with Drew and mentally assessed the cost of the furnishings.

"How d'ya like our combo?" Daphne heard Drew's forced heartiness. "I don't know what piece those cats are playing."

A short pause, then one of the male guests wheezed, "My wife says it's about some broad getting laid so it can't be all bad, Drew!" The other guests laughed nervously.

Daphne ran out into the rain —it was really pouring now — to her car.

As she drove out of the driveway, she passed the first stagecoach which was rocking and wobbling from the Hartley's driveway back onto Mellors Lane, the four horses, unaccustomed to pulling as a team —to doing *anything* as a team —took choppy little dressage-like dance steps as they made the turn.

Far down the lane, turning onto Mellors from Connie Drive, came the second bouncing, wobbling coach, the top-hatted drivers and liveried grooms and footmen all wearing slickers and plastic hat-protectors. Already the puddled driveway and lane were dotted with piles of horse-droppings.

The Burgess's two Dalmatians and three Jack Russell terriers slunk, mud-spattered, along the side of the lane and were peeing on fenceposts as Daphne drove down Mellors Lane and out of Chatterley estates towards town.

Chapter Forty-five

I feel like a traitor, giving aid and comfort to the enemy, Daphne thought, as she loaded into the trunk of her car plastic plates and cups, and paper napkins, all purchased for the CitAct picnic.

She had a dull, throbbing headache, brought on no doubt by the cumulative effect of the rush to complete the Hartley job, the trouble at the Shelter, and now having been drafted into service for the Burgess fund-raiser. The humidity, like masses of invisible feathers, swirled around her, and she fairly dripped with sweat in this typically semi-tropical Pennsylvania June.

She heard her kitchen phone ringing. *Let it ring!* she thought, defiantly. *Let the machine answer.*

After four rings, a woman, speaking very fast, with a trace of a southern accent, said, "Daphne Singleton, you pompous ass, just who do you think you *are,* anyway? With your snotnose attitude —the way you think you're better than everyone else! A lot of other people think you have a snotty attitude and you'd better watch it! You're gonna get it, you little bitch!" The machine beeped off.

A hate call for a change? Almost a threat; well, it *was* a threat. Who could it be? Daphne went over in her mind the women she knew who had southern accents. With the exception of a few Black women —and this woman was not Black —it was one of those things that you just know —she could think of only three women: Liz Heckman, Mrs. Hemsworth Seavers — a former student in her Briarwood Art League-sponsored design class — or Fern Slagle. Fern would never use a word like "pompous"; "ass," yes, but "pompous ass," never.

And Liz Heckman —Daphne felt that she and Liz had always been on good terms. Besides, she had had few dealings with Liz other than at Shelter board meetings — before they became "board members only" meetings. So it had to be Mrs. Seavers, an extremely rich, middle aged woman who had travelled the world over —several times.

Mrs. Seavers had taken over whole blocks of design class

time, telling colorless travel stories that dealt mainly with posh hotel accommodations and annoyances of poor service at various European and Asiatic museums and restaurants. She had informed the class that the Prado in Spain had a terrible rest room.

Martha Iverson had dropped out of the class because of Mrs. Seavers' monologues.

"I didn't sign up for that class just to hear her boring travelogues."

After three classes, Mrs. Seavers also had dropped out. In the interest of diplomacy, Daphne had attempted to "contain" Mrs. Seavers *and* placate the intriguing, free-spirited Martha Iverson, but no amount of persuasive phone calls could induce Martha to return, and her tuition eventually was refunded.

It had been a relief to be rid of Mrs. Seavers, but for a year her hate calls, all worded much the same as that first call, would replace Ted's obscene calls. Ted Mather never called Daphne again.

Thus, one passionate act of one Briarwood woman resulted from Daphne's Briarwood teaching experience. A sheltered, rich woman's hatred moved her sufficiently to express herself with great intensity, for one full year.

But why? Why? Only in Briarwood did Daphne encounter, from women, the pervasive apathy which alternated erratically with dark, brooding malevolence. How could these privileged beings endure living out their lives — apparently successive generations of women —with such low self-esteem when, by the tenets of their own value system, they "had it all"? It was mystifying.

The bookie groupies at the CorBlimey were so culturally impoverished that their almost primitive state of non-intellectuality was somehow understandable, but Briarwood women were constantly exposed to educational advantages.

Still remaining in Daphne's class was one bright spot —New Delhi-born Sugantha, "Sue," Govinda, who each week called out her strident observations from the back of the room, in her clipped, "Hindlish" accent: "No-that-iss-not-so-the-Elgin-marbles-belong-to-the-British-museum-not-to-Greece," or her weekly reminder: "you-haf-told-that-to-us-*last*-wick!"

Daphne missed Martha Iverson and Martha's rain-lamp clippings and Green-Stamp-Catalog taste, her superbly drafted, cross-hatch-shaded, ink drawings of her terrible chairs and sofas.

Years later, in retrospect, the phenomenon of this design class experience came to lodge finally in Daphne's consciousness as the Briarwood Enigma, and always, with this thought, she experienced (instead of anger) profound stirrings of pity for these women, and sorrow and shame for their having thus been so warped despite their lives of security and privilege.

Daphne washed her face, changed into a fresh linen blouse and skirt and drove back to the Hartley's. She turned onto Mellors Lane and drove past the Krock entrance pillars and the little pink-faced jockey lantern holder. At first Ed had the black face painted white, then at Bobbye's insistence, he had it repainted a virulent peach-pink which, given the exaggerated thick lips and flat nose of the nineteenth century cast-iron antique, made the figure an even more ghastly parody.

Daphne thought about Bobbye; they had not spoken since the terrible morning after Ed's fund-raiser. Now their only communication was through Bobbye's attorney whose terse demands for reparations appeared at regular intervals. Designs For Living was a huge-overhead kind of business operation; profit from the Hartley job, and the Screamer, and Yuppie accessory and drapery jobs simply could not cover Bobbye's demands.

Still, Daphne missed her. She was, after all, one of the original shelter staff that had begun operations at the new Bingham location —their dream location —when at long last they moved from the Doncaster building; they had struggled and worked together. She was their first rape crisis director, a pioneer, a fighter like the founders.

Although it had stopped raining now and the sun had reappeared, it was hotter than ever. Over a hundred and seventy-five Burgess supporters strolled unsteadily about the terraces after touring the house's elegant, air-conditioned interior. Drinks in hand, but having had no food, they were directed by Gus to the replicated Mt. Vernon washhouse.

Gus grew more dishevelled with each new coach-load of guests, and the guests themselves became more irritable as the stagecoach novelty began to wear off. Coach passengers had to disembark by jumping several feet to the driveway into puddles, or worse, as the coach drivers, attempting to avoid piles of horse droppings, stopped well past the stone mounting blocks which were too heavy for Gus and the footmen to move to each new disembarking point.

LaVerne Krock suffered a turned ankle as did Miss Dialysis — a.k.a. Nurse Funbuns. The wife of the Republican County Commissioner — a Bitsy Exalted Grand Leader — *sprained* her ankle and had to be carried on the Commissioner's and Drew's interlocked-hands-seat. They staggered into the house with the two hundred-pound woman and summoned orthopedic surgeon — and big A.M.A. lobby contributor — Ambrose Gifford, M.D., who did not conceal his irritation at being summoned from a billiard-room snooker game to minister to the Commissioner's wife. However, he made several offers to Miss Dialysis and LaVerne Krock to " —have a look at that leg."

Earl Roy "Brimmie" Krock could be found under the pergola at the end of the west terrace expounding to members of Miss Dialysis' Kidney Kort on the biblical injunctions concerning Christian Women's marital duties and their failure to take sexual "initiative" — which he pronounced "in-ee-sha-teeve" — resulting in their husbands' battering them. To this wisdom, the Kort members, in their Penelope's Shame Boutique halter tops and draped, wraparound mini-skirts, nodded in grave assent.

By now Gus's white stockings, mud-splattered and bloody

with mosquito and fly-bites, were twisted around his knotty-muscled calves. He had abandoned his hat-doffing flourish and welcome speech after the fourth or fifth carriage load.

His peruke sat askew, its ribboned queue unravelling and unkempt, his long-abandoned tricorn hat was now cocked over the brow of a life-size bronze statue of the goddess Ceres who watched over the revellers from her sheaf-of-wheat pedestal in the center of the rose garden beside the back terrace patio.

Mellors Lane had become so muddy and hazardous that many guests elected to park their cars at the Burgesses' or along Clifford or Connie Drives and walk the quarter of a mile to the Hartley's, rather than to risk the stagecoach ride. They arrived at the big front door perspiring and out-of-sorts.

Daphne and Bronwen spread the wrinkled tablecloths back on the terrace tables, and guests sat down gratefully and sipped their drinks and swatted flies or availed themselves of the beautiful, air-conditioned "poodroozie houses," where they tended to linger too long. Frankie and LaVonda attempted to keep long lines from forming by knocking on the doors and yelling "Next!" Guests were ill-prepared for the poodroozie disaster that would soon take place.

At the washhouse, her mobcap worn atop her fiberglass helmet, Stephanie handed out the gift-wrapped favors from the laundry kettle while the turbanned and aproned washerwomen lounged on the settle-benches behind which they concealed their pewter tankards of Chivas Regal.

There were mixed reactions to the party favors; mainly comments about their being silver-plated and not the expected sterling silver. Through the evening guests could be seen stirring their drinks with the disdained, *plated* candle-snuffers and cigar clippers.

And still no food arrived.

" —but it hasn't been a half-hour," Bronwen told Drew. "I had to mingle with the guests, didn't I? Six different Presto

Presto Pesto Pizza places will be delivering, they promised, in a half-hour. I had to call them all —to get enough delivered."

Drew was agitated. "The guests are starting to get mean. Senator and Mrs. Trumble will be here soon. He called and said they can be here after all! They're making a special trip from D.C. to show their support. I sent Tim to meet their plane. Bert Trumble's a terrific booster, and what a couple they make! The old guy's so dignified and she's such a beautifully-groomed lady! She's not on D.C.'s best dressed list every year for *nothing*, you know. They're both so elegant —so *Old Money!* But there's no more potato chips in Edith's pantry. Everyone scarfed up the three packages —and they were rancid; Jesus, Bronwen," he shook his head at her, as if it were her fault.

A stagecoach lurched into view far down Mellors Lane.

"Another coach approacheth," Drew shouted, "Man the shovel, Gus! Here comes another load!"

Not certain which kind of load his boss was referring to, Gus had been sneaking shovelfuls of manure to the bushes at the side of the driveway and had given Frankie, LaVonda and Nelson each a shovel, and hasty but pragmatic instructions about dumping horse droppings around the espaliered fruit trees by the garage, which instructions, alas, the children either didn't hear or simply didn't heed.

A cry went up on Mellors Lane. The stagecoach had skidded into the culvert and was resting partly on its side. The grooms quickly unhitched the horses, while, in the poodroozie buildings, shovelfuls of horse droppings soon clogged the two toilets (and the ladies' bidet) as the thee children hastened to carry out Gus's instructions in what seemed to them a perfectly logical manner. The splendid, water-saver flush mechanism quickly jammed the toilets under the pile-up, and a deluge inundated the two charming outbuildings, but no one was paying any attention.

Cries could be heard coming from inside the nearly overturned carriage as the coachman and grooms and footmen rushed ineffectually around and around the vehicle. Then Senator Trumble's head and shoulders emerged from the coach window followed by Mrs. Trumble's. The footmen and grooms began to push the coach right-side-up onto its big wheels again, causing the Trumbles to disappear abruptly. Next, the head and shoulders of Drew's aide, Tim Rhodes appeared, then disappeared, as the men rocked and shoved the antique vehicle. Inside the coach, the cries grew louder.

"Wait! Wait! No! No!" Drew shouted, "For God's sake let them get out first! We'll set it back up afterward! Let them get out!" The three Jack Russell terriers were delighted with their master's antics and yipped enthusiastically, rushing about his ankles. The two dalmatians, having leapt onto the coach, which now slid completely onto its side, licked the faces of the Trumbles as they again emerged through the windows.

At the house, guests lined up on the front terrace or lurched down the driveway through the wrought-iron gates, stepping carefully around piles of droppings.

In the living room the Consortium struck up a madrigal. Wilfred Helmeir, the elderly, venerated president of the National Association of Manufacturers, went out onto the terrace in disgust. He had been told that the combo played "old time" music. Three times he had requested pieces: "Jada," "Oogie, Oogie Wah Wah," and "Your Lips Tell Me 'No, No' But There's 'Yes, Yes' In Your Eyes," and they put him off every time, but there was plenty going on down the road so who needed that long hair music?

Wilfred could see what appeared to be Senator and Mrs. Trumble —that *had* to be Bert Trumble's white hair —sitting under a tree by the side of the road. A man was lying on his stomach and reaching into the still-over-turned coach, pulling at another man. Wilfred turned to Daphne who had come out onto the terrace, "That's my accountant, Tyson Tylass! By God, old Tyson's got mussed up this time! His tie's crooked 'n' everything!" Tyson Tylass was being helped across the road as, out of the stagecoach window another head and shoulders appeared. It was Ellen's mother.

"Holy Toledo," Wilfred exclaimed. "If it isn't Eloise

Ames! If her and Tyson's dignity survive this, it'll be something!'' He trotted down the driveway enthusiastically.

The guests were milling around by the haha. The moat-like ditch, a clever barrier that had been copied from Capability Brown's design for the English estate, Greenfields, curved around the main side and front acreage from the pasture. A gate over a small bridge and a ramp controlled the sheep's grazing.

Someone had opened the gate, and the ewes were now filing onto the front acreage. The three dogs, bored with the stagecoach, barked excitedly and nipped at the sheep's hooves.

Daphne could see a white-haired couple being helped into the tractor cart. Gus drove the tractor up over the lawn and onto the driveway. He had discarded his satin coat and weskit but wore still the dickey-type shirt-front and lace jabot. With his peruke turned nearly sideways, in his backless top and clam-digger-like knee breeches, he looked, from a distance, as though he were wearing some sort of bizarre beach attire.

The Trumbles sat with their feet dangling from the cart as the tractor bore them up the winding driveway. The Senator waved, weakly. Mrs. Trumble dabbed at her Trigére lettuce green silk Original. Her large straw cartwheel hat was caved in on one side, its long, green-velvet streamers trailing over the side of the bright red cart. Drew Burgess walked alongside the cart anxiously grinning.

The guests shouted cheers of encouragement. On Mellors Lane Tyson Tylass and Eloise Ames leaned against a tree, and the two remaining passengers crawled out over the side of the mud-caked coach on their stomachs.

It was at this moment that the magnificent curled-horned merino ram appeared around the side of the haha from the back pasture, walked up the ramp, through the open gate and ran and mounted one of the ewes. The crowd wildly cheered the copulating animals.

On the front terrace Bronwen Burgess sank down on one of the stone benches in utter disbelief as Daphne doubled over with uncontrollable laughter. By now, most of the guests had gathered on the upper lawn. Some of the women turned away in embarrassed befuddlement.

"Party's gettin' better by the minute!" a male voice yelled. "Way ta go, yaaaay!" a group of JayCees waved their drinks and shouted, "Up an' at 'em!" While Queen Dialysis and the Kidney Kort disappeared sanctimoniously into the house, Brimmie Krock ostentatiously helped his wife LaVerne to limp to the back patio.

Louise Delaney, the leader of the Bingham County branch of Precious Pink Feet stomped down to her car on Clifford Drive, with six of her PPF followers. They were heard to mutter "appalling" and "tasteless" and other deprecations about "no refreshments at *all,*" "cheap trick," and Louise was heard to say something about stopping payment on contribution checks. Young Nelson, his livery in disarray, nearly collided with the PPF ladies as he ran around the side of the house onto the front terrace.

"Where's Gus at?" he panted. "Shithouse commodes has ran over!"

CHAPTER FORTY-SIX

Strains of Vivaldi floated out over the humid, late-afternoon heat as Senator and Mrs. Trumble, leaning on Tim Rhodes and Drew Burgess, tottered across the brick terrace and into the Hartley's foyer.

The Senator was led off to the bar while Mrs. Trumble allowed herself to be guided to an exquisite bérgère in a corner of the living room. Her muddy feet propped on a comfortable antique gout stool, she accepted a vodka-and-tonic and prepared to enjoy her favorite baroque music, performed as she liked it best, in the intimate, chamber setting of quietly sumptuous eighteenth century-style ambiance, with the promise of the epicurean viands for which Bronwen Burgess was noted —indeed, was famous —impeccably served with Bronwen's Spode, crystal and sterling.

Mrs. Trumble was founder of Symphony Salads, a Bitsy splinter group that contributed thirty to fifty thousand dollars yearly to the Briarwood Concert Orchestra. She nodded now and smiled an acknowledgement to the sackbut player. To her relief there would be *some* redeeming features to this day's incredible succession of indignities after all: a delightful dinner and Evan Peterson's Consortium Antigua.

A quiet circle of music lovers grouped themselves respectfully around Mrs. Trumble as the Consortium began the lovely "L'Autumno" movement of *The Four Seasons*. In the library, half-crazed with hunger, guests circled the hunt table and stabbed at the last of the maraschino cherries and remnants of martini olives.

In grateful acknowledgement of their patroness, the Consortium rendered flawlessly the Vivaldi transcription, the viols, sackbut and electronic piano playing together " — as beautifully as I ever heard you perform" —according to Concert Master Peterson in a later recap of the concert " —in as ghastly an experience as I ever endured."

Upstairs Bronwen and Daphne conducted gaping guests through the six bedrooms and perfectly-appointed sitting rooms,

363

the luxurious baths, each with its superb, hand painted ceramic tile and coordinated wall-coverings, while Bronwen's rain-soaked scarlet shoes bled onto her Vitale Cantini embroidered white panty hose, venous red lines crisscrossing like giant varicosities on her arched insteps.

"Thank God for the Consortium," she whispered to Daphne. " —it's something I *know* Mrs. Trumble loves!"

Halfway into the Consortium's rendition of the *largo* movement of the Vivaldi *L'Inverno,* the distant, raucous piping of a calliope sounded. The piping grew louder. It was playing "O Solo Mio" and grew louder and louder until it seemed to be directly in front of the entrance terrace, which indeed it was; the first Presto Presto Pesto Pizza truck had arrived. Bronwen fled to the terrace where the driver was alighting from a large red, white and green-striped van carrying a stack of grease-blotched boxes. "O Solo Mio" piped on.

No sooner had the first van departed than the second delivery van "O Solo Mioed" up the driveway and another greasy stack was unpacked and served and snatched from the table so fast that the dining room draperies blew as wave after wave of guests streamed into the dining room.

In the living room Mrs. Trumble stirred nervously in her bégère and the Consortium played valiantly on as the third Presto Presto van pulled up, its calliope even louder than the first two.

Guests continued to shove and jostle their way into the dining room where they loaded their plastic plates and lurched onto the patio, tearing at their pizza as they went, dragging out appreciatively the long, melting mozzarella strands. Mrs. Trumble gasped as Lorene Wilton handed her a greasy plastic plateful of pizza and a styrofoam cup of Pepsi Cola.

The Vivaldi work came to a close as the fifth Presto Presto truck pulled up, calliope (and sheep) loudly bleating. At a nod from Evan Peterson, the Consortium struck up a John Dowling madrigal, "A Lover and His Lass," which Peterson himself began to sing, to the delight of Mrs. Trumble and her circle who happily sang-along the Elizabethan song. On the third "Heynonny-no," the sixth Presto Presto van arrived before the fifth van had departed and the ensuing cacophony —A Charles Ivesian fugue punctuated by bleating sheep —assailed everyone's ears.

Then the Consortium simply quit. A red-faced Evan Peterson bowed stiffly, folded up his music stand, picked up his music and his sackbut and walked out. The other musicians followed suit, filing behind their director through the foyer and onto the terrace to their cars, just as the Bingham police arrived, patrol car signal light flashing.

Two police officers entered the foyer. An APB was out, and they had received a tip that Ernest Hartley was somewhere on the property. Bronwen shrank back against the lacquered Coromandel screen —one of a pair flanking the doorway to the living room — as the officers, Berettas drawn, crept up the stairs to the second floor.

In the upper hall, the startled guests' cries blended with the fading "O Solo Mio" strains as the last Presto Presto truck proceeded down the driveway onto Mellors Lane. There was no trace of the doctor.

At dusk, on the Hartley terraces, Gus and Daphne and the washerwomen began to light the lanterns and hurricane torches and the small hurricane candles on the tables. The foliage spot lights were switched on as well as little mushroom lamps lining the garden paths. The Hartley garden glowed in this fantasy: the romance and theater of the flickering candles, the up-lit trees and shrubbery casting dramatic shadows, the brick and stone walls, the windows of the handsome, hybrid Greek Revival-Georgian-Cum-Tudor house providing a rich, tapestry-like background for the scene. Mrs. Hartley would be proud, Daphne thought.

Comfortably satiated, the remaining one hundred or so guests chatted on the terraces amiably sipping after-dinner liqueurs, calling out affably to Bronwen and Drew that it had been " —one of the best parties you every had!" and "We haven't had so much fun in years!" They showed no signs of wanting to leave.

"Do you think you could get your friend, the piano player from the CorBlimey —Ellen what's-her-name?" Bronwen asked Daphne. "We can bring the keyboard out here on the back terrace. It looks as if the rain has stopped for a while." A few stars were blinking through the haze, and a pleasant light breeze blew away the humid murkiness.

"Tell her I'll pay her, of course, and make up any lost CorBlimey wages and *then* some," Bronwen said.

Ellen was scheduled to play at the CorBlimey Lounge. Gino had closed the restaurant section temporarily when he realized that Elwood was totally incompetent to get together even the simplest entrees and had not even ordered any supplies and they had run out of flour and bulk sugar completely; three waitresses were trying to sweeten cheesecakes by tearing open dozens of little individual sugar packets.

"I may get fired, Daphne," Ellen said. "I've never called off before, but I guess I could, this once. Have you talked to anyone at the Shelter? Harriet said Traci's getting a court order so she can get in the building and take over again. She got a look in her office window after dark. She must have seen the roll-away cots in there and the baby and the playpen and Audrey Hopper —a *Black* woman, and the other two women —all the things she hates! All cluttering up her House Gorgeous Magazine-picture-office! She told the police, and she's retaining Agnes Harrison —you know —the attorney that's on the Shelter board, and the word is that the police are coming."

"Oh, Lord. Harriet and Allison could be arrested!"

"I *know*. Traci's her old self again! She has the board completely buffaloed, as usual. They bought her entire confidentiality pitch —she's always hidden everything behind that confidentiality stance and can get away with *anything*. We don't know a thing about her! Where's her husband? She mentioned a husband at her first interview. And what about her references? None of them ever responded to our enquiries. No one's been in her apartment —ever. Is she just a made-up person? Is she for

real? She's come out of nowhere and manipulated us so that
we're powerless! Boy, were we ever *dumb,* Daphne!"

"I know. I tried to warn you and the others —"

"I know you did, I remember. But no one would listen. We
were all naive and trusting and *dumb!"*

"Well, listen, Ellen — how are the shelterees getting
along?"

"They're doing terrifically well —talking together, rapping,
you know. Edith feels a little better. She wants to go home, she
said. Bobbye's been in to see her a couple of times. She got
Edith to agree to bring charges. The doctor's still on the loose.
Herb Haselas has not posted bond and is still in jail. Gino won't
help him out any. Felicia has to stay in the hospital a few more
days. Her doctor is Jerry Gupta —Kamala's husband. Bobbye's
gone to see Felicia, then she's going home. She's exhausted.
Bobbye, I mean. And Harriet and Allison are trying to run things
alone. The one volunteer had to go home —she has three little
kids. Three shelterees were discharged so it's not quite so
crowded. The shopping you did helped out a lot. Now they'll just
stay holed up until we see what Traci's gonna do next, that's the
news."

The lightweight electronic keyboard was carried out to the
back terrace, and when Ellen arrived she found a restless
audience milling about, who were glad to sit and listen to her
jazz improvisations.

They called out their favorite pieces for Ellen to play as
Bronwen and Gus set up two of the Burgess's coffee urns. The
car parking boys had been sent to buy up all the doughnuts they
could find as well as some coffee. The sheep and ram were
corralled again into the back pasture, and the haha gates were
closed. When a light went on in the small sheep barn, it was of
little concern until the police patrol car reappeared around the
end of the washhouse, red lights flashing. They must have
received another tip.

There were shouts from the pasture and a figure was seen running across the field with the ram and two officers close behind. From there it was a matter of just a few moments before the doctor, having been butted smartly several times, was led to the patrol car.

When cowboy-hatted Drew appeared over the knoll riding his favorite Appaloosa — Drew only *feigned* an anglophiliac equitation bias —and gave a western-style riding exhibition in the waning, dusky twilight, complete with a spectacular jump over the haha, the guests, jaded from the afternoon's revels, applauded politely and turned back to the pianist.

In the background were Edith Hartley's pride and joy, the two poodroozies airing out, with their carved, paneled doors standing open and the nearby coiled garden hose a remainder of the cataclysm that had met Gus's eyes after Nelson's announcement.

By the time the doughnuts arrived, Lorene, Melba and Fern, having had no food, but with plenty of Chivas Regal at their disposal, were now amenable to pulling the small buckboard out of the garage and serving the dessert, such as it was, according to Mrs. Hartley's original plan. But Daphne was not prepared for the sight of Fern and Melba pulling the wagon by its tongue and singing "Ole Man Ribber" as Lorene, on the driver's seat, swatted at them with an antique buggy whip. In the wagon, giggling behind Lorene were Stephanie, Frankie, LaVonda and Nelson, who threw doughnuts to the guests.

"Geeee-haw! Yo! Whitie, yo! Blackie." Lorene's slurred commands seemed only to make Melba and Fern laugh all the harder and their singing louder and more raucous. They rounded the gravel walk by the rose garden and wove with the wagon through the avenue between the groups of tables. "Yes Marse, Lorene, Yes Marse," they groaned.

"You an' me, we sweat an' strain, body all achin' an' racked with pain," the two women sang and shouted. When they switched to "It's a long, long way for to tote the weary load," the guest joined in the chorus of "My Old Kentucky Home" with

Ellen's accompaniment.

Nearly all the doughnuts were dispensed when Daphne and Gus carried out the coffee.

"How about "Swing Low Sweet Chariot?" someone yelled. Everyone cheered. Ellen began a moderately-paced version of the old spiritual but picked up the tempo to a boogie beat. When she reached "I looked over Jordan and what did I see —ee?" Fern and Melba abandoned the wagon and boogied onto a cleared area on the terrace where they shook and gyrated expertly in a dance exhibition that had the guests clapping and rocking.

Lorene jumped from the wagon seat and helped the four children down, and Nelson began to do a combination break-dance and salsa as Ellen switched to a Latin boogie rhythm. She speeded up the Latin beat, and Lorene grabbed Tim Rhodes by the hand and began to Mambo, and it soon became evident that Tim was an expert at this Latin dance. Other guests started to dance and the terrace quickly filled with mamboing, shimmying, sambaing, moon-walking, jitterbugging Republicans.

Even Tyson Tylass and Ellen's mother, Eloise Ames, did a dignified but very sexy rhumba. Eloise caught her daughter's eye and, to Ellen's amazement, winked at her. Was it possible that a person's mother could be a sexual entity —a sexual being in her own right?

Ellen segued into some Delta blues while she flipped this idea around. Her mother? A sexy person? A woman? A regular *person?* Well, it *was* a possibility. Would her mother ever work things out with Tyson? It was complex, confusing. Could her mother become a strong enough person to keep Tyson from brutalizing her?

A glimmer of understanding, even empathy, filtered through the din, making Ellen feel disembodied —as if she were floating over the revolving throng looking down, down at them all, like the stories people tell whose hearts have stopped for one reason or another, and they die for a minute and see a very bright light and go through a long tunnel and then they revive and come back and live to tell about it. Was it like that with Ellen and her mother? Could there be some level, some plane on which they could possibly go through a long tunnel and see a bright light and meet and understand each other? Would her own daughters, Kelly and Kitty and Kathy feel about her, Ellen, *their* mother, in this way?

Ellen's consciousness crowded into her thoughts of her mother and her daughters, and she pulled herself back to what she had been playing —Delta blues. She played with such feeling that the dancers began to drift together and pair off and were holding each other now, gently, almost lovingly, tenderly. They were feeling the music tenderly, and that's what she began to play, no matter how it hurt her to play the song "Tenderly," the song that she and Karl had played together and made a tape of —that she couldn't bear to play since he had left home —that he had played with her, annoyed that she could *make* him want to play it with her because the sheer beauty of the melody always captivated —*captured* —him and thus made him captive —to her —a captive *of* her so he'd never get away, never get to Colorado, never escape, never be on his own, *never* it seemed, be on his own, no matter how much he knew that she *did* want him to break away and go.

The three-quarter rhythm of the nostalgic melody was exactly right for this late, late night, the winding-down crowd, and right for her. Ellen played slowly, yet the jazz waltz was imbued with a vibrant, alive summer essence and the soft air and the softer candlelight and the softest recollection. More couples got up to dance as the dream-like melody and mood enticed them, hypnotised them.

Ellen shifted into another key, a little higher, a little brighter. It was Karl's key for "Tenderly," the key in which his harmonica was pitched; the key in which he always played together with her. Somewhere this night, that harmonica was sounding, was playing in ghostly unison with her. It was uncanny!

She smiled to herself, at the way she could maneuver the wonderful little keyboard. She could get almost any sound she wanted from the weighted keys, the sensitive volume control, the refined electronic vibration, but —was her mind playing tricks? Why was everyone looking at her? Almost expectantly, they were smiling. The harmonica sound must be coming from the Yamaha keyboard. But no — the melody was far away, but playing in unison with her; an unmistakably melancholy, very knowing, indefinably familiar harmonica sound.

Ellen looked up and saw him at the edge of the garden; there was a big full moon shining now, and he walked, moon-silvered, down the path slowly, playing all the while, past the wash- house and onto the knot garden path. It had been his harmonica all along! It was Karl. Karl had come back!

CHAPTER FORTY-SEVEN

"More! More!" the guests clamored, as Karl came hesitantly from the shadows and stood smiling at his mother, then walked over to her as she sat blinking tearfully. She knew how touchy he was about any emotional display, and she was not going to ruin things this time! He bent and gave her a flicker of his eyelash on her cheek —what she and her children always had called a "Butterfly Kiss."

"This is my kid!" she called to the audience. She squeezed Karl's hand for a moment. "What a surprise! It's just a such a wonderful surprise, Karl!"

"I got a ride back to P-A with Arnie Pelham. It was sort of a sudden decision. Dad said there was partying going on here, and Arnie lives on Clifford Way, so —"

"More!" the guests cried.

Ellen began "Take Five," and Karl, shaking one knee and tapping six beats with the other foot, came in on the down-beat. The infectious, jump-rhythm stirred the dancers again. They got up and danced with new-found energy. For another hour Ellen and Karl played their special blend of sound, from danceable swing to Gershwin ballads at which Karl excelled — the harmonica so close to the sound of the human voice —then some fifties' and sixties' show tunes, finishing their recital with "La Cumparsita," to which Senator and Mrs. Trumble, remarkably revitalized, tangoed so magnificently that the applause lasted for two full minutes.

An encore of "Blue Tango" brought Troozie and Trev Trowbridge onto the dance area in a tango-exhibition of almost equal grace.

The Trumbles were saying their goodbyes now, and Tim backed Drew Burgess's Mercedes into the driveway to take them to their motel. Soon others began to drift to their cars. Daphne watched from a back table as Bronwen and Drew accepted their guests' enthusiastic thanks. The League of Women Voters' Muffie Palmer and her husband, Bif, were pumping Drew's hand. The Palmers seemed so different here. At the Briarwood debate, they had been guarded and stiff and humorless, but tonight they had "partied" enthusiastically, energetically. What could have been perceived as a fiasco turned out to be one of the hit events of the year, it would be reported all over the district the following day.

Drew's horse was tethered by the haha, and after the last goodbyes were said, he rode home whistling, albeit with Mrs. Trumble's bill for a thousand dollars in his pocket for one Trigère Original and one straw hat, which information Tim had managed to obtain; Tim was going to get a bonus for today's quick thinking.

Maybe it was time to cut Tim in on the apartment building deal that was firming up to close next weekend. "That Nurse Fun Buns or Miss Dialysis — whatever her name is — has an apartment there!" He, Drew, was going to be her landlord! "Hot damn!" he laughed to himself, " —what a pair of knockers! What an ass she has on her!"

Gus and Melba and Fern surveyed the sea of paper and styrofoam. Lorene collected her money and Nelson, Frankie and LaVonda, and departed, but not before the children had exchanged hugs with an astonishingly energized Stephanie.

"She hasn't had one seizure —in over a month —" Bronwen told Daphne. "She's had the time of her life at this party," she said as she and Daphne collected plastic plates from the Hepplewhite sideboard, from the Pembroke tables, the Newport tea table, even from the pair of enormous Oriental porcelain planters flanking the dining room doorway.

The bronze busts — "after Houdon" the provenance had said —on pedestals in the foyer both wore lipstick-smudged styrofoam-cup-hats. In fact, plates and cups dotted the entire property, indoors and out. In the pale moonlight, the lawns looked like fields of giant, white dandelions.

"We'll clean up tomorrow," Bronwen said as she bid all the workers goodnight.

The Raunch Factor

The mud-encrusted stagecoaches were parked at the side of the Hartley garage. Eloise Ames was searching one of them for a missing earring, aided by still-costumed Fern Slagle, the flickering lanterns illuminating what could have been a scene from *Madame Bovary*. Daphne sat watching as Gus extinguished, one-by-one, the hurricane candles and torches.

Karl and Ellen carried the keyboard indoors. The stars winked out and a light rain began again.

"Telephone call." Bronwen beckoned to Daphne. It was Harriet.

"We've been given two hours to clear out. The police came. Mrs. Hartley doesn't want to go back to the hospital, or to stay at the shelter without us. She wants to go home, to her own bed, she says. They've locked up the doctor, I heard. She and Audrey are in pretty bad shape. Harletta's not doing that great, either. Edith wants to have them brought to her house too —for the three of them to stay together, there. They've hit it off beautifully, and Edith has some kind of plan with Harletta and Audrey to open a fashion boutique. Those three have really hit it off these few days."

"Audrey's baby —what about the baby?"

"We have her playpen for her to stay in, at Edith's, with Audrey."

"This is absolutely amazing!"

"Yes."

"You sound exhausted, Harriet."

"I am. Who can help with hauling the women and the playpen and stuff? Allison and I have to load our cars with all of our office stuff. Everything has to be out."

"Well, between Larry and Hal we can get them transported here, I'm sure. Karl's here to help. We can swing it. Tell them to be ready."

And so it has come to pass, thought Daphne, *that the Sojourner Shelter is at last relinquished by its founders, and our most dreaded scenario has indeed happened —the takeover by the*

375

bureaucratic system —in the person of Traci, the embodiment of all we held as antithetical to our original, splendidly democratic concept. Our dream, once realized, is now gone.

At the Shelter, Harriet and Allison finished loading their cars, then turned over their keys to Traci's grim-faced acolyte, Betty Benton. In the parking lot Hal and Larry got out of their cars and opened umbrellas and walked up the walk to the back entrance.

"Juzdt a min't," Edith Hartley said, as she crept to the portable blackboard in Traci's office. "Move zish," she indicated, trying to roll the blackboard towards the center of the room. Harriet pushed the board where she directed, so that it faced the office doorway. Then Edith took a piece of chalk and wrote on the blackboard in big block letters:

"GO POUND SALT IN ASSHOLES"

They filed out to the cars, the seven of them huddled under two umbrellas, Audrey and Harletta each with a supporting arm around the shuffling Edith.

It was nearly morning by the time the three injured women were settled in their individual suites at Edith Hartley's.

The canopied bed and satin-striped chaise-longue and pastel Savonnerie rug were intimidating to Audrey Hopper who sat out in the softly-lighted hallway with her baby.

"I just can't. With Kareema an' her playpen an' diapers an' everything. I just can't, Edith. This fancy place —"

"You honor my home and me by szhtayin' here, Audrey. Plezhe doan disshapont me."

"I love *my* room!" lisped Harletta, "Ith thwanky!"

Audrey stayed.

In the Hartley kitchen Daphne and Bronwen scrounged about to put together some sort of breakfast. The huge refrigerator yielded two cans of frozen orange-pineapple juice and a bowl of moldy vanilla pudding. While Stephanie slept on the library sofa, Bronwen made fresh coffee. She whispered to Daphne, "There are some doughnuts left."

Out on the back terrace, beneath the long roof overhang, Hal and Larry stood with Allison and Harriet and Ellen. Then Karl came out and stood with them. "I set up the playpen," he said.

Everywhere there was a strange, unearthly stillness as the beginning of dawning light rose behind the sheep barn. The verdant Pennsylvania countryside slowly slipped into dim focus.

It makes me think of the Adelaide Creapsey poem, Hal mused to himself. *Why am I thinking of this particular poem? It's dawn, a new beginning; not a sad time, really; yet I'm thinking of it:*

> *These be three silent things:*
> *The falling snow;*
> *The hour before the dawn;*
> *The mouth of one just dead.*

Daphne and Bronwen stepped out onto the back terrace. The rain was feathery-soft and pleasant.

"That's Bobbye's, over there," Daphne nodded toward the Krock acreage. No one spoke.

"I've got an idea," Harriet said. "Let's all go over and wake her up and say 'Hi' and see if she wants to have breakfast with us!" She put her arm around Daphne. "Whatya say?"

Daphne hesitated. Then she smiled.

"Well, why the hell not?" she said.

Bronwen pulled the back door shut. "I know a short-cut. Back over the hill. Come on."

They all started over the knoll, savoring the early morning softness, the fragrance from still-spring-green fields, and they found their energy returning. For some reason they all felt invigorated. They began to run.

They ran shouting down the long slope toward Bobbye's garden, past the domed belvedere, past her prized, circular flower beds, and then they stopped.

In a few moments a light went on in the kitchen. Bobbye

pulled the curtain aside and peered out; then she came out onto her patio. She was wearing her pink jogging suit. Harriet pushed Daphne forward. "Ask her," she prompted.

The two women walked slowly toward each other. "Hi," Daphne said. "Come and eat breakfast with us. At Edith's."

"Well, why the hell not?" Bobbye said. Then, laughing, the two women threw their arms around each other.

At that moment the sun burst through the clouds. The rolling hills that separated the Krock's property from the Hartley's glowed green-gold.

The three founders of the Sojourner Shelter embraced Bobbye, and then the four linked arms and began to climb back over the knoll, followed by Hal, Larry, Bronwen and Karl. And as they climbed the hill, happy to be together, Daphne and Bobbye friends once more, a rainbow appeared. It stretched as far as the eye could see, and they all looked up and felt that, at that moment, they had reached as far as the heart could reach.

THE RAUNCH FACTOR

Book III

CHAPTER FORTY-EIGHT

As her ancestors had done a thousand years before in Palermo, Sicily, Felicia DeCarlo in 1991 in Bingham County, U.S.A., was making an orange salad. She peeled and sliced ten juicy tart-sweet oranges in layers onto a large platter, then scattered a handful of black olives and chunks of artichoke hearts over the slices. Over these she drizzled extra virgin olive oil. A generous sprinkling of crushed dried oregano and chopped garlic, and salt and pepper completed the colorful dish. She worked with happy anticipation, enjoying her immaculate newly-remodelled kitchen. It was her first party in her "new" old house.

Edith Hartley and Harletta Hoskins, having arrived early for the event, opened up and laid the gate-leg table in Felicia's living room. Late afternoon light slanting though the sparkling wavy glass of the many-paned old windows accentuated reddish highlights in Edith's elaborate, newly-colored coiffure and intensified the purple and mauve of the old German glass birds on Felicia's tall Christmas tree.

Edith placed a paper hat and noise maker beside each plate, then stood back and surveyed the table critically. From the kitchen the heady aroma of baked lemon chicken floated enticingly on the pine and bayberry-scented air.

"There's nothing like crystal stemware to make a table look special," remarked Edith. "I remember when I bought them — those —goblins. It was right after the election. I got 'em for Hal and Daphne's wedding supper. Remember? He proposed on election night —right after the returns were in. We were sittin' around my front room listenin' to the radio and watchin' the returns on TV, about three A.M. Then Burgess conceded and Krock won an' Marilee whosis and some of the campaign workers were out in my front hall cryin' and splotchin' up my ten thousand dollar wallpaper, and Hal says to Daphne, 'Let's get married,' just like that, and Daphne says 'Okay,' just like that. Remember? Nine years ago! It seems like a couple months."

"Yeah, it thure duzth," Harletta agreed.

Edith looked haggard. A long faint scar ran from the corner

of her upper lip toward her right cheek, and makeup failed to conceal a bruise-like blotch on her left cheek. She limped as she moved around the table placing fan-folded linen napkins in the Baccarat crystal water goblets. "What time is Audrey closin' up the store, Harletta?"

"I already told you, whenever all the altered dretheth are picked up," Harletta answered irritably. Her lisp had not improved with her ill-fitting upper denture. Her son, Russell's successful dentistry practice and many orthodontic connections had not as yet benefitted the dentally challenged Harletta.

Edith sat down carefully on one of the fragile-looking dining chairs, then said, "Up to now we always charged for alterations. I never heard of a women's wear store doin' them for free."

"Well, menthswear sthores alwayths do them free, sthough Audreyth's makin' it a thelling point for women. We been able to make the three thouthand rent at the mall every month and sthill make a good profit."

"That's because of Asa Helbrun's sales. She could sell Frigidaires to the Eskimos," Edith chuckled at her own witticism, "but she quit workin' in Hal's office just so she could work in our shop and get the discount on all her clothes. Boy that leather shorts and vest outfit looks too young on her! I know she's over seventy."

"Well, she hath great legths. And her fifteen thouthand helped put uth over when we firthed opened Dazzle," Harletta said, adding quickly, "with your hundred thouthand, of corth, but you like the dithcount on *your* outfiths, too."

"Dazzle better get some customers that pay the full price. Makin' first-of-the-year rent is like pullin' hen's teeth," Edith said as she smoothed her teased hair and yawned, and then went on, "but I don't think all them denim separates will do it. Who wants all those —them —zippers? Even zippered pockets on the sleeves? The next new style next week will probly be Gay Nineties with ragamuffin sleeves!"

"Edith, go over the bookths with Felithia next month, and you'll thee profiths and it'll be thipperth that done it. Thipperth, thipperth, thipperth!"

Felicia's doorbell chimed the first five notes of "O, Solo Mio" as outside Daphne Singleton pounded on the door and Hal Renshaw shouted, "Andiam' Andiam' in there! We gotta da vino!"

They entered the house just as Harriet Freeman hurried up the snowy walk to Felicia's small porch, calling out, "Wait up. I made it, you guys, I made it! Barry's coming over around ten."

In the living room Harriet lit a cigarette, flipped her still-lustrous but now-gray-tinged auburn braid and announced, "This is my last pack. I'm smokeless after tonight. Barry's quitting too. We've saved five hundred butts. Butts don't count. Hey, where's Audrey? When do we eat? I'm ravenous. And wait'll you taste the trifle I made! I put in brandy as well as rum!" She stood looking at the glistening Christmas tree for a moment, then said softly, "Norm absolutely *adored* trifle." Edith limped over and put a garnet braceletted, plump arm around Harriet's waist and peered solicitously into her face.

Felicia and Daphne and Hal carried in the wine, a basket of crusty bread and a bowl of mixed vegetables from the kitchen. "Viola!" Hal exclaimed, "the wine, the bread, the grub and thou, belching in the wilderness."

"The pasta needs a couple more minutes," Felicia said, "so let's have some wine." She smiled happily, touching a fork here, a plate there, patting the cut-work white linen tablecloth.

"Bah, Wilderness, Hal," Daphne laughed. "There's a Dickensian Rubaiyat for you."

"The house looks fabulous, Felicia," Harriet observed as Hal drew the cork out of the wine bottle.

"It sure does," he added. "You and Daphne have transformed this dump —er, historical landmark! Last year, when Daph said you bought it, I must confess, I shuddered."

Felicia nodded. "You're right. It was a dump. But, in the old days, if anyone would've said I'd be single again some day and own my own home and be a partner in such a ritzy dress shop as Dazzle, I would've said they were nuts!"

Harriet downed her wine and laughed, "Ritzy? Ritzy? You got that word from your mother, I'll bet." Felicia smiled her wide smile, her crooked but very white teeth lighting her olive skin, a luminous peach-rose glow spreading over her plump cheeks.

Everyone sat down at the laden, candle-lit table. "Start your salad, everyone," Felicia urged. "Audrey won't mind if we begin without her. I'll get the chicken and the mosticiolli."

Mozart's Twenty-First Piano Concerto on the CD player was serene and elegant and soothing.

"You picked a winner this time, Harold." Daphne held her wine glass up to the candle flame. "That cabernet you got at Thanksgiving was sour, and it cost three times what you paid for this."

Hal looked around the table apologetically and explained, "We're a bit short of cash just now, folks. With car repairs after Pete nearly totalled it, and with Celeste's clothing and counselling bills it's been slim pickins for us this holiday."

"Well, I take the blame," said Daphne, as she reached for the vegetable bowl. "I had five good years in a row. My sales were up when we decided to add the two bed rooms and bath-and-a-half to the first floor, for the kids. And I think the added space did help to cut down their fighting. You'll have to concede that, Hal!"

Hal nodded. "Yes, point well taken. After the steel crisis leveled off, an historic era ended here —very painfully for the steel workers —and we entered the Reagan years, a period of a great deal of spending for a relative few. Carl Sagan got it right when he said the eighties gave rise to the glamorization of greed. We were among the ones that lucked out. Your clientele, Daphne, the M.D.s and other health service people and corporate America, of course, were indulging themselves, and we were just lucky that we benefitted. But a lot of people have moved from lower middle into poverty class.

"Now everyone with money is cutting back because of the war. Our Preppy Prez, George Bush, has known since August that we'd bomb Iraq, and believe me, he's gonna do it —declare war —and Congress be damned. He'll do anything to get re-elected —even get us into another war so people will go to the

D.J.Muns-Blancato

polls and vote for the guy who did something powerful and military.

"So now your sales are down, Daphne," Hal continued, "and we have a big second mortgage to meet, and if the kids decide to live with their mother —they're too immature to live on their own —our house expansion was just needless expense."

Somewhat chagrined, Hal glanced around the table, "Please excuse this family finance conference, folks."

Daphne broke a piece off a thick chunk of bread and said, very elaborately, "So, I guess we went overboard. But they're my kids now, too. After all, I didn't want to be the wicked stepmother. I want the children to be happy, but how was I to know they'd turn out to be such little shits?"

Hal mock-choked on his wine as everyone laughed, a little too loudly. Edith, embarrassed, began, "Family's everything. When Audrey takes Kareema home after I baby sit her, my big house seems so —so —"

Harriet interjected, "Don't get discouraged, you guys. Edith's right about families. I have to remind Barry all the time. He's pretty much launched three kids, and has two to go yet. With his youngest in detox and the middle one having just moved back in with him with her two-year-old, Barry's not the contemplative philosopher he used to be. If he didn't come to my place regularly for R and R, I think he'd be in a pretty bad way. But still, they're his family, and he'd be lost without them, I keep telling him. And telling him. And telling him."

"Boy have you changed, Harriet," Felicia said. "About Barry, I mean."

Harriet blushed and helped herself to another piece of lemon chicken. "Yeah. He really used to be my *bête noir,* all right. But *he's* changed too, don't forget." She shrugged and munched.

"It's Ellen and Larry I'm concerned about," Daphne said. "Of all the bad luck! They were making a few gains —got four kids out of six through college —got Kelly happily married, and then all their luck ran out, and Larry gets that terrible illness, and the VA is fighting his disability claims at every turn."

"The VA's gonna claim that his pancreatitis was not service-

385

incurred," Hal said. There are cases like Larry's all over the U.S., all probably traceable to Vietnam — to Agent Orange. They're using the fact that he was a heavy drinker against him."

"Maybe he wath drinking heavily becauth he wath tho thick," Harletta offered.

"Sick veterans like Larry ought to all get together and file a class action suit!" Harriet exclaimed.

"You can't sue any government agency," Hal explained. "It's illegal. It's the same as my situation with Ted Mather — wherever *he* is, he just seems to have evaporated —but, anyway, a law was passed back in the thirties or early forties, protecting all government agencies against any such legal action. That's why we're suing Beckwell Inc., instead of the NSA, for their part in financing the NSA's very successful infiltration and destruction of the Citizen Action Party. And we won't quit until we win. What's twenty million to *them?* They funneled a lot more than that to the NSA to carry out their fascistic control, including depriving CitAct members all over the U.S. of their Constitutional Rights. Beckwell doesn't want anyone rocking the power boat."

"But getting back to families," Felicia said, "I'm happy the way my life is now. Without kids. Two miscarriages were two too many, for me. One controlling husband was one too many. I turned my life around, but I couldn't have done it without you, Daphne, and Harriet and —"

"You did it mostly on your own, Felicia," Daphne said, "you and Edith, and Harletta and Audrey and Lorene, and Bobbye too. It just might have taken you all longer without the Sojourner Shelter."

Felicia laid down her fork and said quietly, "Yes, but without the shelter I might not have lived that long."

A silence fell over the table, broken only by the faint perk-perk-perk of the coffee maker in the kitchen and the brittle click of sleet against the window panes, like frozen knuckles tapping.

Harriet lit a cigarette butt and said, "Hey! Thaddeus Shaeffer told me Lorene's appearing at a comedy club in D.C. tonight. She and Tiffany have been staying with an aunt there for over a year. Her aunt has a cleaning business called 'MoTown Maids.' Thaddeus says their business cards say 'We Whup Windows.' So Lorene whups windows by day and dishes out comedy by night. She's taking a political science course at night too, he said."

Harletta began stacking everyone's dirty dishes. "Nothin' will sthop Lorene. She hath gutths and brainths."

"And she's fearless," Daphne added "She was the best coordinated woman in our karate class, and that's what scares me. She's fearless but small and she's Black and she's a woman —a quadruple handicap."

The door chimes clanged "O, Solo Mio"again, and Daphne winced. Would she *ever* be able to forget the Burgess fundraiser?

"That'll be Audrey," Harriet mumbled, her mouth full of mosticiolli.

Hal laid his napkin on the table and started toward the door, Felicia trotting after him. "Let me just check first, Felicia." He peered through the peephole. "Bill Collectors" had begun appearing at Felicia's door when Herb had been paroled after being jailed for only six months, and it became clear that, from then on, she was being watched. "Yep, it's okay, it's Audrey," Hal said, and he unlocked the door.

Snowflakes clung to Audrey Hopper's thick, curling eyelashes as she shivered into the warmth, handed a canvas bag to Felicia, then took her place at the table. She rubbed her hands together and said, with mock sarcasm, "I appreciate y'all's waitin' for me." She smiled her stunning, wide smile and sipped the wine that Hal handed her.

Audrey seemed serene and focused. Plastic surgery had helped to conceal several of her worst facial scars, and she had let her hair grow to cover the scar from the long gash that ran diagonally from her temple to her hairline. Over the years she had never revealed the identity of her attacker. It was almost as if she were protecting him, or her.

Platters and bowls were passed to Audrey, and as she helped herself to some of each dish she said, "I was nervous carrying that bag o' money," then added proudly, "Due to our free alteration promotion, Dazzle grossed an extra four thousand this past week, folks." Everyone applauded as she beamed. "I'm gonna have to eat an' run, though, 'cause I gotta pick up Kareema at my sister's. But I'm sorry I can't stay for y'all's midnight champagne."

Harriet poured coffee. Audrey picked at her food daintily. In nine years she had not gained an ounce and was slim still. She said, "Thaddeus is at Marva's tonight." Usually rather reticent, Audrey seemed to want to talk. "He's become a happy grandfather since he and Marva patched up all their differences. For a long time he blamed Marva for hastening his mother's death, but I told him Ora *wanted* to take care of Marva's baby. You couldn't tell Ora what to do. That was her great-grandbaby!"

"But she probably did work herself to death," Audrey continued, "and I know her heart was broken when Traci ousted her from the shelter. But at any rate, tomorrow Thaddeus and Kareema and I are going to spend the day together just playin' board games 'n' stuff. Then we're gonna bake bread."

"Bring Kareema here tonight, Audrey," Edith urged.

But Audrey explained, "I promised her and my sister we'd be with them for New Year's. My brother-in-law's in the National Guard, and he was called up. He's leavin' tomorrow." She turned to Edith and said, "Girl, you'll be baby sittin' Kareema when Harletta and me go to summer market next week. You'll be sicka her." She took a sip of coffee.

"Never no chance of Kareema wearin' out her welcome, Audrey," Edith brushed crumbs from the tablecloth, "and Bronwen Burgess and me are takin' Stephanie and Kareema and some Glenview kids to see Phan-thum of the Opera, when you go to market. We got special box seats so the kids that wear helmets can go. We've got the whole week planned. Ya know, Bronwen seems happier now, since her divorce. Things were real bad there for a while when the mister tried to cut her out of getting the house and any money, and she nearly went bezique. She won *some* money, but not enough. Now that he's moved out, things are a little better, though."

Harletta and Felicia began to clear the table while their friends continued to talk.

Gatherings such as this were infrequent, and there was so much happening in their lives —so much to catch up on —that their conversation was more a series of news flashes than sustained dialogue.

Now Harletta placed the big clear-glass bowl of layered liqueur-laced cake, jam and custard before Harriet, for her to serve. Then there was a lull as six spoons clinked against six crystal dessert dishes.

The rich treat was pronounced "sublime," and the news flashes continued. Hal was wound up, trying to talk and take in all the news, all at the same time. It was like old times. But Hal's once-brown hair was now a thinning beige fringe. It fell over his forehead as always, and his face was fuller but with the same healthy color of his youth. He was striding through his fifth decade with an ease with which he surprised himself. As with some men who are angular and lean through their angst-ridden youth, his additional middle-aged bulk now imparted an appearance of compact, rugged handsomeness to him as a sort of bonus, which Daphne often said was " —for fighting the good fight."

"I talked with Bobbye Krock a couple of weeks ago," Daphne said, brushing her silky black bangs from her eyes.

Daphne too was feeling nostalgic. Where, a decade ago, she had been described as "trim," she was now voluptuous, her once-hollow cheeks filled out and almost maternal-looking.

"She's not Bobbye Krock any more, you know. She's Bobbye Taylor now," Daphne went on, " —her own name —and she may leave her Philadelphia firm and move back to Bingham to practice law with Agnes Harrison. Agnes has been winning all those sexual harassment and domestic violence cases, and she's expanding her staff and really wants a partner."

"Oh! Right *ON!*" exclaimed Harriet, clapping her hands. "But I wonder where Bobbye'll live? I still can't believe what's happened to Ed Krock after Bobbye split. She just packed up and moved on without a word to anyone. Then polka-dots and moonbeams enters the scene and starts her manipulation tactics on Ed and —"

"Please, Harriet, we're *EATING!*" admonished Daphne.

Hal, ignoring Daphne, growled, "They deserve each other. Bad cess to them *both.*"

"Yeth, Trathi wath after Ed 'way before Bobbye ever left. When they came in the CorBlimey, they sthneaked in a room in the back. I *thaw* them. Dino took their dinnerth in to them. Herb Hathelas wath told to alwayth cook *anything* Ed wanted. His favorite dinner wath Thpanith rithe and stheack and pineapple yardarmths. Trathi alwayth ordered whatever Ed ordered.

"Thumtimthes hith brother —you know — the minithter, Reverend Krock —came with them. She alwaythe sat between them, an' they were laughin' and jigglin' her an' pawin' her an' she just thmiled that thmile an' the threea them alwayths put away about five yardarmths apieth.

"After the shelter board got Trathi out —you know, when that big contributhion check wath mithing —she an' Ed ate at the CorBlimey every night when he wathn't in Dee Thee."

Hal drained his coffee cup and pushed his chair back. "That big contribution check was from the CorBlimey restaurant chain, wasn't it, Daphne?" he asked.

"Yes. Ten thousand dollars. Remember? They had a big presentation ceremony on TV, with Dino and Herb standing there —Herb in his gleaming two-foot-high chef's toque, and Dino wiping his eyes and going on about how he wanted to help "them poor battered ladies," and Herb nodding and smiling —right after being paroled after being in jail for beating up Felicia!"

"Bobbye went to Phillie right after that, remember?" Audrey said. "She told someone that Ed bought her share of the house from her and he agreed to pretty good alimony. She — excuse the expression —*blackmailed* it out of him. She told me she found out that the nuclear plant paid all their household utilities. So then she was able to go to law school. She was one determined woman."

"I always seemed to be out of town the few times she came back to Bingham," said Daphne. "She called me a couple times a year, but all we talked about was school. She called when she passed the bar exam. She was so happy she was laughing and crying. She said she was going out with some women friends.

"But, truth to tell, even though she thought Ed's political career was laughable, I don't think she's ever forgiven me for that disastrous fund-raiser party she threw for Ed —even though I replaced everything that got wrecked, and for no charge and without complaint and all because of that idiot Robb and those oil lamps. We had a few laughs over it, but the restoration work seemed to take forever! I was over there all the time. We'd have a few drinks. Then we'd heat up some frozen bean sprouts and pita bread —her favorite meal —and have a few more laughs. Once or twice Ed came home, but he went straight down to his basement hideaway and didn't even speak to us."

"What did she ever have in common with him?" Felicia mused.

"I think the only thing was that they had both grown up poor," Harriet answered.

Audrey lit a cigarette. "Growing up poor can be a powerful bond," she observed.

"Yeah," Harriet nodded, "but look at the totally opposite directions Ed and Bobbye went with their lives! She's become a radical feminist activist reformer out to expose oppressors of women —men like Ed —the whole patriarchy! And he's the same political joke-person he always was —only richer."

The door chimed "O Solo Mio" again. It was Barry Spiegel bearing a bottle of champagne and half a chocolate cake. "Oyez oyez oyez, bon soir folks," he said amiably as he divested himself of a seedy-looking parka. Unlike Hal, Barry's physical aging had followed an opposite pattern; he was slimmer than in earlier years, and the somewhat florid coloring of his youth was now a subdued, old world olive, and his hair and beard remained thick and black with only a hint of gray. As usual, he was smoking; this time, a large malodorous cigar. Edith Hartley fanned herself with a magazine as Barry bear-hugged everyone.

"Cigars don't count. I gave up cigarettes, not cigars," was his rejoinder to their jeers. "I have already dined, Felicia," he

said, amid gusts of smoke. "I made vegetarian chili and this cake
for Sarita and my grandson. Then I took some to David, at Peace
Place. They allow clients to have treats on holidays. I was
amazed to see Allison DeVrees there. She acted like she didn't
see me. David said that, according to the staff, she's been in and
out of there numerous times."

"Allison? At Peace Place?" Harriet asked. "Is she a staff
member or a client?"

"A client. She's drying out. She looks terrible —must weigh
about ninety pounds —but I recognized those big eyes and that
red hair. Wasn't she one of the Sojourner founders? I guess she's
not one of the Shelter's many success stories."

Daphne began to fan herself, and Audrey and Edith moved
across the room to dining chairs and Felicia turned on the
ventilator fan in the kitchen, to which actions Barry was
oblivious.

"Barry, I've told you this before," Harriet explained.
"When I was hired to replace Traci seven years ago, Allison
stayed on working at the shelter for a year or so. Then she sort
of dropped out of sight for a couple years. Someone said she was
living with Traci, and the two of them worked in Ed Krock's
Bingham office. Then they showed up at the County Fair last
year doing psychic readings. Remember, Barry? I told you about
how Traci conned a bunch of former shelter board Bingham
Bitsies into financing her trip to Sri Lanka where, she *says,* she
conferred with some Buddhist guru at Katmandu."

Daphne turned to Barry and said, with mock surprise,
"Don't tell us you haven't heard of the AstraLadies, Barry!"

Barry jumped to his feet, and ducking his head, he held up
his arm and moaned, "Protect me from wild women! Hal,
what'll we *do,* Buddy? What'll we *do?*"

"Just keep smoking those cigars," Hal laughed.

"But Hal, *AstraLadies!*" Barry puffed and shouted, "What
NEXT? I finally got Harriet civilized and now a bunch of
overwrought Bingham Bitsies has sprung up. They'll be playin'
tambourines in the Fourth of July parade an' puttin' curses on
people an' sprinkling salt around the courthouse and worshipping

men's jockstraps an' doin' incantations an' —''

A small throw-pillow hit the side of Barry's head. He ducked again, and his cigar fell to the floor. "Aunty EM! Aunty EM!" he howled.

Harriet stood over him, then pointed to the entrance door. *"Out!"* she commanded. "Take that cigar outside. Go to the curb and throw that stinking abomination into the street!"

"Yes, oh wondrous one," Barry intoned, unctuously bowing low. To everyone's astonishment and hilarity he opened the door, bent down and laid his cigar on the old cast iron boot scraper on the porch, returned to the living room and, kissing Harriet, sat meekly beside her.

"See why I love him?" Harriet grinned, " —and hate him." She placed the pillow back on the sofa. "Sorry about your pillow, Felicia."

"No problem," Felicia laughed as she started toward the kitchen with the coffee cups. "It was worth it, believe me. But seriously, Daphne, maybe we should give Traci the benefit of the doubt —maybe she's had a change of heart."

"*WHAT* heart?" Daphne scoffed. "Don't confuse her trendy parapsychology stings and psychic scams with serious spiritual movements — men and women who are searching for a new dimension, a new grasp of and an affirmation of their relationship to the earth and the cosmos — environmental groups, Native American ceremony, Gaia women. You're forgetting what a controlling and manipulative genius Traci is. She's a fraud, but she's not stupid. She's a brilliant and very dangerous con-artist."

From the hallway, Audrey called, "I gotta run. Happy New Year, everybody! 'Bye, ya'll." Everyone clustered at the front door. Outside, the sleet storm had turned into a shower of big wet fluffy white flakes creating nimbuses around the street lights. In the next block a few premature firecrackers went off, anticipating by only a few minutes, the advent of the year 1991.

Daphne and Hal stood at the porch railing, watching as Barry escorted Audrey down the icy walk to her '87 Ford. There was a familiar softness in the air, something nostalgic, to the pair on the porch. The memory came to them simultaneously as they turned to each other. "Do you remember that night?" Hal whispered. "I fell in love with you that night."

Daphne kissed him, "Our first date," she murmured, "How could I ever forget?"

Hal began to whistle John Philip Sousa's march "On the Mall," and linking arms, he and Daphne went into the house.

CHAPTER FORTY-NINE

Long after midnight, after the last horns were blown, after the champagne bottles were emptied, after the noise makers were laid aside, the friends remained in Felicia's living room huddled before the fireplace until dawn, talking. The cannel coal fire dwindled in the grate, Edith snored on the couch beneath an afghan and the talk went on. The subject to which they kept returning was that of the impending war with Iraq, in the Persian Gulf; war that was almost a certainty. Another war.

"It's sickening. I feel physically sick," Daphne said. "And it's not the food and drink I had tonight, either." She laid her head back on the carved walnut frame of the old settee where she was sitting with Hal. "How can you be so certain, Barry? You say it so casually. In reality it means women and children dying, and the old and sick dying, and soldiers —mostly very young soldiers —on both sides, dying in hideous ways. Surely they'll reconsider. Whoever *they* are."

Barry got up and walked back and forth, a mighty nicotine urge engulfing him.

"The Kuwaiti government paid millions to an American public relations agency in 1990 to bombard the American people with the idea of the U.S. intervention in the Kuwaiti situation," Barry said. "It was known then that Saddam Hussein was going to invade Kuwait. It was no secret among the political *cognoscenti* that George Bush was going to declare war. If people would read *The Nation* magazine once in a while or *Political Reality Quarterly* instead of all those slick consumer guides in the doctors' offices — those paeans to materialism —those magazines are so damned slippery they fall off your lap —then people might have a few clues as to what's going on in the world! George Bush has known since last August that he was going to make this move."

Hal leaned forward and poked at the coals in the little grate and said, "Bush's concern is not a noble one —not the prevention of oppression against the Kuwaitis; first of all, he wants to be re-elected. Americans loved Reagan when he okayed our invasion of Grenada, remember? Then, second, Bush sees his own oil interests at stake."

"Right!" Barry agreed. "We dassn't jeopardize the big ole boys' big ole bucks. After all, this country's a respectable plutocracy, ain't it?" He turned to Daphne, "We can't put people before profits, m'girl," watching her warily, to gauge her reaction, but she only smiled wanly and reached for Hal's hand.

"I'm not anyone's *girl*, Barry —I couldn't let *that* pass —but surely, you can't mean that the senseless slaughter of another war is inevitable, and for such appalling, disgusting reasons!" Barry looked crestfallen.

"That inevitability is very manipulable, Daphne," Hal said. "A media barrage is all it takes, and since corporate America pretty much controls the media, they can justify war over and over, in so many ways that not wanting to go to war makes a person appear to be unpatriotic. All the male sports nuts fall right into line. They've already been programmed since birth —you know, the new Dad at the maternity ward with the football and hockey stick —they're programmed from birth to accept, to glorify violence. Sports and war are about guys knocking out other guys; men's brutality towards one another is extolled — admired —by our society as a desireable, he-man thing. Our entire society pays into the ritualized violence of contact sports. And that includes many women. Lots of middle and upper class women think their men's sports addiction is cute, that it's something laughable but benign that they can commiserate with other wives about and —"

"You're talking about rich women. Poor women don't fare so well," Harriet interrupted. "Their boyfriends and husbands, disgruntled about their low-paying jobs or out of work, punch out 'their' women whenever TV gladiators are the losers in societally-approved brutalizing rituals of the Big Game. It's a very short step from the stadium to the domestic setting."

"And it's another very short step from there to the role of Community Leader or corporation CEO or military strategist," Barry added, "and from there it's an even shorter step to economically violent policies on a global level. And all along the way this kind of mentality constantly accesses racism, sexism, ageism, classism and anti-Semitism and homophobia to pay into their dehumanizing system."

"Ruthell — my thun — wath thaying that the Kuwait thituation ith like in Germany," Harletta said, "that we have to sthop the invathion or Iraq will take over the world."

"That 'Get Hitler' analogy is surfacing all over the place," said Hal. "I hear it in the super market, in elevators, and it's so incredible when you realize that we were selling arms to Saddam Hussein —to Iraq —*on credit* —in nineteen eighty-one! Iraq is a third-rate, very small country, militarily ill-equipped, except for the possibility —or probability —that they would use chemical warfare. They are militarily hardly a match for U.S. capability. And certainly there is no similarity to Germany's relative capability in the nineteen thirties; something *had* to be done back then —although World War Two was very very profitable — make no mistake — but today's situation demands talks and negotiating, none of which was seriously undertaken. Bush wants war."

Everyone sat gray faced and subdued in the pale morning light.

Felicia broke the silence. "I'm going to make some coffee," she said.

On the way home, Hal said, wearily, "Ringing in the New Year was sort of a downer, Daph, wasn't it?"

Daphne drove in silence for a few moments, then replied, "Yes and no. It was exhilarating to see everyone and catch up on the news. I loved the dinner and champagne and everything, but I kept turning the thought over in my mind that Americans subliminally *need* wars. Vietnam is history. Twenty-year-olds today don't even know where Vietnam *is*. Nicaragua seems remote to most people. But the twenty-year span is up, and now it's time again for more patriotic institutionalized serial murders. That's all war is, you know?

"We should protest, Hal, the ones who hate it should join

together and try to stop it — make it known that it's crazy, horrible, rotten!" she banged the steering wheel, "useless, disgusting slaughter!"

January 2
1991

Hi Daph —
   Surprise! Yes, it's me, with my semi-annual letter. Been writing my New Year's Resolutions and thinking about the old Sojourner gang. Those were good times. Everything was exciting and new —even with the shit we had to take from Traci and the crap I took off Ed. (Was I out of my mind to put up with him?)
   Here at the office all I do is write depositions for accident cases. Bor-r-r-ring!
   Just before Christmas I moved from my efficiency to a condo with two other women. One's a lawyer, the other's a social worker. We get along great. You should hear our Pan the Patriarchy discussions. That's one reason for this letter. We're fucking sick about the Persian Gulf situation. A bunch of us are chartering some busses to go to a protest march in D.C. Why don't you get a group together and meet us there and march with us? I'll let you know as soon as I find out more details. We've got to make it known, as thinking, feeling, rational beings — as women — that we're against slaughter and violence.
   Boy, Daphne, did I ever learn from the Shelter struggle we all went through —that you have to act, and not hide from the truth. So we better get our asses in gear!

I'll call you in a couple days.
Love —Bobbye Taylor, Esq. (Ha!)

P.S. You gotta come to the
demonstration. It would be so cool
to see you!

CHAPTER FIFTY

Daphne knocked on her stepson's door. Once. Twice. Three times.

"Fuck off." It was a surly baritone.

"Pete, you know that language is unacceptable to me."

"Lemme 'lone. I'm tired."

"It's two in the afternoon! Your father asked me to wake you and make sure you get to that job interview. He had to persuade that man to give you an interview. You have barely an hour."

Daphne went back to the kitchen. At first there was no response, but soon she heard clumping and the shower running, and twenty minutes later Pete slouched into the kitchen, a scowl distorting his handsome face. His wet blond hair dripped onto his fleece-lined denim jacket.

"My father's pressuring his friends about a job really stinks. Man, it really sucks." He drank the orange juice Daphne handed him, then wiped his mouth with the back of his hand.

"Pete, I hope you'll be here for dinner tonight. We're having your favorites —ravioli and pineapple coleslaw. We want to talk to you and Celeste about going to the Gulf War protest march with us, in D.C."

"Ravioli and coleslaw sucks," Pete mumbled. "Activism sucks." He shuffled out the kitchen door and headed down the walk towards the bus stop.

Daphne phoned her shop to check with James, now promoted to shop manager. He answered the phone smartly, a discernable British accent crisping his mild tenor voice. "Hello, Boss, how are you?" he answered, his clipped tones reminiscent of Cary Grant on Late Night Oldies. "Kenny's here going over the books," he said, in answer to Daphne's inquiry. "Ruth Ann's done a good job posting the entries. Now she's straightening the sample room, marking the new Brunschwig samples, and then she's going to dust windows B and C. Gerry's talking to a customer about Scalamandre drapery trimming, and we'll have window A re-done by the end of the day. Kenny's going to help lift that armoire in there. So everything's under control."

"Terrific," Daphne exclaimed. "I think Gerry will work out well, James, even if she only comes in three days a week. She's an experienced estimator, too. With the three of us, we can go after more big money Briarwood work."

It was a fair-sized payroll for Daphne, still her firm's principal designer, to meet and which she had been meeting with relative ease until recently. Debbie Fentriss —the Debbie of the shop's early struggling days —had quit working to marry Yoga Robb, after Daphne fired him, and they were living in a double-wide mobile home in Truschel Township. Debbie was pregnant with their first child, according to the note on the large gold-bordered Christmas card she had sent Hal and Daphne. "Yours in Christ, Robb and Deborah," she had signed sanctimoniously beneath the elaborate, full-color reproduction of a Giotto Madonna and Child. Now Debbie was Robb's Mobile Home Madonna, an image that he could control, as macho medieval and Renaissance painters and sculptors had for centuries controlled visual images of women. But Robb's Giotto and Fra Angelico-inspired Little Mother, instead of virginal robes and modest head coverings, sported Big Hair, Fushsia Frenzy lip gloss and an Esprit wardrobe, and instead of gilded tryptich arches, his little holy family was framed by balloon valances over the Special-Order Triple Picture Living Room Window (optional) that Robb had selected from the Zephyr Coach Co. Feature Book when they had ordered their Deluxe Model Mobile Abode. And there was a King Size canopy bed that just fit —though barely —in the largest of the three bedrooms in which Robb had ensconced his Queen of Heaven, his Baby Maker, his Debbie. And Robb was turning out bran loaves, big time, for local food service industries and trying to handle the rage he felt whenever he thought about the ignominy of the way Daphne had fired him.

It was time for Daphne to pick up Celeste and take her to her career counseling appointment. She was visiting a friend at the County Campus of the State University. Hal still drove every day to the main campus, twenty-five minutes away. At least Celeste hung out at the University, like the faculty kid she was, even if she had refused to enroll there as a student.

Celeste was not motivated, Hal had always insisted. She had barely gotten through high school. Her driver's license had been revoked for repeated speeding, and she had been fired from various store clerk jobs. She was alternately sullen and flippant towards Daphne. Today she probably wouldn't be any different.

The Bingham County campus was dotted with boxy new cement-board buildings painted mauve with bright accent colors: all window trim was turquoise. Stubby columns flanking bright aqua entrance doorways were forest green with cerise triangular neo-classic pediments. It certainly was a cheerful effect. It reminded Daphne of the small wooden wagon full of vari-colored wooden blocks that she had played with as a child. *A wonderful touch,* she thought, *here in the campus quadrangle, would be a giant wagon —a Claes Oldenbourg sculpture with a long pull-cord. It would be a witty statement — which most sculpture seldom is.* There didn't seem to be much wit at the college lately, Hal had remarked. When she told him about the wagon-sculpture idea, later on, he just shrugged and said, "Then the students would just be climbing up into the fool thing and fucking their brains out up there."

Daphne parked in the lot which Celeste had designated, then she walked to the dorm. It would not have hurt for her stepdaughter to be ready and watching at the front entrance, but she had said, in a snotty way, to go to room 203, the room of Barry Spiegel's nineteen-year-old daughter, Shulamith, with whom Celeste had been friends since childhood.

Inside the dorm it was fairly quiet. On the ground floor, in a brightly-lit chrome-yellow-walled gymnasium eight young women did aerobic exercises. Their anorexically-thin leader exhorted them, in Western Pennsylvania patois, to "In-hell, ex-hell, now *in*-hell again, now ex-hell," which instructions she punctuated with pelvic thrusts and sultry, sexually insinuating sensual moans of *"Ohhh,* yeah, *Ohhh* yeah."

Daphne took the elevator to the second floor and walked down the narrow, door-lined corridor looking for room 203. A hairy-chested, muscular young man with only a towel around his loins emerged from a doorway marked "showers" as two nubile young women, also in towel sarongs, entered the shower room. It was a co-ed dorm, Daphne realized, but she was startled to see this casual *deshabille,* after her own strictly-monitored college experience. Her all-girl dorm had been a no-man's-land with an eleven-o'clock curfew.

Loud, pounding rock music pulsated from one of the rooms, and a female vocalist sang-shouted "I feel ya movin' movin' movin', insida me, insida me —do it, do it, do it —" Daphne leaned against the wall for a moment contemplating the blatant eroticism of the raucous song and remembering her childhood confusion while living with her own family. Once, after innocently singing, in her seven-year-old treble "Just Molly and me — and baby makes three — " a favorite song of her two middle-aged aunts, she had been sent to her room in disgrace because, she realized years later, the song dealt with *birth.*

"That's a dirty song," had been her mother's thin-lipped hiss.

There were all kinds of things attached to the doors of the dormitory rooms: stuffed animals, large tablets and slates with pencil or chalk on strings, large posters. One huge poster nearly covering an entire door was a blown up photograph of a long, sleek red foreign car with mirror-brilliant chrome trim punctuating its scarletness. Leaning on the hood, their backs to the viewer, their high heeled shoes wide apart, was a row of five topless, tiny-waisted, voluptuous young women in thong bikinis. *Ten shapely cheeks, all in a row,* said Daphne to herself. "I guess that picture says it all," she muttered aloud.

On the door opposite room 203 hung a square, wood-framed slate outlined with thumb-tacked plastic flowers. A piece of chalk tied with a pink and green braided yarn dangled at one side. At the top of the slate on each corner were drawn smiley faces beneath each of which was lettered, "Hi! I'm Kimberly" and "Hi. I'm Denise." Below, in careful swirley loopy writing was a note: "We're down at aerobics. Please leave a message and we'll get right back to you. Bye!" Beneath this flowing calligraphy was a crudely chalked message: "Suck my dick you butteating hore."

A door opened behind her. Daphne turned to face Celeste.

"You're early, Daphne," she whined.

"*Au contraire,* Celeste. I'm right on the dot." Smiling ingratiatingly, Daphne pointed to her Timex watch.

"Well, I'm not ready. Can you wait in the lounge?" Celeste had masses of blondish hair falling over her shoulders. Her heavy makeup was freshly applied. She wore an overly-large and incongruously — with the elaborate makeup — wrinkled high fashion shirt and voluminous pants and heavy, high-topped laced-up boots. Daphne had paid seven hundred dollars toward Celeste's clothing bill the week before, pressing the check into Hal's hand until he had reluctantly accepted it.

Shulamith was peering over Celeste's shoulder as Daphne edged past them into the cluttered room and set her hand bag on the bed and said crisply, "No. I'll wait here till you're ready, but you don't have much time. Hi, Shullie, how are you, Honey?"

Shulamith Spiegel at nineteen was the image of her father at that age, short and pudgy and round-faced. She wore her thick black hair in a waist-length braid. Her nondescript skirt and sweater proclaimed her thorough disinterest in fashion. She smiled at Daphne and shrugged, "I'm okay. Pop said he saw you New Year's Eve. Some kids and I set off fire crackers at Peace Place with David. Now he's grounded there for a month." She shrugged again and lay down on the other bed. Celeste continued to arrange her elaborate hair, then sprayed it. Clouds of lavender fragrance filled the small room.

A large poster over Shulamith's bed was emblazoned with "Die Gruenen" and the sunflower of the German environmental political party. How had Celeste managed to keep this young woman, long a political activist on campus, as a friend, Daphne wondered. A copy of Emily Dickinson poetry lay open, face-down, on the end of Shulamith's bed. Daphne picked it up. "Are you an Emily fan, Shullie?" Daphne asked.

Celeste whirled around and snapped, "That's *my* book!" and snatching it from Daphne's hand, shoved it into her handbag.

Shulamith smiled and said, "I like Anne Sexton better. Did you know that most of Emily Dickinson's poems can be set to the song 'The Yellow Rose of Texas,'?" she said smugly.

"But that's the amazing thing about Emily Dickinson's work," Daphne replied. "That Victorian woman, incredibly repressed by today's standards, poured her fine intellect and amazing sensitivity and passion and eroticism and a huge capacity for love into that disciplined verse form. She expressed the inexpressible with those carefully crafted lines, as few poets ever have." Shulamith only smiled and shrugged.

Celeste swung a forest green wool-lined khaki poncho over her shoulders, picked up her fringed shoulder bag and turned to Daphne, her face set in her usual expression of elaborate boredom. "Let's go, stepmother."

"Come with us to the Gulf War protest march in D.C., Shullie," Daphne urged. "Ask your pop for details. We're chartering a bunch of busses." Celeste, already out in the corridor, called out, "She's got better stuff to do with her time, Daphne. She thinks demonstrations suck."

Shulamith yelled back, "Speak for yourself, Celeste."

What *do* these two have in common? Daphne wondered again. Well, what indeed? Rancorous divorced parents, hectic single-parent home life, a confusing, shared childhood in a nihilistic, violent, destructive, money-centered society. They had a lot in common, actually.

The fifteen chartered busses were to be boarded at three A.M. and depart at three twenty A.M. Hal and Daphne were in the garage in ten-degree weather, propping Pete up in Hal's car, trying to get him to drink from a mug of hot coffee. Celeste lay sprawled across the back seat, asleep. Hal gunned the car motor, flooded it, gunned it again and flooded it again. They talked briefly about not making the trip at all, dismissed that idea, finally got the car started and fishtailed on snow-drifted roads the five miles to the embarkation point, where they saw to their relief that several busses remained yet. Hal talked Celeste awake over her shrill protesting cries, and with Pete swearing and Daphne cajoling and begging, the two young people were hoisted onto the bus where they promptly fell asleep again.

Hal, wide awake now, and Daphne sipped coffee from their small thermos. Daphne's lower jaw throbbed where, in an emergency appointment the day before, Russell Hoskins had extracted a molar because it was "too far gone for a root canal." Russell had chortled that "We can do a nice bridge for you for only fifteen hundred!" Now pain seeped along her cheek and jaw and down the side of her neck into her collar bone. "Take a pain pill, kiddo," Hal suggested. Then, "Hey!" he said, "There's James —and Kenny Savage on that bus over there!" He waved to them, and they gave the thumbs-up sign to one another.

Daphne was glad she had given James the day off to attend the protest march, and idiotically, she hoped he would drop his British accent for today. She swallowed a Percodan and wrapped her wool muffler around her head and jaw. Her thoughts were a jumble. "Oh Goddess have mercy —oh Venus of Willendorf — this whole trip is a mistake," she prayed and leaned her head against the cold window glass. "Wow, wow, wow" went the pain.

Toward the center of the bus, standing in the aisle, was a tall slender woman, tuning a guitar. "Daph, look," Hal nudged her, "It's Nan O'Reilly, the folk singer."

Strumming her guitar expertly, Nan broke into a nineteen thirties' union song in a resonant bass voice.

Hal studied the passengers, most of whom were asleep, some snoring. There were several white-haired elderly couples, many middle-aged passengers and the rest were in their late teens and early twenties. He recognized several of his former students. No one paid any attention to Nan O'Reilly. To Hal, it seemed somehow a let-down; there didn't seem to be any electricity in the air.

"No one's excited at three thirty A.M., Hal," Daphne explained, burrowing more deeply into her muffler.

Just before the overhead lights went out Hal looked at his children across the aisle. It seemed to him that they had changed back into the seven-year-old and eleven-year-old they used to be, their faces untroubled, innocent, round-cheeked and sweet and vulnerable. Feelings of love for them swept over him with such intensity that he had to open his coat and take off his woolen cap. He smiled at Celeste as she curled into the seat corner, with Pete's head drooping against her shoulder.

Who would have believed there had been a terrible fight every night at dinner about this protest march, usually ending with Pete bolting from the table, shouting "You fucking asshole!" and Celeste screaming "Cocksucker!" at him, at Hal —at her father! Where did she learn such crude things? They had no interest in a war protest march, no passion about it at all, no convictions about anything. To get them to agree to come along, he had promised them that they needn't do any household chores for a month. Rotten, lousy bribery!

Then there were the days of watching the War Show on TV! It had a *title* —first, Desert Shield, then Desert Storm —and a cast of characters just like a Hollywood production, with specially composed scenario music in the background. Hal couldn't believe his eyes. He and Daphne had sat watching the first bomber planes as they took off, one after another. Then every night, some General somebody or other, emeritus, back in New York or D.C., would give his idea of what was happening, usually in sports metaphor lingo; an argot of fun-filled adjectives and chuckles as the General worked himself up to the point where he could hardly contain his joy over the whole thing. One General had burbled on the McNeil-Lehrer Show "To these guys, Robin, it's their *Super Bowl!* It's their big moment —like when they made that big touch-down for the college *team.* " The repugnance on the usually inscrutable newscaster's face was unmistakable. Hal would never forget the contempt in Robin McNeill's eyes.

And the yellow ribbons everywhere! They were tied to every porch post, lamppost, stair railing and tree, and they nearly blinded you! On street after street they dazzled the eye.

Hal settled back in his seat, growing drowsy in the darkness. Nan O'Reilly was singing a song about forest animals and making various repetitive noises as the song-story progressed, about a frog going "Arummpp arrrumpp." It didn't seem appropriate for an anti-war demonstration. There were snoring sounds. Finally someone asked Nan if she knew any anti-war songs, and strangely, she didn't play any. Hal tried to see Daphne in the semi-darkness. Her head was angled uncomfortably toward the window, her muffler fallen away from her rounded cheek, and she was breathing heavily in a deep sleep. She looked about seventeen, Hal thought.

From the rear of the bus there wafted the odor of marijuana. Hal drifted off to sleep. Nan O'Reilly continued doggedly singing her song: " —an' the possum he went puh-puh-puh, and the frog he went arrummph, arrummph."

Voices. Coughing. People mumbling, laughing and coughing. Daphne was groggily aware that, *Jeeze, people cough a lot.* All around her everyone was bustling and chattering, reaching for duffle bags and back packs, buttoning their coats. *My God,* she realized, *This is suburban D.C. We're here!* It was winter in D.C. too.

She shook Hal, then looked across the aisle at the still-sleeping children. Hal was gently shaking them awake. Their bus was passing other busses marked "Chartered" and passengers were waving and giving the thumbs-up sign and the "Right On" clenched fist of the mid-sixties and seventies.

Celeste and Pete had slept through all the rest stops, but

Daphne had brought their favorite sandwiches from home —
peanut butter and banana on whole wheat —and she handed one
to each of her step-children. She poured coffee into four very
politically-incorrect styrofoam cups and managed to smile at Hal.
She winced as pain shot through her jaw.

"We're gonna be a little late. Too many rest stops." Hal
looked at his watch.

"Well, our group will wait," Daphne said. "We're all to
meet at the Air and Space Museum."

The bus was pulling into a large parking lot where there
were dozens of other chartered busses parked. People were
hurrying toward a group of trees ahead. They were to walk to
the Metro station, get tickets and ride into the city. Celeste and
Pete drooped into the bus aisle, Daphne and Hal following, and
they all shuffled out into the damp, penetrating, fifteen-degree
cold.

"Celeste! Celeste!" It was Shulamith Spiegel waving and
shouting nearly a block away. They caught up to her, and all
proceeded into the wide tunnel that led into the Metro.

The huge jam-up of people leading to the ticket machines
would have been alarming if it had not been such an amiable,
polite crowd. There was a pervasive, all-of-one-mind calm that
Daphne, and Hal too, had experienced during other protest
marches since the sixties, particularly the Civil Rights marches.
And there had been the many marches to try to get the
ratification of the E.R.A. Daphne and Harriet had been to Illinois
three times, and to Salt Lake City for a whole month, to no avail.
Utah women had been horrified at the idea of breaking out of
their subservience to the patriarchy.

"You can feel it in the air, Hal, the old familiar feeling!"
Daphne gave his arm a squeeze.

Now the crowds pressed into the Metro entrance as far as
the eye could see, and they were subdued and polite —there was
almost a hush over the crowd —an eerie, reverent hush. They
continued to inch their way towards the machines, machines that
would not accept wrinkled bills and had to be fed money over

and over.

It was impossible to turn from side to side. You had to remain in whatever position that you started in, loin-to-loin or groin-to-groin. The crush was building, and there was no repositioning yourself. There was nervous laughter.

Daphne tried not to allow herself to think of panic —of claustrophobic panicking. But the thought kept shooting fear through her along with jabbing pain in her jaw. She stretched her neck to turn and look back for Celeste and Shulamith. They were chattering happily four or five feet away. But Pete, jammed between two middle-aged women, looked morose and miserable.

They were about twenty feet from the ticket machines, now —had moved less than ten feet in over a half hour! Hal had been talking earnestly to those around him, had gained their complete attention, and was outlining for them —too loudly —the hold that the government had on the populace and the way power rode rough-shod over everyone's civil rights. Bush had declared war personally; Congress had not, Hal said. Our constitutional rights were being abrogated. Daphne caught a word here and there, "Fascist mentality —our government is us —not the property of corporations." There were just snatches of words. Her own derriere was being rammed by a canvas bag full of some kind of projectiles —pointy, jabbing sticks, for God's sake, and two red-faced teen-aged boys had their heads nearly resting on her chest —one head on each breast —and were apologizing at every lurch. She was so dizzy from the ache in her jaw that she probably couldn't have stood alone anyway. They had five feet to go now.

Two young women at Daphne's left were laughing nervously about Hal. "I'm so scared just worrying if my folks will even *be there* when I get home from work each night, I can't think about all this scary stuff —you know, what *that guy's* talking about — I don't know how I even talked myself into coming here today," she tittered, almost hysterically and her companion, wearing furry red earmuffs, agreed, saying over and over, "Yeah. I know, I know." Daphne realized, with shock, that there was fear in this crowd, probably all over the U.S. as well as incredible amounts of moxie and courage, anger and nerve.

Suddenly a youthful-looking man —he was probably an agile forty-five — hopped up on a railing along the far wall and, hoisting himself onto a projection near the low ceiling, began waving his arm leading the crowd and singing loudly, "If I had a Hammer," the song that had so stirred the sixties and early seventies demonstrators. Soon other voices joined in until the entire jam-packed space was ringing.

"If I had a hammer, I'd hammer in the mor-or-ning —
I'd hammer in the evening, all over this laa-aand
I'd hammer 'bout DANGER, I'd hammer out a WARNING
I'd hammer 'bout love between
The brothers and the sisters
Oh —all over this la-a-a-n-d"

Daphne felt hot tears on her cheeks. The swollen glands at the back of her jaw throbbed as her tear ducts opened and the tears kept flowing. She could see profiles of other middle-aged people up ahead, and they too appeared to be gulping back tears as they sang and sang the battle song of their youth.

Suddenly they found themselves facing the sputtering ticket machines which reluctantly inched tickets into their sweaty fingers, and soon the crowd was hurtling smoothly through affluent suburban Washington, D.C., on the sleek, immaculate Metro train.

Pete sat with Daphne and was very watchful, occasionally murmuring, "Cool." She gave him another sandwich, and he continued to watch, wide-eyed and chewing slowly. Hal sat a few seats behind them, with Celeste and Shulamith, who were no longer chattering. At the next stop, two men carrying "Vietnam Vets Against the Gulf War" signs boarded the train. The two young women stared at the grim-faced veterans with frank interest, but it was interest that was not returned.

In contrast to the New York City subway, there was not a rat in sight here, Daphne realized. Here on the fine, new, shining clean D.C. Metro, and in the manicured and trimmed communities speeding by, was lavished the burnished luxury that

410

only money-lubricated white male power can proclaim. Incalculable wealth was concentrated here where the denizens of the Capitol Cosmos —the power brokers —cared for nothing else *but* power, and no living being. For them there was only the choreography, the ghastly swaggering theater of Desert Storm. For a little more than three days, U.S. troops had been wreaking havoc on a third rate country and its demonized leader, Saddam Hussein, because of U.S. oil interests. In TV news broadcasts, futurist weapons called Smart Bombs were being described as "seeking out their targets —the chimney of a deserted factory or an abandoned munitions depot miles from civilians, miles from children and old people and hospitals." It was a clean war where no one would die. These were the lies being dished up by the D.C. power brokers, and no photographers were allowed "for reasons of security." Hal interrupted these disturbing thoughts and smiled at Celeste, and to his surprise, she smiled back.

More and more passengers carrying anti-war signs boarded the train as it neared the Air and Space Museum. Now six sign-carrying Vietnam veterans occupied a row of seats in the back and talked together in low growls. They were rather seedy-looking grim men with down-turned mouths enclosed in deep creases like parentheses. Hal walked back to talk to them and found them surprisingly sanguine about their lot. Among them there were four ruined marriages, seven estranged children, two long stints in V.A. hospitals for damaged pancreas and Delayed Traumatic Stress Syndrome, and one skull that contained a steel plate. "Man, this war is fucking crazy. This war is insane," they said over and over, dragging on their cigarettes and shaking their heads.

Hal's birth date, by sheer chance had kept him out of the Vietnam war. These veterans —in their mid to late forties —had been eighteen, nineteen, twenty when they were drafted, two of them had enlisted —mere boys. They talked with Hal amiably for the final ten minutes of the train ride.

When everyone disembarked at the Air and Space Museum, they could hear it. It was a roaring sound. To Daphne it was as if she had her ear pressed to a gigantic chambered nautilus shell. The roar came from the area up ahead.

None of the Bingham group were waiting for them at the check point, so they half-walked, half-ran, with low cries, block after block toward where the roar was, and it grew louder and louder. Hundreds of people — and then, Daphne realized, thousands —were falling in behind them, beside and in front, and flowing from streets on either side of their group, thousands rushing toward and contributing to the roaring noise of protest, of dissent. These hundreds of thousands were Americans who did not want another war.

As they approached Pennsylvania Avenue they saw Barry and Harriet. Felicia and Audrey and Harletta were in the far distance, disappearing into the crowd, but running toward Daphne was Bobbye in an old L.L. Bean hooded jacket and jogging pants and boots. Daphne, her heart pounding from the ten-block jog, picked up speed and waved wildly until she and Bobbye collided, laughing and yelling. "Asa Helbrun's up ahead pushing Edith in a wheelchair," Bobbye shouted. "I *had* to come back one more time, to get you," she shrieked, to which Daphne shouted in response.

"Why the hell *not?*"

And the roar continued louder than ever. As they surged closer to Pennsylvania Avenue, sporadic band music and fragmented drum cadences floated to them on snowy wind-gusts. The sunlight was brilliant but icy cold. They had reached Pennsylvania Avenue now, the main parade route, and lined up eight or ten deep at the curbs on both sides of the street, and before they entered the march they stood and began to read some of the signs held by rank after rank —twenty-five or more abreast —of marching protestors. Past the cold, hard sun-glinted granite buildings lining the avenue, they marched, past the neo-classic monuments of immutable power, past the guards of Empire. And they would continue to march, rank upon rank all day, for miles, to the speakers' platform.

"Stay with us —Celeste —Pete —'' Hal yelled, " —we don't know what might happen. There might be violence, some crazed patriot, anything can happen.'' And Barry instructed Shulamith to stay with the group.

But there were no police on foot or mounted along the entire parade route, no peace-hating patriots; the streets were empty of uniforms, devoid of any military symbolism. Even the Vietnam veterans —and there were hundreds of them —only wore bits and pieces of uniforms —here and there a jacket or a hat or insignia. Over the roar, Hal called to Daphne, "No police! No truncheons, no elephant fences or Darth Vader bullet proof masks! It's almost as if they thought police would give us too much credibility.''

They began to shout out the names of the groups and states as the signs passed. "Look, Celeste,'' Hal shouted and pointed, "there's Massachusetts, and there's Vermont. There's a Florida group, Pete, and look how many came from Michigan —and there's Louisiana, and California!''

Pete and Celeste stood a little apart from the Bingham group and were obviously enthralled, and still they clung to each other's arms like two seven-year-olds. *She's not flippant now,* Daphne realized, *—this is for real. She'll have to come out of her self-absorption now, this reader of Emily Dickinson's poetry —for we are witnessing poetry here, and she's getting hooked.*

Celeste's eyes widened, and she watched intently as a New Orleans jazz band featuring white and black men and women playing trumpets, trombones, and clarinets, and six male drummers, from about age sixteen to seventy-five, performed a dance-march step, a classic nineteenth century Louisiana parade tradition, to the tune of W.C. Handy's "St. Louis Blues.'' Not far behind the casually dressed, rhythmically gyrating blues musicians were four rows of marchers carrying a wide banner, *OREGON EXPLORER SCOUTS AGAINST THE GULF WAR,* followed by five more rows of marchers mufflered up to their eyes and waving signs from Ohio, Indiana, and Wyoming.

Behind them, persistently, an eerie clacking and rattling sound rose above the roar. It was not drums.

A trumpet sounded, raucous and off-pitch, and rounding the bend in the street, swaying in slow stride came what appeared to be an army of Easter Islander-style papier maché giant sculptured figures thirty feet high in overalls and caps, stick-women in long dresses and aprons and babushka kerchiefs —operated by dozens of men and women running about beneath them with long poles. They were the Bread and Puppets Theater of German sculptor Peter Schumann, who had founded the group in New York's Lower East Side and through which they had begun to make political statements in the sixties. Now, centered in the rows of grieving —obviously ethnic-faced —puppets was a puppet woman with lowered eyes, carrying across her outstretched arms the bloody puppet body of a child. The rattling sound grew louder, and the trumpet fanfare sounded again, followed by blasting heavy metal music. Strutting and boogieing around the bend came a human woman in peasant dress on eighteen-foot tall wooden stilts, twirling and swooping expertly, flinging her arms toward the enormous puppet following her, a male in a three-piece suit, who bore a huge sign: *THE NEW WORLD ORDER.*

Following the somber-faced business-suited puppet was an even taller brown-robed and hooded puppet. With lowered eyes and a beneficent half-smile, he opened his very long arms slowly to reveal a human woman in odds and ends of tacky cardboard armor, galloping forth on a crude stick-horse from which hung assorted, dented clanking metal pots and pans. This medieval "knight" raised a dented trumpet to her lips at intervals and bleated a fart-like fanfare blast. Following her and fanning out from the giant's encircling arms were twenty-five or thirty normal-sized humans in raggedy medieval-looking clothing, blowing on kazoos and twirling wooden ratchet rattles. The ghostly clacking and humming, amazingly, carried over the ever-present roar of the spectators and marchers, unmistakably conveying the patriarchal message: the We're-Going-To-Blow-A-Third-rate-Country-Back-To-The-Middle-Ages message of

Empire.

"Oh God," Bobbye said, and she squeezed Daphne's arm and pointed. Approaching were three massive puppet women wearing long, Middle Eastern chador-like garments and head scarves. The middle puppet carried the bloody-clothed body of a small female child puppet across her outstretched arms. Daphne glanced at Pete. He was hunched over, staring, his hands deep in his parka pockets.

Four white paper doves with vast, trailing wings towered more than thirty-five feet over the crowd and were the last of the Bread and Puppets panorama. The graceful bird forms fluttered and dipped poignantly in time to the rippling flutes and strings of Maurice Ravel's "Introduction to Daphnis and Chloe Suite," which poured from the P.A. system in all its purity, floating above the crowd, above the roar, above the war.

"It was cool," Pete conceded; he actually was smiling. "I thought the whole demonstration was cool." He forked a four-layer slice of syrupy buckwheat pancakes into his rosebud pink mouth. Daphne, her own jaw aching, was aware of her stepson's comely mouth and lips because they were duplicates of his father's, the same rosy lips and even, white, orthodontured teeth.

After sleepwalking through the day, when they returned home from the protest march, Hal and Daphne and the children had drooped to their rooms and slept for ten hours. Now, at brunch, Hal watched with wonder as Pete accepted a third stack of pancakes from his stepmother.

Celeste sat with the family, at the oval pine table in the kitchen, and sipped orange juice and nibbled at a piece of toast. It had been months since she had eaten any breakfast. "Yeah, it was neat," she murmured and spread peanut butter on another piece of rye toast. "And the people who gave talks were good too —you know, at the end of Pennsylvania avenue —up on that platform. But why did they have mounted police there and nowhere else along the street?"

"I guess they thought it was too risky not to have security so close to the White House. I have a hunch that sharpshooters were stationed all along the parade route. I saw a little squib in the back page of this morning's paper about marches that were held in Seattle and Colorado and Missouri. There were plenty more, no doubt," Hal said, "but the people who made it to D.C. really wanted to protest in the Capitol, so they sacrificed a hell of a lot, missed a couple days' work and marched in that awful cold because they cared so much."

"Do you think it'll do any good?" Celeste asked.

"No," Hal admitted, laying down his fork and smiling ruefully, "I don't think they'll withdraw the troops now. They're going to have the war anyway."

CHAPTER FIFTY-ONE

Traci Bilsen-Bloom popped a bright yellow capsule into her glistening scarlet-lipped mouth and then poured herself a triple bourbon into the one remaining clean Orrefores crystal glass. Bright morning sunlight danced on the intricate hobstars and facets of the heavy cut glass tumbler.

It was going to be another freakish, unseasonably hot Western Pennsylvania spring day. Allison hadn't cleaned up after their party the night before and was in bed in her usual near-comatose hangover stupor, but Traci felt great. To her, whiskey was the ultimate restorative, the Elixir of Life.

Audrey Hopper would be arriving at two o'clock to do the laundry and clean both bathrooms. But her payments had been getting later and later over the past few months. Traci had threatened to go to Harletta Hoskins and Edith Hartley. Then Audrey had quickly resumed paying the three hundred a week that Traci demanded.

With Audrey's payments and with what Ed Krock and Ted Mather and the AstraLadies paid her, Traci was able to buy a posh condo, trade in her Porsche every year, and accumulate a sizeable nest-egg besides.

Now Traci pressed a button, and the heavy white linen draperies slowly and silently drew closed on their motorized track. The large cathedral-ceilinged living room was now enveloped in cool shadows. An all-white living room had been a good idea. Those Bitsy Bitches were pop-eyed last night! She straightened the Kilim-tapestry-covered toss-pillows on the couch and smiled as she recalled last night's catered party, free-flowing food and free-flowing drinks.

The AstraLadies had turned out to be a very profitable proposition. Now that the Gulf War was over, Traci's persuasive clairvoyance sessions were again paying off, and some Bingham doctors' wives had discovered her mystical powers. Now she got a thousand dollars for an evening with these rich bored women to whom a hundred dollars was a few minutes' pin money. And there was always plenty of coke sitting around, with the requisite

417

matchbooks and little gold spoons on the glass-topped tables in Mrs. Doctor Bitsy's expensively furnished home.

Now Traci's loyal band of members of the newly-formed AstraLadies rejoiced in anticipation of the Astral Confluence ceremony in Bearcat Park tonight under a full moon.

A whole contingent of female misogynists —women who hate women —had been eager to ally themselves with Traci when she was fired from the Sojourner Shelter. When she had first come to Bingham to take the Shelter CEO position, she had revealed herself to be a woman-hater —just like themselves —and now it was clear that she knew how to put women in their place. Their patron saint was the dead actress, Marilyn Monroe, the sex-fantasy idol of all men, and thus, the AstraLadies ideal after whom they endeavored to pattern themselves: her womanly vulnerability, her dependency, her martyred victim image and, above all, her flashy, sensual appearance. The negativity, the self-deprecation and self-abnegation of this pattern of thought, completely eluded the bourgeois Bitsy-AstraLadies. They wholeheartedly supported Traci's convoluted rationale; after all, it wasn't anti-male, was it? It paid into comfortable middle class white women's status quo and was anti-uppity woman, thus ensuring that the socially secure position of Bitsy women was safeguarded.

Marilyn Monroe was a man's woman! She *needed* men — not like that actress-singer-tramp, Madonna, who made fun of men by being independent and doing muscle-building and putting her own sexual pleasure before that of *men*. And the AstraLadies' uniforms were *fun!* Their signature inch-long blood-red fingernails, which matched their lipstick, plus their platinum blonde M.M. wigs were known all over the Tri-state area and beyond. And their husbands were turned on by their M.M. pointy uplift bras and black and white polkadot negligees that completed their uniforms.

AstraLadies often were joined by their sister organization, the anti-choice Precious Pink Feet or PPF. They often demonstrated together in anti-choice rallies. Being activists against women was *fun* too!

After the AstraLadies pictures appeared in the newspapers and on TV of their anti-abortion rallies, their husbands would notice other men's admiring glances at CorBlimey business lunches, and their husbands knew it was because they had such *womanly* wives. There was no doubt about *their* women! Their women were sex-on-wheels obedient *ladies*.

Even Phyllis Schlafly and the Eagle Forum never dreamed up any thing like *this!* It was even beyond the imaginative rantings and love-hate obsessions of the full-time professional anti-feminist author, Favrile Buglia.

Traci chuckled to herself about these things and had begun to go over plans for tonight's Confluence when the phone rang. It was Louise Delaney, P.P.F. leader, who cooed, "The party last night was lovely, Traci. You went to a lot of trouble with those canapés."

"It was Relinquished Endorphin Synapse, Louise," Traci assured her.

"Oh Uh-huh," said Louise, somewhat anxiously. "Some of our PPFs were worried about paganism in your ministry, but your working against women's freedom of choice has won them over. It's the Christian way. And I want you to know that everyone's coming to the Confluence tonight. But are you sure there is electric at Maple Leaf Pavilion? We want to show our video of the Bellaire Abortion Clinic Massacre — you know, where those doctors were bombed, those doctors who murder babies. I know Elfin Glade has electric for sure."

"It immm-pacted on me, Louise, to access the pavilion with all the best facilities, *and* the all-important Rocky Creek nearby, where the Purification Rites will be conducted. Maple Leaf Pavilion fulfills all of the Astral Ritual requirements. Tonight will be the Definitive Lunar Articulation that all the AstraLadies have been waiting for. Sagittarius is in the Seventh House. So trust me!"

"Oh, we *do*, Traci. We *do!*" declared Louise breathlessly, "We know you have the AstraLadies' best interests at heart!

Now, one more thing, and then I'll let you go: Is the Pledge to our Men and the singing of our Anthem *before* the Purification or *after?"*

"Before, Louise, before." Traci was exasperated. "And remember, Louise, our Sacred Secret Ceremony must remain secret to be sacred. Neptune afflicted by Pluto causes confusion. Your Priestess has spoken."

"Oh I know, Traci. I know!"

"I'm takin' a chance even talkin' on the phone to you at *all,* Ted." Ed Krock held the phone with his chin as he tried to pull himself out of the sunken center of his circular water bed. He had thrown away a thousand dollars on the bed whose center had just now sealed itself off somehow, and now the cushiony water-filled channels circled the bed's outer edges, leaving Ed lying on the rubber-covered wooden center of the platform. The red-velvet-covered half-canopy that tilted over the bed like a coffin lid had long ago come loose from the ceiling on one side, taking the stereo and speakers with it so that the wires trailed onto the bed pillows. And right after Bobbye had moved out, the heart-shaped mirror had fallen out of the lid onto Ed and Traci at a very inopportune moment, and he had incurred some painful and humiliating glass cuts on his rear. Traci had laughed at him and said, "It always immm-pacts on *me* to cover *my* ass, Ed."

"Traci told me this was a by-pass phone line, Ed," Ted Mather slurred into the phone, his voice wavering as though coming from under water or a long way off.

"No, this is not a by-pass line. Where the fuck *are* you, anyway, Ted?" Ed pushed the stereo wires out of his face and managed to sit up.

"I can't divulge that information at this point in time. Is this the Mellors Lane house?"

"Yeah. I'm working at the Bingham County office this week."

"Your Congressional absenteeism record is outstanding, Ed.

How much longer can you get away with it? The Gulf War was your excuse for a while. *Now* what's your excuse?" Ted laughed his snuffling laugh. "But seriously, is Traci still puttin' out?"

"That's for me to know and you to find out, Ted. Now whadya want? I'm busy. I gotta talk to some of my constituents this morning."

This statement elicited such hilarity from Ted that it was a full minute before he was able to control his wheezing nasal guffaws and snuffling giggles. "Tell me another one, Ed," he snorted. "But I'm serious. I gotta talk to you *today* — it's classified stuff, even if I have to fly myself out there, and you know I'm not that good of a pilot. The Cessna is the only plane left on the Key —uh —around this place."

"Then you're callin' from *Florida,* huh?" Ed exclaimed, cheered by his own perspicacity. This James Bond stuff sure was intoxicating! He went on excitedly, "I'll be target shooting this afternoon, Ted, at the Sportsmen's Club, you know, in Bearcat Park, and tonight they're having a barbecue there for me. The powers-that-be want to be sure I vote for the hospital waste dump to go on Leonard Blake's property. He's holding out for big bucks the state will pay him if we give the go-ahead. After the barbecue we're having some action with our feathered friends, if you get my drift. And does the name 'Nurse Funbuns' ring a bell, Ted?"

"Out*standing!*" Ted shouted. "She has rang my bell and everything else. But I thought she was supplying ex-Congressman Burgess with full-time pussy."

"Well, she was stayin' in D.C. with him at the Watergate for a couple months, my snitches told me," Ed said, "and went all over town all gussied up, but now she's back in Bingham at Burgess's horse farm and took up with Ernest Hartley —you know —that doctor who beat up his wife —remember that big rape-in-marriage trial and he got a year in jail? Imagine someone wantin' to rape his own *wife!*" Ed laughed heartily. "But now Hartley can't keep Nursie from sashayin' all over town swingin' them buns in yer face. You *gotta* fly *out* here, Ted!"

421

"Have a car at the County Airport for me around ten tonight. I'm flyin' out there! Rock n' Roll, Dude!" Ted yelled. Then he began to sing loudly, "I'm leavin' —on a jet plane, don't know when I'll be back agai —" and hung up abruptly.

Ed struggled out of the water bed and shuffled across the room to his kitchenette and put the tea kettle on for instant coffee. He stood there in his bathrobe, scratching and yawning as it slowly dawned on him that he spent all his time in the basement, while he had ten carpeted rooms upstairs that he never used. Bobbye and that decorator had fixed everything up and installed the Jacuzzi, and then there was all the trouble at the fund-raiser and all the stuff in the paper about it. It coulda cost him the election! It seemed like a helluva long time ago —but all the damage had been repaired, and then Bobbye got the divorce, and he had laid low ever since those disasters. In the up-coming election he'd probably be a shoo-in.

He took his cup of coffee out to the rec-room bar where he added a shot of whiskey and stood stirring and thinking. The circle of Barca-Lounger recliner chairs in front of the TV looked lonely.

A strange thought kept coming back and crowding into Ed's couple of other thoughts. It was something about the basement — the cellar —his boyhood, and all the time he had spent in his family's cellar back in those days, wishing he had a big red Naugahyde tufted bar back then, with a big mirror and cherry-faced plywood paneling like the Bitsies had in their rec-rooms that he saw whenever he and his dad did plumbing work in Briarwood. And he had worked on plumbing in many basements back then, here in Chatterly Estates too! Now *he* had a big house in Chatterly Estates. But here he was —still down in the cellar. Now he had all the things he had always wanted: a big rec-room. And he had a forty-inch TV and paneling and oak gun cabinets, and he was a *Congressman* besides, and he had all the pussy he wanted, but when Bobbye left, none of the Bitsies ever invited him anywhere and were never impressed with him and — and —it was all too profound for him to contemplate further.

Then he heard the key in the side door and he chuckled. It was Traci, his two jiggly boobs and that great pussy! There'd be the NRA picnic this afternoon and the cockfight tonight and here was Traci and things weren't so bad after all!

"Hello, Ed." Traci rounded the corner. She was wearing her tight-fitting red Mandarin coat and pants outfit, and the three-inch-heeled shoes he liked so much, that made her rear end stick out. She undulated over to him, and he reached out and tweaked one boob and then the other.

"Hi-ya, Babe," he crooned, "hows about a quickie?"

"You need a shave, Ed."

"That never stopped ya before."

"Well, today's not good on our compatibility chart. The morning sun remains in Virgo, and I haven't finished your natal chart."

"Ah Babe," Ed whined, you said you'd have it done last week."

"I need more time. Affiliated Mercury is still in the Tenth House, so we can't fuck yet. Give me a cup of coffee." Traci leaned on the bar, and her top button popped open.

"I have to pick up the booze for tonight, so I hope you have my money. I'll be glad when it's over. Those Bitsies are so worked up they're all nearly peeing themselves."

Ed poured a double shot of Jim Beam in Traci's coffee and handed it to her. She slid onto a bar stool and another one of her buttons popped open. He eyed her cleavage.

"I heard about that circle-jerk you dick-heads are calling target practice — at the Sportsmen's Club tonight — is really gonna be a *cock* fight. That's so illegal it makes my pussy itch. And it has immm-pacted on me, Mr. Representative, that Maple Leaf Pavilion is pretty damn close to the Sportsmen's Club. Don't even think about coming anywhere near Maple Leaf Pavilion. I don't want any of you in any way, shape or form near my AstraLadies."

"Shit, Traci," Ed began rummaging behind some bottles in the liquor cabinet, "I thought you reserved fuckin' Elfin Glade

Pavilion. It's miles from the Club.''

"Elfin Glade has *no* Rocky Creek, Ed. The AstraLadies are gonna dip their boobs and butts in the creek at the end of the ceremony.''

Ed grinned, "No *shit?*''

"No *shit,* Ed.'' Traci held out her hand. "My money, please.''

Ed rummaged some more and brought out a roll of bills, which he shoved down the front of Traci's pants.

"Christ, that tickles,'' she laughed. "You can remove your hand now, Ed.''

"No, I'm countin' the money. And besides, Earl knows you'll be here this morning, and he'll be here any minute. I'm doin' foreplay for he and I both,'' Ed chuckled excitedly.

"Stop it,'' Traci giggled, twisting away from him.

"You made me lose count! Now I have to start over.'' Ed thrust his hand in again and with the other hand began working Traci's pants down over her hips. "My Neptune wants to mingle with your moon, Babe,'' he panted, bending over her bare buttocks.

The roll of bills fell to the floor as footsteps on the stairs announced the arrival of the Reverend Earl "Brimstone" Krock.

"Help, Brimmie,'' Traci giggled, "Ed's Neptune is beginning to move into my Libra!'' She slipped away from Ed and, bare from the waist down, plopped on one of the Barca Loungers.

"Now neither one of you can get at me.'' She stuck out her tongue and spread her legs.

"That's Satanic, Traci! Astrology is wickedness.'' Brimmie scowled and waggled his finger as he removed his gold cross and chain from his neck and laid them on the bar, then poured himself a triple shot of Jim Beam.

Now Ed circled Traci's chair and, standing behind it, tilted it back and shoved his hand down the front of her blouse, while the Reverend Earl removed shiny polyester trousers, folded them neatly and laid them on the back of one of the Barca Loungers.

His almost hairless legs were pasty white in contrast to his red face and hairy red neck. His baggy white boxer shorts were imprinted with an allover design of luscious red parted lips, which pattern a minuscule erection was beginning to push out of alignment.

"The Lord wants me to teach you about His love, Traci. He wants us to pray together, you and me and Ed, for your sin of blasphemy."

The Reverend drained his glass. "We're gonna banish Satan through pre'r." Perching on the arm of Traci's chair, he stared at her crotch.

Traci, crossing her legs, drawled, "You're so holy, Brimmie, you're going to an illegal cockfight tonight, but the Lord'll forgive you for it, right? Like He forgives your fornicating. You're a Virgo, Reverend, and Virgos are obsessed with sex!"

"Stop your blasphemin', Traci," Brimmie warned, as he removed his day-glo green nylon fishnet shirt.

"Make me!" Traci challenged.

Ed had unbuttoned her red silk Mandarin coat down to her waist and now her pallid flesh spilled out.

Together, Brimmie and Ed lifted Traci from the Barca Lounger and carried her toward Ed's bedroom, the Reverend shouting, "We're gonna *pray!*" The two men's hoots and Traci's laughter rang up the basement stairs, the ghostly echoes floating through the empty upstairs rooms.

CHAPTER FIFTY-TWO

The familiar hubbub of Bingham's Stop and Spend Super Market had swelled to a frenetic din by five forty-five P.M., punctuated by the same querulous cries as always, of hungry toddlers being pushed in the same hugely-loaded shopping carts by the same tired mothers, with the same tired Muzak accompaniment. Today the BeeGees' seventies hit "Stayin' Alive" seemed, to Daphne's ears, a particularly laconic exhortation. As she approached the hamburger counter, having abandoned all hope of any jiffy nouvelle cuisine —she had two jars of Cheez Whiz in her cart —she heard a familiar voice behind her, reciting, of all things, " — when what to my wondering eyes should appear but a miniature sleigh, and *Daphne!* Hi, stranger!"

Daphne spun around. "Ellen! Why, what*ever* are you doing at the *hamburger* counter?" she laughed.

Ellen flung three pounds of Extra Lean on top of two boxes of Hamburger Helper, and then the two friends pushed their carts into a Toidey Babe Bathroom Cleaner display area that was conveniently deserted. And no wonder. The crazed grin of the life-sized cut-out cardboard photo of a hypermammiferous house slave —in a bikini, yet —was a real turn-off as her cardboard motorized arm and cardboard hand dipped a phallic toilet brush obscenely in and out and in and out of a real toilet. The two feminists leaned over their carts, weak with laughter, stared at the Toidey Babe and the toilet and then burst into laughter again.

"What lunatic fringe ad executives got off on *that* fantasy? And the funniest part is the joke's on *them!*" Ellen gasped, wiping her eyes.

"Remember when Harriet gave that phamacist a hard time in that drug store," she said, "when we were at the Springfield Illinois rally for the E.R.A. extension?"

"You mean where they had that FEMININE HYGIENE sign with five-foot high letters clear across the front of the store?" Daphne said, "and the vaginal spray sign that flashed on and off?"

427

"Yeah, Yeah," Ellen wheezed with laughter. "And Harriet cornered the pharmacist at the cash register where there was a long line of customers, and she said 'Where's the MASCULINE HYGIENE department? *Men* stink. They can stink real *bad,* so where's all the crotch sprays and that kind of stuff, for *men?'* And some women started to mutter, *'Yeah.* What about that? She's right.' And the pharmacist sort of hid behind the cash register and mumbled, "We-l-l-l-l, we got some powder for jock itch, over there by the pipe tobacco."

The two women hooted so noisily that passing shoppers began to stare.

"About ten people got Instant Consciousness-Raising *that* day!" Ellen blew her nose. Daphne could see that her friend's eyes were filling with tears.

"I almost forgot it was possible to laugh like this, Daphne. I haven't laughed —haven't joked in so long —" She turned and faced the wall for a moment, then regained her composure. "Boy, those were the days!"

They talked for a few minutes: Today was Mark's birthday; they were taking a cake to the VA hospital after dinner to celebrate with Larry —Larry was being fed intravenously —and was "hanging *in* there." Daphne realized they'd have to change the subject. Quickly.

Then Ellen said, "I heard from Betty Colvin —*The Bingham Herald* reporter — that Traci's witches' coven Astral whatsis group, is meeting in Bearcat Park tonight, at midnight. Betty had heard a rumor so she looked it up in the Park Reservation Office and, sure enough, Traci had reserved Maple Leaf Pavilion *months* ago! Betty's taking a *Herald* photographer out there tonight. And the word around our neighborhood is that there's going to be a *cockfight* at the Sportsmen's Club tonight, too, *and* we heard that the Reverend Earl is involved in a *ménage à trois* with Ed and Traci. With his *own* brother, if you can believe it!"

Daphne shrugged. "I can believe it. There's always sleaze, always raunch, Ellen. Ordinary people try to get along from day to day, and maybe they work for some noble cause once or twice in their lives —even experience grace a few times in their lives. And then there are people like Ed Krock. And Traci. And Earl Krock. They're the raunch factor, Ellen, without whom this pock-marked derelict of a world can't seem to keep on spinning."

The two friends parted, vowing to get together at the hospital, soon —just a pleasantry, they both knew, since visitors tired Larry and worried him. It had been many months since he had joked with Ellen, punning, when his friends visited him, that they should "pass around the bier." There was very little joking any more. Even a CD that Ellen had made of their favorite jazz classics —"Ain't Misbehavin," "Sunny Side o' the Street," and her Errol Garner-style arrangement of the Pittsburgh-born jazz genius's "Misty" —only depressed Larry all the more.

Ellen did not let herself think of the times —on some other planet, in some other world —when she and Larry had fallen asleep in each other's arms with "Misty" playing softly and rain drumming on the tin roof of their bedroom, their six healthy children asleep in their rooms just down the hall.

Without faltering, Ellen was going through the motions of living, now; motions that her difficult life, her capacity for love, had taught her. They were lessons that she had learned well.

In the bright moonlight, their Marilyn Monroe-style platinum wigs glowed almost phosphorescently as forty-five AstraLadies stood with bowed heads in the clearing in Bearcat Park. They were bounded on one side by Maple Leaf Pavilion with its booze-laden picnic tables and on the other side by the gurgling and splashing Rocky Creek. Around the perimeter of the clearing, trees dipped and swayed in the warm, pleasant breeze.

An owl hooted in the distance as the AstraLadies, at a sign from Traci, formed semi-circular rows before the altar, their identical black and white polka dot negligees seeming to wink and shift, starlike, with each movement. The Sacred Secret Ceremony had begun.

It was taboo for AstraLadies to touch one another, touching being a sacrament and privilege reserved for the Sanctified Male; therefore the celebrants were careful to stand well apart from one another.

Traci was attired in a full length, pink-satin-lined white woolen cloak, from the hood of which escaped a few silken platinum tendrils —her own hair, not a wig. She flung open the cloak revealing a silver sequinned bra and matching garter belt and black lace panties and rhinestone-studded black lace stockings with seams. Now she removed her cloak and handed it to Allison and turned toward the altar, her rounded buttocks defined by the glittering garter belt. She lifted high a scroll-like tube, calling out names and astrological signs, one by one, and each celebrant, one by one, moved in a slow procession to the pink-satin-draped altar, where she received her scroll, which contained a candle and a black elastic lace-trimmed one-size-fits-all garter belt.

From stereo speakers perched on nearby trees came strains of Traci's sixties' recording of "Aquarius." Now she reached behind the altar, her spangles sparkling in the moonlight, and turned on a bright spotlight, focussing all attention on a gilt-framed life-size color photograph of Marilyn Monroe in her most familiar pre-orgasmic pose, with half-shut eyes and open wet mouth and the top of her golden lamé gown split to the waist. She was Everyman's dream of ceaseless copulatory nirvana and every AstraLady's love-hate dichotomy. She was the embodiment of everything the AstraLadies wanted to be, that they had to be because Marilyn Monroe was the woman men wanted. Women's libbers were just jealous of her.

Traci stood facing the mesmerizing photograph and lit a phallus-shaped pink wax candle and raised it on high, a signal for each celebrant to drop her polka dot negligee, revealing a long white gown. Then each celebrant drew a phallus-shaped candle from her garter belt scroll and solemnly glided, Druid-like, toward Traci, where each lit her candle from Traci's candle. They all raised their phallic tapers toward the photograph and began to sway, never taking their eyes from their gold-and-white icon.

Then a low moan rose from their midst as the AstraLadies slowly became aware — aware of something glistening on Marilyn Monroe's cheek! Her eyes shone like liquid, and then her eye opened and closed! Could it be? Was Marilyn crying? A sigh rippled through the celebrants, and as if in a trance, they moved past Traci and clustered at the base of the tree from which the photograph was suspended.

Their low cries rose, "Ahhhhhh." The celebrants stretched scarlet-tipped fingers toward Marilyn's tears, tears that were far beyond their reach, just as she was now beyond the reach of the men who defined her womanliness, beyond sex, beyond life. Their idol was crying for her loss and crying for all the AstraLadies, and crying for *every* woman too ugly to be worthy of the life-giving protection and copulatory acts that only the Sacred Male could bestow and only through which true womanliness was possible. Their idol was crying —as a plaster Jesus had done a few years ago in a Kincade Township church when it wept and closed one eye, and people had travelled from all over the U.S. and even from Europe to witness the miracle. Now this moment was the AstraLadies' Epiphany, their *raison d'etre*. Their martyred idol had wept and winked for *them!*

Traci inserted a cassette in the tape player, pressed the "On" button, and with her candle bravely flickering, glided over a knoll toward Rocky Creek as strains of the AstraLadies' hymn wafted over the trees. The celebrants, singing along, followed her in single file.

Lining up along the bank of the creek, the AstraLadies lifted their voices in their hymn, eagerly anticipating their immersion in Rocky Creek, after which they were entitled to don their garter belts over their long white gowns —gowns symbolizing their purity and WASP heritage. The AstraLadies had been well-prepared for these bold ceremonial acts back in the seventies in the Fascinating Womanhood movement when they had wrapped their nude bodies in clear plastic to titillate their turned-off

husbands. Additional experience, which had emboldened the
Bingham Bitsies in preparation for tonight's ritual, had occurred
in the late seventies when some of the Bingham church services
featured women of the congregation doing the Islamic *belida,* or
belly dance, as they called it, in which staid matrons in jewelled
brass hip belts and harem pants and skimpy brassieres shimmied
and gyrated in the chancel, accompanied by the bongo drumming
of slavering church ushers wearing burlap loin cloths over their
three-piece polyester suits. Now this stirring spiritual Astral
Confluence was the transfiguring climax that Traci had only
hinted about.

"Can you see anything?" Howard Fletcher shifted his
camera bag and pulled Betty Colvin's shirttail.

"Shhhh," she cautioned him. "They're leaving the clearing
now. I see moving lights. We have to get in closer."

They groped through the dense underbrush and locust trees
and wild grapevines, Betty trying to store in her memory all that
was happening. Wait till her editor saw *this* feature story!

Howard pulled Betty's shirttail again. "Look," he
whispered, "a police car just passed, down there on the road
where we parked the car."

Betty turned and squinted through the branches. "Oh shit!
they're gonna wonder about our car! But no —no —they're going
past. It's funny they didn't drive up to Maple Leaf Pavilion.
Look! There's the S.W.A.T. team van...and another squad car.
What the fuck is going *on?"*

Howard peered down at the road and whispered, "There's
nothing illegal about partying at a pavilion if it's reserved ahead.
That's how you found out about this witches coven in the *first*
place, Betty. It was in the reservation book."

"Yeah, but alcohol and pot are illegal in the park, and those
women have plenty of booze, and we saw them passing roaches
around."

"Apparently it's not Traci's coven the police are after."

Betty and Howard pushed into the brush. Little by little, they edged closer. "I can see the lights better," Betty whispered. "and — what's *that?* I hear singing. My God, they're singing 'Stand by Your Man'!"

Betty crept closer, pushing jagged vines and underbrush aside as Howard stumbled behind her adjusting his camera lens. The singing grew louder, and now the sound of gurgling water mingled with the voices. The full moon was bright as daylight.

"Can you see anything else?" Howard whispered, fitting flashbulbs in his camera.

"Yes, yes. There's a whole bunch of them. They're wearing white wigs and long white gowns! They're lined up along Rocky Creek. What *are* these women doing? They're just standing with their candles and swaying and singing. We don't dare get any closer."

Howard whispered. "It's nearly midnight. Maybe they're gonna do something *Satanic.*" He was standing beside Betty now, breathing hard from the exertion, sighting through his view finder.

"They're going in the water and stooping down!" Betty whispered excitedly. "The water's over their knees! Their gowns are getting wet. Now they're all going in deeper."

"Let's move parallel to them," Howard whispered hoarsely, "and get closer to the creek. If we're far enough downstream, they won't see us, and I could get some great shots."

Betty nodded, "Yeah! Yeah!"

They grabbed at the increasingly tangled wild vines and, forcing aside a cluster of Scotch pines, pushed themselves slowly sideways until the gurgling creek seemed almost directly beside them.

"What's happening?" Howard tugged Betty's shirttail again.

"They're lined up — there must be at least forty of them — in the water, stooping and then standing — up and down — Traci's on the shore, waving her arms. I can see her. Good God — she's all tricked out in a bra and garter belt and — What's *that?* It's some *other* music. It's coming from over there —" she pointed, "and from the beat, it sounds like Country and Western."

It was coming from the Sportsmen's Club.

Ed Krock and Ted Mather took their pork barbecue sandwiches and beers and joined other NRA members at the cockfight ring which was in a copse of pines and locust trees about fifty yards behind the Sportsmen's cabin. The bright moonlight illuminated the area sufficiently, and few additional lights were needed.

Fresh straw was being spread in the ring to absorb the blood from the last round, and now metal spurs were being attached to the legs of docile-looking roosters who were to fight the next round. Ed had bet plenty on the losers of the last two rounds and was looking the birds over now and betting more carefully.

All in all, it didn't seem to be Ed's lucky day. Ted was acting rotten. He was mad about the Citizen Action Party's law suit against Beckwell Corporation, and Beckwell was mad at Ted, and Ted was taking it out on *Ed!* And Nurse Funbuns, a.k.a. Kidney Kort Kween Dialysis, had disappeared into the woods with the Truschel Township Fire Chief for an hour and twenty minutes, and most of the sportsmen were drunk and getting pretty loud.

"I'm leavin' after this next round," Ed said to Ted Mather, then held out a package of Tums. "Want one?" he said, and tossed three into his own mouth.

"It's only midnight, Ed. Ya gonna be a party pooper? You been tossin' Tums like they was peanuts, today."

"I don't feel so good, Ted." Ed wiped his badly sunburnt face with a red bandanna and swatted at the gnats that wouldn't let his ankles alone. He was sorry he had worn his Bermuda shorts; they wouldn't say up with just a belt, and now his damned suspenders were cutting into his shoulders. He belched and wished he hadn't come.

Allen Cope, Ed's aide, and several Truschel Township fire

fighters pushed wheel barrows laden with plates of sauerkraut and mashed potatoes, and plastic bowls of strawberry shortcake over to where Ed and Ted were standing.

"Oh *man,*" Ed groaned, "I can't resist this shit!" and balanced two bowls and a plate on his left arm and, with his right hand, set his beer on the ground. Ted watched him contemptuously.

"I hear you guys at the Truschel Fire Department are in trouble with that fundraiser yer tryin' to put on," Ted sniggered to the shortcake server. "Township don't want them topless dancers, I heard!"

"How do you hear all this local stuff, Mather, spendin' all your time at them fancy island resorts," replied Strawberry Shortcake.

"He heard it from *me,*" Ed said, helping himself to a second plate of sauerkraut.

"Listen, that really hurts the fire department," Mashed Potatoes said, "Our bingo is down, and last year we only made two hundred dollars on our wives' apple butter and piccalilli, but the wet t-shirt show last year made nine hundred dollars! *Now* the Truschel Planning Commission has gone and ruled to amend the zoning ord'nance, and topless shows cannot be held within five hundred feet of a home or a thousand feet of a church, school, park, or library."

"Well, that seems right to me —about people's homes and churches and schools and parks, I mean," said Ed as he finished his sauerkraut, "but I can't see the part about the library."

"Yeah, that's really shitty," Ted drawled, "Ole Ed might want to go in the library with some of them girls and *read!* Right, Ed?" Everybody laughed and hooted. Ted was really getting out of hand!

"Listen," Ed sputtered, "with all the crime n'all, we can't have filth near the churches or around our schools and parks, why —why —kids have to be protected from —"

Ted, beginning to hit his stride, explained, "Ole Ed wants all the filth for *himself!*" The hoots and catcalls and laughter were getting *to* Ed. But *how* to shut Ted up?

Ed needn't have worried. A Country and Western band, The Southern Comforters, had started up again, and members and their girlfriends were hopping and stomping on the porch of the Sportsmen's log cabin. Allen Cope and the others, all nuts about Country and Western line dancing, wheeled their barrows over there. Ed could hear raucous shouting and thumping coming from the porch, and Allen was yelling, "Yeeeeeee —haw!"

Some kind of argument was going on at the cockfight ring. The two trainers had put their birds face to face in the ring, but nothing happened. The roosters stood staring at each other, then one bird fell over. "What the *fuck?*" one of the trainers said.

"Who's been messin' with these birds?" the other trainer shouted. He stood up, his fists clenched.

"Come on! Get 'em. *Get* 'em," someone said and threw some pebbles at the groggy birds. Ted Mather got a long stick and poked at the supine bird. Then others got sticks and began poking the birds.

Ed was unhooking his suspenders when he noticed the headlights of the squad cars and the S.W.A.T. van winding up the hill toward the club parking lot. The Southern Comforters had drowned out the sirens at first. Someone had snitched to the police! They were being raided! They'd all be goners if they were caught. Holding up his pants, Ed ran to the fight ring to warn the handlers to cover the bloody straw and get the crates and birds and run into the woods.

"Grab your birds and run!" Ed shouted. "It's the *police!*"

CHAPTER FIFTY-THREE

It was all in *The Bingham Herald* the next day: "CONGRESSMAN IN BEARCAT RAID" shouted the gleeful headlines. "KROCK'S PARAMOUR NAMED IN ANIMAL SACRIFICE" screamed the next line. "SATANIST LEADS MATRONS IN MIDNIGHT ORGY" stunned Bingham Countians as they read Betty Colvin's lurid page-one account and studied a two-page spread of Howard Fletcher's clear and surprisingly well-composed photos: Ed with his Bermuda shorts down around his ankles; frenzied NRA members fleeing into the trees behind Maple Leaf Pavilion; Traci in her sequins and lace, smacking at a crazed rooster; flustered AstraLadies being attacked by a blur of feathers.

There were shots of other AstraLadies in long, wet, bloody, form-revealing white gowns over which garter belts were a clearly-defined feature of some obviously nefarious practice; a shot of a sheepish Ted Mather staring blankly into the camera as he and other men wearing cowboy hats and shorts and NRA tee-shirts were herded into a S.W.A.T. van, and the caption "BINGHAM SPORTSMEN PARTICIPATED IN OCCULT RITUAL." There was a large clear shot of Ed, Ted Mather, the Truschel Township Fire Chief, and several others holding bloody roosters, but most sensational of all were five or six be-wigged, recognizable Precious Pink Feet members and, in the foreground, Ed and Traci all staring open-mouthed at the camera, with the caption "PPFs AND CIVIC LEADERS EXPOSED IN DEMONIC PRACTICES LED BY ED KROCK (D. PENNSYLVANIA) AND AGENCY HEAD."

Particularly déclassé was a close-up of one of the booze-littered picnic tables with its centerpiece of melting but clearly discernible phallic wax candles —a new low for *The Bingham Herald*, whose staff found their newspaper moving inexorably toward tabloid journalism.

Families of the once-respectable Bingham Bitsies found their mothers' and sisters' and wives' behavior alarming and scary, for which the blame was easy to place: *that infamous women's shelter*. It had ruined the wives and mothers of Bingham County, they said, and nothing would ever be the same.

"They all went bezique!" Edith Hartley exclaimed about the AstraLadies' denouement to Asa Helbrun at lunch at the Copper Bottom. "Traci's so lascivicious, a real control freak. But none of those PPFs' bombs and murders are ever given as much newspaper coverage as that."

Asa nodded and sipped her Bloody Mary. She was wearing a white cotton sweater with "Women Are People" imprinted on the front in bright red, and a short red leather skirt and white stockings. She had let her curly hair grow out to white and wore it in a frizzed-up-in-back ponytail. Intelligence and vigor illuminated her lightly-made-up, finely wrinkled face. She reached over and speared a cherry tomato from Edith's salad and said, "Yes, and did you see the eleven o'clock news? They're going to get off with only a big fine, because of the drug and alcohol ordinance, and the S.P.C.A. is citing mistreatment of the chickens. Then they interviewed Ed —he looked awful —all dishevelled —and his lawyer tried to step in front of him, but Ed blurted out, 'You can't prove *anything!*' Oh, it was a circus! But you know, it's only because she's Krock's paramour," here Asa snorted, "that Traci got all the publicity. She wasn't even *evil* on her own! She had to be linked with a man! And as usual, everyone says the Sojourner Shelter is to blame for the Bitsies' indiscretions. But I think Krock's Congressional career is finished. Ellen Kirschner will be a shoo-in when she runs against him in ninety-four."

"Yes," Asa nodded, in answer to Edith's questioning stare. "Hal Renshaw has persuaded her to run."

"I thought *he* was gonna run, on the Citizen Action Party ticket," Edith said.

"No, Edith, he said he's not going to run for office for a couple of years. The CitActs lost their ballot status. When Hal got twelve percent of the vote in the eighty-two election, the

Pennsylvania Legislature was really jolted, so they hurried up and passed legislation, and now the law says that third parties have to have *five thousand members* in order to get on the ballot. Ellen will have to run as an Independent. But she can get all the CitAct issues out —get 'em discussed and in the forefront again.''

"I've heard that voters don't like a third party to take votes away from the Democrats and Republicans," Edith said, fishing the olive out of her martini.

"Balderdash!" Asa snorted. "That's their agitprop they use to keep new ideas from taking hold. The CitAct idea of People, Not Profits has the Republicrats —right now there's no difference between the two parties —scared to death.

"Bingham County's hardly a haven for iconoclasts," Asa went on as she sawed at the thick steak the waitress had set before her, "and when most of the steel industry folded and Blake castings and the other manufacturers moved south, all that's left in the tenth district is the medical community, the university and public utilities, and service industries. The few high-tech companies that do move into the area come here to service what little is left in Bingham, so it's not a great growth area just now. But interested people are around the County yet. I still run into them. They haven't forgotten those great CitAct Party days, the debates, the idealism. We could start up again. We'd get members.''

"Maybe Ellen *will* do it, stir up the CitAct ideas, I mean," said Edith, "with all us old timers helping and rooting for her. My land, Asa, working in Hal's office sure was an education for you, wasn't it?''

Asa smiled and sipped her tea, then replied, "Yes, I learned a lot. But I taught Hal a thing or two, don't forget. When I was growing up in Nebraska, all kinds of history were being made. That was Willa Cather country, you know, and —''

"Willa *who?*" Edith interrupted.

"Willa Cather, the author. The writer. Early in this century, she wrote novels about the people who were shaping thought — ideas —in the areas that my Norwegian ancestors helped to settle.

My grandparents were sod-busters!'' Asa finished the last bite of steak, then went on, ''My mother actually spent her childhood in a house dug out of the prairie —with grass growing out of the roof! My relatives were tough and determined! She told me that she and my aunt Solveig used to climb up on the roof and pick wild flowers!

"Some of them settled in Montana," Asa continued, ''and Kansas, too, and had big farms. My uncles started up a coal mine — a sort of co-op, with some Swedes and Norwegians and Hungarians and Italians. A real progressive idea, with all of them being co-owners. I was pretty young, but I remember Big Bill Haywood and Carlo Tresca and Elizabeth Gurley Flynn coming out there from New York to help 'em get organized. Flynn was about twenty! A thin little thing, but feisty, and so alive, and such a good speaker!'' Asa's eyes sparkled.

"But their organization didn't last. Big money boys came and just took over everything, and the original founders lost out and ended up working in the mine for the new owners —for peanuts! When Haywood tried to help them organize a union, the money boys ambushed him and took him in a barn and tortured him —tied him up and burnt him all over with lighted cigarettes. My family headed back east to P.A. to work in the iron foundries here, and later in the steel mills. It seemed pretty tame here after all those prairie winters."

"Well, that's why you're so tough, Asa."

"Maybe, Edith, maybe. I was the baby, so I'm the last of the family. It must be partly in my genes to endure and survive. But the human mind can give strength to the body. Your own life is proof of that."

"I feel awful tired some days, Asa. My leg will never be right again."

"Oh, pooh! You're walking great since your physiotherapy!"

Asa patted Edith's hand, then stared into space saying dreamily, "I feel myself slowing down some. And I never did get to Ankor Wat. Too late now."

"Where's that, Asa?"

"It's in Cambodia. A beautiful partially buried ancient city I've dreamed of all my life — since early childhood. Boy, I wonder what Carl Jung and his collective unconscious would have said about that?"

"You could still go," Edith suggested.

"No. Cambodia's a good place to stay out of right now. But there are ancient ruins in Mexico I'd like to see, if I could afford it." Asa shrugged.

"Let's *us* go to Mexico. My treat!" Edith exclaimed. Asa laughed, but her eyes were sparkling again.

They were finishing large slabs of strawberry cheesecake when Daphne Singleton waved to them from the Copper Bottom vestibule, then joined them at their table.

Daphne was wearing a red wool blazer, white sweater and red and white plaid pants. The warm May sunshine slanted through the restaurant's mullioned windows highlighting her lustrous black hair. "I have only a few minutes. I'm picking up Celeste at the college. She's taking a secretarial course!"

Daphne studied the menu for a few moments and then said, "A big scandal just broke here in Bingham."

"Fancy that, Hedda," mumbled Asa, her mouth full of cheesecake.

"What? What happened? Tell us!" Edith laid her hand on Daphne's and leaned toward her.

"After nine years, they're going to exhume Leonard Blake's wife's body — you know, Lucille Blake. A reliable source has just informed the police that she probably was poisoned."

"Poisoned?" Asa said. "She was poisoned?"

Daphne answered, "You remember the case, then?" It was nearly ten years ago."

"Oh, yes. Lucille Blake, of the Blake Castings Blakes. The poor thing. It was hushed up, it seemed to me. A lot of people thought it was hushed up," Asa said. "But who on earth tipped off the police?"

"Yes, who on earth?" Edith echoed.

"Emily Ann Buterbaugh," Daphne replied.

"And *who*, pray tell, is Emily Ann Buterbaugh?" Asa asked.

"My dears, Emily Ann Buterbaugh is a.k.a. Nurse Funbuns and a.k.a. Queen Dialysis, of the Kidney Korner Kort!"

Edith, thoughtfully stirring her tea, mused, "We had a janitor at my high school by the name of Floyd Buterbaugh. He was called 'Panties' Buterbaugh. He was always stealin' the girls' panties out of their gym bags! Why —my land —I'll bet he's her father!"

"Her grandfather, more likely," said Daphne. "Emily Ann's only about twenty-five, I think."

"So did Leonard Blake make a pass at her, Daphne?" Asa asked.

"Well," Edith added, "about every man or boy in the county did, at one time or other. Ernest used to say if he could bottle whatever it is she puts out on the air, he'd be a billionaire. Imagine! Panties Buterbaugh's granddaughter mixed up in something like this! But I'm not surprised. That krinkly stuff runs in families."

Asa made a "tsk" noise and said, "You mean 'kinky,' Edith, and it doesn't necessarily follow that Emily Ann —boy, that name doesn't suit her at all —that it's a genetic defect that she displays herself like some sort of exhibit. Her low self-esteem comes from distorted values. She defines herself solely through the male value system as do ninety percent of American women."

"It's sad, but it's so true!" Daphne concurred. "When *are* women going to wake up to the reality of their own full personhood?"

"It shouldn't take repeated beatings for women to wake up," Edith entreated, staring at Daphne searchingly.

"Was being physically battered the turning point for you, Edith?" Daphne asked.

Edith remained silent but slowly nodded her head.

Daphne sighed. "I'll never forget the despair on Lucille

Blake's face, that day at her home. I still see her in my dreams. She was a client of mine, you know. Oh, *why* don't we *act* when we encounter women who are that desperate?''

Asa leaned forward. "Daphne, if she was poisoned, Lucille Blake was sick, and her judgement would have been impaired. No matter what anyone might have said or done, she probably would have wandered away *anyway,* and no one could have saved her!''

"Yes, Daphne, think of all the women the Shelter *did* save,'' Edith said earnestly. "When I was in the shelter, in all my pain, just them few days I spent talkin' to Harletta and Audrey —why —why —a whole life time was in them few days! All the abuse I took from Ernest —how he hit me whenever he felt like it, an' I just *took* it and believed I was *nothing*. Even with my expensive clothes, I was *nothing!* An' there didn't use to be anyone to help ya, like nowadays —''

Asa stirred uncomfortably, shuffling her feet beneath her chair, then said, "Is it known for sure —I mean, is there *proof* of poisoning? Do you know if cyanide was used? A chemical engineer like Blake would have access to plenty of chemicals — through Blake Castings.''

"Yes,'' Daphne replied, "you'd think he'd use something like that. But he must have known cyanide is detectible through DNA tests of the hair of the deceased. Lucille Blake was probably done in by a mushroom — the Deadly Amanita, sometimes called the 'Angel of Destruction,' and it is lethal!''

"My *land!''* Edith exclaimed.

"A *mushroom,* Daphne? How'd they find out that weird fact?''

"Well, Emily Ann told police that Blake was harassing her. She didn't like his type — she told some other people, too. Thought he was too old. He was enraged that she rebuffed him, and once while he was drunk, he bragged about the murder. He took Funbuns —er —Emily Ann out to the little thicket in back of her house and showed her the mushrooms growing in the moss there. He said they grow all over Pennsylvania. He threatened to put the lethal powdered Amanita into her well —into her drinking water if she didn't 'put out.' She was terrified. What Blake didn't know is that the mushroom Amanita phalloides —particularly in Amanita virosa —the active principle, known as Amanita toxin, *is* detectible for as long as ten years! The incredible thing is that by the time any symptoms appear — it could take as long as fifteen hours or more —it is virtually too late. The victim, very disoriented and thirsty, and maybe throwing up, simply dies. Vomitus material was found by the entrance of the shed where Lucille's body was found. A medical examiner would have questioned *that* immediately, I would think."

"The coroner was paid off by Blake, I heard," Asa said. "But exhumation of a body is a rarity, I've heard."

"Well, they're going to do it. And the statute says the evidence cannot be speculative, so they're quite sure that a poison substance will be found. Then they'll find the Amanita residue, you see. The court granted a petition for the exhumation. It was at last week's hearing. Blake denied everything, of course. Funbuns' testimony was labelled 'hearsay,' but since they didn't trust the funky local medical examiner, a pathologist from Phillie was called and swore that 'to the best of my medical knowlege and beliefs, Amanita mushroom residue can be detected in the liver of the deceased. So then the court granted a petition —a process that usually takes about ten days —but the judge signed it right away, making it a legal document, and it was taken immediately to the prothonotary to be signed, and it became law. To guard against any more coroner pay-offs, the prosecution said he 'abused descretion,' and a request was made that a different medical examiner do the autopsy after exhumation. So the court considered this case to be the 'extraordinary circumstance' required by Pennsylvania law, and Blake will be found out! He's done for!"

"How do you know all this, Daphne?" Asa said, incredulously.

"I was there. As I probably was the last person Lucille Blake spoke with before she wandered to that shack, the D.A.

required my possible testimony. It turned out they didn't question me. Didn't need to because the court made an exception to the hearsay rule. They're actually going ahead with the exhumation pretty much on the basis of Funbuns' trip to the police."

"But —but —what was Blake's motive?" Asa asked.

"I know this is a real cliché —but —he had a huge insurance policy on Lucille! Couple of million dollars."

Daphne pushed back her chair and stood up and, swinging her blazer over her shoulders, smiled at her two rather dazed friends.

"Who knows?" she said. "It was the end for Lucille, but maybe now it'll be a beginning for —for — Emily Ann."

May 20
1991

Hi Daphne —

Yes, it's me. Can't believe this much time has passed since the D.C. protest march. It was so great seeing you. I called you a couple of times. I'm sick of talking to your machine. Don't you ever stay home?

I'm still undecided about going into law practice with Agnes. We both have huge phone bills from all our midnight discussions. Don't know if I want to move back to Bingham.

*Mainly I'm writing you about the big Gulf War victory celebration Agnes said they're having there in the city in June. There's talk of one here in Phillie too, but I'd rather protest there with you guys. It's disgusting. U.S. citizens hardly know ONE THING about what happened in that war. And there were no pictures. All the media were blacked out and all we saw were those creepy generals. That pig, Swartzkopf! Ugh! And they never even **got** Hussein! God knows how many Iraqi women and children we bombed. And Bush urging those poor Shiites to rebel against Hussein and then not giving them any military back-up or support! Hussein will subject those Shiites to a hideous death to get* *revenge. It'll be a holocaust.*

Agnes said we should get a group of dissenters together and march in the fucking parade —behind one of those giant erections —those guns. Wish we had PUPPETS, like at D.C.

So if you and Hal are organizing anything there in the city, I want to be part of it. So let me know so I can ask for time off. I have vacation days coming.

When I come out, I may stay with Agnes and her husband. They have an extra bedroom. I can't believe they bought a house in Chatterley Estates, on Mellors Lane, a block from where I used to live. It's close to Bronwen Burgess's house. It's all so ELITIST but Agnes said why shouldn't she and Tom live nice? Good point. But — MELLORS LANE???? Well, why the hell not? Did you hear Bronwen's getting married again? Some guy from the Glenview School. Nick something or other. Forget his last name. And I guess Agnes handled a tricky zoning variance for Bronwen so she could make a Bed and Breakfast out of the Burgess house. It's very hoity-toity, I heard, with string quartets every weekend. On Sundays, she has a buffet called "Bronwen's Brunch," and it's getting famous. I can hear the Chatterleyans saying "There goes the neighborhood," like they said when I first moved in there.

I rambled on enough for now. Work here is still bor-r-ring as hell, but there are some terrific women here and even the few men in the firm aren't bad.

Call me. I really miss you and can't wait to see you again.

Love, Bobbye

Hal put Bobbye's letter back in its pale green envelope and laid it aside. Daphne had left it out on her desk for him to read. Now he picked up a post card postmarked "Cancun." Inexplicably, it had a picture of a Koala bear in a palm tree. The card, written in a flowery hand, read:

Olay —We're having fandangle! Fine hotel. Great service. Chinese quizene. Taking Viennese waltz lessons. Do not have

446

to leave hotel. Everything in hotel just like home incl American TV! Asa went to ruin. (Aztec). I take needel point lessons love to all Edith.

Hal had seen Daphne twice, briefly, in the past four days. Either he or she was always asleep, it seemed, when the other came in —after midnight every night. Daphne was wonderful about driving Celeste to appointments and classes —his daughter actually was passing a computer course —and the change in his indolent child seemed to Hal to be miraculous. Celeste was slowly rejoining the family. Now if Pete could only keep his act together —

It was time for Hal to change clothes for work. In the bedroom he laid the letter on Daphne's night table. Her camisole and panty hose festooned the back of her tufted velvet slipper chair. She seldom wore a bra. He gathered up the wispy undergarments and buried his face in them, breathing in their Daphne-and-Balenciaga fragrance. Hal had given her the classic Prelude cologne every Christmas. He wondered if they'd have to go to a motel for some privacy.

There were some big changes in their household. Celeste and Pete didn't want to go to their mother's, Doreen's, any more, and her jock-husband's hang gliding and Cayman Island scuba diving no longer had the cachet they once had with the two kids. It was astonishing.

The phone rang. It was Hal's secretary, Louise Sharp, whining about a lost file. Hal wished he could lose Louise. How he missed Mrs. Helbrun! *She* never lost a file.

Louise went on to say, in that irritating nasal tone, that the Students For Peace wanted to see him that afternoon and so she had set up the appointment. Hal flung on his jeans and blue denim shirt and tie.

On the way to the college, he called Daphne on his car phone, and she agreed to round up some of their activist friends to meet at his office. He'd have to run the risk of incurring disapproval for having a political meeting in his office. He already was under university surveillance for having attended the

447

Gulf War protest in D.C.

The motor of his Toyota was coughing. And he had just gotten a tune-up! The temperature gauge was edging up. Ever since Pete's accident, the Toyota had been a financial drain. But Pete hadn't been hurt, thank heavens. Not a scratch! And, on his own, Pete had registered for summer session at the college. He was ambling into Hal's building now, with several young men and women, as Hal pulled into the parking lot.

My God, Hal thought, *Pete looks so much like his mother — a handsome version —he's not so damned skinny. He and Doreen are the same, yet completely different. Kids are just* **themselves** *after all.* Pete had told Hal in an offhand way that he had joined Students For Peace, and he volunteered at the Salvation Army Homeless kitchen two days a month. Would wonders never cease?

CHAPTER FIFTY-FOUR

On a big cutting table at the Designs For Living workroom, Daphne rolled out thin, very cheap, black upholstery cambric. Not the linen cambric dust sealant for chair bottoms of olden days, this stuff was a non-woven plastic with a strange chemical odor. All the protesters might swelter in hooded robes made of this junk, if the June heat wave continued. It had been over ninety degrees for three days.

Consulting her list of height measurements, Daphne began to cut out caftans and hoods. Nearby, Kenny Savage and James McInnes stapled the hoods onto neck cut-outs.

Harriet Hoffman and Felicia DeCarlo dipped plaster-soaked orthopedic gauze in water and molded masks on the vaseline-coated faces of Hal, Audrey Hopper and Shulamith Spiegel, who lay side by side across Daphne's two pushed-together work tables. The ghostly white masks lent a strangely sinister air to the three "victims."

Harriet quipped, "This looks like a scene from *An Evening at Home With the Marquis de Sade* —but seriously, I'm really surprised the Students For Peace chickened out of wearing robes and masks and marching with us."

She began patting wet white strips of gauze around Audrey's shapely dark nose.

"Maaaaa mmy!" Audrey sang, waving her hands, "I'm Al Jolson in reverse —'ole sun shine east, de sun shine west.'"

Harriet smacked her lightly, "You're bustin' up my work, girl!"

Audrey held her arms in front of her face and wailed, "Yas, Marse Harriet, but I don't *want* no whitie face, Marse Harriet."

It was good to hear Audrey joking, but later it was sobering to see accurate impressions of the scar tissue of her damaged face on her finished mask.

"Students For Peace said they want to do their own protest, in their own way," Hal mumbled. Felicia shut his mouth with a wet plastery strip.

Celeste, her plaster mask nearly set, sat to one side, staring silently at the others, with uncharacteristic patience.

Shulamith spoke up. "I happen to know the Students For Peace are all scared. Some of the members told me they think robes and death masks symbolizing the dead Iraqi women and children would be too radical a statement for them. The parents of most of the Students For Peace never did any political activist stuff. Our parents," she nodded toward Celeste, "have been activists all the while we were growing up, so it's not a totally new thing to *us,* but hey, it *is* scary. There'll be a lot of gung-ho pro-war types at this parade, and it could be dangerous, according to my pa, Barry Spiegel, PH.D."

"Yeah," said Kenny Savage, "I'm not looking forward to marching four miles in these sweat suits, without a permit. Not that this is my first demonstration or anything."

"I told you all that I tried to get a street permit ten days ago," Daphne explained, "but they arbitrarily refused when I told them we were a protest group. Refused to issue a sidewalk permit, too." She handed the last caftan to Kenny, then began to clear off the table.

Harriet, laying dripping gauze strips across Shulamith's high cheekbones, mused, "I can't help thinking how much food could be bought with that hundred and fifty thousand dollars the city's spending just to have that bomber fly over during the parade. We should explain things like this —talk it up —to parade spectators while we're marching. Don't you think?"

"No," mumbled Hal, as Daphne gingerly loosened his nearly dry mask. "Silence is better. Silent, black-robed figures will make spectators think, and maybe question the mindless festivities —a celebration because of *killing* might start to seem distasteful —who knows? And we can give statements to the press."

"Dream on, Dad, dream on," Celeste said, removing her mask, and everyone looked at her, startled to hear the usually reticent Celeste speak so vehemently. "If the media report it at all, it'll be some little back page insert," she said, laying the dried mask on the table and then wiping the oil from her face,

The Raunch Factor

"or maybe it'll be a complete news black-out, like the D.C. march was. Word power is awesome, Dad. Remember those TV commentators, during your campaign, in eighty-two? They said your words were like droplets from your bleeding heart. Instead of giving balanced reporting, they downplayed your win. You *did* get twelve percent of the vote, and they reported it wrong, and you couldn't get them to issue a correction —remember, Dad?"

"Why don't you do a press release, Celeste?" Hal urged, trying hard to keep his enthusiasm in check. "It's short notice, I know, but I think you could do a great job. Try to have it on my desk in my study at home by Friday night. Okay?" Celeste shrugged, but she didn't refuse.

A terse, concise, grammatical and neatly typed press release was on Hal's desk when he sat down wearily to sort his mail at eleven thirty Friday night. The article's lead sentence, *An Iraqi child has dreams and joys and hungers and can feel pain —like any child,* stunned Hal and brought tears to his eyes. It was as if he and his daughter had spoken to each other, had really communicated, for the first time.

He read the short piece and then realized that Celeste had written from her informed heart, and what she had written was poetry.

The official temperature in Western Pennsylvania at seven Saturday morning was ninety-three degrees and was expected to go higher. It was a cloudless day with an eerie brilliant stillness. Pete had departed for the city at six A.M. Hal and Celeste sat in the kitchen, sleepily eating Daphne's mandatory scrambled eggs breakfast.

"We'll need energy! Scrambled eggs will stick with us all morning," she instructed.

She passed a plate of whole grain toast. "Roman armies used to march hundreds of miles on just such whole wheat bread as this."

"Yeah, right, Daphne," Celeste said morosely. I have a

451

headache and cramps and I don't *wanta* march today."

"You'll be okay. You'll see," Daphne coaxed.

"Take some aspirins, Honey," Hal urged, "and *please* come with us. Shullie's counting on you. Barry said she can hardly wait."

"This whole thing will be fuckin' *dangerous!*" Celeste blurted it out, nearly in tears.

Daphne patted Celeste's shoulder, then set the aspirin bottle on the table, suddenly realizing that, for years, the family had feared Celeste's ill-tempered outbursts and that perhaps a more caring attitude on their part might help to ease her through her fears and help her to get through the questioning, searching period she was going through now. It was a big step for Celeste. Going into a crowd of strange hostile people took courage. Celeste was new at it. She looked at Daphne searchingly, and Daphne saw fear in her gray eyes. "We'll all be in it together, Celeste," she assured her.

At seven thirty A.M., wearing black shorts and tee-shirts and carrying their robes and masks and thermoses of ice water in their shoulder bags, they drove through Bingham to the subway, where Bobbye met them. Then they rode the subway to the city to the appointed meeting place of the protesters behind a warehouse, not far from the starting location of the parade.

Crouching behind the warehouse, they struggled into their robes and masks, then crept to the front of the building, and concealed behind shrubbery that lined the street where the parade was assembling, they watched and waited.

Members of several high school bands and drum and bugle corps fell into place. The drum major of the lead band blew his whistle, and the parade began to move along to a jazzy street beat. Daphne thought of Ellen, who had apologized for not participating in this march. Ellen would have loved the music today and had often said that it was the percussionists who were the soul of most bands and almost *all* of rock and roll's popularity was directly the result of brilliant drummers. "The instrumentalists know maybe four chords, and then they twang away on those same four monotonous electronic chords backed up by —actually carried by —that incredible percussion.''

They were two protesters short of the twelve they had planned for —Ellen stayed with Larry after he had had a bad week, and Barry had learned through the grapevine that he would jeopardize his job if he marched. But no matter.

They waited, concealed, as more high school bands and majorettes strutted and pranced by. There were a few ''Welcome Home Gulf War Veterans'' signs, and a sizable crowd was gathered all along the curbs lining the streets that followed the long, once-cobbled slope leading into the downtown area.

There was crowd noise —big noise, but not like the roar that had filled their ears from the moment they had disembarked from the Metro in D.C. the previous January. This was an entirely different crowd today —a different sound. It was a celebration, yet it seemed hostile; the atmosphere was sinister. Daphne felt the hairs on the back of her neck begin to prickle.

Weapon-laden trucks and tanks began to move into the parade from a side street. It was the beginning of the ''festive military display'' promised by the media. The protesters planned to fall in line behind the largest of the big phallic guns, and march single file, Harriet leading, carrying her life-sized dummy of a dead child across her outstretched arms.

At a signal from Hal, the group ran into the street and lined up behind the biggest gun. Immediately three policemen with truncheons shoved them all toward the curb, growling, ''AWright, c'mon, c'mon, get outa here.'' There was booing from the crowd.

The protesters pushed into the crowd, then reentered the parade a block ahead, this time behind a high school band. Their ghostly figures were a marked contrast to the eight Dallas Cowgirl-style majorettes.

Spectators' boos and catcalls became louder as the group followed the parade toward the downtown reviewing stand. They had two more miles to go. They were sweating and breathless, their vision impaired by their masks, the sun's heat searing their backs.

"My *feet!* My feet! How much further?" Shulamith groaned.

Celeste said, "Shut *up,* Shullie, shut *up.* "

Two men ran alongside Audrey, kicking at her as they yelled "Whaya think yer *doin,* asshole?"

Audrey and Felicia dodged their harassers and ducked through the crowd and out onto the street again, where they fell in line behind a large open limousine carrying five decorated Gulf War veterans, who turned around and stared at them impassively. On both curbs, young men and women shook their fists and chanted, "U.S.A., U.S.A., U.S.A.!" Now Bobbye, Hal, Harriet and Kenny ran out and lined up behind Audrey and Felicia. About ten yards ahead, the police stepped out into the street and started walking back toward them, swinging their truncheons.

On the sidewalk, Daphne, Shulamith, Celeste and James McInnes felt the crush of the spectators. "Assholes! Fuckin' *assholes,* "growled the increasingly hostile voices. Shulamith was crying, moaning softly behind her mask.

Now a group of sixteen- to eighteen-year-old boys, their fists clenched, walked alongside the sidewalk protesters, bumping into them and taking up the U.S.A. chant. On the street, the police hurried the spectral figures over to the curb.

Daphne and the others pushed their way through the crowd to the next block and reentered the parade again, behind the big gun. The police didn't catch up with them for another two blocks.

Now all ten specters formed to single file again and pushed and groped their way through the crowds along the sidewalk. The booing and cursing became increasingly menacing. The throng of spectators gradually increased block by block as the parade neared the reviewing stand.

Daphne realized afterward that all along the way there were low voices, scared-sounding people who had pressed close, momentarily, and said, "Keep it up, whoever you are. Keep it up," and "God bless you all," and a well-dressed, fresh-faced pretty young woman had inquired brightly, but sincerely, "What do ya *stand* for? —Like what do your costumes *mean?* What are you people supposed to *be?*" The fact that this wholesome young woman didn't have a clue was astonishing and discouraging to Daphne.

Many children asked, with piping shrill voices, "Are they from Halloween, Mom?" Some of the parents answered, "No, they're not from Halloween. They're demonstrators —people who are against the Gulf War."

One tall man explained to two ten-year-olds, "Those people have the right to object to this celebration of war. The United States Constitution guarantees that they can do this non-violent protest. These people are called dissenters."

One of the boys said, "Well, if they have the right to not like it, why are the police pushing them out of the parade?"

Once more the specters were herded to the sidewalk, and once more, they reentered the parade, this time falling in behind a straggly group of red-faced, sweating, but valiantly erect World War II veterans wearing moth-eaten odds and ends of uniforms, their wrinkled overseas caps rakishly tilted. From the sidewalks came the shouted chant, "U.S.A., U.S.A.! Love it or leave it, dick heads!"

Quickly the word passed through the ranks of the VFWs that an unpatriotic act was being committed. They turned and waved their fists at what they perceived to be robed traitors. The VFWs, out of step, finally broke ranks and, swearing and shouting, shoved the protesters over to the curb. "You ACLU Commie Fags don't deserve to take part in the American way," they jeered. "We oughta lock yunz up and throw away the key."

Their vision obstructed by their sweat-soaked masks, the robed figures continued to weave and stumble in and out of the parade until they neared the end of the route. There a crowd of several thousand pressed around the reviewing stand. A group of eighteen or twenty young men in cut-offs and fishnet shirts and tee-shirts and billed caps inscribed with the names of pro football teams began to circle Bobbye and Celeste. Was it because these two were the shortest in the group? —and obviously women? With clenched fists, the men stalked them, moving closer and closer, yelling obscenities and threats.

Hal, about ten feet ahead of Celeste, whirled around, saw what was happening and ran back and charged the harassers. Waving his big plywood "The Shame of Our Nation" sign, he dispersed some of the taunters, but Celeste, panicking, began to tear off her robe and ran sobbing to the curb and disappeared into the crowd.

Hal started to follow Celeste, but Audrey hurried to him, shouting, "No —no —stay in line! She'll be okay now, without her robe and mask!"

Shulamith began to cry again and headed for the sidewalk, but Bobbye and Audrey pulled her back. "Come on! There's the Students For Peace group over there on that hill, Shullie. See?" Audrey said. "And the Veterans Against the Gulf War. See them? Celeste will go over there. See their banners? Don't worry. Celeste'll be okay!"

Reluctantly, Shulamith moved back into the line, Bobbye and Felicia holding her hands.

Hal passed the word along that they all should run up onto a deserted grassy hill —some distance away —that overlooked the reviewing stand and from which the ten specters, standing in a row like sentinels, could be seen by the crowd below.

Panting from the exertion of the run up the hill, all of the group turned around and were dismayed to see that Harriet, slowed down by her rag-stuffed dummy, had not come with them, but had been overtaken by the men in cut-off jeans, who surrounded her, kicked and pushed her, then grabbed the dummy and began tossing it up in the air and chanting the U.S.A. chant. Harriet broke away and stumbled, gasping, up the hill to where the others stood.

At the bottom of the hill, on the Marriott Hotel outdoor patio behind the reviewing stand, waiters were setting out a huge buffet luncheon for the Gulf War veterans, and from the reviewing stand, snatches of civic leaders' speeches floated up the hill. Diagonally across from the group on the hill stood the silent, motionless Students For Peace and Veterans Against the Gulf War, lined up on another grassy knoll with their huge banners, visible but inaccessible to spectators. At the bottom of the hill, on a side street, two police cars pulled to the curb and the occupants sat there, watching.

Shulamith and Harriet begged, "Can't we *run?* We have to *run!*" Shulamith was crying again.

Already halfway up the hill, the men in cut-offs —this time accompanied by a few enthusiastic young women —began to climb the rest of the way up to the protestors, chanting the U.S.A. chant and rhythmically waving their fists in the air.

"Sieg Heil! Sieg Heil! You fuckers," Hal shouted. "Why not Sieg Heil?"

The taunting phalanx advanced steadily, and still the police did nothing. At the bottom of the hill, a TV station van pulled up, and to the left of the protestors, a young press photographer approached cautiously as the reviewing stand crowd stood watching the hillside drama.

Suddenly the hecklers picked up speed. Shulamith, screaming, ran over the hill and disappeared. Hal, holding his plywood THE SHAME OF OUR NATION sign like a shield lined up with Kenny and James, and behind them, the others began to back up. Now the chanting hecklers spread out to surround the group. "Run, all of you! Run!" Hal shouted. *Where* were the fucking *police?*

The hecklers charged into Hal and knocked him to his knees, broke his sign and were swinging the wooden pieces at Kenny and James when the police finally sauntered up the hill toward them.

CHAPTER FIFTY-FIVE

Under the newly leafed locust trees in Daphne's back yard, Felicia and Barry stood over the slowly turning rotisserie spit and brushed barbecue sauce on six chickens. Daphne dispensed vodka and lemonade from her little portable bar to the protesters as, one by one, they hobbled into Daphne's house to take showers, then limped back out again.

Shulamith, Celeste and Pete preferred to hose one another off at the end of the yard, occasionally shooting a spray at Hal, who reclined on the wicker chaise longue, his wounds neatly bandaged, a pitcher of vodka and lemonade on a table by his side. "It was ninety-six degrees today, folks," he called out, "and we were walking furnaces out there today, and none of us are the worse for wear!"

"Speak for yourself, Dr. Renshaw!" Shulamith shouted from the picnic table where she and Celeste and Pete, dripping wet, were ladling potato salad onto their plastic plates. "I was petrified — and still am," shuddered Shulamith, "and I'm exhausted, and my feet are ruined!"

"I'm exhausted too," Celeste exclaimed, with only a remnant of her old whine. "That guy chased me for four blocks until I doubled back and finally got up to where the Students For Peace were. I was never so happy to see you in my life, Pete!"

"Yeah, it was cool," Pete agreed. "But you're never gonna find your robe and mask. Why'd you put them in a trash can?"

"Because I couldn't run properly. And believe me, I was freaked, Pete."

"You kids were so brave," Daphne clucked maternally as she handed them plates of barbecued chicken.

Audrey and Bobbye, freshly showered, limped across the lawn from the house, carrying their black robes folded neatly, their white masks resting on top.

"I'll treasure this outfit for the rest of my days," Audrey said proudly. "I'm a warrior — excuse the military-type expression — and this here is my armor!" She laid the bundle carefully on the grass beside her chair. "Girl —" she slapped Bobbye on the shoulder lightly, "I can't believe what we all just done!"

"I wouldn't have missed it for anything," Bobbye murmured, then took a noisy slurping drink of her lemonade.

"Amen to that," Audrey agreed, feeling relaxed and mellow. "Preach it, girl," she yelled.

Kenny Savage and James McInnes, having showered at home, rounded the corner of Daphne's garage and walked across the lawn saluting the picnickers. *"Laisser les bon temps rouler,"* James called out. "Today was almost as bad as Stonewall! That was before your time, Ace." James laid his arm across Kenny's thin shoulders.

"Well shit, James, I was only six years old at the time," Kenny groused.

"The good times really *are* rollin', you guys. Have some vodka lemonade." Daphne filled tall glasses and handed them to the two men.

"When I saw what was happening to all of you, and Dad," Pete said, "I was just about ready to come over there. The police sure took their good old time. But standing stock still was what our group had decided we were gonna do. So did the Veterans Against the Gulf War. Incidentally, three of those veterans are homeless. Can you *beat that?*"

"I know," Barry said, waving his sauce brush. "Shullie told me. I'm going to get them on the college landscaping crew for the summer. I'll shame Chancellor Eldridge into doing it. He has clout, if he puts his mind to it."

Felicia brought a casserole of baked beans from the kitchen, set it on the picnic table and sat down on one of the old Newport-style wicker chairs.

Long afternoon shadows slanted across the lawn and soon the moon would begin its slow slide up over the cluster of locust trees, trees whose shapely foliage always reminded Daphne of her favorite Constable landscapes and of the lush pastoral paintings of Corot, Bouché and Fragonard. She thought back to the time when Pete was in high school and he and his buddies had played their guitars every night under these locust trees for one whole summer and didn't seem to have a care in the world.

She tried to remember the poem she had written back then —it was a sonnet, sort of —and she remembered thinking at the time that it was rather good, which was no doubt an indictment against it, she realized. She tried to recall the first line: "Midst trees in the Fragonard manner / backyard Pierrots strum their lutes." That period in their lives seemed so long ago.

The heat had not abated, but everyone's physical pain seemed to be lessening. The vodka helped. If anything, the air was hotter now and more humid.

Daphne turned on the sprinkler along the side of the yard, and soon a cooling mist began to drift across the lawn on the occasional breeze, diffusing the light from the citronella candles and mosquito torches, which James had thoughtfully provided. What a wonderful detail person James was! Without James, she could not have run Designs For Living all these years.

An element was missing. What was it? Memories came flooding back. Music! That was it: Ellen's get-down piano blues, Lorene swinging her ample behind in her unforgettable dance, the buck board wagon being pulled through Edith's garden. Had nearly a *decade* passed?

Through the sprinkler mist, Daphne could see three figures rounding the corner of the house: Harriet, Thaddeus Shaeffer, and Audrey's Kareema were strolling across the lawn toward the flickering candles. Hal was laughing about something; Bobbye was doing impressions of her boss; the young people were tossing a frisbee; Felicia was asleep in the hammock. Harriet began to dance, doing *tours jetés* across the lawn.

It's my own Commedia del Arte, Daphne said to herself, *all the fragments of the American Dream.*

"La Commedia de la Sogno Americano," she said, out loud, surprised that she remembered the Italian word for dream. She eased the squeaky kitchen door open and went to the refrigerator for another jug of lemonade.

"What did you say?"

Daphne, startled, yelped and jumped, the lemonade sloshing in the pitcher. She peered into the shadows. Audrey was sitting at the drop-leaf table in the darkened corner.

"Wow, you scared me," Daphne said.

"I'm sorry, Daphne. I thought you could see me here." Audrey lit a cigarette. The match flare made a momentary voodoo mask of her perfect features.

"You know, Audrey, Thaddeus is here, with Kareema —"

"I was expectin' them. He picked her up at my sister's. He said blacks fought that Gulf War. He and my sister didn't want nothing to do with that war."

"I don't blame them. What they say is true," said Daphne. "The number of African-Americans in the military is way out of proportion to the total population. It's an economic ghettoization of blacks because they don't have any choice. They have to survive."

Daphne filled a plastic bucket with ice cubes. "What are you sitting in here for, Audrey? It's nice outside. I turned on the sprinklers." She went over to the table and bent down and saw that her friend was crying.

"Whoa! Audrey. A while ago you seemed so *up!* What happened? This whole day was too much for you, wasn't it? The heat, all the stress. You've had enough violence in your life without —"

"Daphne, this day was one of the best in my whole life!" Audrey said it angrily. "If you could call it a life. If just doin' nothin' but workin' six and seven days a week is living. Work. Work. Work. Just to get money to *pay off* somebody. I'm so damned tired of working for Traci. I'm fuckin' *tired!*"

Audrey laid her head on the table, on her folded, scarred arms. Her shoulders shook as she wept. The crystal beads with which she had ornamented her dreadlocks trembled and sparkled.

"What do you mean, you're paying Traci?" Daphne sat down beside Audrey. "Oh God, is she blackmailing you for something?"

Audrey looked up and nodded wearily. "It was bound to come out. I'm so drunk, I don't even care anymore. Now ya'll will know I'm a jail bird. I did time at Muncie, an' Traci found out, an' I been payin' her ever since. When she started comin' on to me, when I was cleanin' her fuckin' house —I do housework

for her too. She love to see me on my knees, scrubbin' her floors
—I hit her, an' that's when she beat me up."

"It was *Traci*? *Traci* injured you like that?" Daphne was
horrified.

"Oh, she a tough one, all right. I had a knife an' was gonna
cut her good an' she got it outa my hand *that* quick." Audrey
flicked her long fingers. "She a karate champ."

"Oh, Audrey, Audrey."

"Ya'll thought it was Thaddeus cut me, right?" Audrey had
reverted from her usually relatively accentless language and was
slipping in and out of Bingham darktown jive talk, as Thaddeus
had done when he and Daphne first met.

"We —we —didn't know, Audrey. You and he had broken
up just before the beating —the battering —but you didn't bring
charges against him, and we couldn't figure out —"

"Well, for the record, Thaddeus is Kareema's daddy, an'
I'll always love him, but he's bi-sexual, an' thought he was in
love with a guy whose kid was in the Special Ed Program. But
I think he still love me. He'll come back to me some day, I know
it."

Audrey stubbed out her cigarette and stood up and smoothed
her wrinkled shirt. "Now you know the whole story. When Asa
and Edith and Felicia find out, my Dazzle days'll be over."

"Why? Why? They won't judge you!"

"They'll never trust me again, neither. I committed a
serious crime. I stole five thousand dollars from a woman I did
housework for. I was twenty-two. I never had any decent clothes.
I wanted a car —a *car!* Never had nothin'. She drove this big
maroon Cadillac! When I saw the money in a drawer, I didn't
think. I just took it. She was a black woman too! One of the
sisters. A sister! She was a numbers writer. She had me arrested.
Wouldn't let me work it off. I begged her to let me work off the
debt. *Begged!* But she hated me. It was such *hate!* But I did my
time. I took my punishment."

"It was your beauty, Audrey. Your looks have caused you
a lot of sorrow. Traci shouldn't get away with what she did to
you. She could have killed you!"

"Yeah. If only I was ugly or a fuckin' singer, like Lena Horne, or a dancer, or an actress. But I can't sing an' I can't dance an' I like men, and sex, but the wrong men started messin' with me —from the time I was twelve years old. Black men and white men both. I never really ever was a child! I never got no money from men. I got a mixed son. Mixed-racial, you know. Fifteen years old now. I gave him for adoption. He somewhere in this state. I ended up incarcerated because I had been dealin', too. Had a record.

"But I won't bring charges. An' I'm not payin' Traci no more, and it won't matter. I'm gonna tell my friends before she tell on me."

"That's exactly right." Daphne put her arm around Audrey. "Don't say anything tonight. Let's just have our party tonight. Let's party, Audrey. You've won your own personal war!"

In the yard, a light breeze was stirring. The young people laughed as they ran through the sprinklers, their apparently limitless energy sobering to their elders, who sat squishing their aching feet in the soaked grass.

The conversation continued as Pete and Thaddeus set up speakers on a picnic table and hooked up Daphne's tape player. Daphne slipped in a tape. Now Ellen's piano interpretation of Duke Ellington's "Sophisticated Lady" supplied the evening's missing element.

The timeless mood-inducing imagery once again delineated jazz for what it indisputably had become —a major twentieth century art form.

"Man, that music say it all," said Thaddeus.

"Sho'nuff?" Daphne quipped, leaning over and slapping high-fives with the laughing Thaddeus.

"Sho'nuff," he quipped back. They had remained friends since that day when they had first met in the Glenview Gym nearly a decade ago.

Ellen's Bill Evans-style jazz chords ended her Ellington piece, and there was a pause, and then the strains of the concluding act of the opera *Der Rosenkavalier* began. Pete had found the tape in Daphne's tape box and, at random, started it playing. What would it do to Harriet to hear this music —Norm's beloved Silver Music —out of nowhere, with no preparation, no warning?

Daphne pressed the "OFF" button and went and sat with Harriet. "Are you all right? she asked quietly.

"I'm okay, thanks. You can play it," Harriet assured her. "But a short synopsis might help everyone to enjoy it more."

"You're right," Daphne agreed. She tapped her glass to try to get everyone's attention. They listened half-heartedly as she described Hugo von Hofmannstal's libretto of the opera that Richard Strauss had written approximately seventy-five years ahead of his time, in 1911 —a story of the love affair of an older woman and an adolescent boy and the lovers' dismay when they realize that the boy has fallen in love with a girl his own age.

"The older woman, a noble woman called a Marschallin — she's the wife of a field marshall —and the boy, Octavian, and his young girlfriend, Sophie, tell of their mixed feelings in a beautiful trio they sing, standing together on the stage, in the final act of the opera," Daphne explained.

"They say that stuff all in one song?" Pete was skeptical. He and Shulamith and Celeste were scuffling in the wet grass, not really paying attention.

"Yep. All in one song, Pete," Daphne assured him. "But there's one comic scene after another, leading up to this gorgeous trio: people in disguises, people popping out of trap doors, a buffoon Baron leching after Sophie, a bunch of loud kids claiming the Baron is their father — the guy's involved in a paternity suit —all set in an elaborate eighteenth century court. There's a little servant, or page boy, about eight years old, named Mohammed, who runs around in satin knee breeches, a tail coat and ruffled shirt and a big turban. They had these little kids in noble houses back then. They were Moorish or Ethiopian or Islamic. They called them blackamoors. They were like household mascots.

"They were *slaves* is what she mean," called out Audrey, not unpleasantly. "The little black dude in the turban nothin' but a slave, like Nelson at Edith's fund-raiser party that time —

remember? Now Nelson a fuckin' soldier!"

"Well, uh, to get back to the opera," Daphne said loudly, "Strauss set this incredible story to even more incredible music."

"Yeah, sure —if you like that kind of music," Pete grinned. "Give me heavy metal or a good rapper any day."

"Don't be so gauche, Peter!" Shulamith rubbed a handful of wet grass into his hair.

"Listen, people, listen. It's worth it, honest. Come on!" Daphne said. She caught sight of Kenny Savage yawning, his angelic face rosy and beautiful. "Yo! Kenny! 'Attention must be paid,' as Arthur Miller said," she admonished.

"Arthur Miller?" Kenny looked blank.

"The playwright, you barbarian!" James mock-smacked the top of Kenny's blond head. "It's a line from *Death of a Salesman!* You want to be a cultural illiterate all your life?" he demanded. "All Kenny cares about is food, folks," James explained to the others.

"And sex," Kenny said sheepishly. He and James had been lovers for eight years. Domestic and devoted, they had spent years remodelling an old Art Deco era gas station and asphalt parking lot into a much-photographed mini-estate for themselves.

"Priceless glazed terra cotta gryphons edge the barge boards of the very unique neo-classic main living area informing the splendor of the tranquil sculpture garden beyond," the architecture critic of the city Sunday supplement had gushed. His historically inaccurate description had ignored James' and Kenny's months of hard labor. They had spent a year, each night after work, just chipping paint off the gryphons, and another six months jack-hammering the parking lot asphalt to make the walled garden.

Kenny yawned again, then smiled apologetically. In the distance, thunder rumbled.

Daphne resumed her synopsis, ignoring the boredom of her audience.

"Anyway, the sexy Octavian —he's been a very busy guy —has the hots for the teen-aged Sophie but remembers the risky but great sex he had with the married Marschallin, so he's torn between the inexperienced, beautiful Sophie and his more experienced and charismatic older lover."

Daphne noticed that everyone had begun to quiet down. Even Pete and Shulamith had stopped horsing around. *Put it into a pop-culture format, and they're all ears,* Daphne thought wryly.

"Well, anyway, in this trio you're going to hear this young hunk, Octavian, who feels some remorse for his older lover but not *much* remorse — after all, Sophie is a *Babe.* Octavian is singing in the German *Eine softig bod mine bod weltschmertz gelayen,* which translates "lay your warm and tender body next to mine —"

Immediate loud hoots of derision rose from the audience.

"You're making that up, Daphne!" Harriet shouted.

"Cut out the fractured German," Barry laughed.

"Well, that's basically what's going on," Daphne explained.

Bobbye reached over and took the libretto booklet and began to read the English translation as Daphne resumed her synopsis.

"Strauss' music is complex, yet simple; elegant, yet playfully ornamented; joyously sweet, yet bitterly nostalgic," Daphne said, "all these qualities at once."

Sketching in the action of the final scene of the opera, Daphne explained that the hugely obese Baron has discovered that he has been duped by Octavian and "wisely, Baron Ochs — which means 'ox' in German —prepares to depart but is waylaid by a caterer who presents him with a huge bill, and then the kids appear, calling out 'Papa, Papa, Papa,' and the Baron, fearing a paternity suit, bids the Marschallin goodbye, and he splits.

"The Marschallin and Sophie and Octavian are now the only ones on stage; *he's* hot to trot, and demure Sophie's ready for a relationship but feels guilty that she's busting up the Marschallin and Octavian, and the Marschallin is pretty depressed but resigned to giving up Octavian. They stand in a row about ten or twelve feet apart and, facing the audience, sing the very famous trio. I should point out that the role of Octavian is traditionally always sung by a woman —usually a mezzo soprano —and such a role is called a 'pants role' or 'trouser role.'

"So, let's listen," Daphne said, and she pressed the "PLAY" button.

A very sonorous bass note segues into the Baron's signature rollicking Viennese waltz as he exits.

Next, sweet string phrases, and very Straussian, answering woodwinds recall the opera's earlier themes of the two teen lovers —the same poignant melody that had impelled a shocked and grief-stricken Harriet to dance her goodbye to her dead son; the solemn, beautiful funeral dance that she had danced with Thaddeus, in the Glenview Gym, so long ago.

Now piercing trumpets and blended strings announce the Marschallin's haunting theme of loss: four notes that she first sings, repeated by the violins, which Octavian and Sophie then repeat alone, and then together, and again with the Marschallin, interweaving these notes over and over into many different harmonic structures. Slowly these themes ascend, and with each repetition, they soar upward and upward to the trio's peak: a celestial, high major chord sublimely blending the three voices in intervals of thirds, and then slowly descending with the strings, resolving triumphantly all the opera's preceding tonal explorations, consoling the Marschallin and ecstatically releasing the two young lovers and leading them to the closing love song — a gentle lullaby-like Germanic folk melody, which they sing in a tender duet, "I am yours and only yours." During this duet, the Marschallin slips offstage, leaving the lovers alone onstage, in each other's arms, after which they too exit hand in hand.

Deep chords in the strings ending in G sharp and C natural with rolling tympani dissolve into a brief, playful lilting woodwind and string capriccio ending in a deep tympani-accented bass chord to conclude one of the most stirring musical dramas ever written or performed.

The visibly moved listeners —Bobbye was in tears —were somewhat dazed and smiling, but they did not speak.

Daphne waited for a few moments, then said, "At the very end —during that woodwind section —visualize this: Following their duet, Octavian and Sophie have run offstage. Now the stage is empty and nearly dark. Then little Mohammed, the blackamoor, in his satin knee breeches outfit and his turban, skips on stage holding a candle. He picks up the Marschallin's handkerchief that she had dropped. Then he turns and skips offstage again, and then there's a quick curtain. *The End!"*

"Neat!" Celeste and Shulamith chorused, clapping their hands.

"All *right!"* Kareema said. "I'd like to hear the whole opera."

Another thunder roll and a sprinkle of rain alerted Pete and Thaddeus, and they hauled the tape player and speakers into the house. The picnic moved indoors.

In the living room, Daphne opened to their widest the windows that overlooked her small rose garden, and now a refreshing perfume-laden breeze drifted through the room. Here and there, pools of light from ceiling-mounted track lights dramatized Daphne's collection of paintings. The deep blue walls made the room intimate. White linen slipcovered armchairs and couches were arranged invitingly on the polished, bare yellow pine plank floor. A colorful Indian dhurrie hearth rug replaced the winter kilim rug and accented the simple grain-painted mantel.

Daphne dimmed the lights and went around the room lighting the candles in her collection of ruby votive glasses.

"We set out coffee and dessert in the kitchen, so help yourself and bring them in here," she suggested.

A four-foot square oak kitchen table cut down to make a coffee table was centered in a large grouping. Everyone gravitated there, and the thunder and the steady rain were counterpoint to the resumed conversation.

Barry, addressing a plate of strawberry shortcake on which he had slathered nearly a pint of whipped cream, turned to Harriet and said amiably, but not without apprehension, "Didja enjoy hearing *Rosenkavalier* again? Huh? Huh? Huh?" Without waiting for an answer, he continued, "Talk about *déjà vu.* The little blackamoor character reminded me of what I heard about the spectacle of the Burgess fund-raiser. *That* certainly rocked our little hamlet!"

Hal interjected, "The English novelist Samuel Butler said that the history of art is the history of repeating."

Audrey scoffed, "If Lorene and Fern and Melba did a ree-peat of them Aunt Jemimah outfits *today,* there'd be picketing out front."

"Hot damn! You're right, Audrey," Barry said. "There probably would be pickets. You can take credit for a lot of activism in this region, Hal. You and all your campaign workers — and all those who fought Traci — were all point people, venturing into *terra incognita.* You almost got shot down creating a women's shelter in this hot bed of misogyny — excuse the metaphor —and a third political party almost got off the ground in this xenophobic enclave. That's some kind of feat! It shouldn't be taken lightly." He lit a cigar and puffed at it earnestly.

"Well, Bingham County will never be the same," said Felicia.

"*None* of *us* will ever be the same either," James added, draining his coffee cup. "At least we nailed a few villains. Hey! Does anybody know what time it is?" He sang the old rock song.

Kenny sang back, "Does anybody care?"

"It's only ten o'clock," Pete said. "I've been going strong with activism for sixteen hours!" He said it with pride.

"I only know it's time for Traci to surface again with some new scam," said Harriet, "since her sortie into the occult has bombed, a weeping winking Marilyn Monroe picture notwithstanding. The latest news is she's gonna lead the Bitsies in a twelve-step format to help them examine their childhood abuse —real or imagined.

"She's already got some churches in town to put up her huge posters showing a picture of a cowering child reaching out to Traci. Only this time she's not wearing a garter belt. She's wearing a diaphanous gown —veree sexee —and standing with outstretched arms, and a crucifix is floating in the misty background."

"After all the AstraLadies and witches' coven stuff?" Felicia asked, incredulous, "*Now* she's going into *religion?*"

"Yep. And she'll maneuver plentee trendee holee monee,"

Harriet laughed.

"Did you say religious robes and a *crucifix?*" Barry asked in disbelief.

"Yep," Harriet said. "She'll manipulate a bunch of confused, superstitious, out-of-work wretches into sitting in a circle in the Methodist Church basement and sobbing together about how they were victimized and ruined in childhood and how all their pitiful fuck-ups are somebody else's fault. And any seriously unbalanced people that really have delayed traumatic stress disorder possibly could be badly harmed. But, hey! There's money in programmed martyrdom, and Traci Bilsen-Bloom, Girl-Therapist, will pull it off!"

"I can see it now," James smirked. "The *Herald* headlines: Tots in Terror Conference Reveal Bitsies Abused. Do you *love* that acronym? T-I-T! It's perfect!"

"Oh, the lengths people go to, just to get money and feel powerful!" said Bobbye.

"She's a real strategist. Scapegoating is a major manipulative tactic used by megalomaniacs," Hal said, " Stalin, Hitler, Ku Klux Klanners, the religious right with all their hatred of women, hatred of blacks, hatred of Jews, hatred of any religion that's not as hateful and judgmental as *they* are! And it can occur on a global level, to demonize entire masses of people in preparation for annihilating them — as was done to the Vietnamese and Iraqi, and the Jews, and who knows how many yet to come."

"One thing that would help defuse a world full of hate and guns and bombs would be for more women to run for political office," Bobbye said. "Every day in the media there's just this sea of male faces everywhere — especially in government. They're dick-heads, most of them. Where are the women? Nineteen ninety-two is supposed to be the year of the woman!"

"Well, listen, y'all," Audrey said, "look what happened when Traci got power. An' ain't she a woman?" She glanced significantly toward Daphne.

"No, I think she's a female impersonator," growled Barry.

Daphne had brought a fresh pot of coffee from the kitchen

and began filling the empty cups.

"I heard what you were saying. I think Traci's one of those exceptions that inevitably occurs when huge historic breakthroughs happen, such as the massive shift women have made in the last twenty years, the shift toward personal empowerment —away from dependency. It's a change that men fear so much that we're seeing *men* fronting anti-abortion groups, advocating bombing abortion clinics. We're seeing an increase in rape and a great increase in sexual harassment. There are many symptoms of men's fear. But Traci's behavior, I think —" Here Daphne glanced at Hal. "I think it's pathological."

Celeste, who had been licking strawberry juice from her plate, now spoke up, "There should be a money fund or something to help women get a fair start in politics."

"That sucks!" Pete said disgustedly.

"Shut *up,* Pete!" Celeste shot back, "or at least say something intelligent."

Barry, waving his cigar, said, "It could happen! Money funds for women, I mean. It sure could lead to a shake up in the so-called free enterprise system. What I think women politicians should address is the fact that there's always a certain percentage of the adult population that will always remain unemployed —a percentage that really need jobs, I mean.

"There's something very wrong with a system that says 'If I have a job and I have money, then somebody else better fail — and fail *big time!* and *not* have a job or any money.'"

"Women think that's silly," Harriet explained. "They think it's just *mean,* and dumb, and impractical."

"Well, the trouble is —our competitive system is not free enterprise at *all,"* said Hal. "For example, look at all the monopolies."

"You look at them, Dad. This is boring." Celeste stuck out her lower lip in her old spoiled-kid petulance.

"Go on, Dr. Renshaw. What *about* monopolies?" Shulamith asked.

"Well, take public utilities, nuclear power —they should be safer and the rates lower, but just the opposite is happening. And then there's agribiz. About five American corporations monopolize —control —almost all food production in the U.S. What's competitive about *that?*''

"It's bor-r-r-r-ring!" Celeste groaned.

"Well, *I'm* interested, Dr. Renshaw," Shulamith said.

Hal, finishing his strawberry shortcake, said, "Where was I? Oh, yeah, agribiz. The interested environment-conscious farmer is history. Now the big chemical fertilizer companies are making big bucks but are causing a serious decrease in soil fertility."

Barry nodded as he stubbed out his cigar on his saucer. "And tobacco companies are working night and day trying to influence the U.S. State Department to put pressure on foreign countries —Taiwan, China, Japan, and others for these countries *not* to conduct campaigns against smoking! The State Department *can* exert power against these countries by threatening to withhold American subsidies or refusing their exports."

"Man, that really sucks," Pete observed.

Outside the rain continued its steady downpour, and the first cooling breeze of the evening was refreshing.

Hal put his bare feet on the end of the hassock on which Pete was sitting. Shulamith sat on the floor, and Celeste came and sat beside her.

"There're all kinds of pressure from American and international banks — it's a world bank now, you know — to create receptive markets for U.S. business," Hal said, "and this subverts governments and denies human rights. It inhibits progress in overcoming poverty, disease and ignorance because so much energy goes to the accumulation of money-slash-power. You just can't think of one without the other: it is always money-slash-power."

Thaddeus and Audrey moved closer to the sofa and sat on the floor, listening. Then Thaddeus spoke up, "None of this wealth is geared to addressing human need —say, to national health care, or the arts —the arts are *so* vital to the human spirit. The chief aim of money-power is *more* money-power for only a very few, very rich people. The rest of us folks be damned."

"What's the matter with you, Thaddeus?" Bobbye said sarcastically. "That's the democratic way!"

James said, "What gets me is the way money and power are always being equated with democracy, like they're inseparable — one and the same!

"They keep saying we need to *buy* more. Then democracy will work. It's very simple. Go shopping, folks."

"Hey!" Shulamith said. "There's a talking doll for sale at the mall, and it has lifelike rooted dynel pubic hair that's cut in a heart shape! It's called Robo Babe, and it says 'Let's go shopping' whenever you press a button. Robo Babe comes with different hair colors and a plastic shopping cart and a seventy-five dollar miniature plastic shopping mall complete with shops. One of these little shops sells leather masks and whips — you know, sado-masochism junk — and there's even a recorded message that announces 'Attention, shoppers' and then gives a spiel about a sale of night gowns and bras and garter belts. Penelope's Shame is really pushing the set. It's called Dolls and Malls."

"Are you serious, Shullie?" Daphne asked.

Thaddeus said, "That's gross, man!"

Kareema, who had been dozing on the couch, sat up suddenly and said with new interest, "That's cool!"

Felicia said, somewhat apologetically, "Speaking of competition and about free enterprise and all — I saw this TV show last week about how America doesn't know how to compete in the world market and all."

"I saw that program too," Shulamith said. "It was creepy. All these Japanese kids in uniforms, riding bikes to school — none of them have cars — and when they graduate from high school, they have a hundred percent job placement because of work-study courses they took.

"Then, in a German high school," she continued, "the film showed the work-study program with the Mercedes Benz Company, where the students — all boys — have a million dollar robot to learn on. Everywhere it was boys. It was plainly sexist. And they pushed and pushed the Mercedes company."

Felicia interrupted, "Yes, but they interviewed an American boy, too, who had no focus at *all*. All he wanted was to get a car. His high school work-study program had him working each day at a fast-food place. He used his pay for his car. In the next scene he's telling his high school counselor —a woman who was counseling *over a thousand kids* —that he's decided to go into police work, law enforcement, y'know? Then the next thing they show is he's in an army recruiting office, and he's decided to go in the *military!*"

"Who sponsored the TV show?" Hal asked.

"It was on PBS. There weren't any advertisers," Felicia said.

"Oh, there were sponsors, all right. American corporations control most of public TV by underwriting —just paying for the programs outright —and their chief concern is profit in a global market, making the most money with the smallest investment," Hal explained.

"The Japanese and Germans are ahead in global competition because, from the first grade on, they've geared public education to turning out students —mainly males —to be workers —just workers —to work in technology. Sexism was quite evident in the show's message, right?" Hal asked.

"Yeah. Oh, yeah," Shulamith said. "It definitely was. In the German segment of the show they visited a typical middle class home with the father and three sons seated comfortably at the dinner table and the wife-and-mother — you know — the hausfrau robot, dutifully serving them —flitting in and out of the kitchen."

"Well, anyway," Felicia went on, "at the end of the show, they interviewed an American principal of a middle class American high school. He seemed to be getting backed into a corner by the interviewer. He —the principal —looked confused, even ashamed."

"The hapless principal just may not have had a corporate mentality," Daphne said. "Maybe he thinks education should be about creative thought, not lock-step regimentation that starts at kindergarten to produce nothing but computer technicians, starting at the first grade! *Jeeze,* what a sickening idea!''

"How do these oppressive ideas get started in the first place?" Celeste asked.

"They've always been around," Barry said. Power groups manipulating unsuspecting, less-venal *normal* people and exploiting them, or worse yet, deliberately limiting the kind of education the majority of the population has access to. Like what that TV show advocates. Technology should help everybody, should make possible a shorter work week! That's why it's vital to keep dissenting, disagreeing, and demonstrating like we did today —to keep some vestige of democracy. Life should be better for the *majority* —not just for a handful of super-rich consumers with superficial values!''

Through the open windows that faced the backyard could be seen a lemon-slice of yellow moon, which shifting clouds revealed, then concealed, then revealed again. The rain had diminished to a fine drizzle.

James and Kenny and Felicia said their goodbyes and departed, trudging wearily across the backyard in single file along a narrow curved stepping-stone path that led to their cars.

The little mushroom lights with which Daphne and Hal had outlined the path across the lawn plus the bright moonlight inspired Harriet to go out and start dancing again, and prompted Pete and Shulamith to put up the badminton net. The racquet-wielding young people laughed, their voices mingling with Thaddeus's and Audrey's low voices as they sat outside talking with Barry and Hal at the picnic table, Barry's glowing cigar circumscribing the air as he emphasized a political point.

In the kitchen with Daphne, Bobbye hung up her dish towel and helped to finish loading the dishwasher.

Both women stood now in the dim living room, watching the candles flicker.

"You should have used plastic cups for the coffee and dessert," Bobbye said.

Daphne, plumping up the toss pillows on the sofa, shrugged

and said, "I think coffee tastes better in a porcelain cup. And strawberry shortcake is too hedonistic for a styrofoam plate. It's a bourgeois attitude, I know, but I still have *some* sybaritic vestiges, kiddo!" She laughed, but it turned into a hiccup.

Bobbye moved to the end of the room and stood with her back to the fireplace, the row of flickering votive candles on the mantle shelf casting her shadow across the floor. She had let her hair grow out to its natural light brown. A loosely tied black and white print scarf kept her damp thick curls under control.

Bobbye was as shapely and stylish as ever, though a bit plumper now. She wore simple white cotton shorts and a black halter and black sandals and, in the dim light, looked about sixteen years old.

"Oh, Daph," she said, "it's been *so cool!*" She smiled and twisted her heavy gold link bracelet. "It's been like old times!"

Daphne went to the window and stood looking out at the badminton game. The palpable tension in the room was making her uncomfortable.

"I'll be staying at Edith Hartley's tonight," Bobbye continued, clearing her throat, "with Audrey and Kareema." Again she cleared her throat. "We're house-sitting while Edith's in Mexico. Boy, it'll seem odd to be back in that neighborhood."

"I can imagine," replied Daphne.

What was happening here? The whole atmosphere of the room was so charged with —with —*emotion,* and something else indefinable. Daphne felt sweat breaking out on her forehead and neck. Her tee shirt stuck to her back. She picked up a magazine and began to fan herself. Out in the yard, excited laughter indicated that the badminton game was heating up.

Bobbye lit another cigarette with a shaking hand, and cleared her throat again.

"Remember the night of the Burgess fund-raiser and you all came and stood in my backyard?"

"Do I ever! It was the first time you had spoken to me in weeks, Bobbye, after the —after the —"

"Well, for a while anyway," Bobbye said, "I *did* think you had deliberately engineered that whole fiasco at Ed's fund-raiser party, you know, to sabotage his campaign. To help Hal."

"Bobbye! Why would I risk nearly bankrupting my business? That whole mess was a terrible financial setback for me. I just tried to do good professional work on your house. You were my friend! I wouldn't have done anything to hurt you. How could you *think* such a thing?"

"Well, I was pretty naive in those days. Ed paid the bills. I had never really had a job. I was just beginning to come out of my dream-world and starting to experience feminist consciousness. Wow! I was going through so many changes!"

"We all were, Bobbye."

"But now I realize how hard you had to work to earn a living. How much shit a single woman has to take. You were dynamite back then —actually supporting yourself while I just took my big house and my car and my clothes for granted. I was fuckin' *dumb,* that's all!"

Bobbye made no move to sit down but continued to twist her bracelet. Her face glistened with sweat.

"It's funny, your bringing it up now, Bobbye, your feelings, I mean," Daphne said. "All these years we never really discussed it. The money I lost was quite a serious loss for me, quite a struggle."

"I know. I was a bitch. You never blew up. You were so wonderful, so patient. But...at the fund-raiser —" Bobbye waved her hands around. "All these lights —these candles, here tonight — God, how they bring it all back. I was so *enraged!* So humiliated!" She was getting louder. "I wanted to put on a showy party. That snooty neighborhood was so full of all those Chatterley Estates Presbyterians —the Frozen Chosen Ellen called them —and those Episcopalians —that one Episcopal group that hates gays and Lesbians amd broke away from the main diocese because of it! And then when all hell broke loose at my place and there was all that damage —the smoke —the soot, and the police, and it was in the *paper!*"

"All your guests said it was the best partying they ever *did,* Bobbye."

"I know, I know. But look at the pain I caused you. I feel

such *guilt*, Daphne! I can't stand that I feel this guilt!"

"Oh, well, it's all past, now," Daphne said, relieved, hoping they could change the subject.

"But all the money you lost, hon, because of me!" She was going to go on with it. "You replaced all that ruined stuff and didn't make a cent."

Why was Bobbye dragging this out? What did she want? When was she going to stop?

"That was all a long time ago, Bobbye. Remember in *Goodbye, Columbus,* the Philip Roth novel, when the heroine's father writes her a letter forgiving her for sleeping with her boyfriend before marriage? And he says in the letter, 'Let's let buy gones be buy gones'? You know, he spelled it b-u-y!"

"Yeah. I remember. Wasn't that the novel where the father has a wholesale plumbing supply company called —called —"

"POTEMKIN SINK!"

They both shouted it out together, laughing, bending over, really laughing.

"Oh God, I remember how we laughed about that. And I remember when you nagged me all the time about reading and learning, getting an education. And you were right, Daph, and I'm getting educated and I'll be a better lawyer —a better person —because of it. I got some *culture,* because of you.

"We had so many great experiences together, Daphne — doing over my house, working at the Shelter, the Gulf War demonstration in D.C. —our protest march today. Don't you see? We've been together these past few years, even though we've been physically apart. We've always been in each other's hearts."

Bobbye was crying.

"It's true. We've been friends for a very long time, Bobbye —in spite of that fund-raiser disaster. It was just bad luck, really, and I —"

"No, no, Daphne, you don't *understand*. We're more than friends. You know it. We're more than that to each other!" Bobbye's tears were blotching her cheeks and her small chin trembled.

The screen door squeaked, and then Hal appeared in the living room doorway.

"Oops. Excuse me," he said. "Wrong moment —I'll come back later." He started back to the kitchen.

"No, no, Hal. It's all right. Come in," Daphne said, hoping to lighten up the scene —hoping Bobbye could collect herself. But it didn't work.

"You might as well hear it too, Hal," Bobbye said. She was sobbing.

"Good heavens! What happened?" Hal said, bewildered.

"Sit down, Bobbye," Daphne placated. "I'll get you some vodka lemonade. We'll all have a drink, okay?"

"I don't want any fuckin' vodka lemonade! I just want you both to know. I want to say it. I've loved you, Daphne, since the first time I ever saw you. And I think she loves me, Hal."

"Aw, Bobbye — kiddo — we're all pretty tired, and muddled," Hal began.

"I'm not *muddled,* godammit! I know what I feel. Let Daphne speak for herself," Bobbye cried, drawing in her breath in little gasps between each word. "But she'd never leave *you,* Hal."

Daphne was aware that they were, all three, standing in a row, about eight feet apart, each of them staring out of one of the three windows that faced the backyard, and voicing their feelings about their lives, and it was like the end of the last act of *Der Rosenkavalier.*

We're living an opera, Daphne realized, *Sophie, Octavian, and the Marschallin —doing our trio.*

As if on cue, Bobbye, still weeping and twisting her gold bracelet, said, "I read that opera translation while you were playing it tonight, and I feel like that Marschallin. I know what she meant when she said she knew the time would come to give up her lover, and I know what she meant when she said she didn't realize it would hurt so much —"

Hal turned, in some alarm, saying, "Give up her *lover?* You and Daphne have been —" He stared searchingly at Daphne, but she only shook her head in the negative and put her finger to her lips.

Bobbye, staring out the window, sighed deeply and went on, "Over and over I told myself that I'd even love Daphne's love for you, Hal, just as the Marschallin felt when she's looking deep into her soul and knows she's *got* to love the love that Octavian feels for Sophie or she can't bear the pain of losing him.

"Jesus — it's like that Rilke poem, Daphne," Bobbye continued, "that poem says we have to learn to love the questions that we can't find the answers to. 'Love the questions themselves,' Rilke says. God! *You* gave me that book of Rilke poems, Daph."

Bobbye took a deep sobbing breath, then went on, "All the best things that have ever happened in my life have been because of you, but I couldn't tell you until now. Why'd you think I stayed away from you all these years? But I had to get it out in the open."

Daphne, crying now herself and moved by Bobbye's recollections and introspections, looked sideways at her friend and said hesitantly, "I really love you, Bobbye, but not the way you think —or want —I guess. I'm not erotically attracted to women. I *love* women, but as friends, not sexually —"

"Wahhhhh!" Bobbye wailed, digging her knuckles into her eyes like a child. "Don't *say* that!"

"Don't you think, Bobbye," Hal began, "don't you think your terrible experience —the bad experience you had with a man, when you were young, you know, *that* experience might have affected you —so —you're —you're drawn to women more —I mean —men turn you off, uh, offend your sensibilities, perhaps?"

"Jesus Christ no! You fucker!" Bobbye shouted. "I got raped by that slime-bag because he *knew* I had always been attracted to women and the *dick-head* said he'd straighten me out once and for all. I've loved women as far back as I can remember, and you're a dick-head too, Hal!"

She started to wail again, and Hal turned to Daphne and said, *soto voce,* "Well, as they say, Daphne, I'm outa here, M'Dear," and he walked into the kitchen and out the back door and into the yard.

"Bobbye, oh Bobbye," Daphne entreated, *"Please* don't cry. We'll always be friends! You know that. There's some wonderful woman out there for you, you'll see. You're sweet and beautiful and courageous and fun and —"

Bobbye turned and looked directly into Daphne's eyes, her own swollen eyes streaming, her face blotched and red.

"How-can-you-say-that-to-me," she gasped.

"Please. Please. Oh please, Bobbye! Think of all the things we both stand for and believe in. We love all those things together, don't we? Just think —you can have your pick of all the finest women. There'll be *one* who'll be worthy of you, and together you can have a very special love — loving all your similarities — the physical *and* the mental — " Daphne was sobbing now, too. She couldn't stop the tears, simply couldn't stop them. "Men and women who can love, Bobbye, mostly love their differences. Men and women try to understand the ways in which we're not alike, and they love the ways in which they are alike too, of course, but you and your women-loving-women lover can have so very much, so much that's absolutely *unique,* because you'll be so alike! Think of how you'll love all the questions with *her,* as you and I do now, only it will be even more wonderful —please —please." Daphne was nearly shouting now, her tears were streaming, and she couldn't stop them.

"But don't you see," Daphne went on, "I love *Hal.* I just *do.* But you're gonna *have a wonderful life!"* she howled. The two women stood staring at each other, panting.

Bobbye, suddenly subdued, murmured, "Will you kiss me goodbye?"

"Goodbye? Kiss you goodbye? Let's not part as enemies. We'll always be friends, always, Bobbye. Am I not going to *see* you ever again? Is that what you're saying?"

"I have to go now, to Edith's, with Audrey and Kareema, and I'd like to kiss you goodbye, that's all."

"Sure. Okay. Why the hell not? We'll just say goodbye for now, Bobbye, okay?"

Daphne turned to Bobbye. Then realizing that her friend was

not going to come to *her,* she went to Bobbye and turned her tear-soaked cheek to her to be kissed. But Bobbye gripped Daphne's shoulders with her small, strong hands, and kissed her lips softly, softly, and Daphne knew that she would not see her friend ever again after this night. They stood now, not touching, and Bobbye whispered, "Oh, God, Daphne. Oh God," and then she was gone.

In a few moments, Hal came into the living room and put his arms around Daphne, and they stood there together, not speaking, as the back door opened and Kareema, carrying a candle, her wet hair wrapped in a towel, skipped into the darkened kitchen and picked up the scarf that Bobbye had dropped, then skipped outside again.

978-0-595-38230-9
0-595-38230-4

Printed in the United States
60617LVS00002B/175-180